WAITING
for the
MESSIAH

WAITING
for the
MESSIAH

STORIES TO INSPIRE
JEWS WITH HOPE

Mordechai Staiman

JASON ARONSON INC.
Northvale, New Jersey
Jerusalem

This book was set in 12 pt. Bembo by Alabama Book Composition of Deatsville, Alabama, and printed and bound by Book-mart Press of North Bergen, New Jersey.

The author gratefully acknowledges permission to use the following:

"A Basketful of Miracles," by Avrohom Shmuel Lewin, reprinted in *L'Chaim* weekly publication. Copyright © 1993 Lubavitch Youth Organization. Reprinted by permission of the publisher.
A Treasury of Jewish Folklore, Nathan Ausubel, ed. Copyright © 1948, 1976 Crown Publishers, Inc. Reprinted by permission of Crown Publishers, Inc.
"The Rebbe's Life and Vision: A Chronology of Events," by Rabbi Boruch Jacobson, printed in Algemeiner Journal 23: 1169. Copyright © 1994 Algemeiner Journal. Reprinted by permission of the author.
"The Sparks that were Redemeed," *L'Chaim* weekly publication. Copyright © 1991 Lubavitch Youth Organization. Reprinted by permission of the Publisher.
"When the Stork *Benshed Gomel*," *Talks & Tales, xliv; 539*, Nissan Mindel, ed. Copyright © 1984 Merkes L'Inyonei Chinuch. Reprinted by permission of the publishers.
"Potential Messiahs of their Generation," *Moshiach Forum #2: Moshiach in Every Generation*, Copyright © 1994 International Moshiach Center. Reprinted by permission of the publisher.
Safed Spirituality, by Lawrence Fine. Copyright © 1984 Lawrence Fine. Used by permission of Paulist Press.

10 9 8 7 6 5 4 3 2 1

Library of Congress Cataloging-in-Publication Data

Staiman, Mordechai
  Waiting for the Messiah : stories to inspire Jews with hope / by
Mordechai Staiman.
        p.   cm.
  Includes bibliographical references and index.
  ISBN 1−56821−986−5 (alk. paper)
    1. Legends. Jewish.   2. Messiah—Judaism.   3. Hasidim—Legends.
  I. Title.
  BM530.S83   1997
  296.3'36—dc21   96−51939

Manufactured in the United States of America. Jason Aronson Inc. offers books and cassettes. For information and catalog write to Jason Aronson Inc., 230 Livingston Street, Northvale, New Jersey 07647.

Dedicated
to my one and only
Rebbe

Rabbi Menachem Mendel Schneerson of Lubavitch

and

my wife Ada,
Lisa and Michael Fullerton,
Ari and Sachiko Staiman,
Charles Weisbard,
Heather Staiman and Tom D'Agostino,
Burton Milenbach,
and my favorite Mom-in-law, Sophie Weisbard,
who was born in Yekatrinislav
where the Lubavitcher Rebbe was raised.

CONTENTS

ACKNOWLEDGMENTS

Now that American playwright Edward Albee has said it first, I too can respond in truth to the question:

"How long did it take you to write this book?"

"All my life," I tell you, plus, along the way, timely moments freely given from the following persons:

To Arthur Kurzweil with love: May God bless you for all your encouragement and helpfulness with this book project and others. And, to Jason Aronson's production editor, Leabe Berman, a lovely voice of encouragement and inspiration all the way through.

For story leads and "Moshiach" ideas, I am indebted to Ariella Benayoun (who also taught me the deeper meaning of "*Yechi Adoneinu Moreinu V'Rabeinu Melech Hamoshiach L'olam Vo'ed*"), Yisrael and Sara Tova Best, Rabbi Moshe Borisute, Sandra and Daniel Botnick, Rabbi Shmuel Butman, Rabbi Eli and Yehudis Cohen, Rabbi Heschel Greenberg, Rabbi Leibel Groner, Rabbi Benjamin Heitler, Rabbi Boruch Jacobson, Librarian Lora Keister of the Buffalo, New York Bureau of Jewish Education, Rabbi Yosef Y. Keller, Rabbi Shloma Majesky, Levi and Raizel Reiter, Rabbi Yosef Y. Shagalov, Rabbi Lazer Spira, and Shlomo Yitzchak Weiss.

Everyone needs a cheering section and sympathetic ear. Here's to the following persons who supplied that, plus helpful criticism on my story book: Rabbi Reuven and Devorah Leah Blau and family, Jim Blier, Rabbi Kasriel and Nechama Kastel, Tamar and Daniel Ramniceanu, and Levi and Raizel Reiter and family.

Thanks also to my friends who insisted that nobody should be the ultimate editor of his own work, and who generously gave of their time to edit, proofread, scan, and translate foreign language material for my manuscript. These include Kim Aarmodt, Michael Gorelick, Murray Kahl, Rabbi Avrohom Keller, Rabbi Yosef Y. Keller, Ed Sader, and Rabbi Yosef Y. Shagalov.

Special thanks to Richard Basil Mock for his unusual artwork that further deepened my appreciation for the heroism and holiness of the Skulener Rebbe.

Thanks also to *Beis Moshiach* Magazine for publishing "The Mountain Jews" and "Everything Ends in a Song."

Let is also be noted that, during the researching and writing of this book, Dr. Harvey (Tzvi) Lang's holistic approach to medicine helped keep me alive, and Burton Milenbach, Ph.D., helped me maintain a sane family environment.

Especially, I want to thank—again and again—Rabbi Reuven Blau. Because whenever I felt the need to start a new writing project, I'd drop over to his house for *Shabbos* lunch and say, "Reuven, Reuven, I need to write a new book, but what?"

"*Gut Shabbos,*" he'd calmly say. "Sit down, and later, after a few *lechaims* and *niggunim*, we'll come up with a new book for you."

He never failed me. So, thank you, Reuven, for the *lechaims*, *niggunim* and suggesting this book, and all the others I'm working on.

And since, thank God, nothing's changed since I finished my first book *Niggun*, I repeat whatever I said then about my S.O.P. (Significant Other Person): To my wife, Ada Staiman, a true woman of valor, who day and night got up like a trooper to read my stories, make corrections in my manuscripts, and make innumerable suggestions to improve the stories. It was her enthusiasm, vitality, and perceptive understanding that helped bring this book to fruition.

First, last and always, I thank God for coming to me every *Shabbos*—my special time with Him, when He invariably filled me with the creative thoughts to enrich my life and my writing.

And, finally, a special thanks to our Creator, who is sending us our Messiah. May he come before this book gets published!

INTRODUCTION

If you haven't already done so, walk over to the cashier and buy this book—please. God knows you've waited long enough. I'm talking about a wait of two thousand years. For whom, and for how long? For the Jewish Messiah, of course, and, I hope, this book will take some of the wait out of the wait.

Let's face it: "Every wait is a wait for him."[1] As it is written, the world was created only for the sake of the Messiah, that he might bring redemption (Talmud, *Sanhedrin* 98b). As such, the coming of the Messiah has been a basic tenet of Judaism, one of the thirteen principles of faith, as stated by Maimonides.[2] Even more exciting: "The messianic idea is the most glittering jewel in the glorious crown of Judaism,"[3] and if reading this book makes you feel like a prince or princess all over, you've learned your Jewish lessons well.

Never have we been so close to greeting one holy man who, God tells us, will redeem us all. Never has this redeemer, our Sages tell us, been so close to greeting us. Never have the Jews, the "Sons of the Compassionate," been so close to seeing God's emissary on earth, for the Holy One gave His robes—glory and majesty—to him.[4] I'm talking about the Messiah, the man of our Jewish dreams and hopes come to love and guide

---

1. With special thanks to Elie Wiesel for the phrase.
2. Commentary to *Mishnah, Sanhedrin* 1168, 10:1; *Thirteen Principles*, # 12.
3. Joseph Klausner, *Messianic Idea in Israel*, 1955.
4. *Numbers Rabbah* 14:3.

1

us back to God. And if we believe the holy predictions of modern-day prophets, such as the Rebbe of Lubavitch, Rabbi Menachem M. Schneerson, then "the time of our Redemption has arrived" and "the Messiah is on his way!"[5]

What Redemption? What Messiah?

Although it may not always be wise to wish everything explained, it cannot but help to know that God, in His infinite wisdom, created the world with words, rather than thoughts. He used words to the Jewish people, whom He married to the Torah—in the same way that married couples must learn to transmit their needs through the dynamics of words. No man can read another's mind, and that is the way God foresaw it. His chosen people, therefore, God said, would best use their time to digest the Torah, Talmud, and Kabbalah (the hidden secrets of the Torah) on their way to making this earth a holy place for God to dwell in. One day, perhaps, if God chooses to redo His Creation—and that's always a possibility—He will pronounce aloud the Messiah's name instead of only thinking of his name among the six things that preceded the world's creation.[6]

In the meantime we have a nameless Messiah. Yet many of you probably have heard, along your own path, there was *this* false redeemer, and *this* wannabe Messiah, and *that* great pretender,[7] all tending for a time to depress the Jewish spirit.

The Messiah may yet be nameless, but the endless waits, the exiles of the Jews, weren't nameless. Each had its own name. In Jewish history, there were four such exiles beginning with the Israelites' stay in Egypt, which they exited in 1230 B.C.E., or as the Jews called Egypt in those days, *Mitzrayim*. The post-Egypt era was an astounding time for Moses and the Israelites—their exodus remaining "forever the springtime of the entire world."[8] They crossed the parted Red Sea. They received the Torah at Mount Sinai—on the eve of 6 Sivan, 2448 (May 14, 1313 B.C.E.). God

---

5. *Shabbos Parshas Shoftim*, 5751 (August 17, 1991).

6. The other five things include Torah, the throne of glory, creation of the fathers, Israel, and the Temple. Some also include repentance, the Garden of Eden, and *Gehinnom* (Purgatory). That all these came before the creation of the world described in Genesis is based on Proverbs 8:22, Psalms 93:2, Hosea 9:10, Psalms 74:2, Jeremiah 17:12, Psalms 72:17, Psalms 90:2–3, Genesis 2:8, and Isaiah 30:33. Also see *Genesis Rabbah* 1:4.

7. See my Appendix B.

8. Rabbi Abraham Isaac Kook. Tzoref, *Hayye HaRav Kook*, 1947, p. 191.

was the groom, Israel the bride, Torah the marriage contract, and Moses the best man. They worshipped (not all Jews) the Golden Calf—since then, there is no generation that does not share the sin of making the Golden Calf.[9] And they entered the Promised Land without their leader Moses—yet, as *Chassidus* reminds us, "Every day we must leave Egypt to reach the Promised Land."

Their feeling for their Promised Land lasted until 586 B.C.E., when they lost more than that feeling and went into exile again, this time to Babylonia. That was the second exile, which lasted seventy years. Along the way they saw their beloved Jerusalem and Holy Temple set ablaze. As our Sages teach us, "God has overlooked [even] idolatry, incest and murder, but did not excuse the neglect of Torah study."[10]

The third exile, in Medea (Persian Empire), lasted about fifty-two years. In 538 B.C.E., Persian king Cyrus and later (after Cyrus's death) his son Darius released the Judean exiles to return to Jerusalem and rebuild it as part of their tolerant policy toward religious and ethnic groups. Princes Zerubbabel and Sheshbazzar, members of the Judean royal family, were assigned to repatriate the temple vessels.

Maybe Rome wasn't built in one day, but the Jews wished it never had been built at all. Not that the Romans hated the Jews—they didn't. They just couldn't put up with a fly in their ointment. The Great Jewish Revolt of 66 C.E. (Common Era) and the siege of Jerusalem constitute one of the most important and horrifying events in Jewish history, and by the time it was over, in September 70 C.E., Roman general Titus Flavius Vespasian and his legions had wasted Jerusalem, burned down the Temple, and scattered the Jewish population every which way. That might have been the swan song for any other nation, but Jewish sources tell us that the moment the Temple was destroyed, the Jewish Messiah was born[11] and would never leave the Jewish people again. He would be there spiritually for them, in one holy physical, living body or another on earth, waiting for God to tap him on the shoulder and say, "Go out and redeem My people," and he and his followers, in turn, would proceed to inform all

---

9. *Lamentations Rabbah.*

10. Jerusalem Talmud, *Chagigah* 1:7.

11. "From the day the Temple was destroyed, an individual was immediately born whose righteousness is such that he can be the Messiah. And when the time comes, God will reveal Himself to him and send him and then pour forth upon him the spirit of the Messiah, which is hidden and reserved above" (the *Chasam Sofer*, Rabbi Moshe Sofer Schreiber, 1762–1839, *Responsa*, vol. 6, ch. 98).

other Jews.[12] And that hasn't changed as you read these words, unless, of course, God has mercifully revealed the Messiah before this, and happy days are finally here.

Jewish sources also point out that Titus, as long as he lived, regretted the day he scorned the God of the Jews. Another so-called fly in the ointment came back to haunt him, obsess him, and ultimately to drive him mad. God avenged His people. Picking it up in the middle of a midrash, we learn that when Titus triumphantly returned to Rome, he later took a bath, and when he finished washing himself, he swished down a cup of wine. At that very moment, when Titus thought he didn't have a care in the world, a gnat appeared, entered through his nose, and proceeded to burrow into his brain for the next seven years. When Titus died, his skull was split open; inside a creature resembling a sparrow was found![13]

The Roman exile is the fourth and longest—almost 2,000 years!—lasting to this day. Since 70 c.e., the Jews have been dispersed all over the world. This dispersion is called the diaspora; we Jews call the exile *golah* and the redemption *geulah*. An interesting Jewish tidbit to this is that the Hebrew word *geulah* contains the word *golah* plus an *aleph* (the letter "a"), for once the "*Aluf* of the world"—the Creator—reveals Himself in the universe, the *golah* itself will become *geulah*.[14] This is most welcome news even to the most Orthodox of Jews who live in the *golah*. The worst thing—and I say this humorously—that could happen when *geulah* comes is that our world will be perfected. The Empire State Building, the Eiffel Tower, the Suez Canal, Disneyland—they'll all be there, yet they'll have a new shine, the divine light of God revealed. In brief, "*geulah* will simply restructure the world as it was meant to be, directing all energies toward goodness and sanctity."[15] We will keep everything we want and

---

12. Why the hints from a potential Messiah? Numerous Torah sources point out that the soul of the Messiah descends into the body of the *tzaddik* who is destined to be the Messiah—in stages. (See *Midrash Rabbah, Parshas Shemos*; also *Pirkei Geulah*—Rabbi Schachne Zohn.)

13. Hayim Nahman Bialik and Yehoshua Hana Ravnitzky, *The Book of Legends—Sefer Ha-Aggadah*, trans. William G. Braude (New York: Schocken Books, 1992), p. 192.

14. From a talk by Rabbi Menachem M. Schneerson, seventh Lubavitcher Rebbe, on *Shabbos Parshas Acharei-Kedoshim*, 5751/1991.

15. Menachem M. Brod, *Days of Moshiach* (Kfar Chabad, Israel: Chabad Youth Org., 1993), p. 142.

have from the *golah*. We've nothing to lose and everything to gain when the Messiah comes. And so, too, God willing, when *geulah* finally comes, may we forever cement that *aleph*—or *Aluf*—in our lives!

According to the scenario made in heaven, in due time God will finally name the Messiah and he will free the people of Israel from their suffering in exile, lead them back to Jerusalem, and establish peace over all the nations of the world.

Why would God do all that for his chosen people? Maybe the answer is contained in the question. Because His chosen people have not yet carried out their earthly mission: to make the earth a holy place for God to dwell in. And yet there is another reason: We are also told that, for whatever reason(s) God has extended the fourth exile of the Jewish people, "God hates the exile, as He knows that in the exile the Jews are lacking—and indeed, He understands their lack better than the Jews themselves do. Even though a Jew knows of the ultimate state of the era of Redemption, since he lives within the confines of a physical body and the confines of this world, he cannot understand these concepts fully. Nevertheless, since a Jew knows that God hates the exile, he also hates the exile."[16]

Interestingly, over the centuries the very thought of the Messiah appearing anywhere was enough to trigger a tidal wave of Jews rushing to get where he was. Having bags, they traveled. There is a little-known story about a man named Theudas, who was executed as a would-be Messiah by the Roman procurator Fadus, in 44 C.E. What set Theudas up for the kill? As a mob of Jews joined him, Theudas marched down the Jordan Valley to the Jordan River, which, he had all his followers believing, he would part at his command. It didn't work out that way at all,[17] and, because the procurator wasn't taking any more chances that Theudas would dry up the Jordan river, he put Theudas and his many followers to death.

Maybe, also, there's really something to the Jewish thought that when one closes one door, another door opens. Almost at the same time the Roman Empire was overrun by the Huns in 479 C.E., in "about 448 a Jew appeared on Crete announcing that he was Moses and that he would

---

16. Rabbi Menachem Mendel Schneerson.

17. Josephus Flavius, *Antiquities* 20:45; Judah Gribetz, Edward L. Greenstein, and Regina S. Stein, *Timetables of Jewish History* (New York: Simon & Schuster, 1993), p. 60.

repeat on a much larger scale the miracle performed by Moses at the Red Sea: he would part the waters of the Mediterranean and lead the Jews of the island dryshod to Judea! When the hour he fixed for the miracle arrived, he ordered his followers to jump into the sea, which they did, with the result that many of them drowned in the waves."[18]

No, not all Jews would jump in a lake at the sound of the footsteps of the Messiah, but Moses set a great example as a leader and redeemer. Anyone who emerged as a potential Messiah in the coming generations was always compared to Moses, and although comparisons are odious, they usually came off second-best. Skepticism abounded no less thousands of years ago than today. By the time Rabban Yochanan ben Zakkai (*tannaic* sage, first century c.e.) appeared on the scene, Jews heard his warning loud and clear: If you have a seedling in your hand, and they say to you, "Look, here comes the Messiah!" go on and plant the seedling first, and then come out to meet the Messiah.[19]

Yet when the "Messiah for certain" (*Moshiach vadai*) shows up, well, that's a different story. Rabbi Shneur Zalman of Liadi (1745–1812), the founder of *Chabad Chassidus*, was once asked: "Who is greater, Moses or the Messiah?" He answered, "The Messiah. Moses is compared to a physician without experience, whereas the Messiah is compared to a veteran and experienced physician."[20]

Yet from Moses to the Messiah, this much can be said with great certainty: "Moses, the first redeemer of the Jews, was known as the redeemer in Egypt prior to the actual exodus. Likewise, the Messiah, the final redeemer of the Jewish people, will also arrive some time prior to the actual redemption and the ushering in of the Messianic Era."[21]

Yet with much less certainty can we say why the Jewish people longed for a messiah in the first place—unless, of course, we accept certain statements. For one, God said we needed one. Yet somebody must have asked the big unanswered question. What does our service to God still lack to make us long for the Messiah? After all, before the Jews finally opted for kingship, they had a theocracy, with God making all the rules

---

18. Socrates Scholasticus, *Historia Ecclesiae* 12:33, as quoted in "Messianic Movements," *Encyclopaedia Judaica* (Jerusalem: Keter Publishing House, 1971).

19. *Abot de Rabbi Nathan*, ed. Solomon Schechter (London, 1887), ch. 31, p. 34.

20. *L'Chaim* weekly publication, no. 180 (Brooklyn, NY: L.Y.O., Sept. 13, 1991), p. 3.

21. *Sfas Emes*, Rabbi Yehudah Aryeh Leib Alter of Ger, 1847–1905.

and his chosen people following them. Why go from that perfect Godly civilization to a manmade kingship? At the time they did, there wasn't much else they could do. As one historian notes, "When the powerful Philistine forces struck at the heart of the Israelite settlements, inflicting humiliating defeats, even capturing the Ark itself and (it seems) destroying the Shiloh shrine,[22] it was natural that the people should turn to [the prophet] Samuel[23] and that he should play the critical role in deciding whether, and if so how, the Israelites in their desperation should embrace kingship."[24] Sorely did the Israelites need King Saul and eventually an obscure, young shepherd who carried a slingshot. David, of course.

During the reign of King David (tenth century B.C.E.), the belief developed that his House would rule forever, not only over Israel but also over all the nations.[25] Out of this came the belief that any true Messiah had to be descended from the House of David.[26]

Still, many things had to be set in place, concerning why the Jewish people need, anticipate, and even must continue trying to hasten the Messiah's arrival.

God said the Messiah would bring the Redemption.[27] According to the prophet Amos (Amos 5:18–20), the great Redemption would come, God would directly and miraculously intervene in the affairs of the nations, and He would bring about the succor of Jerusalem, the return of the exiles, the conversion of the gentiles to a belief in the God of Israel, and the resurrection of the dead.

Hearing all that, the Jews of that time must have given out a collective "Wow!" Holy party-time! That great messianic banquet—a favorite

---

22. The central Sanctuary during the period of the Judges.

23. Eleventh century B.C.E. Jewish prophet.

24. Paul Johnson, *History of the Jews* (New York: Harper Perennial, 1988), p. 52.

25. Psalms 18:42–52 and 2 Samuel 22:48.

26. God swore to the Jewish people that this was to be so, and we read this every day as a concluding blessing for the reading of the *Haftarah*, during the Shabbat morning service in synagogue. See, for example, *Siddur Tehillat Hashem*, trans. Nissan Mangel (Brooklyn, NY: Merkos L'Inyonei Chinuch, 1990), p. 188.

27. "Nor does the Redemption follow immediately upon the appearance of the Redeemer. After he is revealed, he is hidden, and only upon his second appearance does the great global process of Redemption begin." Raphael Patai, *The Messiah Texts* (Detroit: Wayne State University Press, 1979), p. xxxi.

imaginary event on which the Jewish messianologists lavished attention—
would be within the grasp of every Jew holding a fork or not. Many times in
the Talmud, the Sages mention the Leviathan (*Livyasan*—the Great Fish)
banquet (for example, Midrash: *Vayikra Rabbah* 13:3; Talmud: *Bava Bastra*
75a), and Jewish sources, including the *Maharsha* (Rabbi Shemuel Eliezer
Eidels, 1555–1631) and Rabbi Menachem M. Schneerson (1902–1994),
believe this banquet is not just a parable—it will indeed occur.[28]

Leading up to this, Jews were only too happy to hear the prophet Isaiah
envision a future era of universal peace that would be ushered in by "a
shoot out of the stock of Yishai [King David's father]" (Isaiah 11:1). In
short, the splendor of a future Jerusalem would soon be at hand.

Yet the Jews eagerly, breathlessly, hopefully, anxiously, patiently,
desperately (add any other adverb to describe their feelings for the
Messiah this side of heaven), continued to wait for the right man—but
then, it could be a woman[29]—who had to come but had not yet. So
where was he? Jews wanted to know. And if he hadn't come in 2,000
years, what was holding him up?

The first thing we have to know is—surprise!—the Messiah is already
here. He's been here all the time, walking the same streets as you or you
or you or I. Now, two things have to take place: God himself must reveal
the Messiah to the Jewish people and the Jewish people have to accept the
Messiah. But not necessarily in that order. It can very well be that, at first,
the Jewish people have to acclaim a holy man as the Messiah and then
God will give His own thumbs-up—*but in God's time.*

Which brings us to: Who are these holy, hidden men, potential
Messiahs all, who stand ready for the call? Most of them have one thing
in common. Like Moses, who was reluctant to lead his people out of
Egypt, so too these hidden saints are generally reluctant to become the
Messiah, and for good reason. It's a lifetime of nonstop holy work, of
devoting one's total energy to transforming this world to the Coming
World, of showing all Jews that "Judaism enjoins 613 duties, but knows
no dogmas."[30]

The Messiah is a human being, extraordinary as he is in his study and

---

28. Brod, *Days of Moshiach*, p. 156.

29. See reference to the messianic figure called "Daughter of Joseph," by
Sondra Henry and Emily Taitz, *Written Out of History: Our Jewish Foremothers*
(New York: Biblio Press, 1990), pp. 75–76.

30. Samson Raphael Hirsch, *Nineteen Letters*, no. 15 (1836), p. 146.

grasp of Torah. The only qualification about his origins is that he be a descendant of King David, through the lineage of his son Solomon. As for when he will arrive to claim his heritage, any time is a potential time for his coming.

All that aside, what is holding him up? This is one of the few questions with many answers. Excuses, excuses, Jews offer one after another, but in this case all of them *were* true.

At various times we heard the Messiah was prevented from coming because the generation was unworthy. Or, "When man will rise above the earthly, when human worms will turn into human eagles," then the Messiah will appear.[31] Then the machinations of Satan held him up. Or else the pious were unable to complete prayers that would have brought his advent. Then, he couldn't come until all the unborn souls were born and the celestial Hall of the Souls, the mystical *Guf*, was emptied. Then, the Messiah himself told the famous Baal Shem Tov (1698–1760)[32] that he wouldn't come till all the teachings of *Chassidus* had been spread to the far corners of the globe. Or, Jews had not wept sufficiently over the Divine Presence's[33] exile. Another holdup: If Israel would keep one Shabbat properly the Messiah would come at once (*Midrash, Shemos Rabbah*). At other times the Talmud (*Sanhedrin* 97b) informs us that all deadlines for the coming of the Messiah have come and gone—that the thing depends solely on our returning to God. The famous chassidic rebbe, Rabbi Nachman of Bratzlav (1772–1811), also had something to say about the Big Wait: "When faith will take the place of rationalism, the Messiah will come."[34] Czech writer Franz Kafka, a modern-day admirer of Rabbi Nachman, left us this thought: "The Messiah will come only when he is no longer necessary; he will come only on the day after his arrival."[35] We're even told, the prophet Elijah (who's considered the harbinger of the Messiah) was forbidden to gather the three patriarchs— Abraham, Isaac, and Jacob—to beg for redemption, for they three alone

---

31. I. L. Peretz, "The Day," 1906, *Alle Vork*, xii, p. 319.

32. Rabbi Israel ben Eliezer. Founded *Chassidus*. Charismatic, legendary, immensely influential and revered, the Baal Shem Tov is credited with many miraculous cures.

33. In Hebrew, the *Shechinah*. Often used as a synonym for God.

34. Aaron of Apt (Opatov), *Keter Shem Tov* (Lemberg, 1865), p. 9a.

35. *Parables*, trans. Greenberg, p. 65.

could have brought the Messiah before his time.[36] And not for a moment should you think that Elijah's job was easy. In between preparing to stop off at people's house for seders, fighting for social justice, and "reconciling parents with their children and children with their parents" (2 Kings 3:23–24), he has had to hold many a nervous hand, including the Messiah's. One *aggadah* relates how Elijah comforted the Messiah in one of the halls of *Gan Eden*. He held the Messiah's head against his chest and said: "Bear the suffering God has imposed upon you till the end of days because of the sins of the Jewish people; courage, the end is near."[37]

Almost from the day the Jews had a leader—and Moses is a good example—there has always been a lively debate about who is the real potential Messiah of his time. Moses clearly was. Queen Esther[38] was considered such a redeemer. Also Hezekiah,[39] Bar Kokhba,[40] Yitzchak Luria,[41] the Maharal of Prague,[42] the Vilna Gaon,[43] and so many others. Generally, disciples tended to name their own leader as the Messiah,[44]

---

36. H. N. Bialik and Y. R. Rawnitzky, *Stories of the Sages*, trans. Chaim Pearl (Tel Aviv: DVIR Publishing House, 1991), p. 152.

37. *Midreshe Geulah*, pp. 307–308; and Aharon Wiener, *The Prophet Elijah in the Development of Judaism* (London: Routledge & Kegan Paul, 1978), p. 63.

38. Rabbi Berekhya, *Midrash Abba Gorion*, in Adolph Jellinek, *Bet haMidrash*, 6 vols., 2nd ed. (Jerusalem: Bamberger & Wahrmann, 1938), 1:5.

39. Talmud, *Sanhedrin* 94a, 98b, and 99a.

40. See my Story Four of the Exile, "Son of a Star—or Son of a Liar?"

41. See my Story Seven of the Exile, "The Ari from the 'Old of Days.'"

42. See my Story Eight of the Exile, "The Golem Speaks Out."

43. See my Story Twelve of the Exile, "The Spiritual Aristocrat."

44. Originally, the term *Moshiach*, whose Anglicized version is *Messiah*, was applied to any person anointed with sacred oil—kings ("God's anointed") and priests. The Temple high priest, in particular, was termed "the Anointed [*Moshiach*] of God" (Leviticus 4:3, 5, 16; 6:15). The title was even given to the Persian king Cyrus, a non-Jew chosen by God to liberate Israel from Babylonia (Isaiah 45:1).

Moshiach later was applied to a prophet, or anybody God sent forward with a special mission. This second type of the divinely elected also had to undergo the ceremony of anointing: 1 Kings 19:16 tells us that God commanded Elijah, for example, to anoint Jehu as king over Israel, and Elisha as prophet in his own place.

Then came King David, and *Moshiach* designated the awaited Deliverer of the Jews from their bondage and oppression, who will establish or restore the kingdom of Israel.

and, it should be noted, not all leaders rebuffed the wishful thinking of their followers. Indeed, it was not only the students but the sages themselves who made such claims (Talmud, *Sanhedrin* 98b). Writes the Torah and Talmud commentator Rashi (1040–1105 C.E.): "Each [such] sage said that the name of the Messiah was his own name."

Is there an author's message in this book? Sure, and, if up to now, you've given little or no thought about the Jewish Messiah in your life, may I suggest you read on, in a book that will give you a chance to meet some potential Messiahs of past generations and of the potential Messiah of this very generation we live in. In between you'll read a collection of stories. Some are more like glimpses, essays, short biographies, parables, all, God willing, rebuilding our inner fortress of hope as Jews. First, you'll walk through almost 2,000 years of "Stories of the Exile"; then, suddenly, as you approach the "Stories of the Coming World," you'll begin to see, as the first rays of the sun shoot over the rim of the horizon, the Jewish Redemption come, like the rising sun, gradually, slowly, until it appears in the sky in all its dazzling radiance.

In 1989, after I myself had wandered forty years, far from Judaism, I finally returned to my religion. Then and there, I found a holy man—the Rebbe of Lubavitch—in a pocket of Brooklyn, New York, called Crown Heights. He kept emphasizing that while waiting for the Messiah we Jews should study Torah and do good deeds and acts of kindness, to hasten the arrival of the very God-sent man whom I was waiting for most of my life.

So welcome, fellow Jew, and may this book be just what you have been waiting for, while waiting for our Messiah.

Finally, *Moshiach* came to mean the savior who will make the world acknowledge God's sovereignty, thus ushering in the World-to-Come. In that context, *Moshiach* will be the dominating figure of an age of universal peace and plenty. Then, in the words of Isaiah's promise, "The world will be filled with knowledge of God as the waters cover the ocean bed."

STORIES OF THE EXILE

1

TODAY

No one knew for certain why, in the very old days, Elijah the prophet hung around the entrance to the cave where Rabbi Shimon bar Yochai (100–160 c.e.) was buried. But a good guess might be (if you knew Elijah the prophet): he was waiting for Rabbi Yehoshua ben Levi to come by and ask him a question. And why not? Rabbi Yehoshua liked to ask questions, and Elijah liked to answer them.

"So where is the Messiah already?" Rabbi Yehoshua finally asked Elijah one day at the cave's entrance.

At first the prophet hesitated. He remembered only too well Rabbi Shimon's hideous physical condition. Accused of treason by the Romans, Rabbi Shimon and his son Eleazer hid themselves in a cave for twelve years, studying Torah. They achieved such an exalted level of holiness that when they emerged at last, their gaze alone was enough to scorch the surroundings, which appeared mundane to their holy eyes. So God sent them back to their cave for yet another year, for fear they would destroy His world. And when they emerged for good, Rabbi Shimon's body was covered in painful, ugly sores from sitting immersed in the sand of the cave for so many years.

Which was quite similar to the Messiah's physical condition at the time of this story. No one suffered more, and willingly suffered for all Jews, than the Messiah. Could Rabbi Yehoshua handle seeing the Messiah at his worst? Would the rabbi wither in his holy sandals?

"I'm ready," Rabbi Yehoshua said.

"Today?" asked Elijah the prophet.

"If not now, when?" Rabbi Yehoshua earnestly asked again.

"Forgive me," said Elijah the prophet, shaking his head. Why had he ever doubted the rabbi's intention? "I should have known, Rabbi, what stern stuff you are made of."

"Then I'll come right to the point, holy prophet. I must know: Will I attain the World-to-Come?"

Just like that, Elijah had been asked. It was not quite the question he'd preferred to be asked. Clearly, the question begged for an answer, yet he himself knew he couldn't speak for God. Now, if Rabbi Yehoshua had asked him about the Messiah, well and good: more than willingly would he respond positively and frankly to that. But about the World-to-Come?

Elijah the prophet looked up to the sky. "I'm at a loss to answer that. *Teku!*"[1] he cried, repeating the ancient plaint all sages lament when they cannot solve a talmudic problem. *Teku*—the answer for all ages. *Teku*—the answer (all answers to unanswerable questions in our time)—would have to wait for the Messiah to come.

But Elijah the prophet could see Rabbi Yehoshua was still waiting for an answer.

"So what is the answer?" he who loved to ask said.

It was neither the voice of Elijah the prophet nor Rabbi Yehoshua ben Levi who said, in a powerful thrust, like an echo that had bounced off a lot of walls of a cave and came full strength to rest on the lips of the trembling prophet: "If God so desires it."

And he who loved to answer immediately turned the tables and asked his own question: "Then where does that leave you?"

Rabbi Yehoshua ben Levi was stunned, but not speechless. "Here stand two persons—you and I—but I heard the voice of a third from your lips, holy prophet."

For some reason Elijah then pointed to the cave. "As Rabbi Shimon bar Yochai is our witness, I ask you now, do you care if your question is right?" asked Elijah.

In response, Rabbi Yehoshua said he would like to make two questions from that question.

---

1. The term *teku* is used in the Talmud at the end of a discussion when no definitive answer was reached. Its basic meaning is that the question is unanswerable despite all attempts. It is also an acronym for four Hebrew words that mean: "Elijah the Tishbite will solve all difficulties and inquiries," that is, we will know the answer when the Messiah comes.

"Well?"

"Is this a wise question for me to ask?"

"Well?" the prophet again said impatiently.

The rabbi then asked him, "When will the Messiah come?"

Ah, the question was finally out in the open! Elijah was pleased. "Well and good!" he said, showing his pleasure.

"Well?" now the rabbi asked.

"Go and ask him yourself," was Elijah's reply.

"Where is he sitting?"

Elijah: "At the entrance to the city of Rome."

Rabbi Yehoshua: "And by what sign may I recognize him?"

Elijah: "He is sitting among the lepers burdened with sicknesses."

Rabbi Yehoshua: "How will I recognize our beloved Messiah?"

Elijah sighed. He always sighed when he didn't like what he had to say. Yet he'd have to tell it like it is and let Yehoshua fend his feelings for himself. "It won't be a pretty sight," said Elijah. "At first, Rabbi, close your eyes deeply, pray, then slowly open them, and expect to see—"

"What?" Yehoshua wanted to know.

Elijah: "All of the lepers first untie all the bandages over their sores and then retie them. That's what separates the Messiah from all the other lepers. He unties and reties each bandage separately, saying to himself: Should my God call me, I must not tarry."

And Rabbi Yehoshua also tarried no longer. Bidding goodbye to the prophet, exuberantly he made his way through the seedy bevy of people who milled near the gates of Rome: all faces, in pain, designed as private faces in public places. Sometimes he saw a face he hadn't seen in years. Yet other bodies seemed to the rabbi to be sleepwalking, perhaps dreaming their own questions and answers. In the sordid scheme of life lived then, every man had a question. *When?* And an answer: *Today.* Was he not happy who he, Rabbi Yehoshua, could ask his question directly? For suddenly— there—he saw the Messiah. Untying a single bandage. Nothing could stop Yehoshua now. He advanced close, closer, as close as he could get. Sickly or not, the Messiah was truly a sight for sore eyes.

Face to face finally with the Messiah, Rabbi Yehoshua greeted him, saying, "Peace be upon you, my master and teacher."

"Peace be upon you, O son of Levi," the Messiah replied.

"When will you come, O master?" Rabbi Yehoshua asked.

"Today," was the Messiah's answer.

Today. Of course! The answer was as plain as plain.

Still, he found himself saying, "Today?" as if he were a sleepwalker himself and had to rub his eyes. "This truly will be a day like no other!"

"Yes, today," the Messiah said with much pain.

Today—was it said to emphasize the painfulness of the Messiah's suffering physical condition? Or was the answer itself a pained one? Such a subtlety was too much for the rabbi to grasp. He thanked the Messiah profusely, having nothing further to ask of him.

"Today! Today!"

Now the rabbi skipped past the mob of people. With taxed eyes, the Roman guards took in the rabbi. They let him pass undisturbed. To them, the lighthearted rabbi was just another mad Jew out in the noonday sun. But there were other impediments along the way that held him up. He had to stop for a few hours here to tend the sick, a few hours there to pray for the dying, and sometimes he'd kneel for long periods to pray to his God for his people's final deliverance.

But the Messiah did not come.

When Rabbi Yehoshua came back to Elijah, Elijah asked, "What did he say to you?"

Rabbi Yehoshua: "Peace be unto you, O son of Levi."

The way he nodded, Elijah seemed pleased with that answer. "Then, it's my guess, Rabbi, that he thereby assured you and your father of a portion in the World-to-Come."

Rabbi Yehoshua was less sure. "How can I believe that, since he lied to me?"

Elijah: "He—the Messiah—lied? Never! He's eminently trustworthy."

Rabbi Yehoshua: "I just don't know, after what he said. I just lost my trust in him, and I'm sad about that."

"What, this is unheard of!" Elijah was beside himself in disbelief. "Not my redeemer. Nor yours."

"Well," Rabbi Yehoshua said, folding his arms on his chest in a defiant gesture. "I do not make up these words, but he told me in a word, 'Today,' that he would come today, yet he did not come."

"One word? Aha!" Elijah had answered many questions in his time. But no answer seemed as crucial as this. So now he had to choose his words well.

"The Messiah said *today* and he meant just that."

"Easily, Elijah, I could have lived with the Messiah's saying that he regrets that he cannot come today. At this time in our history, what's one day more or less between friends?"

"Rabbi, I tell you, he really meant today."

"Then why do I have the feeling his today is not the same as my today? Eh, eh? Pretty bad times, today when one can't trust the Messiah?"

"But that's exactly it, in a nutshell. What he said to you, Rabbi, was the beginning of the verse, 'Today—if you would but hearken to His voice'" (Psalms 95:6).

And, holy Messiah, as you sit at the gate of Rome, removing one bandage at a time and wondering when your day will come, you too cry out in pain to your Creator, "Today—if I would but hearken to Thy voice."[2]

2. This story is based on Talmud tractate *Sanhedrin* 98a.

2

MENACHEM THE COMFORTER

It often seems as if the entire Jewish people have been sitting and weeping over graves for two thousand years. And on no day does it seem worse than on the ninth of Av, when even the Western Wall wails and the stones mourn for the destruction of the Holy Temple in 70 C.E. Yet one consolation took place on that day: On that same day when the Holy Temple was destroyed, a boy named Menachem—let us all call him the Comforter!—was born. Yet, between the Temple's destruction (surely a scene right out of hell) and the baby's birth (truly a message from heaven), his inconsolable mother chose to focus on the sad theme. Which left the birth up in the air. Whom would Menachem comfort, if not his mother?

It happened that while a certain Jewish farmer named Ezra was plowing, his heifer began to low unusually loud, like a wail, it can be said with finality and alarm. The lowing echoed in the valley and attracted the attention of a passing Arab, who then approached the Jewish farmer.

"Why do you continue to plow?" he said to Ezra the farmer.

"Dig I must," answered Ezra.

"Jew, O Jew," the Arab said, "unharness your heifer and unhitch your plow and go into mourning."

"Why?"

"Because the Temple of the Jews is destroyed."

News of the wasted Temple was spreading like wildfire but had not reached the ears or eyes of Ezra, so he asked the Arab how he knew this.

"From the lowing of your heifer."

While they were conversing, the heifer lowed again. "Jew, O Jew," the Arab said, "harness your heifer and hitch up your plow, because the Messiah, deliverer of Israel, has been born."

"What is his name?"

"His name is Menachem. Everyone calls him 'the Comforter.'"

"What is his father's name?"

"Hezekiah."

"Where does he live?"

"In Birat Arba, in Bethlehem of Judah."

Suddenly Ezra turned to his right. He went over to a little stream and washed his hands, saying the *hatov v'hamaytiv* blessing in honor of very good news for the world. Then he again turned to the Arab, who stood there as if he expected a small reward or some good news himself.

"I must go and serve this Menachem child. To do what I can to comfort his mother."

"Yes, Jew, you must make your presence felt," advised the Arab.

"That's it," the farmer said exactly.

"What's it?"

"I shall listen to you and make my presence felt. What more natural way than to sell garments inexpensively for children!"

"Well, I'm on my way again," the Arab said, as he headed toward the right fork in the road.

"And I am on my way," Ezra said as he left his heifer to graze in the field, and, bidding his family farewell for now, he became a merchant for expensive-looking children's garments at bargain prices. It was his intention to journey from one region to another and from one city to another city till he reached that place in Birat Arba. This he carried out, building a solid word-of-mouth reputation as an honest and God-fearing merchant with low-cost, quality children's garments.

When word came of his arrival in the marketplace of that section in Birat Arba, women came from all the villages in the area to buy garments from him, except for one woman—the mother of Menachem the Comforter—who bought nothing. Instead, she stood there, stoically, sadly, at the outer rim of the marketplace, apart from everyone else. Her eyes were very red, tears continuing to stream down her face, as if she had just heard the bad news about the Temple right then and there. In front of her there was no marketplace, no Ezra the merchant, no bustling of women and vendors, nothing save the Temple burning into large ashes and then into smoldering littler and littler ashes.

As the other women urged her to buy garments from Ezra, he heard one woman call out to her, "Mother of Menachem, come and buy these beautiful garments for your son."

There he had it! Now Ezra knew he found her. Only a mother's grief for a dead child could grasp the melancholy of her heart and soul. Yet, seeing the woman, Ezra knew it was she, and even her baby son at her side didn't seem to comfort her—yet.

"No!" she suddenly cried out, wringing her hands, "this is no time to buy clothes. I would rather have Israel's enemies strangled."

All the other women gathered around her, leaving Ezra alone with his goods. "Why do you say such things?" they asked her. "Your son lives! He's everything we expected him to be."

"Because . . ."

Now, Ezra wanted to hear what she had to say, so he quickly joined the crowd of women around her.

". . . the day he was born . . ." she said.

By the time she had said that, Ezra had squeezed his way through the crowd and reached the mother whose son was beginning to make a difference in the lives of Jews everywhere. "The Messiah is born," Ezra joyfully murmured to himself.

And she said, ". . . the Temple was destroyed."

Suddenly she collapsed.

When she came to, Ezra was by her side. The other women had made her as comfortable as they could.

When she acknowledged his presence, Ezra, who wanted nothing more than to serve his Messiah, said to her, "I am confident that even as at your son's arrival the Temple was destroyed, so, because of his arrival, the Temple will be rebuilt."

"'Tis small comfort," she cried and called out to her God.

"We must go on. Menachem will rebuild the Temple. He'll bring all us Jews together again."

"Yes?" She sounded as if she agreed—or wanted to.

Ezra sensed she was slowly coming around to his way of thinking. So, he said goodnaturedly, "Yes, Menachem's our savior, our comforter, but meantime he needs to be clothed and fed, eh, eh?"

Now standing on her own two feet, the mother said, "But I have no money."

"That is of no concern to me," Ezra said warmly. "Come and take for your son whatever he needs. After a time, I will come to your house, and you will repay me, if you can. If you can't, let me have the *mitzvah* of doing some good by you and your son." Ezra knew that he had to see the child again.

When he returned home to his family, the Jews there were ecstatic. What stories he told them of their Comforter. Cradling both hands, he showed them how he rocked the baby before he left the side of the mother. "I held him close to my chest. This way. I gave him clothing. The finest. The best quality."

That night, at the festivities, many wanted to know the same thing: "When will Menachem the redeemer come for us?"

"I don't know, but surely I shall ask the mother."

However, perhaps allowing the mother and son time enough to gain new strength and get over past hurts, Ezra went back to his plow and heifer for a few months. And waited.

A year later, he said to himself: "I will go and see that child to find out what has been happening to him."

So again Ezra made the journey. When he came to the mother he asked, "Your child—what has been happening to him?"

She replied, without a trace of bitterness, "Right after you saw me, winds and storms came, snatched him out of my hand, and carried him off and away."

Ezra examined the mother's face. Was she telling him the truth? Of course. Her calm face told him everything he wanted to know. There was no reason to believe otherwise. Her son Menachem, if only for a short time on this earth, had comforted the entire Jewish nation. Yet, in leaving the mother, Ezra knew that God Himself was surely comforting Menachem the Comforter wherever he was as he prepared himself.

The Messiah was not yet here, but in the name of Menachem the Comforter the Messiah would come another day. "This time for good," said Ezra, as he went back home to wait. As for Ezra, he eventually gave up his former life and returned to selling inexpensive quality garments for children. "I'm glad I listened to that Arab. Who knows," he dreamed aloud, "what life I will touch next?"

That is the whole story. Of course, as you read these words, you and I are sitting and weeping over the graves of two thousand years, still waiting, with the likes of Ezra the farmer, for the Messiah, and that is the way it has to be. Hence it is written, "Menachem the Comforter is far from me, even he who should revive my spirit" (*Lamentations Rabbah* 1:16, sect. 51).

This story is based on Palestinian Talmud, *Berachot* 2:4, 4a, and *Lamentations Rabbah* 1:16, sect. 51.

3

WHEN THE STORK BENSHED GOMEL

I

After Jerusalem—"beautiful in elevation, the joy of the whole earth" (Psalms 48:2)—was sacked again in the year 70 of the Common Era, "new winds later began to blow in Rome," according to one storyteller,[1] who also told us that the Roman emperor issued an order that the Jews should rebuild the *Beis Hamikdosh* (the Holy Temple) in Jerusalem!

Great was the joy among the Jews, and many who were living abroad decided to return to the Land of Israel to participate in the rebuilding of the Holy Temple.

At that time there were living two wealthy and generous brothers, Pappus and Lulianus. They set up tables with money on the entire road between Antiochi and Acco, and provided food, water and other help for all the Jews who were returning to the Land of Israel from the north. Antiochi was the capital of Syria and Acco was on the northern border of the Land of Israel.

---

1. This story is based on Rebbi Nissan Mindel's version in *Talks and Tales* monthly magazine, ed. Nissan Mindel, 44:539 (Brooklyn, NY: Merkos L'Inyonei Chinuch, Tammuz 5745 (July 1985)). The words *bensh gomel* loosely translate "to give thanks for deliverance from danger."

But the Jews had terrible enemies who were always ready to do harm to them. Those were the *Kuthim* (Samaritans), who decided to put a stop to the Jewish venture. They went to the Roman king and said to him: "Your Majesty will be making a big mistake if you allow the Jews to rebuild their Temple, for they will surely take the opportunity to fortify the walls of Jerusalem at the same time, and will be in a position to rise up in revolt against the ruler of Rome. Rome will then lose much income from them through the loss of the Head Tax and other taxes."

The king immediately regretted his order to the Jews, and asked the *Kuthim* what they would advise to enable him to withdraw his order without "loss of face."

"Very simple," they said. "The king need only order that he wants the Jews to set up the Temple in a different place, not where it stood previously, or to make it either smaller or larger than before.

"The Jews will surely not want to do this, so the king's edict will naturally be left unfulfilled."

The king was pleased with the suggestion, and decided to follow their advice.

II

The Jews were gathered together in the Valley of Beth Rimon to discuss and plan the very important details of the rebuilding of the Holy Temple.

In the middle of their earnest discussion, the order arrived from the king that the Sanctuary in the new Temple must be five cubits larger than the previous one—so that it should be larger and more beautiful than the previous one.

A huge cry rang out from the Jews. They knew that it was obviously a trick of the king to nullify his first order, knowing that the Law of the Torah forbids any change in the size of the Sanctuary.

Their great hopes were dashed to the ground. Their anger toward the false Roman ruler increased by the minute, and voices called for an uprising against Rome. The situation became very critical.

The Sages knew what a dangerous situation such a revolt could lead to, and they tried to calm down the agitated assembly.

In desperation they turned for help to Rabbi Yehoshua ben Chananiah [a close disciple to Rabban Yochanan ben Zakkai], a very learned Sage, a very wise scholar. They begged him, "Go out and speak to the assembly. Try and calm them and soften their bitter mood."

When Rabbi Yehoshua stepped forward, all eyes turned upon him, and a breathless silence filled the air as the people waited to hear him speak.

"I shall tell you a parable," he began. "A mighty lion caught a lamb and wanted to devour it. A bone stuck in its throat and he called out: 'Whoever will remove the bone from my throat will receive a big royal reward.'

"The stork jumped eagerly forward, stuck its long beak in the throat of the lion, and pulled out the bone. The stork demanded the promised reward.

"'What *chutzpah*! What insolence!' shouted the lion. 'It's a reward you still want? Is it not enough that you had your head in the mouth of a lion and come out alive? Away with you before I reduce you to a bag of bones! You've had your reward!'

"You see, my friends," Rabbi Yehoshua continued, "the Almighty sent us into exile—into the 'mouth of the lion'—so we must be glad to be alive. When the Almighty finds it to be the right time, He will help us to rebuild our Holy Temple without the help of the wild beasts amongst whom we now live."

"Amen!" called out the Jews in unison and quietly went their way, realizing the time had not yet come for the restoration of the *Beis Hamikdosh*. But their faith was unshaken that the time of the third *Beis Hamikdosh* would surely come, and come it will—any day, with the coming of the Messiah.

4

SON OF A STAR—
OR SON OF A LIAR?

Simeon Bar Kokhba
(died 135 C.E.)

PRESENTING A POTENTIAL MESSIAH
IN HIS TIME . . . SIMEON BAR KOKHBA

When Rabbi Akiva beheld Ben Koziva, he exclaimed, "'A star . . .
has risen out of Jacob' [Numbers 24:17]—Koziva [hence, not kozeva
("false hope") but *kokhba* ("star")] has risen out of Jacob. He is the king
Messiah." Rabbi Yohanan ben Torta responded: "Akiva, grass will be
growing out of your cheeks and David's son the Messiah will still not
have come" (*Lamentations Rabbah, 2:2–4*).

It couldn't have been the setting—a hot, sultry day in the Brooklyn
Botanical Gardens. It couldn't have been the Japanese garden setting—a
thousand millennia removed from a battlefield. It couldn't have been the

---

This short bio is based on information from the following books: Yigael
Yadin, *Bar-Kokhba* (New York: Random House, 1971); "Bar Kochba, 'The
Star,'" *Treasury of Jewish Folklore*, ed. Nathan Ausubel (New York: Crown
Publishers, 1948), pp. 233–237; Yehoshafat Harkabi, *The Bar Kochba Syndrome*
(Chappaqua, NY: Russell Books, 1983); Michael Grant, *The Jews in the Roman
World* (London: Weidenfeld and Nicolson, 1973); Ralph Nunberg, *The Fighting
Jew* (New York: Creative Age Press, 1945); *Encyclopaedia Judaica* (Jerusalem:
Keter Publishing House, 1971), vol. 4.

nice Jewish couple in front of me, wheeling a baby carriage, who together agreed out loud—perhaps they wanted everyone around them to hear—"that the government burns down whole cities while the people are forbidden to light lamps."

Why, I asked myself, as I heard these shocking words by another revolutionist of his day,[1] on Tisha B'Av[2] of all days! And then as I sat down on a park bench I realized that it was meant for me to hear these words. Because I was thinking of the man they called Bar Kokhba, or Bar Kosiva, or Bar Koseva or Bar or Ben. It was all the same to me. "Desolate lay Zion, in ruins moldered Jerusalem; the temple was but a heap of stones. Where once stood the sanctuary now grew weeds, and jackals howled in the Temple court where once David the Psalmist and his vast choir of Levites plucked the harp strings and raised their voices in songs of praise to the Eternal."[3] Heaping humiliation upon humiliation on the Jews, the cruel Romans thoroughly prevented the Jews from lighting their Godly lamps.

Sixty years after destruction of the Second Temple, the Roman emperor Hadrian[4] decided to solve the Jewish problem for all time. He banned circumcision, in effect legally equating the Jewish ritual with

---

1. Mao Tse-tung, 1893–1976. Chinese communist leader of the People's Republic of China, 1949–1976.

2. The Ninth day of the month of Av. Known as the "blackest day in the Jewish calendar," it's a day of fasting and mourning that commemorates the destruction of both the first Holy Temple (586 B.C.E.) and second Holy Temple (70 C.E.) in Jerusalem, post-Temple disasters, catastrophes, and horrors; Hadrian's leveling of Jerusalem; the death of Rabbi Akiva and nine other martyrs; the Crusades and their unholy massacres, rapes, and depredations; England's expulsion of the Jews in 1290; and Spain's expulsion of them in 1492, to name a few.

3. *Treasury of Jewish Folklore*, p. 233.

4. 76–138 C.E. Roman emperor, 117–138 C.E. There's a midrashic story told about the emperor Hadrian. One day, as Hadrian was being carried through the streets of Rome, a Jew passed by.

"Long life to you, great Emperor!" said the Jew, in greeting him.

"Who are you?" the emperor asked.

"A Jew."

"How dare you, a Jew, greet me?" raged Hadrian. "Off with his head!" he told his soldiers.

Chancing by was another Jew. Seeing the calamitous results, he decided not to greet the emperor.

At once Hadrian demanded to know who he was.

"I am a Jew."

castration. There could be no Jewish continuity, of course, without the mark of the Abrahamic covenant.

Then Hadrian, known in history books as a just and compassionate philosopher-king, replaced Jerusalem with a pagan city named Aelia Capitolina. On the site of the Holy Temple he built a new temple dedicated to the Roman god Jupiter. None of this sat too well with the local Jews, who bided their time as long as Hadrian was nearby in Egypt and in Syria.[5] But vengeance would be theirs one day, they vowed.

Worst was Tinnius Rufus, the Roman governor of Judea, who sadistically persecuted and excessively taxed the war-torn Judeans with the frank cruelty of a conqueror.

No wonder, then, taking in all the cruelties to his people, the greatest Jew of his generation, Rabbi Akiva,[6] "the Crown[7] of the Torah," the eternal optimist, set out to find the potential Messiah of the generation. All Jews prayed for a deliverer. Was Akiva not a Jew of the same yearnings and measure of faith? Yes, and a man of action. He knew what he had to do: He had to find a national warrior-king arisen to conquer and destroy Rome. Rabbinical tradition envisioned a warlike Messiah of Joseph who would precede the peace-making Messiah of David.

Out of the blue, a stranger showed up.

"Who are you?" Rabbi Akiva asked him.

"I am called Simeon bar Koziva," responded the stranger, and whatever else he said, he swept the great sage Akiva off his feet.

Right from the outset, Rabbi Akiva had no doubt that Bar Koziva was the

---

"Aha, I knew it. For passing me by without greeting me, chop off his head," he ordered his soldiers.

Seeing all this, the emperor's advisors were astonished. What did this all mean? they asked. "If you had the first Jew decapitated because he greeted you, then why did you the same thing to the second Jew because he did not greet you?"

The emperor Hadrian roared back: "Are you trying to teach me how to handle my enemies?"

5. Yigael Yadin, 19.

6. Rabbi Akiva ben Joseph, 40–135 C.E., Jewish sage and martyr in Palestine.

7. "A legend related that Moses in heaven saw God making crowns for the letters of the Torah and asked for the reason. God replied, 'A man called Akiva will arise who will deduce rules of Jewish law from every curve and crown on these letters.' His innovativeness in the field of Jewish law led to the saying, 'What was not revealed to Moses was discovered by Akiva.'" Geoffrey Wigoder, Dictionary of Jewish Biography (New York: Simon & Schuster, 1991), p. 21.

King Messiah. Bar Koziva, a powerful, dominant personality, regarded himself as the "savior who had come down to the Jews like a star from heaven, to deliver them from their somber troubles."[8] "And Akiva saw that this man's spirit was like flame and that his words were like sparks falling on kindling wood. He marveled greatly, and his heart was filled with gladness."[9]

Then Rabbi Akiva spoke these words of Scripture: "There shall come forth a star [kokhba] out of Jacob and a scepter shall rise out of Israel and smite the corners of Moab and destroy all the children of Seth" (Numbers 24:17).

Promptly, Rabbi Akiva renamed him Bar Kokhba, to fulfill the scriptural passage concerning the Messiah's arrival. Then, turning to the multitude of his twenty-four thousand disciples who were ready to follow the great sage in life or death, Akiva declared: "This is King Messiah!"

Bar Kokhba called, and volunteers arose from all parts of the country. He had most of the Jews believing God was on his side.[10]

Who was this King Messiah, this Son of a Star? According to one source, "he was a young and courageous man, with an altogether fascinating personality...a man of imposing stature, of enormous physical strength and possessed of decisive talent in military strategy."[11] In battle, he "catapulted stones on one of his knees and threw them back, killing several people" (Lamentations Rabbah 2:56). He may also be described as a quick-tempered leader who, in charge of both the economy and the army, ruled imperiously, concerned himself even with minor details, and did not refrain from threatening senior officers of his army with punishment or even from inflicting deterrent punishment. Bar Kokhba selected his fighting men by having each of them cut off a finger or by having them uproot a cedar tree (Lamentations Rabbah 2:2).

Except for Rabbi Akiva, all the other sages were up in arms. Very few would dare go against Akiva's wishes, but they watched Bar Kokhba develop an elite rebel army through harshness and cruelty. True, the Jews were now united under the leadership of a single commander in chief, but at what price? The Aggadah tells us that when he went to battle, he relied on his own powers rather than on help from heaven. By any other name, said the sages, that was arrogance—"self-aggrandizement against God." What other Jewish leader would say, to God, in battle after battle,

---

8. Encyclopaedia Judaica (Jerusalem: Keter Publishing House, 1971), 4:231.
9. Treasury of Jewish Folklore, p. 234.
10. Ralph Nunberg, The Fighting Jew, p. 44.
11. Ibid., p. 46.

"Neither assist us nor discourage us"? Yet Rabbi Akiva stood by his star. He truly "believed that Bar Kokhba's revolt against the Romans was but the first signal for a decisive political revolution that would create another world, in which the Jews would be able to live freely and to worship their God without interference."[12]

The Bar Kokhba rebellion lasted three years. Even in later generations, despite the disappointment engendered by his defeat, his image persisted as the embodiment of messianic hopes. This is evident from Maimonides,[13] who,

> in his codification of the laws of the Messiah, cites the story of Rabbi Akiva and Bar Kokhba as proof that the Messiah need not work miracles: "Do not think that the King Messiah will have to perform signs and wonders and bring about novel things in the world, or resurrect the dead, etc. It is not so. This is seen from the fact Rabbi Akiva was a great sage of the sages of the *Mishnah*, and he was an armor-bearer of King Bar Koziba and said of him that he is the Messiah King: and all the sages of his generation considered him to be the Messianic King until he was killed because of his sins, and when he was killed they realized that he was not; but the sages had not asked him for any sign or wonder."
>
> Despite the fact that Bar Kokhba did not actually redeem the Jews, the *Midrash* (*Asara Harugei Malchuf*) explicitly states that Rabbi Akiva made no mistake. Bar Kokhba was the potential Messiah of that generation, and had the generation merited it he would have redeemed them. It was only "because of sins" of that generation that he was killed.

Maimonides also sought to explain the failures of Akiva and of his contemporaries by citing the old claim that world order is not changed when the Messiah comes. Only Israel's suppression by the nations then will cease, and all will be free to study Torah.

In the end, Bar Kokhba, facing certain humiliation and death by the Romans, took a poisonous snake and wound it around his arm. "I prefer dying by the bite of a snake to dying by the sword of a Roman," he cried, and then collapsed.[14] A greedy Samaritan chanced upon the body of Bar

---

12. *L'Chaim Moshiach No. 6* publication (Brooklyn, NY: L.Y.O., 1993), p. 1.
13. 1135–1204. Jewish philosopher, jurist, and physician.
14. *The Fighting Jew*, p. 51.

Kokhba and cut off its head. And seeing this, the Romans, who wanted to capture Bar Kokhba alive, could not take any pleasure in their victory.

Soon little remained of the Jewish Revolt, except Bar Kokhba's minted silver coins, invalidated by perforation and hung around the necks of young Jewish girls as charms."[15] And soon, down through the centuries, historians—many Jews included—flipped a coin: "Heads, Bar Kokhba was the son of a star; tails, he was the son of a liar."[16] Who knew, and who will ever know!

And as I got up from my park bench, I realized that it was evening now,

---

15. Not by a long shot has everyone agreed that Bar Kokhba was a bona fide Messiah. Writes Rabbi Newman: An unbeliever asserted to the Rabbi of Berditchev [Levi Yitzchak, died 1809] that the great masters of old were steeped in error. For instance, Rabbi Akiva believed that Bar Kokhba was the Messiah, and enrolled under his banner. Thereupon the Berditchever narrated this parable: "Once upon a time the only son of an emperor fell ill. One physician advised that a piece of linen be smeared with a burning salve and wrapped around the bare body of the patient. Another physician, however, discouraged this, because the boy was too weak to endure the pain the salve would cause. Thereupon a third physician recommended a sleeping-draught; but a fourth physician feared this might endanger the heart of the patient. Upon this, a fifth physician advised that the sleeping-draught be given by teaspoonsful to the patient, as often as he awakened and felt the burning of the salve. And this was done.

"Thus, when God saw that the soul of Israel was sick unto death, he wrapped it in the biting linen of poverty and misery, but laid upon it the sleep of forgetfulness, in order that it might endure the pain. However, lest the spirit expire utterly, he awakens it from hour to hour with a false hope of a Messiah, and again puts it to sleep until the night shall have passed and the true Messiah shall appear. For such reasons the eyes of the wise are sometimes blinded" (Martin Buber, "Rabbinic Wisdom," *The Reflex*, May 1929, p. 65). Newman also points out that (in *Nifloath Beth Levi*, published by A. J. Kleiman, Piotrkov, 1911, p. 22) we find the same story, and the lesson drawn from it is as follows: "The Jewish nation—God's firstborn—became dangerously ill with immorality and wickedness. The Prophets and the later Sages were unable to achieve any improvement, with the result that God prescribed Exile to purge us of our spiritual maladies. In order, however, that we, in our weakened state, may be able to bear it, He has permitted false Messiahs to mislead even the noblest Jews in order to sweeten the Exile by a hope of Redemption." Louis I. Newman, *The Hasidic Anthology* (Northvale, NJ: Jason Aronson, 1987), p. 250.

16. From the recently discovered letters, we know today that his true name was Kosba or Bar Koseba, not "Bar Kokhba" (Aramaic for "son of the star") as Akiva had called him. By altering one letter, the sages, in a punning allusion, referred to him as the "son of falsity," *Bar Koziba*; perhaps, they were alluding to his proving a false hope, a "cause of disappointment." *The Bar Kokhba Syndrome*, p. 43.

and the lamppost lights were on. Quickly leaving the Botanical Gardens, I found myself on the long stretch of Flatbush Avenue, separating the Gardens from Prospect Park. And as I walked along gazing up at the lampposts, on an otherwise wistful, dark path, I reassured myself that one day, as our sages tell us, Tisha B'Av will be a day of great rejoicing. And why not! The Messiah's birth[17] started on such a night as this—with a little light.

No, Bar Kokhba's lamp was not extinguished, nor ever will be. After two thousand years, each of us still carries the messianic torch. Just one more light. Just one more summer day or winter night. Just one more mitzvah. Just one more star.[18] And the Messiah will be here!

---

17. The Messiah was born on the Ninth of Av, upon the destruction of the Second Temple. Likewise, every year on Tisha B'Av, the Messiah is born, for in every generation there is one soul worthy of being Messiah, if the generation merits, as we find in the Talmud (*Sanhedrin* 98b). Also: "Our Sages teach [The Jerusalem Talmud, *Berachos* 2:4; *Eichah Rabbah*, 1:51] that *Mashiach* [or *Moshiach*] was born on Tisha B'Av. This is not merely a description of past history. On the contrary, the intent is that every year, Tisha BeAv generates a new impetus for the coming of the Redemption. . . . Herein lies one of the differences between the future Redemption and the previous redemptions in our history. In the exodus from Egypt, the Jews who were not found worthy of being redeemed died in the plague of darkness [see Rashi on Exodus 13:18]. Similarly, in the return to Zion led by Ezra [fifth or fourth century B.C.E.], the majority of the Jewish people remained in Babylon. In contrast, the future Redemption will include all the members of our people: every single Jew will leave the exile. . . . In an expanded sense, the Redemption will also affect those Jews who have not yet been born, for their birth will be hastened, and it will also affect the souls of the previous generations who will arise in the Resurrection of the Dead." *Sound the Great Shofar: Essays on the Imminence of the Redemption*, adapted from the Addresses of the Rebbe of Lubavitch, Rabbi Menachem M. Schneerson (Brooklyn, NY: Kehot Publication Soc., 1992), p. 74.

18. "The star . . . alludes to both *Moshiach* and to every Jew . . ." as the Baal Shem Tov taught, "that within each and every Jew there is a 'spark' of the soul of *Moshiach*." Rabbi Abraham Stone, *Highlights of Moshiach* (Brooklyn, NY: S.I.E., 1992), p. 17. See also Rabbi Heschel Greenberg, who wrote: "The soul of every Jew is comprised of five distinct levels, ranging from the lowest aspect of the soul to the highest. The first four levels represent the soul's different modes of expression: action, emotion, intellect and will. The fifth level—*yechidah*—represents the soul's very essence. While every Jew possesses a soul comprising all five levels, it is *Moshiach*, the *yechidah* of the Jewish people, who makes it possible for the essence of every Jewish soul to be revealed." "*Moshiach*: A Cornerstone of Jewish Belief," *Di Yiddishe Heime*, vol. 9, no. 4 (Brooklyn, NY: N'shei Ubnos Chabad, Summer, 5751), p. 10.

5

THE PRINCE OF SAND

Yehudah HaNasi
135 C.E. – 200 C.E.

PRESENTING A POTENTIAL MESSIAH
IN HIS TIME . . . RABBI YEHUDAH HANASI

"Rav said, 'If he [Messiah] is from among the living, then he is
Rabbeinu Hakadosh [Rabbi Yehudah HaNasi].' (Comments Rashi:
'If Messiah is alive today, he is definitely Rabbeinu Hakadosh.').''
Babylonian Talmud, *Sanhedrin* 98b.

Rabbi Yehudah once said, "Some win eternity after years of toil, others
in a moment."[1] To the ancient Jews of the Common Era, Yehudah the
Prince[2] always had a great future, because he understood where he and
his people were going at all times. How did he know this? The Torah,
which is the map of the world, told him so. In compiling the *Mishnah*,[3]

---

1. Talmud, *Avoda Zera* 10b, 17a.
2. Yehudah HaNasi was also known as Yehudah the Patriarch, Rabbi, and
Rabbeinu Hakadosh (our holy teacher).
3. "Why did our teacher [Rabbi Yehudah] the Patriarch [write down the
Mishnah] and not leave matters as they were? [It was] because he observed that
the number of disciples was diminishing, fresh calamities were continually
occurring, the wicked kingdom [of Rome] was extending its domain and
increasing in power, and Israelites were wandering and emigrating to distant
countries. Therefore he composed a work to serve as a handbook to all, the

the basic part of the Talmud, he also earned the undying gratitude of the Jewish people. No wonder, then, it's recorded there, "From Moses until Rabbi Yehudah HaNasi, there was not another man who combined Torah and worldly greatness to such a degree" (Talmud, *Sanhedrin* 37a; *Gittin* 59b).

Not all the Jews of his time, however, could see his holy light and what it meant for them. To some, Yehudah the Prince was a prone-to-anger, holy man who would give you the shirt off his back, yet he was often misunderstood. Much of this had to do with his suffering in silence from numerous illnesses. In silence, did I say? It was the kind of silence that spoke more clearly than speech.[4] On his face was the "sublime poetry of pain"[5]—translated into a kind of *ahavas Yisrael* that endeared him to his people,[6] the holy face and even-handed humility that Jews came to expect from him.

Such a time was when he invited Rabbi Chiya bar Abba and his twin sons, Yehudah and Hezekiah, to a feast at his home. If Rabbi had left well enough alone, the two lads probably would have remained absolutely quiet for the night. Yet the Prince bade them to drink "plenty of wine, to induce them to speak."

When they were feeling the wine's effect, they began by describing the time of the Messiah's arrival, saying: Messiah will not appear before the two ruling houses in Israel—the Exilarch in Babylonia and the Nasi [Yehudah HaNasi was the current patriarch] in *Eretz Yisrael*—came to an end, for it is written, "And [the son of David] shall be for a Sanctuary, for

---

contents of which could be rapidly studied and not forgotten." Ira Robinson, *Moses Cordovero's Introduction to Kabbalah: An Annotated Translation of His Or Ne'erav* (New York: Yeshiva University Press, 1994), pp. xiii–xiv; and Moses Maimonides, *Mishneh Torah*, introduction.

4. "Rabbi Yehudah said: Suffering must be regarded as a precious experience. He himself suffered for thirteen years, six of them from bladder stones and seven years with diseased gums and teeth." Pearl, *Stories of the Sages*, p. 149. Compare with the later words of the Kotzker Rebbe (Rabbi Menachem Mendel of Kotzk, 1787–1859), who said, "When one feels like shouting and doesn't, that is when one truly shouts."

5. Heinrich Heine, *Harz Journey*, 1824.

6. "Rabbi Jose ben Abin said: All the time that Rabbi Yehudah was ill and suffered terrible pains, no woman ever miscarried or suffered a difficult pregnancy. This was because the rabbi's sufferings were an atonement for the community at large." Pearl, *Stories of the Sages*, p. 149.

a stone of stumbling, and for a rock of offense to both houses of Israel"
(Isaiah 8:14).

Hearing this, Yehudah the Prince felt deep pain—this time, emotional. He had to remind himself that this was a party, so he did not
remove the twins from the house. But he told them, "You thrust thorns
into my eyes!"[7]

At this, Rabbi Chiya remarked: Master, don't be angry—it's not
entirely their fault, for the numerical value of letters in *yayin* is seventy
[*yod* (10) + *yod* (10) + *nun* (50) = 70], and likewise the letters in *sod*
[*samekh* (60) + *vav* (6) + *dalet* (4) = 70]. Take no notice of them, I bid you.
After all, when *yayin* ("wine") goes in, *sod* ("secret") comes out.[8]

Rabbi Yehudah understood and was ready to forgive. Were not these
twins also named Hezekiah and Yehudah—one his namesake? Yes. So,
now, he put everyone at ease by making a little joke at his expense.

"King Hezekiah[9] 'broke in pieces the brazen serpent that Moses had
made' [2 Kings 18:4], and that Hezekiah's predecessors had spared when
they suppressed every form of idolatry. Hezekiah's ancestors left something undone whereby he might distinguish himself, and my ancestors
left room for me to distinguish myself!"[10]

With the mention of "Hezekiah" and "Yehudah," their own names,
the twins smiled, their father smiled, Yehudah the Prince managed to
smile through his pain—indeed, everyone else smiled, too—and the
party went on. Later that night, Yehudah HaNasi, in mentioning the
incident again, admitted he took his own advice that night: "He is great
who is not ashamed to admit he does not know" (Jerusalem Talmud,
Hagigah 1:8), he said.

By every account, Rabbi Yehudah's beginnings were dramatic. On
the very day Rabbi Akiva died, he was born.[11] He succeeded his father,
Simeon ben Gamliel, as patriarch (Nasi) at the crucial period following

---

7. Talmud, *Sanhedrin* 38a.

8. *The Book of Legends*, p. 264.

9. "Jews have no Messiah to expect, for they already had him at the time of
Hezekiah" (Talmud, *Sanhedrin* 99a). However, see also *The Book of Legends*, p.
339, where it points out that Hezekiah was rejected as the Messiah because he did
not sing a hymn of praise to God after the Almighty performed "all manner of
miracles" for him.

10. Talmud, *Hullin* 6b–7a.

11. Talmud, *Kiddushin* 72a; see also *The Book of Legends*, p. 261: "As soon as
R. Akiva died, Rabbi was born."

the unsuccessful revolt of Bar Kokhba against the Romans. The sixth to hold the title of Nasi in an uninterrupted chain that went back to Hillel's descendants, Rabbi Yehudah was the only one who is called "the prince" of Palestinian Jewry.

In a moving tribute to the Prince, Rabbi Shimon bar Yochai[12] once said: All of the seven qualities which the sages attributed to the righteous—handsomeness, strength, riches, wisdom, longevity, honor, and children—were established in Yehudah HaNasi and his sons.[13]

Witness that his authority as patriarch lasted fifty years. He was responsible for the appointment of all judges and teachers and devoted himself to the religious and economic reconstruction of Jewish life after the tragic period through which it had passed.

A wealthy man in his own right, he owned large tracts of land on which he developed agriculture and raised cattle. He also owned his own boats, which put him in an excellent position of exporting and importing wool and linen products. As for his generosity, in times of famine he often opened his private storehouses to the public.

It might be said Yehudah the Prince could do almost no wrong, and that's because his judgments and instincts were very good—and his connections to the Roman ruler "Antoninus"[14] certainly helped. Undoubtedly, this won a period of peace for the Jewish community. In a reference to Psalms 121:4, he once noted: "God is called Protector of Israel though he protects all men" (*Sifre* to Deuteronomy, # 38), and there was something that suggested that Yehudah the Prince was a universal man who'd willingly bring salvation to the whole of humanity—or else what's a Messiah for!

No one knows for certain whether all the stories (read: legends) about his friendship with Emperor Antoninus are true, "but they reflect his close links with the Roman authorities, and his open quasi-royal status, and were perhaps even intended to show that the Jewish leader was on a

---

12. Author of the mystical classic, the *Zohar*— *The Book of Splendor*. Flourished circa 100–160 C.E. Two of his famous sayings include: "Three people who dine together and do not exchange words of Torah are considered as though they have eaten an idolatrous sacrifice" and "There are three crowns: the crown of Torah, the crown of Priesthood, and the crown of Royalty. The crown of a good name is superior to them all."

13. *Avot* 6:9.

14. Presumably, Marcus Aurelius Antoninus, 121–180 C.E., who greatly respected the ideas of Torah and its sages.

par with the Roman emperor."[15] However, he "saw his chief task not in nurturing Roman friendship for political advantages, but in concentrating on the internal structure of the Jewish community in Palestine, and particularly on its unity around the central authority of the Sanhedrin and its *Nasi*."[16]

He also united the Jews of Palestine by stressing the use of Hebrew in their everyday language, even though Aramaic was the official language in his time. However, with Roman officials, he spoke Greek. There's a story about one of his female servants who "was able to teach some visiting scholars the meaning of some obscure Hebrew words."[17] It was hardly unusual for Rabbi Yehudah to keep a staff of highly intelligent female household servants. After all, "woman," to use his own words, "was endowed with more intelligence than man" (Talmud, *Niddah* 45b).

For most of his life, sickness dogged him, and he remained bedridden during his last years. Most of his adult life he spent in Bet Shearim, in the lower Galilee, where he had his academy. In his later years, however, he lived in Sepphoris, where the climate was easier for him to deal with, what with his protracted illnesses (bladder stones and diseased gums and teeth, among others).

At long last, heaven intervened, and he received a respite from his ailments. One day, goes the story, one of his female servants was cleaning a room, and she found a nest of small mice. She was about to destroy them when Yehudah the Prince stopped her and said, "No, let them live; the Torah teaches us, 'His mercies extend over all His creatures' (Psalms 145:9)."

Thus, seeing his compassion for even animals, heaven relented and eased his pains.[18]

Not only did many disciples flock to him, but also the prophet Elijah always sat among them, at the Bet Shearim academy, to hear him expound Torah."[19]

It happened that one day, on *Rosh Chodesh*, Elijah the prophet was not on time.

Rabbi Yehudah asked him why he was late.

---

15. Wigoder, *Dictionary of Jewish Biography*, p. 245.
16. Pearl, *Stories of the Sages*, p. 326.
17. Ibid., p. 328.
18. *Book of Legends*, p. 262.
19. Talmud, *Bava Metzia* 85b.

"I took a long time to arouse Abraham to wash his hands before prayer. Then I had to get him back again on his bier. I do the same for Isaac and Jacob."

Rabbi Yehudah was not certain he understood what Elijah the prophet meant by that. So he asked him, "Why couldn't you attend to all of them at the same time instead of separately?"

A great look of wonderment filled Elijah's face. "I was afraid," he said, "that if they all prayed together at the same time, they might bring the Messiah before his time."

Reluctantly, both Elijah the Prophet and Rabbi Yehudah accepted the inevitable: this generation of Jews was not ready for the Messiah. Still, the Prince and the Prophet dared to hope . . .

As he neared his end, Rabbi Yehudah said things that were not altogether understood by some of his peers—certainly not by the multitude of Jews who loved him no less for whatever he said and did. He counseled them to "die that you may not die; live not that you may live. Die here where you must die, not hereafter where you need not die."[20] He also once said—which was shocking even in those days, according to Jewish law—"Let my coffin be open to the public" (Talmud, *Ketubot* 12:3).

As with the recent passing of the seventh generation Rebbe of Lubavitch, Rabbi Menachem Mendel Schneerson,[21] many of whose chassidim expected and wanted him to live forever, so it was with the Palestinian Jews, who couldn't fathom life without their holy prince.

But the Torah always has the first and last word, Rabbi Yehudah counseled his people. Note, he pointed out, "As the waves of the raging sea hurl themselves against the earth, but their force is broken by the sands on the shore, . . . so do the nations roar and fume and seek to overwhelm the world, but recede, broken and powerless, when Israel cleave to God" (Zohar, *Exodus* 225b). "Cleave to God," Yehudah the Prince came to teach and stayed to learn; he intended to illumine and was himself illuminated (a paraphrase of the Talmud's *Pesachim* 25b).

In the end he joined the sands of all time—the Jews being the sand, and he, their Prince.

---

20. Talmud, *Avot de Rabbi Nathan*, ch. 32.

21. After a very long illness, he passed away on *Gimmel Tammuz*, 5754/June 12, 1994.

6

Now Bring Me A Minstrel

Dark dark dark—what comes next? More darkness. And more darkness. Then, suddenly—suddenly—the Prophet Elisha said: "Now bring me a minstrel. And it came to pass when the minstrel played, that the hand of God came upon him"—and first a sound, who knew where it came from or who played it, but yet it arrived unheralded and hung up on a tree, like a star from afar; it might have been a blue note; then from nowhere a red note appeared, fainter and trail blazing, a fresh scent, like the whiff of a buck, alerted, in a dry river bed that might be turning at the coming of a weekday on the Sambatyon River—and then a drift of light and a sound or two or three—green da yellow la brown re—a purple Mozart had never discovered, played on the very harp of David itself!

At early dawn, when the whole world lay hushed in sleep, two rabbis walked home together. Suddenly the morning breezes began to blow, and under their touch the harp strings stirred and played of themselves.

Finally, the walkers noticed that the slight mist disappeared, the leaves of the trees let go of their burden, and a light rain gave in. When the wind blew the dark away, they beheld the morning burst. Banners and streams of colors of October welcomed them.

All night the Sages of the Talmud, Rabbi Hai the Great and Rabbi Simeon ben Halafta, had been traveling in the valley of Arbel, and now,

41

as the first rays of the sun shot over the rim of the horizon, Rabbi Hai was filled with rapture. "Rabbi," he cried to his companion, "this will be the way the Jewish Redemption will come, like the rising sun, gradually, slowly, until it will appear in the sky in all its dazzling radiance."

7

THE ARI FROM THE "OLD OF DAYS"

Isaac Ashkenazi Luria
The AriZal
1534–1572

PRESENTING A POTENTIAL MESSIAH
IN HIS TIME . . . ISAAC ASHKENAZI LURIA

In the works *Shivchei Ha'ari* (9b) and *Eimek Hamelech* (11:4), it is quoted in the name of Rabbi Chaim Vital, o.b.m., that "Rabbi Luria was *Moshiach ben Yosef*." Also see *Toldos Ha'ari* (Jerusalem, 199, 258), on what the holy Ari said about himself concerning this.

"Angels came bearing baskets full of flowers"[1] and the whole city of Safed, in Palestine, joined in the holy festivities. It was that kind of marriage of merit, when the daughter of Rabbi Isaac Luria[2] Shlomo, and

---

This short bio is based on the following books: David Rossoff, *Safed: The Mystical City* (Jerusalem: Sha'ar Books, 1991); Geoffrey Wigoder, *Dictionary of Jewish Biography* (New York: Simon & Schuster, 1991); *Safed Spirituality: Rules of Mystical Piety, the Beginning of Wisdom*, trans. Lawrence Fine (New York: Paulist Press, 1984); and *Encyclopaedia Judaica* (Jerusalem: Keter Publishing House, 1971), vol. 2.

1. Apochrypha, 3 Baruch 12:1.
2. A kabbalist reverently known as Ari HaKadosh, the holy Ari (from the initials of Ashkenazi, Rabbi Isaac, or Ari, meaning *lion*).

the son of Rabbi Yosef Karo,[3] married in 1570: "almost as if the two aspects of our one Torah, the hidden and the revealed, were united. . . . Together, the two different, yet inseparable aspects of Torah were revealed to the world by these two Torah personages, and symbolized by the marriage of their children."[4]

Probably nothing would have made the Ari happier than if this union produced the Messiah of the generation. Why do I say this? Because, based on certain allusions made to his disciples, he believed himself to be "the Messiah, the son of Joseph," destined to die in the fulfillment of his mission.[5] And within two years, on July 15, 1572, when he was thirty-eight, a cholera epidemic snuffed out his life. His grave in Safed, with a large lantern atop it, was and remains a place of pilgrimage for successive generations.

Till the end of his days the Ari acted as if he had to prepare the world of Jewry for Messiah ben David. There were times when he was driven by inner forces that he could not reveal to anyone except his closest disciple, Rabbi Chaim Vital (1543–1620).

At the same time, the Ari carried on his everyday business affairs. He was born in Jerusalem from a German (or Polish) Ashkenazi father and a Sephardi mother. When he was very young, his father died, and his mother moved to Cairo, where she raised him in the home of his uncle, Mordechai Frances, a wealthy tax collector. As he grew into a man, the Ari earned his living as a merchant.[6] (Later, like many of his contemporaries in Safed, the Ari continued to conduct his business there; indeed, three days before his death from the plague, as sick and weak as he was, he made up his accounts with his customers.[7])

While living most of his life in Cairo, the Ari, for seven years following

---

3. 1488–1575. Codifier of *halachah* (Jewish Law). Popularly known as *Beis Yosef* and *Shulchan Aruch* ("The Set Table"), for his major works. Concerning the Redemption, he once said, "Anyone who does not mention the 'Kingdom of the House of David' in the blessing of 'He who rebuilds Jerusalem' does *not* fulfill his obligation of prayer. Therefore, we must make reference to the Kingdom of Heaven, the House of David, and the Holy Temple. Indeed the Jewish Nation will not be redeemed from Exile until we demand all three" (Rabbi Yosef Karo, *Beis Yoseph, Tur Orech Chaim,* ch. 38).

4. Rossoff, pp. 65–66.

5. *Encyclopaedia Judaica,* 2:574.

6. Wigoder, p. 313.

7. *Encyclopaedia Judaica,* 2:573.

his marriage, isolated himself throughout the week in a house on the island Jazirat al-Rawda, on the Nile River. Only on the Sabbath did he return to his home.

He spent another seven years studying the Talmud. Legends about him abound. One tells us that even while sleeping, the Ari "studied Torah with the souls of *tzaddikim* in *Gan Eden*. For every secret that was revealed to him, the Ari confessed that he had cried out to the Lord until tears flowed down his cheeks and into his beard. All this Rabbi Luria had earned by perfecting himself from his youth, little by little, until he reached the level of divine spirit and was privileged to study with Elijah the prophet."[8]

Not too many people know that before the Ari's theoretical teachings became known, he won fame as a poet.[9] As the poet Robert Frost once said, "Writing a poem is discovering." In the case of the Ari's poems, "writing a poem is revealing," and continues to reveal the inner secrets of the Torah. Here's one of his major mystical efforts:

HYMN FOR SABBATH EVE

I sing in hymns
to enter the gates,
of the Field
of holy apples.
A new table
we prepare for Her,
a lovely candelabrum
sheds its light upon us.
Between right and left
the Bride approaches,
in holy jewels
and festive garments.
Her Husband embraces Her
in Her foundation,
giving Her pleasure,
squeezing out His strength.

8. *Toldos Yitzchak*, ch. 6; *Shivchei Ari*, pp. 10b–11a; Rossoff, p. 86.
9. *Encyclopaedia Judaica*, 2:577.

Torment and trouble
are ended.
Now there are joyous faces
and spirits and souls.
He gives Her great joy
in twofold measure.
Light shines upon Her
and streams of blessing.
Bridesmen, go forth
and prepare the Bride's adornments,
food of various kinds
all manner of fish.
To beget souls
and new spirits
on the thirty-two paths
and three branches.
She has seventy crowns
and the supernal King,
that all may be crowned
in the Holy of Holies.
All the worlds are engraved
and concealed within Her,
but all shine forth
from the "Old of Days."
May it be His will
that He dwell among His people,
who take joy for His sake
with sweets and honey.
In the south I set
the hidden candelabrum,
I make room in the north
for the table with the loaves.
With wine in breakers
and boughs of myrtle
to fortify the Betrothed,
to strengthen the weak.
We plait them wreaths
of precious words
for the crowning of the seventy

in fifty gates.
Let the *Shechinah* be adorned
by six Sabbath loaves
connected on every side
with the Heavenly Sanctuary.
Weakened and cast out
the impure powers,
the menacing demons
are now in fetters.[10]

Here the entire poem's structure (as well as all of Lurianic *Kabbalah*) is
laced with messianic tension. "Written in much the same Aramaic style as
the *Zohar*, this song dramatically depicts the welcoming of the beautiful,
adorned Sabbath bride. In rich mystical symbolism and vivid erotic
imagery, Luria describes the love between male and female that occurs on
the Sabbath and the joy that love creates."[11]

The year 1570 had to be a good year for the Luria family. Besides
moving to Safed in Galilee, he married off his daughter and continued his
mystical studies with the famed kabbalist Moshe Cordovero (the Remak),[12] to whom he referred as "our teacher whose light may be
prolonged" and "my late teacher" (after the Remak shortly passed away
that same year).

For six months the Ari lived in Safed before he revealed his greatness
to his divinely predestined disciple, Rabbi Chaim Vital, a young man at
the time. Their union as mentor and disciple/scribe would radically alter
the dimensions of mystical thought. Deeply revered and possessing strong
charisma, he soon had the reputation of a saint enjoying divine inspiration, and it was even believed that he understood the language of animals,
the chirping of birds, the rustling of leaves, and the speech of angels.[13]

Other reliable sources tell us he knew "everything that happened in a
man's lifetime and what type of damage he had caused in the upper
worlds. He divined the source of a man's soul, and his purpose in this

---

10. Fine, pp. 78–80. Reprinted with permission from Paulist Press.

11. Ibid., pp. 64–65.

12. 1522–1570. Popularly known as the Remak, the initials of Rabbi Moshe
Cordovero.

13. Wigoder, p. 313; *Shivchei Ari*, p. 11a; Rossoff, p. 111.

world, as well as his earlier *gilgulim* [reincarnations], and thereby would prescribe guidelines to rectify one's soul."[14]

Truly this holy man, the Ari, was from the "old of days." And a rereading of the above poem makes me wonder how much he is revealing about himself. The stanza

All the worlds are engraved
and concealed within Her,
but all shine forth
from the "Old of Days."

could easily be applied to the life of the Ari. How else can one explain such a holy mystic—in whom "all the worlds are engraved and concealed within" him—if there is an explanation at all! On Friday afternoons, he used to go with his thirty-five (more or less) disciples and prostrate himself on the graves of talmudic rabbis to unite with the souls of the dead. Why? What comes readily to mind are the words of the *Chabad* Rebbe, Rabbi Shneur Zalman of Liadi, the Alter Rebbe (1745–1812). Once, he was overheard saying, "Dear God, I don't want your paradise, I don't want your World-to-Come. I just want you."[15]

Do I go too far in connecting the Ari's actions and the Alter Rebbe's? No, and here's why: The Ari founded a school of Jewish mysticism known as the Lurianic *Kabbalah*. According to Wigoder and others, the chassidic movement was strongly influenced by Lurianic *Kabbalah* and adopted the special liturgy that developed from his doctrines.[16] "Thus," adds Fine, "long before the phenomenon of charismatic leadership emerged in Eastern Europe among the *chassidim* (as evidenced by that sect's impressive line of vivid religious personalities), Isaac Luria established himself as mystical master par excellence. Indeed, there is ample evidence that the figure of this sixteenth century teacher served as a prototypical model among some of the chassidic masters."[17]

Which would put the Ari not only in the "days of old," but also in the "days of new"!

---

14. Rossoff, pp. 85–86.

15. Rabbi Chaim Meir Heilman, *Beit Rebbi* (Berditchev, 1903); Avraham Yaakov Finkel, *The Great Chasidic Masters* (Northvale, NJ: Jason Aronson, 1992), p. 76.

16. Wigoder, p. 313.

17. Fine, p. 64.

The Ari wrote almost nothing, explaining that when he held a pen, visions appeared before him like a great river and he could not channel this river through a mere pen. Still he had a lot to say. Every person, he pointed out, had a part to play in the messianic drama and every action had national and messianic significance.[18]

The Ari's method of teaching was unique. He would introduce a topic and then walk away without delving into it. That was a clue for Rabbi Chaim Vital to continue the discourse in depth to the other disciples.

Here's not so much a story as a revelation: Rabbi Yaakov Arazin was one of Rabbi Luria's outstanding disciples. One night Rabbi Arazin went, distraught, to the Ari's house. "I am Rabbi Chaim's senior," he told his master. "Why must I listen to him deliver the discourse? It does not seem fair."

The Ari looked at him. "Of all my disciples," said the Ari, "only Rabbi Chaim is able to understand my wisdom. I have come into this world only to teach him."[19]

A sad story: One Friday afternoon, in the midst of singing with his disciples, the Ari suddenly said, "My comrades, would you like to come with me now to Jerusalem and have *Shabbos* there?"

Jerusalem was a long way off. Still, some responded affirmatively at once; others hesitated.

"We're ready, Master," they answered, "but let us first tell our wives that we won't be here for *Shabbos*."

Suddenly the Ari looked crestfallen. He shook and cried out, "Heaven help us! Had you all answered yes yes yes! without any second thoughts, the Jewish people would have been redeemed. But as soon as you hesitated, the moment passed and now the Messiah will not come."[20]

The Ari lived in an age "that ushered in an altogether new era." Rabbi Isaac Luria declared that as of then "it is not only permissible but a duty to reveal *Pnimiyut haTorah*, the esoteric part of the Torah."[21] As the Ari's thoughts emerge through Rabbi Chaim Vital's work, *Etz Hachaim*, his revelations of Torah were intended to usher in the era of Messiah. Based on the *Zohar*, they deal with such esoteric concepts as *tzimtzum* (the

---

18. Wigoder, p. 312.

19. Rossoff, p. 97; *Shivchei Rabbi Chaim Vital*, p. 29a.

20. *Shivchei Ari—The Praises of Arizal*, pp. 9b–10a.

21. J. I. Schochet, *Mystical Concepts in Chassidism* (Brooklyn, NY: Kehot Publication Soc., 1979), p. 16.

voluntary restriction of Divine light), *klippot* (shells, "evil covers" of man's spiritual core, that form a barrier between man and God), and the four worlds of Emanation, Creation, Formation, and Action (referred to in *Kabbalah* as *Abya*, the acronym of their initials: *Atzilut, Beriah, Yetzirah, Asiyah*).

Yet instead of the Messiah, the plague came, and the Ari knew he had little time left to divulge the Torah's secrets. Were he to live another five years, he said, he would be able to achieve rectification for all the world and bring about the Final Redemption and Messiah. But his generation wasn't found worthy, and the Ari was taken away in his prime.

So we Jews went on, then. It would have to be another Messiah of his generation to "shine forth from the 'Old of Days' . . . May it be His will that He dwell among His people."

8

THE GOLEM SPEAKS OUT

Judah Loew ben Bezalel
The Maharal of Prague
1520–1609

PRESENTING A POTENTIAL MESSIAH IN HIS TIME . . . RABBI JUDAH LOEW BEN BEZALEL

A letter to the *Maharal* of Prague, written by his student, Rabbi Yisroel, appears in Volume II of the *Maharal's* work, *Nesivos Olam*, in section "*Nesiv Halashon*," p. 83. "The Angel of God in our midst, may he dwell with honor in our land, our Righteous Messiah, the King at our head, King of Judah...the remarkable Gaon, Rabbi Judah Loew, may our Master live forever."

Wherever Jews dwell, somewhere it must be—or should be—written that the most public life of a man is the most private. Such a man created the Golem . . . life! . . . a man whose kabbalistic powers could control the Angel of Death and—dare we say—affect God Himself.

This pedagogue, this saintly rabbi, this philosopher, this moralist, this mathematician . . . this Judah Loew ben Bezalel was known to us as

---

This bio is based on the following books: Ben Zion Bokser, *From the World of Kabbalah: The Philosophy of Rabbi Judah Loew of Prague* (Philosophical Library, 1954); B. L. Sherwin, *Mystical Theology: The Life and Works of Judah Loew of Prague*, 1982; Yudl Rosenberg, "The Golem," *The Great Works of Jewish Fantasy*

the Maharal[1] of Prague, a king's confidant,[2] a descendant of famous rabbinic scholars, who could trace his lineage back to King David.

The same holy man who was a genius from early childhood, engaged at the age of ten to an equally remarkable girl named Perl.

Everything in the Maharal's life came from the Word, the Bible. More than any other philosopher before him, he deepened and expanded "the idea of Israel's historic uniqueness as a nation." He viewed Israel[3] as the primary link in the drama of creation for which all else came into being.[4] We, who attended his every word,[5] wanted to believe he was God's human Torah on earth. If he were not the Messiah himself, then who was! Right from the outset, nay, even before he was born, he was already protecting the Jews of his generation. That was probably why, after birth, "he was named Judah Liva [Loew, Loewy], the Lion, for he would be like a lion who does not permit his cubs to be mangled."[6]

A truth—for I was there, in spirit if not yet in form. Let me tell you what happened. Rabbi Bezalel and his *rebbetzin* (who was pregnant) were having a party. A party, did I say? Please excuse my mixed-up wires—

---

and Occult, trans. Joachim Neugroschel (Woodstock, NY: Overlook Press, 1987); Geoffrey Wigoder, *Dictionary of Jewish Biography* (New York: Simon & Schuster, 1991); Yaakov Dovid Shulman, *The Maharal of Prague: The Story of Rabbi Yehudah Loew* (Lakewood, NJ: C.I.S., 1992); Rabbi Dr. Aaron Mauskopf, *The Religious Philosophy of the Maharal* (New York: Bernard Morgenstern, 1966); *Hasidim: Continuity of Innovation*, ed. Bezalel Safran (Cambridge, MA: Harvard University Press, 1988); Frederic Thieberger, *The Great Rabbi Loew of Prague* (London: Farrar, Straus and Young, 1955).

1. The name "Maharal" is formed by the initial letters of *Moreinu Harav Rabbi Loew*, which means, "Our teacher the master Rabbi Loew."

2. Emperor Rudolf II of Hapsburg.

3. "Israel may be considered as contributing the element of form to the world's otherwise chaotic and undisciplined character. And if Israel should, God forbid, perish, the whole world will fail." Quoted in *From the World of Kabbalah*, p. 170.

4. *The Religious Philosophy of the Maharal*, p. 79.

5. A characteristic story is told of Rabbi Mendel Menachem Morgenstern of Kotzk (the Kotzker Rebbe, 1787–1859). "He once heard the Rabbi of Gostnin complaining in a room next to his own that the Maharal of Prague often repeated himself in his writings. He opened the door and said: 'We take great pains to understand every word of the Maharal, and for you it is too much if he repeats his words!'" *The Great Rabbi Loew of Prague*, p. 28.

6. *The Great Works of Jewish Fantasy and Occult*, p. 164.

—I was still not assembled in those days—

—the party was actually a Seder, one of those ritual meals the Jews hold on the festival of Passover. I daresay Rabbi Bezalel, who was a very religious man, could have used my help during those days, too. The Jews were forced to live in a cramped, walled-in ghetto and wear yellow badges. Expulsion orders banned them, and pogroms separated one Jew from another Jew. Christian nations persecuted them, often accusing them of using the blood of Christians when preparing the matzos for the Passover festival.

When I think of it, I foam at the mouth. What lies! What *chutzpah!* Those Christians could look it up in the Bible and the Talmud. It says right there that Jews are to regard blood as an unclean thing. Jews are strictly commanded to avoid blood even more than fat, for the Torah calls blood an abomination.

Yet scarcely one Passover in Austria and Hungary passed without the body of a dead Christian child being discovered in a hidden spot belonging to a rich Jew, where it had been thrown so that the man might be accused of killing the child in order to use its blood for ritual purposes.

So it also happened in Worms. On that Passover night, when all Jews would collectively leave their prison called Egypt, one sacrificial lamb was secretly being prepared—a ritual accusation against the father of the Maharal, Rabbi Bezalel.

From where I stood, in the spirit of things, I saw a Christian man, I would say he was thirty-something, carrying a dead child in a sack; from shadow to shadow he moved through the ghetto. To me, there was no doubt he was up to no good. If no one saw him, and the darkness of the night and deserted streets were in his favor, he intended to throw the body through a small window into the cellar of the Rabbi's house.

Inside, the people were just sitting down to the *Seder*, when the wife of Bezalel was suddenly seized with labor pains. Quickly the women got up from their seats and attended the *rebbetzin*. As for the men, some had the presence of mind to rush out of the house to fetch the midwife.

Ach-aveee, at that moment that fiend with the dead child was across the road from Rabbi Bezalel's house. Suddenly he saw a mob of men running toward him. Quick—quick—he had only time to act, certain he was that they intended to seize him. Quick—quickly he turned on his heels and fled toward the Christian section of town.

Spotting a man running with a sack and racing behind him the people from Rabbi Bezalel's house, the sentinels thought that a thief was being chased. Once they saw the Jews overtake and dart past the thief, they scratched their heads. What was going on? But they decided: Act first, ask questions later. So they nabbed the man, searched his sack, and found the body. It didn't take long: the sentinels and their captain had their ways to make him confess his evil design.

As it is written, the report of this deliverance immediately spread through the whole town. Rabbi Bezalel had prophesied his newborn son would comfort us and free us from the ritual accusation. And he named him Judah Loew, as it is written: "Judah is a lion's whelp; from the prey, my son, thou art gone up" (Genesis 49:9).[7]

I guess, then, Rabbi Bezalel really didn't need me at that time. In the year 5272[8] from the creation of the world, the holy Maharal was born in Worms[9] (southwest Germany), and it was a night most Jews would never forget, and now you, too, know why.

And you should also know that my master, the Maharal, may he rest peacefully until the Messiah comes, once said: "Man, being incomplete, is not at rest and is therefore always striving for his completion. . . . And this itself is his perfection.[10] This is what this holy man was about. And nothing is lost in the transition from the legends about him—his magical halo—to his actual life.

After a long twenty-two-year courtship with a woman named Perl,[11] which can rival any true romance in today's world, in 1553, he was

---

7. *The Great Rabbi Loew of Prague*, p. 147.

8. "According to the family chronicles, he is supposed to have been born in 1512, but his first biographer, Nathan Gruen (1885), puts the date ten years later. He does so because the brother Chayim, whom he considers much older, was a schoolfellow of [Moses] Isserles [the Rema, the greatest rabbinical authority of his time] and the latter was born in 1520. Today [1954], it is generally accepted that Isserles was born about 1510; if so, the objection to 1512 as the year of Rabbi Liwa's birth falls to the ground." Ibid., p. 12.

9. According to family tradition, Worms was considered the birthplace of the Maharal, although other accounts place his hometown as Posen or Prague. See *The Great Rabbi Loew of Prague*, pp. 8–9.

10. *Netibot Olam*, 1595, quoted in *From the World of Kabbalah*, p. 69f.

11. According to the family chronicles, after their betrothal—he at ten, she at six (which was a common happening in those days)—Perl's father lost his complete fortune. Naturally, the father freed my Master from all obligations, but he would hear nothing of the kind—he would not give up his beloved Perl. Meantime, Perl supported her parents by selling bread and pastries. Then suddenly something wonderful happened. In a letter written by Perl to Judah Loew's parents, she said: "About six weeks ago, I was carrying a large

Landesrabbiner (chief rabbi) of Moravia in Nikolsburg (Mikulov), after which he went to Prague. There he founded a yeshivah called *Die Klaus*, organized circles for the study of the *Mishnah*, to which he attached great importance, and regulated the statutes of the *chevra kaddisha* (burial society), founded in 1564.

I know you might be amused by what I am about to say, given who is saying it, but if Rabbi Judah Loew had not been born, the Jews of his day would have had to create him. Wherever he served he introduced widespread reforms in community organization and Jewish education. "Each congregation of thirty members is bound to provide for six talmudic students and six apprentices."[12]

But the true greatness of the Maharal, who lived in a spiritual world without losing sight of the realities of life, was that he restored the *Mishnah* to a major role in Jewish educational curriculum and that his whole life's work was a new interpretation of the *Aggadah*. I cannot count all his authored Torah and kabbalistic commentaries and seminal works that will serve as guideposts on the highways of Jewish thought until the Messiah arrives and explains all the rest.

The Maharal based his beliefs on Jewish thought, especially kabbalistic concepts, but he himself wrote in a style comprehensible to any thinking Jew. And here, according to Gershom Scholem, is why the Maharal is forever linked to *Chassidus*, because he popularized kabbalistic ideas.

---

basket of bread loaves through the street to bring them to the marketplace, a soldier rode right up to me on horse, holding his sword in his hand. I grew very frightened and turned to run away, but before I could do so, he took his sword and thrust it through a loaf of bread from my basket." . . . Perl caught the horse by the bridle and demanded payment. She was poor, she pleaded, and had to support a family. "I looked up at the soldier. His face was pale and his eyes were not evil, as are the faces of most soldiers." . . . The horseman replied that he was hungry and had no money on him. As Perl would not let him go, he pleaded with her: "If I do not have this bread, I will die. Take this pouch from my saddle. I will come back within twenty-four hours to pay you for the bread, and if I do not, you may keep whatever is in the pouch."

The soldier did not return, and, after a month of trembling, Perl finally opened the pouch and found therein a heap of shining, solid gold coins. Now Perl and her parents were well-off again, and the wedding took place, he at thirty-two, she at twenty-eight, in 1544. Quoted material comes from *The Maharal of Prague: The Story of Rabbi Yehudah Loew*, pp. 35–37.

12. Quoted by M. M. Yoshor, *Saint and Sage* (New York: Bloch Publishing, 1937), p. 92.

Basic to his thought was, the Torah mediates between God and the world. As for the Messiah, he notes, "The essential function of the Messiah will consist in uniting and perfecting all so that this will be truly one world."[13]

So, when will he come? Even I want to know. As far as any Jew knew, along the path to the Messiah, "The world is to exist six thousand years: two thousand years of desolation, two thousand years of Torah, and two thousand years of 'the days of the Messiah'" (*Sanhedrin* 97a). The Maharal explains that "before 'the days of the Messiah,' even if the Jewish people had merited the Messiah, he could not have come. But now that the two thousand years of 'the days of the Messiah' have commenced, it depends on us: Once we merit it, *geulah* [redemption] will come immediately, but even if we never become worthy of it, it must occur during this period (*Netzach Yisrael*, ch. 27)."[14]

Yet he also stressed that the role of the Jewish people in this process is crucial. Always maintaining that the diaspora is "a perversion of the divine order, which assigns to each nation its own suitable place," he stressed that "the return of the Jews to their own land is an essential precondition to mankind's eventual redemption."[15]

I know, sooner or later, you're going to insist I identify myself, the narrator of myths and facts, or you may think you already know who I am. Really, I prefer to remain as anonymous as a piece of clay, but please think what you like! Whoever or whatever I am, the Maharal took a special liking to me and confided many items to me. Neither can I speak nor sing a song, but I am a good listener. On me he tried out his ideas before he wrote them down in his notebooks, and that seemed to work out nicely for him. After all, he had nothing to lose. I had no mouth in those days to refute anything, let alone to form even a little *o*.

So I'll tell you the what but not the why about my Master. He remained in Prague until the year 1584. The next years made my head whirl. In 1584, he became a rabbi in Posen, then shortly returned to Prague for four years; then went back to Posen as chief rabbi of Posen and of all Greater Poland, and finally returned to Prague, becoming its chief rabbi, and remained there for his last eleven years until his death.

---

13. Quoted in *From the World of Kabbalah*, p. 176.

14. Menachem M. Brod, *The Days of Moshiach* (Kfar Chabad, Israel: Chabad Youth Org., 1993), p. 52.

15. Geoffrey Wigoder, *Dictionary of Jewish Biography*, p. 246.

And now I come to the sad part of my story: the death of the Great Rabbi Judah Loew. Like a good storyteller, I have two versions. One, appropriately, is called the Posen version, and you can look it up in various books, including Frederic Thieberger's *The Great Rabbi Loew of Prague* (pp. 174–175): It begins . . .

One night before the High Holidays, Rabbi Loew noticed a light in the synagogue opposite his house. He went there and saw on the praying dais a man of sinister appearance, sharpening a glittering knife in front of a scroll with a long list of names. Rabbi Loew ran away in terror, but when he recovered his self-possession, he saw clearly what was the matter. The plague had begun to spread amongst the community and that apparition in the synagogue was the Angel of Death, threatening the members of the community. He took courage, went again to the synagogue, snatched the list away from the Angel of Death, and hurried back to his room.

He looked at the list containing the names of the men and women of the community whom he had saved from death by the plague. But a piece of the list had remained in the hand of the Angel of Death, and on it was the name of Rabbi Loew. When the holy days were over, the Rabbi fell ill and died.

I also tell you, in my capacity as teller of legends, the Prague Version. It begins . . .

Rabbi Loew was very old. His kabbalistic power had always prevailed over the Angel of Death whenever he had approached. Death therefore tried a ruse. He hid in the heart of a magnificent dark red rose, which the Rabbi's favorite grandchild presented to her grandfather. (Or perhaps it was his own wife who gave him the rose to remind him of his youthful happiness.) As my Master accepted the flower, half gladly, half reluctantly, Death claimed his victory.

On August 22 (18 Elul), 1609, at the age of ninety-seven, my Master, whose mind remained active right to the end, died. Nine months later, Perl followed him. The rest is legendary.

Which brings me up. Whatever you may think about me, a golem should have nothing to do with the Maharal. Just as my Master said (about another matter), "It is most unworthy to suppress books or silence teachers,"[16] so I've been given a little time to speak out. Did my Master give me life from nothingness, from a lump of clay? That's what is said.

---

16. Beer HaGola, 1598, ch. 7.

But I'll never tell. This I shall say: In 1745, Meier Perles, a descendant of the Maharal, first published the family chronicles under the title *Megillath Yuchasin*, as a supplement to his work, *Mate Moshe*. As Frederic Thieberger (*The Great Rabbi Loew of Prague*, p. 8) notes, "In view of the relationship between Perles and the subject of his chronicles . . . it is, however, remarkable that a work published [more than] one hundred and twenty years after the death of the Great Rabbi Loew makes no mention of any of the famous legends attached to his person, for instance that of the Golem."

So let's put this story to bed. I've nothing more to say. Whether the Maharal created me, I'm no longer the golem I used to be, and the blood libels against the Jews are a thing of the past. What's left of me is—and I neither deny this nor admit it—may be lying in wait in the attic of Prague's famous Altneushul synagogue, awaiting either a new threat to the Jewish people or the advent of the Messiah. And I wouldn't be the least surprised to see both the Messiah and my Master at the same time, in the same body and soul, as the same person. For me it'll be like old times. Or else what's a golem for?

9

SOMETIMES THE ANSWER IS NO

D oes God always answer prayer?" the holy man was asked. "Yes,"
he said. "And sometimes the answer is—'No.'"[1] If we are to
believe the essentials about us Jews, then we also have to
understand our legends and myths. Such is one, hundreds of years ago,
when the most legendary pious man in the city of Safed, Palestine, Rabbi
Yosef de la Reina, said no to God.

"Yes," he affirmed as he had always affirmed every day, "I believe with
perfect faith in the coming of the Messiah; and though he may tarry, I will
await daily for his coming,"[2] but he no longer wanted to wait and see what
happened. He determined to storm heaven—if need be—to bring back the
Messiah.

Of course that didn't sit too well with God, nor with the dutiful
Messiah. Unfortunately, at the time, the Messiah had his own problems.
Rumor had it that he lived in the most beautiful palace in heaven, but his
hands were fettered with golden chains![3] Why was this so? Our sages tell
us we'll have to wait for him to come to get an answer to that.

---

1. Alistair Cooke, BBC Radio 4, "Letter From America," March 8, 1981.
2. Moses Maimonides (the Rambam), Commentary to *Mishnah; Sanhedrin* 10:1. Twelfth Principle of the Thirteen Principles of Faith.
3. Manasseh ben Napthali, quoted by poet Heinrich Heine, *Ludwig Boerne*, p. 130f.

Well aware of the Messiah's ordeal, through their rigid kabbalistic practices, were Rabbi Yosef and his disciples. Still, by freeing the Messiah, the rabbi reasoned, he'd be relieving the suffering of all Jews for all time to come. All the more reason to go on with the plan.

But how did he hope to accomplish this? Against an army of countless evildoers headed by Satan and his wife Lilith, Rabbi Yosef had five good men, all disciples, all, like him, who were pure in heart and intention. Together, they would pool their kabbalistic resources and overcome all the obstacles, each of them agreed. God, they truly felt, was on their side. With that ever present in their hearts and souls, they worked it out spiritually to prepare for their ordeal.

The plan included keeping their bodies spartanly cleansed, their thoughts focused, and their clothes immaculate. Nothing was to come between them and their Maker. They also had to prepare to travel light and carry enough provisions to last for a long time. "And be ready in three days," Rabbi Yosef told them. "All Israel is depending on us."

But was the rabbi himself ready? Who could say? Certainly none of his followers who found him crumbled up like a ball, in a state of collapse, in the local synagogue. No one dared touch Rabbi Yosef when he was in such a state of *dveikus*. But of course he was ready, as he stood up to greet them. The dazzling radiance streaming from his face told them so. Besides food and drink, Rabbi Yosef had also completed his other preparations, including taking along with him a writing quill and parchment.

"We are ready to reach the highest regions of heaven," he said as he limbered up his body. "Let's be on our way." One by one the troop of holy men left town for the wilderness. "And may the Lord be with us," they all said as one.

During the first part of their trek, there were no songs among them. Their business was too serious for that. Yet certain singers are irrepressible, and surely Rabbi Isaac, one of the five disciples, with a wisp of a body, was one: he finally found his voice again as they made their way through a dense wooded area and finally came in silence to Meron where all of them prayed at the grave of Rabbi Shimon ben Yochai, the teacher of all kabbalists, the author of the *Zohar*.

There they spent three days and three nights. All that time they touched no food or drink, but delved into the mysteries of the *Zohar* and sent up flaming prayers to God. As the day's activities went on, Rabbi Isaac, whose voice seemingly grew in baritone as his body melted away, managed to sing some of the holiest music this side of heaven, to accompany the prayers and fasting. And there were other good sides to

Rabbi Isaac's music: for one, it soothed Rabbi Yosef and put him to sleep—in a good way, of course. And oh the things he dreamt of! That night, he got more than he bargained for; that night, in a haunting dream, Rabbi Shimon and his son Eleazer came to him, looking as if they were in a fighting mood. He remembered the legends about them. Once, in a hidden cave they fled from the Romans, where they remained for twelve years, constantly learning Torah. It is said that they achieved such "an exalted level of holiness that when they emerged at last, their gaze alone was enough to scorch the surroundings which appeared mundane to their holy eyes. God sent them back to their cave for yet another year, for fear that they would destroy the world."[4]

Now Rabbi Yosef saw it all again, in his dream. The two holy men left the cave and approached—or God sent them to—the waiting Rabbi Yosef, who had no idea what to expect. But what they said was designed to put the fear of God in anyone.

"Your task is impossible. Turn back. You won't come back alive." Yet the two rabbis, whose gaze was still enough to scorch the surroundings, nonetheless blessed Rabbi Yosef and wished him well.

"I know our cause is right," Rabbi Yosef told his disciples upon waking from his dream and relating what happened while he slept. All five men agreed with him, and promptly, to show their determination, once they reached another forest near Tiberias they delved into the profoundest mysteries of the *Kabbalah*, studied the sacred formulae, calculated *gematriot*, and drew mystic designs of God's ten emanations, the *Sefirot*. We're not certain of the exact number of times—either twenty-six or thirty-three would be a good guess—the rabbis immersed themselves in the Sea of Galilee, but they did purge themselves of every impurity. And one day as Rabbi Yosef prayed ardently for the prophet Elijah to come and help them in their noble quest, Rabbi Isaac also took the time to record the whole sequence of dream and events in a hastily made-up song, which he then filed away in his head for some future time when he might express all that had happened to him. What did the other disciples think of the activities of the eccentric Rabbi Isaac? For now they looked the other way. But nothing escaped the all-seeing eyes of Rabbi Yosef, who meticulously jotted down every happening on his parchment. To emphasize the importance of his call for the prophet Elijah, the

---

4. *L'Chaim* publication, No. 266 (Brooklyn, NY: L.Y.O., May 7, 1993), p. 2.

harbinger of the Messiah and the Redemption,[5] Rabbi Yosef cried out
with tears that unlocked the gates of heaven, "O Elijah, come and teach
me the right approach to reach the Messiah. My people cry out for him
20,000 times in their prayers each year. The *Kaddish*, the *Shema*, *Lechoh
Dodi*, *Aleinu*—they're all based on the Messiah.[6] O Elijah, I cannot say
how many Jews have died with the song '*Ani Ma'amin*' on their lips!"

Perhaps Rabbi Isaac was the best singer among them, but Rabbi
Yosef's prayers reached the heart of the prophet Elijah immediately, and
at once he appeared to the rabbi.

"Whatever you wish, beloved Rabbi, I will help you do, but I fear for
your lives if you go on with your quest," Elijah said.

From his prison behind the wall, the beleaguered Messiah was deeply
moved by Elijah's offer. How he wished it could be himself appearing
before this rabbi and his holy five, to help them. He had a certain feeling
about this Rabbi Yosef. What was it? This was a man prepared to be
mesirus nefesh (willing to give up one's life) to bring the Messiah. As it is
written, "The Messiah is standing on the other side of a wall that is already
cracked and crumbling. He is[7] "watching through the windows, peering
through the crevices." And it surely goes without saying that a glance
from the Messiah gives a person the energy that he particularly needs to
complete the required preparations so that he can be privileged to greet
the Messiah."[8] From that moment on, the Messiah kept both eyes and
ears on Rabbi Yosef. He witnessed everything. He heard the rabbi plead

---

5. "As we know, *Eliyahu HaNovi* will announce the Messiah's arrival, in
keeping with the verse, 'Behold, I am sending you Eliyahu the prophet before
the coming of the great and dreadful day of God' (Malachi 3:23). As we say in
birkas hamazon, 'May the Mericiful One send us Eliyahu the prophet (may he be
remembered for good), and let him bring us good tidings, deliverance and
consolation.'"—Menachem M. Brod, *The Days of Redemption: The Redemption
and the Coming of Moshiach in Jewish Sources* (Kfar Chabad, Israel: Chabad Youth
Org., 1993), p. 126.

6. Rabbi Heschel Greenberg, *Shlichus: Teaching about Moshiach, a Resource
Handbook for Shluchim* (Brooklyn, NY: Nshei Ubnos Chabad, 1994), p. 26.

7. *Shir HaShirim*, 2:9; cf. *Kiddish Levanah* in *Siddur Tehillat HaShem*, p. 239.

8. *From Exile to Redemption: Chasidic Teachings of the Lubavitcher Rebbe Rabbi
Menachem M. Schneerson, Shlita, and the Preceding Rebbeim of Chabad on the Future
Redemption and the Coming of Mashiach*, compiled by Rabbi Alter Eliyahu
Friedman, trans. Uri Kaploun, vol. 1 (Brooklyn, NY: Kehot Publication Soc.,
1992), pp. 107–108.

with Elijah. "Oh Elijah," cried the rabbi, "you who shall turn the heart of the fathers to the children and the heart of the children to the fathers,[9] lend me your help to make all Israel feel the Godliness of their lives. Help bring the Messiah. That's why you've come to me now. Why don't you admit it, please?"

From the sidelines, the Messiah blew his *shofar*, as if to say, "Elijah, help the rabbi. Help him to the Promised Land and Redemption. Can't you see how determined he is? It's obvious that all he wants is the best for our people and for the glory of God. Oh, Elijah, help him, for the rabbi must do what he has to. His 'character is shaped by deeds.'[10] He aspires—he dares—he lives!"

Do not think, for one second, that the Messiah would hold back his speech. We know only too well, "Each time he hears Jews groan, he tries to break his chains. . . . But God has vowed not to release him till the Jews . . . tear the chains from his hands."[11] We can safely assume the Messiah has always spoken up for the Jews. To what extent and to what degree? Over the millennia both the Messiah and Elijah the prophet have held secret talks with God[12] about the Redemption of the Jews, and many differing remarks have been leaked out. By who it would be hard to say. But some of what has been said is known.

"The Son of David will come when all the souls destined for earthly bodies will have been born."[13]

---

9. Malachi 3:23.

10. Moses Montefiore, *Liberal Judaism*, 1903, p. 119.

11. Sholom Asch, "Epilogue," *Sabbatai Zevi*, 1930, p. 130f.

12. In the *Midrash* (*Yalkut Shimoni*) a discussion is recorded between God and the Messiah. "These Jews who are protected by you," God says to the Messiah, "their sins will one day bring about your imprisonment in an iron yoke, make you like a calf whose eyes are blinded, and stifle your spirit under the yoke. Through their sins your tongue will cleave to your palate. Is this your will?" God asks the Messiah. "Lord of the Universe," the Messiah answers, "with joy I accept it . . . on condition that not one Jew shall perish. And not only shall the living be saved, but also all who died from the days of Adam till now. And not only those, but also the prematurely born shall be saved in my days. And not only those, but even all whom it entered Your mind to create, but who were not created. On these conditions I am willing to suffer . . . on these conditions I accept it." As printed in *L'Chaim Moshiach*, no. 9 (Brooklyn, NY: L.Y.O., April 1994).

13. Talmud, *Yebamot* 62a.

"Messiah will come in a generation for extinction."[14]

"The Son of David will come at a time of such want that even a fish will be unprocurable for an invalid."[15]

"Messiah will come in a generation all good or bad."[16]

"The redeemer will come when men despair of the redemption."[17]

"When will Messiah come? 'Today, if ye hearken to his voice.'"[18]

These remarks passed through the lips of the Messiah, and God passed them on to His people; then He said, in His own way, which was later paraphrased by Maimonides, to wit: "All these matters concerning the Messiah's advent will not be known to anyone until they happen."[19]

"And so," Elijah the Prophet, growing sad because he saw it as a lost cause, said to Rabbi Yosef, "I'll help you, but you hardly stand a chance. Satan will run ragged over you. Still, there is a way, slight chance as it may be."

"Yes?" eagerly asked the rabbi. "Yes? . . ."

Said the prophet: "This is what you must do if you do anything at all. You must be as holy and as pure as the angels, and have the street smarts of Satan and his army of wild dogs. Nothing less in your makeup will do."

So Rabbi Yosef and his holy five followed the advice of Elijah the prophet and remained where they were for twenty-one days, each day eating less and less. If his "troops" wavered, he rallied them by reminding them they had chosen this path, "for we have sworn before God that we won't rest until we have driven Satan from the earth and have brought Messiah. We won't rest until we've restored God's holy presence on earth—the way it was when the Temple stood in Jerusalem. We won't rest and, to that end, we're ready to sacrifice our lives."

Ah, self-sacrifice—*mesirus nefesh*—the very words that warmed the cockles of the Messiah's heart! "Yes, now more than ever, Rabbi Yosef is my man," beamed the Messiah as he shook his golden shackles in the gleaming palace in the sky.

For the next three weeks, the Messiah and his heralder Elijah observed the rabbi and his disciples never touching food or impure things, bathing

---

14. Eleazer ben Pedat, *Pesikta Rabbati*, ch. 1, ed. Friedmann, p. 4b.

15. Talmud, *Sanhedrin* 98a.

16. Talmud, *Sanhedrin* 98a.

17. Talmud, *Sanhedrin* 97a.

18. Talmud, *Sanhedrin* 98a (Psalms 95:7).

19. Moshe ben Maimon (the Rambam), *Yad: Melakim* 180, 12:2.

twenty-one times a day to purify their bodies in the Sea of Tiberias. "So that you become as holy as the angels," is the way Elijah put it. The Messiah especially watched them very closely, and when the three weeks were up, the holy men recited *Minchah* wearing *tallis* and *tefillin* and intoned "Flaming angels surround the Holy One, blessed be He!" Slowly it was dawning on the holy travelers that God was still very much on their side; slowly the silent, imperceptible manifestation of God, the still, small voice, the inevitableness, the regularity of nature, the starry field, the simple flowers bearing witness, in every breath, in the four elements of substance, new aspects of the Torah were unfolding constantly in front of them. And if the eyes of the Messiah were on Rabbi Yosef, there was also no doubt that the eyes of Rabbi Yosef were on the Messiah. So reasoned, for better or worse, the holy rabbi, who began to feel more and more certain that he and his disciples were on the right path—these "men with ascetic eyes and sensual lips" who "dandle eternity on their fingertips."[20]

With so much going for Rabbi Yosef and his five disciples, it was inevitable that, through kabbalistic formulas, they deliberately invoked the angel Sandalfon and his angel hosts to appear along a fiery road, the very earth trembling and shaking underfoot, as Sandalfon stood regally in a holy fire with a whirlwind sweeping up everything in its path around him. Terrified and very weak themselves, Rabbis Yosef and Isaac managed to keep their feet under them, despite the winds, and held up the other four holy men, who fell at once into a swoon. "Praise be His Name whose glorious kingdom is forever and ever!" Rabbi Yosef and Rabbi Isaac kept saying.

Helpless to do anything himself, the Messiah could hear the angel Sandalfon speak in a voice so low that it was almost inaudible—yet it sounded like distant thunder, something that frightened mere mortals. But no longer were Rabbi Yosef and his holy five such men. Their rigorous training so far paid off—they could speak and act like angels. Except for one thing: Rabbi Yosef lost his voice. After all, who wouldn't have, hearing Sandalfon thunder, "Insolent mortals! How dare you cause such turmoil in all the seven heavens? You are mad, mad, mad, mad!" So what were the holy men to do without their spokesman, who was too terrified to speak?

That was when Rabbi Isaac's singing came through. Opening his mouth wide, he let go of sounds never heard on earth. "Ya ya na pa la la la—la la la pa na ya ya!" But the angel Sandalfon knew the song—he had

---

20. Judah Stamfer, "Kabbalist," *Jerusalem Has Many Faces*, 1950, p. 16.

composed it a long time ago and had left it on a shelf in the treasurehouse of heavenly music. And now? Here was the rightful singer of the music, tiny, wistful, no longer timid, singing it for the rightful owner of the song. With this turn of events, there was only goodwill bestowed upon the rabbis by the angel Sandalfon.

"Holy rabbis," said the compassionate angel, "I know you're not doing this for your own glory, but for our Father in heaven. I know you desperately need my help, but I must tell you that only the archangel Metatron can help you defeat Satan. Yet, Rabbi Yosef, I'm afraid you may have reached the end of your road: no person on earth can endure the presence of Metatron and live. So I don't know what to tell you."

"Tell me how to be worthy to reach the Messiah," said Rabbi Yosef.

"Rabbi," said the angel Sandalfon, "how easy those words come off your tongue."

"O Sandalfon, you misunderstand our rabbi," protested Rabbi Isaac.

"With all due respect, I do not," said the angel to both Rabbis Isaac and Yosef. "You can be certain that all angels in heaven are in agreement that the Messiah should come and bring the Redemption for the Jewish people who suffer in Exile. Yet—and it's a big 'yet.' I myself cannot help you. My one duty is to guard the way along which the prayers of the righteous mount to heaven and to bring them before the Throne of God. So far, as I see it, there is nothing but the Almighty between you and Satan's planned torturous death for you. Even the angels cannot beat Satan, and the Lord knows we've tried enough times. Only if God Himself stands by you will you be able to achieve your aim."

"God is on our side," all five disciples said at once, coming to the aid of Rabbi Yosef.

"Spoken like high-minded men," the angel said. "But how can you expect God to support you unless He believes that the right time has come for the Messiah?"

With another blast from his *shofar*, the Messiah spoke out, this time to the angel Sandalfon, who heard it loud and clear.

"Rabbi," the angel advised him, "even angels have a right to change their minds. I've just been advised that your next step is to meet the archangel Metatron—with your eyes closed. 'The angel of death is all eyes.'[21] Keep your eyes and those of your disciples shut tight, I warn you, as you focus solely on the fear of God. You should know that God has

---

21. Talmud, *Avoda Zeira*, 20b.

given over the task of preventing Satan from growing stronger to Metatron and his hosts. But I don't know if this information will help you one bit. Still—" and again the angel lifted his head as if he were heeding a higher voice than his, which in fact he was—the Messiah's *shofar*. Then, nodding his head, he said, "It's still worth a try."

"Yes," said Rabbi Yosef, "we must pray to the Almighty One as we've never prayed before. We must make our prayer a window to heaven."

"Your prayer must reach the seventh heaven right next to the heavenly throne. That is where the archangel Metatron is," said Sandalfon.

"Then we'll do it, we'll do it," lilted Rabbi Isaac, and the other disciples joined in on the refrain.

"Don't be fooled," Sandalfon cautioned them. "Not all prayers reach him. Metatron's so very busy with all his underlings. And, I must warn you, even if he hears you, the terror of his presence can kill you. It's really not worth the gamble."

"I am a Jew," Rabbi Yosef said very slowly. "Now and forever, I am a Jew."

"He's a Jew," sang Rabbi Isaac. "Now and forever, he's a Jew. And had there been no Jews, there would have been no Torah.[22] And had there been no Jews, there would be no Messiah. So he's a Jew, now and forever he's a Jew," Rabbi Isaac sang and danced before the angel.

"Say no more," thundered Sandalfon. "I must go. May God be with you." Then he disappeared as fast as he appeared.

The holy men knew what they had to do. Into the desert they went, where they found an enclosure in the rocks. There, they remained for forty days to learn how to live life without food. In the enclosure they also found an underground stream where they bathed—some say twenty-one, some say thirty-three, days—to make their bodies holy. They studied the *Kabbalah* and prayed nonstop. What they had to do and face seemed like a superhuman task. But they carried out all that prescribed by the angel Sandalfon, including reciting the Ineffable Name of God formed by seventy-two letters and calling upon Metatron, the angel of this mystic name, to appear before them.

For better or worse, it worked, and Metatron the archangel whose look could kill anyone, hid his own face from Rabbi Yosef, while his holy five cowered behind him with their eyes closed.

---

22. Judah Halevi, *Kuzari*, trans. Hartwig Hirschfeld (New York: Schocken Books, 1964), 2:117.

With the help of Metatron, Rabbi Yosef and his disciples flew to heaven in a whirlwind.

Speaking of whirlwinds, Satan got wind of it and was in a rage. But what could he do? The rabbis were heading in his very direction, and if Rabbi Yosef got past his army of evildoers there was no stopping him from reaching the Messiah and bringing on the Redemption. It was enough that nothing else was spoken of but this rabbi's daring attempt to bring the Messiah down to earth. Even the Messiah himself was pacing back and forth in his heavenly palace, hopeful that soon he would be free from his golden chains and descend on his white donkey to the children of man.

Soon word came to him that Rabbi Yosef and his holy five had entered Satan's hemisphere, which was entrenched behind two mighty barriers, one of iron, stretching from heaven to earth, and the other formed by a great sea. This was the great wall of the sins of the Jewish people. How could anyone break through that where others had failed? Yet that was exactly what Rabbi Yosef was doing. Well, damned if Satan would let him go farther!

But, then, another messenger brought in more bad news. Miraculously the holy men were heading toward Mount Seir.

Satan's wife Lilith cried out, "Quick, Honeybun, there's no more time to lose. Send out the dogs." When word got back to Satan that Rabbi Yosef had rendered his dogs useless, he hurried off to press his complaints before God.

"What kind of God are you to let a mortal being push you around?" Satan put it straight to God. "Behind your back, the angels are up to dirty tricks. Trying to bring on the Redemption of the Jews when you're squarely not for it now. Trying to knock me off, too. Lord of the Universe, don't let them do it. You need me as long as the Jews still sin."

God agreed with Satan—the time was not right. "Your arguments have merit. And surely I know that the Messiah would love to help his people. Truly, a real people pleaser he is. Yet, I tell you, every day I take many things into consideration. Then along comes a saintly man, and it makes me wonder, if I'm not being overly harsh with my people. Any people who possesses a Rabbi Yosef de la Reina is indeed worthy of the Messiah's quick coming."

"Or never coming!" shouted Satan.

All the angels disagreed with that. They were ready to dance with joy and party for the Redemption.

"I don't believe it." Satan was fit to be tied. "How can you call such a man a saint? He's impudent. He's turning heaven and earth upside down, going against your very laws and precedents, your history, your logic. If anything, he's a sinner, like all his people. Stiff-necked people."

"Satan, you go too far," cautioned God. "Indeed, to my ears, you sound a bit anti-Semitic."

Satan protested, throwing out every reasonable reason why the Jews were not ready at that time for the Messiah, which caused the Messiah, listening to the arguments, to weep in his palace. Nor was Elijah the prophet too thrilled about what he was hearing.

God decided to pacify the Evil One. "All right, Satan, I'll make you this one concession. Should Rabbi Yosef stray from his holy course even by the thickness of a hair, I shall grant you the power to thwart his plan!"

Satan was delighted with God's answer. "Heh, heh," he confided to his wife as they transformed themselves into two huge black dogs and raced toward the holy men ascending Mount Seir, "heh, heh, sometimes His answer is no."

Rabbi Yosef was ready for these mad dogs. Metatron forewarned them what to do and what not to do. He told them they would succeed, through mystical formulas and incantations, in capturing Satan and Lilith and thus drive all evil from the world. "If you do all this, the Messiah will surely come!" the archangel said.

Of course there was so much more he had to teach him. "You don't subdue mighty Satan with a wing and a prayer," he cautioned. So he also had Rabbi Yosef inscribe the Ineffable Name on a plate and showed him how to use it in the face of Satan.

And by God he did it—the holy Rabbi Yosef and his small band of saints subdued the mad dogs, Lilith and Satan, outside a small hut on a towering mountain!

And of course Satan and Lilith used every trick in their book to get the rabbis to show them kindness, "even a morsel of bread, even a whiff of spice, please," begged Lilith. "Please have mercy," sobbed Satan. "We're so hungry."

But to give in at all to these fiends meant failure and well the rabbis had been warned. With all the evil in the world tied up in knots, Rabbi Yosef and his disciples were ecstatic for the first time. As Satan and Lilith cried crocodile tears, Rabbi Isaac broke out into two wonderful songs—one in praise of God, the other a musical diary about how they stormed the gates of heaven and lived to tell about it. How proud the Messiah in his palace felt! At any moment he fully expected Rabbi Yosef de la Reina to open up the palace gates with a key handed him by God Himself. The Jews, wherever they were on earth at that moment, had every reason to celebrate and expect the Messiah. From his window the Messiah could see his white donkey bray, eager to be let out of the heavenly stable. From the distance, he heard the strains of the great *shofar*, which he had two days before given to Elijah for just such a time. "Ah, that Elijah, he plays a mean *shofar!*" he said. "There's no doubt he'll be ready to announce my arrival."

All along the way to Mount Seir, tied up like two escaped convicts, Satan and Lilith begged to be given "a smell of your spices or we'll perish!"

But at that moment when the Holy One was about to give "His robes—glory and majesty—to Messiah,[23] Rabbi Yosef took pity on these hapless creatures, who, tied behind the rabbis, were too weak to walk on their own and almost had to be dragged on the ground. Although the other disciples reminded Rabbi Yosef to show no pity, it was Rabbi Isaac who persuaded Rabbi Yosef to give them a bit of frankincense to smell, just to keep them going.

Seeing this, the Messiah cried out, "No, no, no!" but it was too late. As it is written, "Satan enters through a needle's eye"[24]—"Never give Satan an opening."[25] Gaining their former strength, Satan and Lilith shot searing flames from their nostrils. Shrieking demons and devils, the worst of mankind's fears incarnate realized, scared two of the rabbi's disciples to death, so great was their terror. Two more disciples went mad. In the end, only Rabbis Yosef and Isaac were left. Nobody really knows what happened to the two, separately or together, but legend has it that they lived out their lives in disgrace, with Rabbi Yosef renouncing the God of Israel in his grief and moving to Sidon, in Lebanon, to finish his memoirs on the parchment.

As for the other rabbi, he continued as a will-o'-the-wisp troubadour, his songs passed down through the generations of kabbalists, and one day, if you're lucky, you'll come across the words to one of his songs that tell how it all ended.

> Hear O Israel, how a terrible wailing was heard in heaven
> Hear how the angels went into mourning.

---

23. *Numbers Rabbah* 14:3.
24. Rabbi Moses Hagiz, *Leket HaKemah* (1697), 1897, p. 103a.
25. Talmud, *Bathra* 16a.

Listen well how the Messiah became more dutiful
And how his white donkey was led back to its heavenly stall.
Hear the prophet Elijah grieve—hear him wail as he never
wailed before
And hide the great *shofar* from the sad eyes of the Messiah.

Now hear the voice of the Almighty proclaim:
"Pay heed, O Yosef del la Reina! Pay heed!
No human has the power to end the Exile!
I alone, God, will hasten the Redemption of the Jewish people
When the right time comes!"[26]

But enough of this sad song!
Of course we Jews all know the Messiah will come. But sometimes even
in our prayers, God's answer is no.

---

26. The original story comes from an old Yiddish *groschen* (penny) book.

10

OVERCOMING THE MESSIAH

She heard him coming, running fast and hard along the path, his breathing very heavy, and within moments after slamming the gate he stormed into the house. She could see her husband Itzik, the landowner, was beside himself, and if he was so, heaven help the rest of the Chelmites! she thought to herself.

"What's the matter, Itzik? Who died?"

Itzik stopped in his tracks, closed his eyes, and blurted it out. "Chashe, the Messiah's coming, Chashe, the Messiah—at this very moment he's said to be only a few hours' journey from Chelm."

Taking a cue from her husband, a leading citizen of Chelm, she asked him if that was good or bad.

"Good? Bad? Eh?" Itzik seemed genuinely dismayed. "Chashe, I want the Messiah to come just as much as any other Jew, but . . . but, you know, we have only recently built this home, and have invested our funds in cattle, and, besides, I have just finished sowing our crops! What a time for the Messiah to arrive!"

Chashe calmed him, declaring philosophically, "Don't worry! Think of

---

Based on Chelm tale, "Overcoming the Messiah," from Nathan Ausubel, ed., *Treasury of Jewish Folklore* (New York: Crown Publishers, 1948), pp. 337–338. Reprinted with permission from Crown Publishers/Random House.

the trials and tribulations our people have met and survived—the bondage in Egypt, the wickedness of Haman, the persecutions and pogroms without end. All of these the good Lord has helped us overcome, and with just a little more help from Him, we will overcome the Messiah, too!"

11

THE BIG SURPRISE

It was hard to say where they were going.

Their riding cart, constructed twenty years before this journey began in 1756, rolled along at a slowpoke horse's pace, seemingly going nowhere in particular. Aboard the wagon, two men—a young talmudic scholar and his mentor, who was none other than the Baal Shem Tov[1] (the Besht) himself—were, at that moment, speaking about how the holy Ari[2] (1534–1572) and his disciples/kabbalists in the Holy Land, would, attired in white raiment, sing and dance as they marched along a fertile field of grains, ready to greet the Sabbath Queen. That was then and this was now, hours before the Sabbath began. Too early to greet the Queen. Which is why it was hard to say where they were going.

They had left town one Friday afternoon and crossed an open field—but no, the wagon didn't stop, but kept on moving, and the men

---

This story is based on texts from Jacob Kadaner, *Sefer Sippurim Noraim* ("Book of Terrible Stories") (Munkacs: M. Herskovics, 1912), pp. 9a–9b, 10b; and Raphael Patai, *The Messiah Texts* (Detroit: Wayne State University Press, 1979), pp. 31–32.

1. Israel ben Eliezer. Known popularly as the Baal Shem Tov, Master of the Good Name and the Besht. Founder of *Chassidus*. 1698–1760.

2. Isaac Luria. Considered a potential Messiah in his time. Founded a school of Jewish mysticism known as the Lurianic Kabbalah, whose teachings brought about a new messianic hope and was a major factor in the popular acclaim for the pseudomessiah, Shabbetai Tzevi.

kept on talking, way past the field and through a wooded area. When they reached an opening they spotted a small village.

Was this where they'd stay for the Sabbath? wondered the Torah scholar. The village—anywhere but out in the open—suited the scholar well. There was another thing: we should also know, this far along the trip, that, unlike the Besht, the Torah scholar never liked surprises. Many times he had told his parents that, and right at the outset of this trip he pedantically confessed to the Baal Shem Tov his distaste for the surprise element. Nothing surprised the Baal Shem Tov, however, so he smiled warmly at the young man. "We'll keep surprises to a minimum, eh?" And the Talmud scholar liked that.

Yet—and who can blame a horse that had a mind of its own!—as they went into the village, the horse went on of its own and did not stop at any house.

Anticipating the youth's response, the Baal Shem Tov shrugged his broad shoulders and said, "Seems as if we're not, after all, stopping here."

"It would have been nice to spend the Sabbath in this village," the Torah scholar entertained.

"May there be no more surprises," said the Baal Shem Tov.

"Amen," added the young man.

Yet there continued to be one surprise after another. Surely they had to stop somewhere to greet the Sabbath Queen. Surely. Surprise: When the horse reached the end of the village, it stopped at the edge of a lake on which a houseboat was anchored. Surprise: the horse drank some water and moved on. Surprise: there were no known villages for the next ten miles, the Baal Shem Tov told his young traveling partner. Surprise: the young Torah scholar began to accept that he was traveling with a man whose middle name was Surprise. Yet it was no surprise that the Sabbath was just around the next bend. Won't we have to hurry, Rebbe? Do you know where we're going, Rebbe? Why can't you tell me, Rebbe?

Oh, the unanswered questions on this scholar's mind that he would've liked to press the Baal Shem Tov for answers. Now, if only the horse could talk!

And that's exactly what the horse did. It neighed when it finally stopped at the ruins of a house. Immediately the Torah scholar took that as a sure sign that there would be no more surprises. Here the two, in privacy, could welcome the Sabbath, to keep it holy. And in everything the young man thought he was absolutely correct—for now. But let's face it: nothing could be taken for granted when you traveled with the Master of the Good Name.

Once the two alit from the wagon, the Baal Shem Tov entered the ruin, and the youth went in after him.

There they—or, to be more precise, the youth—found another surprise waiting for them. Living in the ruined house—hovel—cabin—hut—call it what you will!—lived an old man, a leper; from head to foot, /he was covered with boils and wounds, and he barely saw. Yet when the Baal Shem Tov embraced him, the leper immediately knew what he had in hand. The Torah scholar, on the other hand, was frightened and shrank from any such embrace, nor did the circumstances call for him to reach out. Yet, as he gazed on the happy leper, he remembered a line from the Talmud: "When daylight comes, the sick man rises" (*Bava Batra*). Why suddenly should he recall that now? he wondered. This sick man, whose very skin seemed to be rotting away at the moment the Besht was introducing him to the young man, was—quite the opposite—rising in the twilight, for he was grinning from ear to ear at the sight of his beloved Rebbe, the Besht. What could the young man make of this?

He hardly had any time to give his question thought when, all of a sudden, he was also introduced to the leper's wife and children, who walked about in torn and tattered garments. Yet they seemed blissfully happy, and he who saw not their joy has never seen joy in his life.

And while the wife bade the young man sit down at her table and brought him a cup of hot water, in which she squeezed the last drop from an almost dried-out lemon, the Besht and the leper went into a separate room, and talked there about half an hour.

When the two men returned to the waiting family and young scholar, they took their leave and parted from each other in fierce love, like the love of David and Jonathan. And then the Baal Shem Tov and the Torah scholar, still wondering where they'd spend the Sabbath, took their seats in the cart, and the horse trotted along on its own.

On the way back home—if that was where they were going—the young scholar asked the Baal Shem Tov: "Remember, Rabbi, you promised me no surprises . . ."

Patiently the Besht smiled, as he always did when asked a question. "I could tell you that I kept my promise," he finally said, "but would you believe me?"

"Rabbi, you were meant to believe in and be believed. It's just that it came as a big surprise to me, the . . . well . . . this whole trip."

"Perhaps to me, too," said the Besht. "But tell me," he said, shifting closer in the cart to the young man, "what surprised you the most?"

"The most?"

"Yes, out with it, young man."

"Well," he labored to get out the words, "Er, eh, the meaning of the joy—that's it—the joy that your encounter with the old leper caused to both of you? . . ."

By now, they were approaching their own village, with the horse hip-hop-hippiting along at a fast clip. And by now the Baal Shem Tov saw no reason to hold anything back from his companion. So he said, "As for what happened between me and the old man in the ruins, as it is known, there is a Messiah in every generation in this world, in reality, clothed in a physical body. And if the generation is worthy, he is ready to reveal himself; and if, God forbid, the generation isn't worthy, he departs.

"And yes, that old man was ready to be our True Messiah, and it was his desire to enjoy my company on the Sabbath."

"Then why didn't you take advantage of that event?" the young man wanted to know.

As the Baal Shem Tov was alighting from the cart, which had come to a halt in front of his shul, he looked up at the young man, who was assisting him off the cart, and he said to him, "Because I foresaw that he would depart at the Third Meal [which is taken at the outgoing of the Sabbath], and I did not want to endure any pain on the Sabbath. Therefore, I took my leave from him before the arrival of the Sabbath."

And that night the young Torah scholar dreamed he was marching with the holy Ari on a fertile field of grains, dressed in white garments, singing and dancing, ready to greet the Sabbath Queen. Which was, in his touched way, a big surprise to the Torah scholar. For the Messiah came to greet him instead. He was a leper. And the two embraced joyfully.

12

THE SPIRITUAL
ARISTOCRAT

The Vilna Gaon
Rabbi Elijah ben Solomon Zalman of Vilna
1720–1797

PRESENTING A POTENTIAL
MESSIAH IN HIS TIME . . . THE GAON OF VILNA

In the book *ha-Tekufah ha-Gedolah* (*The Great Era*), by Mendel
Kasher, Reb Hillel of Shklov, a disciple of the Vilna Gaon, writes in
the sefer, *Kol ha-Tor* (*The Sound of the Dove*): "Our Great Teacher
[Rabbi Elijah] is the one to be appointed and designated as the
shining beacon of the Messiah ben Joseph for this last generation."[1]

---

1. "Two *Moshiachs*? When we say '*Moshiach*,' we mean the descendant of
David who will restore the Davidic kingdom and rectify the world. As we pray
three times daily, 'Speedily cause the scion of David Your servant to flourish.'
This is the *Moshiach* we all await. However, the Talmud, *Midrash* and *Zohar*
mention a second *Moshiach*, a descendant of Yosef who precedes the Davidic
Moshiach and is killed while battling the *Gentiles*.

"According to *Chazal* [our sages of blessed memory], 'The land shall mourn
every family apart . . .' (Zechariah 12:12) refers to the death of *Moshiach ben
Yosef* (*Sukkah* 52a). The *Gemara* even relates that *Hashem* [God] tells *Moshiach ben
David*, 'Ask of Me, and I will give you nations for your inheritance . . .'
(*Tehillim* [Psalms] 2:8), but when he sees *Moshiach ben Yosef* slain, he says to
Hashem, 'Master of the universe, all I ask of You is life.'

"Here we find an explicit reference to *Moshiach ben Yosef*; he is killed, but

Once, when the Chabad chassidic rebbe, Rabbi Shneur Zalman of Liadi (1745–1812), was in a light mood he was asked, "Tell me, Rebbe, do you think the Messiah will come as a *chassid* [a follower of a chassidic rebbe] or as a non-*chassid*?" The Rebbe said he hoped it would be as a non-*chassid*.

Moshiach ben David lives on." Menachem M. Brod, *The Days of Moshiach* (Kfar Chabad, Israel: Chabad Youth Org., 1993), pp. 107–108.

Also, Jewish tradition speaks of the Messiah ben David and the Messiah ben Joseph. The term *Messiah* (*Moshiach*) unqualified always refers to the Messiah the descendant of David of the tribe of Judah. He is the actual final redeemer. The Messiah the descendant of Joseph of the tribe of Efraim (also referred to as the Messiah the descendant of Efraim) will come first, before the final redeemer, and later will serve as his viceroy. The cooperation between the two Messiahs signifies the total unity of Israel, removing the historical rivalries between the tribes of Judah and Joseph. J. I. Schochet, *Mashiach* (New York: Sichos In English, 1992). Typical of the love and esteem Jews had for the Messiah ben Yosef is found in this story told by one *chassid*:

> "Once Rabbi Yehudah Zevi of Stretyn (died 1844) said to us at table: 'Today the Messiah the son of Joseph will be born in Hungary, and he will become one of the hidden *tzaddikim*. And if God lets me live long enough, I shall go there and see him.'
>
> "Eighteen years later the rebbe traveled to the city of Pest and took me with him along with other *chassidim*. We stayed in Pest for several weeks and not one of us disciples knew why we had come.
>
> "One day a youth appeared at the inn. He wore a short coat and his face was as beautiful as an angel's. Without asking permission, he went straight into the rebbe's room and closed the door behind him. I remembered those words I had heard long ago, kept near the door, and waited to greet him as he came out and ask his blessing. But when hours later he did come out, the rebbe accompanied him to the gate, and when I ran out into the little street, he had vanished. Even now after so many years, my heart still beats with the living impulse I received from him as he went by." (Martin Buber, *Tales of the Hasidim, Book Two: The Later Masters* [New York: Schocken Books, 1991], p. 151.)

This bio was culled from source books that include: Mendel Kasher, *Ha-Tekufah Ha-Gedolah— The Great Era* (Jerusalem: Machon Torah Shlema, 1968), vol. 1; S. M. Dubnow, *History of the Jews in Russia and Poland* (Philadelphia: Jewish Publication Society of America, 1920), 3 vols.; Leonard Oschry, *The Story of the Vilna Gaon* (Brooklyn, NY: Torah Umesorah Publications, 1976); Menachem Gerlitz, *In Our Leaders' Footsteps: The Gaon of Vilna* (Jerusalem: Oraysoh

"Why do you say that?" he was asked. "Because," he responded, "the non-chassidim would never accept anyone but a non-*chassid*, whereas the *chassid* would gratefully accept any Jew as the Messiah."[2]

Such a totally acceptable non-chassid, or more precisely, *misnaged* (an opponent of *Chassidus*) in his time had to be Rabbi Elijah, whose extraordinary story must have been told over and over on the Golden Floor of Heaven long before he made his first appearance on earth. Here was a holy man; even the Torah, seemingly, had waited for him to appear. He was unlike any other religious. It can be said with some certainty that if God had designated him as the Messiah, even his so-called archrival, Rabbi Shneur Zalman, who founded Chabad Chassidism, would have welcomed him as such.

It can also be said with certainty that, in those days, Jews throughout the world honored him as the rabbinic genius of the age and the greatest living Torah giant—perhaps of all time. Even such accolades didn't sit too well with him, though. He never held the position of *rav* or *rosh yeshivah* (principal or rector of a *yeshivah*)—in fact, not even *maggid shiur* (a lecturer in Talmud). Others, his critics, saw him otherwise. They called him an anachronism, a man out of time, a throwback to a bygone era, yet probably he himself disdained any association of himself as the Messiah—*ben David* or *ben Yosef*!

Why deny himself such a singular distinction? Because, in his lifetime, Chassidism was sweeping large parts of Eastern Europe, led by such chassidic rabbis as Rabbi Shneur Zalman, and the Vilna Gaon took the lead in combatting its spread. Jew fight Jew? Why? What was it all about? According to Geoffrey Wigoder,[3] the Vilna Gaon "was appalled by the apparent levity of the *Hasidism* in their attitude to the Torah and

---

Publisher, 1983), vol. 2; *Vilna Gaon Haggadah*, trans. Yisrael Isser Zvi Herczeg (Brooklyn, NY: Mesorah Publications, 1993); Geoffrey Wigoder, *Dictionary of Jewish Biography* (New York: Simon & Schuster, 1991).

2. Another version of this anecdote involves the Kotzker Rebbe, Rabbi Menachem Mendel of Kotzk (1787–1859). Said the Kotzker: "I believe the Messiah will come as a '*misnaged*.' If he comes as a *chassid*, the *misnagdim* would not be likely to accept him, whereas the *chassidim* would quickly recognize him as Messiah, even though he came as a *misnaged*, and would gladly accept him." E. Bergmann, *Kotzker Maasiyoth* (Warsaw: 1924), p. 33; Louis I. Newman, *The Hasidic Anthology* (Northvale, NJ: Jason Aronson, 1987), p. 251.

3. *Dictionary of Jewish Biography*, p. 134.

concerned that it might develop into a pseudo-messianic movement that would be as disastrous as that of Shabbetai Tzevi."[4]

Yet, like his main opponent, Rabbi Shneur Zalman, the Vilna Gaon also had a wry sense of humor. Once, he summed himself up by saying, "It may be proper to call me a *kosher* Jew, but as to being a *chassid*, a saint—I haven't reached that stage yet."[5]

By stages—at very early ages—he became known as a genius (later appropriately dubbed the *Gaon*, which means "genius"). Born to a family of talmudic scholars, by the time he was three-and-a-half years old he had an undeniable grasp of the entire Torah, *Neviim* (Prophets), and *Kethuvim* (the Holy Writings, beginning with Psalms).

It fared him very well when he was six. One *Shabbos*, in synagogue, he was called upon to give a Torah lecture, which his father had taught him. Who was in the shul? Considering that almost every man in Vilna studied Torah, "[t]here were old men who had been learning *Gemorrah* for more than sixty years; there were younger men, too, who were learned scholars."[6] To every question, he offered the right answer. Later, for *Shabbos* lunch, he was brought to the house of Rabbi Heshel, the head of the *Beis Din*, the Jewish law court, of Vilna. Now confronted with the newly gained fame of the boy and his father, the rabbi played down the boy's wisdom of Torah. "This morning," he said to the boy, "you repeated what your father taught you. It is not so hard to do that. Let us see if you can make up a Torah lecture by yourself."

With that he led the boy into his library, pointing out all the "books you'll need to make your own Torah lecture," and left him there.

An hour later, the boy reemerged, and delivered his own Torah

---

4. 1626–1676. A Jewish pseudo-messianic figure who proclaimed himself, through his so-called public relations director, Nathan of Gaza, as the Messiah, in 1648, when it was predicted by knowledgeable Jewish sources that the Messiah would come. He married a woman named Sarah who had earned her living as a prostitute and had declared that she would wed only the Messiah. Understandably, then, at their wedding Shabbetai Tzevi called Sarah "the bride of the Messiah." Although, near the end of his life, he completely betrayed the Jewish people, one group of followers, the Donmeh, continued to exist in Turkey until the twentieth century, still believing that Shabbetai Tzevi was the Messiah who would return one day.

5. Quoted by Glenn, *Israel Salanter*, p. 31; *A Treasury of Jewish Quotations*, ed. Joseph L. Baron (Northvale, NJ: Jason Aronson, 1985), p. 168.

6. *The Story of the Vilna Gaon*, p. 4.

lecture. Now there was no denying that this boy was truly born for greatness. "Some of the explanations which Eliyohu [Elijah] gave when he was six years old were afterwards published. They were so good, that they were preserved for all time."[7]

To what heights, then or in the years to come, would this holy man rise? He could have had any position he desired. The Jews of Vilna furnished him with a newly built house of study; there, after he had spent eight years in his twenties wandering anonymously—a self-imposed exile for penance—in Jewish communities in Poland and Germany, he spent most of his life with his family (except for a brief, unsuccessful attempt to travel to the Holy Land), refusing any public office and devoting himself to scholarship.

So convinced that he could "serve God also without a world to come," he wanted only that which he had worked for. "Were an angel to reveal to me all the mysteries of the Torah," he said, "it would please me little, for study is more important than knowledge. Only what man achieves through effort is dear to him."[8]

After he was settled down with his wife and children in Vilna, he stuck close to home; yes, even to *davening* in his home. "It is better to pray at home," he maintained, "for in the synagogue it is impossible to escape envy and hearing idle talk."[9]

In truth, he had very little use or concern for the secular world revolving around him. Who knows how few times he actually walked the streets of Vilna! In every way he was a private man. To things outside Torah, he responded: "This mundane life is like a drink of salt water, which seems to quench, but actually inflames. . . . Life is a series of vexations and pains, and sleepless nights are the common lot."[10]

Yet there were holy men with ways to reach the Gaon, to bring him back down to earth, as it were. Such a person was the Maggid of Dubno (Yaakov ben Wolf Krantz, 1741–1804).

Once, when the Gaon welcomed him to his home, he said to him: "I am told that you speak to the very hearts of those who listen. Now from time to time, like anyone else, I am in need of admonition. Therefore, I beg of you, give me a lesson in *Mussar* (ethics), for I need it badly."

---

7. Ibid., p. 6.

8. See *Reflex*, Dec. 1927, p. 57; *A Treasury of Jewish Quotations*, p. 477.

9. *Alim LiTerufa*, 1836, in *Hebrew Ethical Wills* (Philadelphia: Jewish Publication Soc., 1926), p. 321.

10. Ibid., p. 313f.

Considering whom he was faced with, the Maggid must have taken a very deep breath before he spoke thus:

"In this week's portion of the Torah—*Vayeira*—we read that God said to Abraham: 'If there are only fifty righteous men in the midst of the city of Sodom, I will save her.' Now what does the Torah mean by explicitly mentioning '*in the midst of the city*' (Genesis 18:26)? The Lord says: 'It is not pleasing to Me to see righteous men living in seclusion, and poring over My sacred teachings in the privacy of their homes without taking any notice of the troubles and sorrows of their neighbors. I need men who are outstanding, but who will not stand apart from their neighbors. I need men who will live in the very midst of the city not only in body, but also in spirit, who will devote their energies to being a good influence on their fellow-men and who will work to the end that the entire community should live in keeping with My commandments.'"

Hearing this, the Vilna Gaon wept. Whether it was part of his greatness or a grave weakness of his, he knew he had shown little interest in the affairs of the community, almost continuing his earlier life as a recluse, except for the coterie of disciples he "learned with."[11]

The real question here is not what becomes a legend but what becomes a man—the kind, considerate, and loving man that Rabbi Elijah really was in the face of being called too intolerant by his critics? Was there a place for *ahavas Yisrael* in his life? Did he have—or did he desire to have—a kernel of leadership, the kind that was needed in the Messiah to lead the Jewish people out of exile? Clearly, he showed that leadership in every way to combat the *Haskalah*, or Enlightment, movement, insisting on the primacy of Torah and Halachah (Jewish Law). If we are to believe the historian S. M. Dubnow, Rabbi Elijah was a "spiritual aristocrat" who "felt bound to condemn severely the 'plebian' doctrine of *Hasidism*. The latter offended in him equally the learned Talmudist, the rigorous ascete, and the strict guardian of ceremonial Judaism, of which certain minutiae had been modified by the *Hasidim* after their own fashion."[12]

Imagine for a moment that you're living in September 1796, in the month of Elul, and you receive the following epistle—a Jewish New Year's message?—from none other than the greatest Torah scholar of his, and your, generation, Rabbi Elijah, the Vilna Gaon:

---

11. Benno Heinemann, *The Maggid of Dubno and His Parables* (Jerusalem: Feldheim Publishers, 1978), pp. 188–189.

12. *History of the Jews in Russia and Poland*, 1:236.

Ye mountains of Israel—cried the great zealot—ye spiritual shepherds, and ye lay leaders of every Government, also ye, the heads of the Kahals of Moghilev, Polotzk, Zhitomir, Vinnitza, and Kamenetz-Podolsk, you hold in your hands a hammer wherewith you may shatter the plotters of evil, the enemies of light, the foes of the [Jewish] people. Woe unto this generation! They [the *chassidim*] violate the Law, distort our teachings, and set up a new covenant; they lay snares in the house of the Lord, and give a perverted exposition of the tenets of our faith. It behooves us to avenge the Law of the Lord, it behooves us to punish these madmen before the whole world, for their own improvement. Let none have pity on them and grant them shelter! . . . Gird yourselves with zeal in the name of the Lord![13]

Strong fighting words![14]

If you were a Jewish "soldier" from Lithuania, White Russia, Volhynia or Podolia, you were waiting for just this kind of letter to join in the fray with other *misnagdim* against the late Baal Shem Tov's followers. In Jews the call to arms brought out the best and the worst of times. The Vilna Gaon's call-to-arms letter continued to circulate in many communities, "and gave rise to severe conflicts between *mithnagdim* and *hasidim*, the former as a rule taking the offensive."[15] Still, it was more than a bit much to hear or see, on the day of the Gaon's funeral, that "the local Hasidic society met in a private house and indulged in a gay drinking bout, to celebrate the deliverance of the sect from its principal enemy."[16]

We cannot leave this unfortunate time when Jew fought Jew tooth and nail without coming to a happy end, for the sake of the memory of the Gaon of Vilna, and for the sake of *ahavas Yisrael*. As time went on, most *misnagdim* laid down their arms, realizing the *chassidim* had become one of the greatest forces for spreading *Yiddishkeit*, furthering of Jewish education, and hastening the arrival of the Messiah. As time went on, the Gaon of Vilna, if not openly, surely quietly in the inner recesses of his heart and

---

13. Ibid., pp. 373–374.

14. According to Yehoshua Mondshin, the Vilna Gaon never penned this letter. Then, who did? Other *misnagdim* with an axe to grind. *Kerem Chabad* (Kfar Chabad, Israel: Machon Oholei Shem Lubavitch, 1992), No. 4, p. 208.

15. *History of the Jews in Russia and Poland*, 1:374.

16. Ibid., p. 375.

home, retracted his fiery attacks on the "other Jews." "The tongue's sin weighs as much as all other sins together." Inevitably, he returned to the Torah—"Like rain, the Torah nourishes useful plants and poisonous weeds"—and he wrote commentaries and all sorts of "annotations" to biblical, talmudic, and kabbalistic books. The introduction to the *Vilna Gaon Haggadah* takes note, "But even more important is his contribution in terms of technique. His unique method of deep analysis in tandem with fidelity to the simple meaning of the text was institutionalized by his student, Rabbi Chaim of Volozhin,[17] in the *yeshivah* which he founded. It went on to sweep the intellectual world of Lithuanian Torah Jewry and remains one of the predominant approaches to the study of the Talmud to this day."[18]

Greater love hath no man than the love Reb Hillel of Shklov must have felt for his mentor, the Gaon, when he wrote those prophetic words: "Our Great Teacher is the one to be appointed and designated as the shining beacon of the Messiah ben Joseph for this last generation." Messiah ben Joseph—he would prepare the way for the real Messiah, Messiah ben David. He would come first to prepare for the final redeemer.

If called upon, was he prepared to be the Messiah ben Joseph? Who really knows! Yet, knowing his intolerance for certain types of people, we can well imagine him to agree: "When the real Messiah comes, all the sick wil be healed—but fools will remain fools."

---

17. There's an interesting messianic anecdote attributed to Rabbi Chaim of Volozhin. He was sitting with his disciples, discussing the ultimate redemption and the coming of the Messiah. One of them said, "Rebbe, I read the *Avkas Rochel*, describing all the terrible troubles that will befall the Jews in the Messiah's time, and I wonder if Israel will be able to bear them."

"Do you think," said Rabbi Chaim with a smile, "that in the Messiah's time God will leaf through the *Avkas Rochel* page by page?" Shmuel Himelstein, *A Touch of Wisdom* (Brooklyn, NY: Mesorah Publications, 1991), p. 67.

18. *Vilna Gaon Haggadah*, vii.

13

IN PRAISE OF THE
FROG'S SONG

What things they once learned in Mezritch!

"So what did you learn in Mezritch?" an interested party once asked Rabbi Aharon of Karlin (1736–1772).

In response, Rabbi Aharon, a chassidic rebbe himself who attracted tens of thousands of followers, said with unparalleled piety and humility, "In Mezritch, I learned nothing at all."

"Are you pulling my leg?" asked the curious one. "What do you mean—nothing at all?"

"That's right," said Rabbi Aharon. "In Mezritch I learned that I am nothing."

Another time, three men—and the number of curiosity seekers was increasing—asked Rabbi Levi Yitzchak of Berditchev (1740–1810), "Well, what did you discover at the *shul* of the Great *Maggid* of Mezritch [1704–1772]?"

Said the Berditchever Rebbe, "I discovered that there is a God Who is the Master of this world and all other worlds."

"But, Rebbe, everyone knows that!" they all chimed in.

"No," said Rabbi Levi Yitzchak. "They say it everywhere, but in Mezritch they know it."[1]

---

1. Rabbi Yisrael Berger, *Eser Orot*, Warsaw, 1913; and Avraham Yaakov

According to chassidic tradition, the Great *Maggid* had three hundred disciples, whom he called "noble tapers that need only to be lit to burn with a pure flame." Other great scholars he rejected[2]—their ways were not his way, he said—yet they remained in Mezritch, performing services for him and his disciples. In the exacting world of Mezritch, he called them "stokers, because tending the stoves was part of their duties."[3] To a man, every one of them was certain that the *Maggid* was none other than the potential Messiah of their generation. He had assumed the leadership of nearly all chassidic Jews when the Baal Shem Tov (1698–1760), founder of *Chassidus*, cured him of "teaching without a soul."

The *Maggid* passed on all that the Baal Shem Tov taught him, including the language of birds and trees. To which the *Maggid* added: "Rabbi Yohanan ben Zakkai received Torah from Hillel and Shammai. . . . He used to say: If you have a sapling in your hand, and someone should say to you that the Messiah has come, stay and complete the transplanting, and then go welcome the Messiah."[4]

In short, the *Maggid* became the thinking teacher, the one man designated to lead all the other leaders—the greatest *tzaddik* of his generation.

Ask any of his followers. He lit up their lives, they said. If he could do that for them, surely he could do it for all *Yidden*, indeed the entire world; if not lighting all candles at one time, then one candle at a time. That had to be what a Messiah was for! That had to be their *Maggid*!

Yet you'd never know it by them! They were generous, saintly men, but very secretive.

And what made their *Maggid* so special? Many of his disciples said "that he had only to open his lips and they all had the impression that he was no longer in this world, that the Divine Presence was speaking from his throat." Everything he taught them was in preparation for the coming of the Messiah. "I believe with perfect faith in the coming of the Messiah. Even if he delays, I will wait every day for him to come."[5]

Finkel, *The Great Chasidic Masters* (Northvale, NJ: Jason Aronson, 1992), p. 11.

2. Martin Buber, *Tales of the Hasidim, Book One, The Early Masters* (New York: Schocken Books, 1991), p. 107.

3. Ibid.

4. *Avot de-Rabbi Natan* B 31; and *A Garden of Choice Fruit*, ed. Rabbi David E. Stein (Wyncote, PA: Shomrei Adamah, 1991), p. 81.

5. The twelfth principle of the Rambam's Thirteen Principles of Faith.

And he taught them well. Once, for instance, the *Maggid* told Rabbi
Meshullam Zisha of Hanipol (1718–1800), one of his favorite disciples:

> I cannot teach you the ten principles of service. But a little child
> and a thief can show you what they are.
> From the child you can learn three things:
> He is merry for no particular reason.
> Never for a moment is he idle.
> When he needs something, he demands it vigorously.[6]
> The thief can instruct you in seven things:
> He works quietly without others knowing.
> He is ready to place himself in danger.
> The smallest degree is of great importance to him.
> He labors with great toil.
> Alacrity.
> He is confident and optimistic.
> If he does not succeed at first, he tries again and again.[7]

And before the Great *Maggid* began to teach the two brothers
Shmelke[8] and Pinchas,[9] he told them how to order themselves all day
long, from rising to falling asleep, and by command and prohibition made
manifest his miraculous knowledge of their ways, as if they had been
known to him long before. In the end he said: "Before retiring to rest at
night, the Disciples of the Wise are accustomed to cast accounts of their
doings during the day. And if a Disciple's heart swells within him at the
thought of having made excellent use of the day, the Angels in heaven
knead all his good works into a ball, and hurl it into the abyss."[10]

"Another disciple said: 'Whenever we rode to our teacher—the
moment we were within the limits of the town—all our desires were

---

6. Buber, *Tales of the Hasidim, Book One*, p. 105.

7. *Hayom Yom—From Day To Day*, compiled and arranged by the Lubavitcher Rebbe, Menachem M. Schneerson (Brooklyn, NY: Otzar Hachassidim
Lubavitch, 1988), p. 50. In *Hayom Yom*, Rabbi Y. Y. Schneersohn noted that he
learned these seven principles from Rabbi Meshullam Zisha of Hanipol.

8. Rabbi Shmuel Shmelke of Nikolsburg, about 1726–1778.

9. Rabbi Pinchas Horowitz, the *Baal Haflaah*, 1730–1805.

10. Louis I. Newman, *The Hasidic Anthology* (Northvale, NJ: Jason Aronson,
1987), p. 351; and Martin Buber, *Die Chassidischen Buecher* (Hellerau, 1928),
p. 412b.

fulfilled. And if anyone happened to have a wish left, this was satisfied as soon as he entered the house of the *Maggid*. But if there was one among us whose soul was still churned up with wanting—he was at peace when he looked into the face of the *Maggid*."[11]

Still another: "Our master spent many hours at a nearby pond. Do you know why he went to the pond every day at dawn and stayed there for a little while before coming home again? . . . He was learning the song with which the frogs praise God. It takes a very long time to learn that song."[12] It was this song the *Maggid* so much wanted to teach his followers to *daven* with, perhaps even to greet the Messiah with.

So why did these loving disciples keep quiet once, thereby betraying their master?

Nobody can really say, but the truth is both sad and funny—if you can find it in your heart to laugh at the human foibles of saintly men.

In heaven, there was a big to-do going on. Most angels, God willing, might have overlooked it, but Satan, having his own steamy fit, insisted they look, and what they saw was not pleasing to their eyes. Once more, the Great *Maggid*, Rabbi Dov Ber, was insisting and demanding that the Redemption finally come from heaven.

The earth may be trembling, but nothing could shake the rafters of heaven. God had passed the word that the Messiah wasn't ready to mount his donkey, they said, and that's that. Still, the angels knew well enough that they couldn't disregard the *Maggid*'s personal effort. He had to be heard, or, better yet, with their Master's permission, they would hear him out, by questioning him. So the angels, led by Sandalfon, Gabriel, and Michael, requested a showdown with the *Maggid*, and God granted it. Satan was ordered not to butt in on this situation.

Their voice from heaven found the *Maggid* in the solitude of dawn, as usual, near the pond, listening to the sounds of frogs. Near his side was a dark lantern, with its shutter closed to hide its light. He greeted each angel by name, so attuned he was to all heavenly sounds.

Speaking for all of them, the angel Sandalfon wanted to know why the *Maggid* was trying to hasten the Redemption.

"Sandalfon, you should know better than to ask me that question. After all," said the *Maggid*, "I am considered the *tzaddik* of my generation, and that's my task—hastening the Messiah."

"Who told you that?" said the angel Michael.

---

11. Buber, *Tales of the Hasidim*, Book One, p. 102.
12. Ibid., p. 111.

The *Maggid* took his time to answer that. He heard a sound he'd never heard before from a frog, and he didn't want to lose it. After mouthing it a number of times, he finally said, "Dear angels, my students will surely testify that the *Maggid* is the *tzaddik* of his generation. Will you accept that?"

Each angel looked at another. What could they lose giving the *Maggid* a chance to prove himself?

"Well, I think that would be a workable solution," said Gabriel, and then adding a bit of humor, said, "Having blown many horns myself over the aeons, I'm certain, Rabbi Dov Ber, you're much too much of a *tzaddik* to toot your own horn."

Said the *Maggid*: "All I'm after is the promised Redemption—and the Messiah!"

No angel could fault him for that, so in heaven they agreed to this, on condition that his students instantly recognize him as the *tzaddik* of the generation. If they did, the angels, God permitting, of course, would bring on the Redemption.

Picking up his dark lantern, right away the *Maggid* went to summon all his students who were also great *tzaddikim*. When they were gathered together in his dimly lit room, he asked the disciples, "Is it true that I am the *tzaddik* of the generation?"

Now this question confused all of the students because they were not used to hearing such questions from their Rebbe, who was a great and humble man.

Understandably, then, no one responded to the question.

Perhaps it was still too dark in the room where they were, thought the *Maggid*. Perhaps a little more light shed on the subject and them would help. When he partly removed the shutter of the dark lamp, the room took on a darkly orange hue. Yet, so focused were they on their master that they hardly saw anything else save him. As far as they were concerned, the grayness in their lives was a color that always was on the verge of changing to some other color whenever they gazed into the face of their master. Now was no different.

So the Great *Maggid* asked them a second time. "Tell me, I beseech you, is it true that I am the *tzaddik* of the generation?"

This time also no one answered.

What was going on here? The *Maggid* couldn't believe his ears. Not only that—the angels folded their wings and wept, and God stared into an abyss. Even Satan couldn't make sense out of it.

Yet these men before the *Maggid*, who would follow him to the ends of the world to help bring the Messiah—these were the very lamps of a new dynasty that the Great *Maggid* had waited all his life to ignite. These were the very men who were in search of the man when he was a boy of five and a fire consumed his parents' home and its contents. Noting his mother's grief, the child asked her:

" 'Mother, is it right to grieve that much for the loss of our home?'

" 'Heaven forfend,' his mother answered. 'I do not grieve over the loss of our home, but over the document of our family-tree that was burned with it. For this document traced our descent to Rabbi Yochanan Hasandler, who was a direct descendant of King David!'

" 'If so,' said the young boy, 'I shall start for you a new dynasty. . . .' "[13]

And so, now more determined than ever, the *Maggid* fully opened the shutter of the dark lantern and, when he asked a third time, the room never seemed brighter in his presence.

But what could the disciples say! No one dared to answer. The answer was so obvious that any response would ridicule them and their beloved *Maggid*! Of course, he was the *tzaddik* of his generation. Of course, he had the right to petition the Messiah to come. Of course, he was their pure flame, these noble tapers, these willing stokers. Of course, of course! . . .

And of course, the angels turned their back, to the glee of Satan, and left the *Maggid* and his disciples at their pond. From this misunderstanding, Satan drew new strength to resist the *Maggid*, and nothing came from his whole effort. The Messiah did not come.[14]

> Yet, as our Sages remind us:
> Even those things that you may regard
> as completely superfluous to Creation—
> such as fleas, gnats, and flies—
> even they too were included in Creation;
> and God's purpose is carried out through everything—
> even through a snake, a scorpion, a gnat, or a frog.[15]

---

13. Jacob Immanuel Schochet, *The Great Maggid* (Brooklyn, NY: Kehot Publication Soc., 1990), vol. 1, p. 19; and *Sipurei Chassidim*.

14. Shin Nisanzhan, *The Royal Chasidut of This Nation of Rizhin* (Warsaw: Chasidut Furland, 1937), pp. 5–6—as related to me by Rabbi Avrohom Keller, a Lubavitcher chassid who lives in Crown Heights, Brooklyn, NY.

15. Midrash *Genesis Rabbah* 10:7.

It is also written that after the *Maggid*'s death, his disciples came together at the pond "and talked about the things he had done. When it was Rabbi Shneur Zalman's turn, he asked them: 'Do you know why our master went to the pond every day at dawn and stayed there for a little while before coming home again?' They did not know why. Rabbi Zalman continued. 'He was learning the song with which the frogs praise God. It takes a very long time to learn that song.'"[16]

As they stood solemnly, perhaps trying to suppress a feeling of shame for not having helped their master bring the Messiah, suddenly one disciple broke out into a *niggun*, then another disciple began to sing the song, and then another disciple and still another until every last note of the song of the frog was sung by them in praise of God.

Truly, the *Maggid* had taught his disciples, his real dynasty, well. More than ever, they were ready to greet the Messiah.

---

16. Buber, *Tales of the Hasidim*, Book One, p. 111.

14

INSIDE THE MESSIAH'S CHAMBER

The Rizhiner Rebbe
Rabbi Yisroel Friedman
1797–1850

PRESENTING A POTENTIAL MESSIAH IN HIS TIME . . . RABBI YISROEL FRIEDMAN OF RIZHIN

"The holy Rabbi, Rebbe Yisroel of Rizhin, o.b.m., sent letters to the *tzaddikim* of his generation for their consent that he was the Messiah. Rebbe Meir of Premishlan, o.b.m., even agreed to give him the *spodek* (fur hat) that had belonged to his father (the holy Rebbe Aharon Leib, o.b.m.)." Rabbi Mordechai Slonimer, *Stories of Our Master, the Ramach* (Bnei Brak, Israel: 1989), p. 228.

Whenever I think of the Rizhiner, I cannot help recall the famous oil painting by Jacques-Louis David (1748–1825) sitting in the Louvre Museum in Paris. Called "The Coronation of Napoleon," it depicts a feeble, old pope trying to crown Napoleon Bonaparte (1769–1821) emperor of France. But Napoleon, being the impatient man he was, has seized the crown from the pope's hands and crowned himself.

So, too—with all due respect to one of the great chassidic rebbes, Rabbi Yisroel Friedman of Rizhin–the Rizhiner was such a man of destiny, seated on pillows of luxury, waiting for the arrival of the Messiah. Himself impatient for that biggest of days, the final Redemption, he was also willing, with the help of his friends, to name himself the Messiah. Anything to stop his fellow Jews from suffering so much.

Perhaps this might also be said of Napoleon, who seemingly offered a hand of peace and freedom to all Jews who supported his bid for power.[1] Yet, the Rizhiner gave not only his hand but all of himself to his fellow Jews, and no Jew who knew him doubted that he'd give his life for them, too.[2]

So, now, let's leave Napoleon in St. Helena, or wherever he happens to be, and travel to the Court of Rizhin where Rabbi Yisroel Friedman ruled, where his loyal Jewish subjects celebrated this royal personage as they had never celebrated any chassidic rebbe before, during, and after the Rizhiner.

Perhaps to Rabbi Yisroel of Rizhin, the Jews of his time were like a Jewish book wanting a handsome cover. Such a book needed to be written, packaged royally, and sold at an affordable cost. To speak of a chassidic rebbe in these terms in no way is meant to cheapen the Rizhiner's effect on Jews. Yet, in direct contradiction to the custom of his parents, the Rizhiner made no bones about his being "forced" to live in great splendor.

Why can't you be like us? a rabbi once asked him. Why? asked the Rizhiner: "Because I have three kinds of funds: one is from the real *chassidim*, and this goes for my necessities. One is from the householders of middling piety; this I give away to the needy. The third is from habitual sinners; and this goes for luxuries. Is it my fault that the third fund is the largest?" (It is said that the real reason was the same which prompted the

---

1. "Napoleon's outward tolerance and fairness toward Jews was actually based upon his grand plan to have them disappear entirely by means of total assimilation, intermarriage, and conversion. In effect, his was a benign 'final solution' to the 'Jewish problem.'" Berel Wein, *Triumph of Survival* (Monsey, NY: Shaar Press, 1990), p. 71.

2. When Rabbi Chaim Halberstam, the Sanzer Rebbe (the *Divrei Chaim*, 1793–1876), visited Rabbi Yisroel of Rizhin, he offered these words of praise: "Why was the Temple built on Mount Moriah (where the binding of Isaac took place) and not on Mount Sinai (where the Torah was given to Israel)? Because the place where the Jew is willing to offer his life for the Sanctification of God's Name is more sacred than the place where the Torah was given. At all times, Rabbi Yisroel is ready to offer himself for the Sanctification of God's Name." Harry M. Rabinowicz, *Hasidism: The Movement and Its Masters* (Northvale, NJ: Jason Aronson, 1988), p. 155.

command to the high priest to wear gold-embroidered vestments, and the Tabernacle to have gold appointments, namely to gain the deference of the people.)[3]

Why? The Rizhiner offered another explanation for living like a prince. He explained his manner of life by declaring that when a *tzaddik* lives in poverty, he has only limited ideas of people's needs, and prays for mere sustenance. When, however, he enjoys riches, he feels bold enough to pray that his adherents also may have a life of comfort.[4]

Now we come to the Rizhiner Rebbe and the Messiah, a case worth its weight in gold, although not worth discussing, perhaps, if one thinks for one moment that this rebbe considered himself to be the Messiah. Worth discussing, on the other hand, if one can imagine that the Messiah could and should have considered himself to be the Rizhiner Rebbe—or to live like him as a prince in a richly appointed home on earth. And why not? As one writer recently noted, "But when the Messiah (*Moshiach*) will arrive, rectifying and completing what Adam did not, he will be called the *B'chor*, the first born of royalty (*Shemos Rabbah* 19:7)."[5]

Of royalty, yes, but was he an excellent rebbe? Neither did he write learned books nor make any notable contribution to chassidic thought, some scholars maintained.[6] Yet others point to the compilations of his commentaries, which were published under the titles *Irin Keaddishin* (Bertfeld, 1907), *Knesset Yisrael* (Warsaw, 1907), *Beit Yisrael* (Piotrokow, 1913), *Nifla'ot Yisrael* (Warsaw, 1884, 1924) in and *Pe'er Layesharim* (Jerusalem, 1921). "His comments, many of which are based on kabbalistic themes, attest to his great wisdom and piety."[7]

But Rabbi Yisroel was all heart and soul—in short, a rebbe for all reasons. To this day he remains one of the most beloved rebbes of all time,

---

3. Louis I. Newman, *The Hasidic Anthology* (Northvale, NJ: Jason Aronson, 1987), p. 294.

4. Ibid., pp. 294–295.

5. *Moses in the Twentieth Century: A Universal Primer* (Springfield, NJ: SJR Associates, 1994), p. 32.

6. Among others, Rabinowicz, *Hasidism: The Movement and Its Masters*, p. 154; Elijah Judah Schochet, *The Hasidic Movement and the Gaon of Vilna* (Northvale, NJ: Jason Aronson, 1994), pp. 92–93; and Aaron Wertheim, *Halakhot veHalikhot haHasidut* (Jerusalem, 1961), pp. 92–93.

7. Avraham Yaakov Finkel, *The Great Chasidic Masters* (Northvale, NJ: Jason Aronson, 1992), p. 144.

and one of the humblest; his door was always open to all Jews. And handsome and debonair, he was the best-looking book cover the Jews had in his time.

Which meant the book on the Rizhiner had to be a kind of Messiah Primer. A book in which the beleaguered Jews could find solace in a heartless and Jew-baiting world. A book with a taste of the World to Come. A potential best-seller. Indeed, "[t]he messianic idea and dream were so deeply rooted in the Rizhiner that he—or his son David-Moshe of Chortkov, opinions vary on this—prepared a special room in his apartment called the 'Messiah's chamber.' All his most valuable and valued belongings were stored there and no one was allowed inside."[8]

If such a book could be found now inside the so-called Messiah's Chamber, we'd know much more the effect the Rizhiner had in hastening the Messiah. Still, until that time comes, we know a good deal about him, however clouded in myth he remains to this day.

This much is certain: Rabbi Yisroel Friedman of Rizhin, the Great *Maggid*'s[9] great-grandson, became a legend who contributed greatly to the spread of *Chassidus* to the Austro-Hungarian Empire. He also founded the Rizhin-Sadigora-Chortkov-Boyar and other dynasties.[10]

Long before that, he was orphaned at five, engaged at seven, married at thirteen (to Sarah, daughter of Rabbi Moses, head of the Talmudical College of Berditchev and later rabbi in Buchan); and at the age of sixteen, he succeeded his brother Abraham, who passed away in 1813 and left no children; eventually, the youthful Rabbi Yisroel settled in Rizhin, where he established his fabulous Court.

We also know, privately, he avoided pleasure and even tended toward asceticism. It's said he walked on hard peas he placed inside his leather shoes. Often he fasted and slept only three hours each night. A visitor to his Court easily learned more about this dedicated holy man. Often without much prodding, the Rizhiner would tell him: "Coarse trades are held in contempt. A tinsmith is little esteemed, and a bricklayer less, for they handle lowly substances. How do matters stand with me? What is coarser

---

8. Elie Wiesel, *Souls on Fire* (New York: Summit Books, 1972), p. 160.

9. Rabbi Dov Ber of Mezritch, 1704–1772.

10. All these dynasties "are keeping alive the Rizhiner tradition today with large *yeshivot* and chassidic centers in *Eretz Yisrael* and the United States." Finkel, *Great Chasidic Masters*, p. 144.

than a clod averse to spiritual elevation? And yet do I not work with this material, for the greater glory of God?"[11]

Pressed further by the visitor how he viewed his role in Rizhin and later in Sadigora (after he was jailed on trumped-up charges in Russian prisons for twenty-two months and fled Russia to what is now Poland), the Rizhiner would say: "The true *tzaddik* should be like quicksilver which instantly records a change of temperature. He must, likewise, instantly recognize the lack of tranquility and peace of mind among his followers."[12]

If there were two things he felt deeply about, one had to be the coming of the Messiah. The other, the diamond called "Jew." Once, in citing the verse "But all the children of Israel had light in their dwellings" (Exodus 10:23), the Rizhiner said: "Each one of us possesses a Holy Spark, but not every one exhibits it to the best advantage. It is like the diamond which cannot cast its luster if buried in the earth. But when disclosed in its appropriate setting, there is light, as from a diamond, in each of us."[13]

With such an embracing attitude to all Jews, Rabbi Yisroel's ability to draw *chassidim* to him was legendary. Yet there were times he had to draw a line when confronted with phony kinds of characters. Once, a *chassid* complained to the Rizhiner that he lacked fine garments, a fine dwelling, and a beautiful wife, the three things that serve to broaden understanding according to the Talmud (*Berachot* 57). "But," replied the Rizhiner, "these things only serve to broaden a man's understanding not to create it in him. Therefore of what use will they be to you?"[14]

Indeed, the Rizhiner had endless ways to endear himself, even if he was accidentally on the short end of a "joke." Here's one story recently told to me: On one Tisha B'Av, in Reb Yisroel Rizhiner's shul, the young people finished *kinus* and were passing the time on a long fast day. As the day wore on and the young people grew restless, they decided to "make *freilach*" a little. So they went up to the women's balcony, and they made a lasso out of a rope. When a friend would enter the shul unsuspecting, they would lasso him and lift him all the way up to the balcony. This helped pass the time, and as you can imagine, the hilarity

---

11. Chaim Bloch, *Gemeinde der Chassidism* (Vienna, 1920), p. 289; and Newman, *Hasidic Anthology*, p. 80.

12. Newman, *Hasidic Anthology*, p. 119.

13. Ibid., p. 172.

14. Ibid., p. 296.

and boisterousness grew louder and more *freilach* with each new "victim."

Suddenly, the Rizhiner himself walked into the shul. Laughing and confident, the *bochurim* didn't realize who it was and they caught and lifted the Rebbe himself, high into the air! Halfway up they saw who it was, and in a panic, they almost dropped him to the ground. The shul went from loud laughter to a terrified silence in a split second.

After he was lowered to the floor, the Rizhiner walked over to the *aron kodesh* and began to speak. The *bochurim* responsible for the prank shrank, certain they would now get a well-deserved public blasting. Instead, Reb Yisroel Rizhiner opened the *aron kodesh* calmly and said, "Master of the World, if you don't like the way your children are keeping this special day—take it away from them!"[15]

As the many books in Hebrew about the Rizhiner get translated into English, the book on the Rizhiner must be getting fat. But, in between, there were lean, tragic days for him. At forty, he was arrested and jailed for twenty-two months, summarily charged with treason and complicity in ordering the death of two Jewish informers, and he was linked with a vaguely formulated plot aiming to crown him "King of the Jews."[16] After his release, he was still in grave danger, until he managed to move his Court from the domain of the czar, in Rizhin, to Sadigora, under the rule of the Hapsburgs.

Later, he told his *chassidim* of his harrowing time. Worsened because, in jail, he was stuck with his *yetzer hora*: "When I was imprisoned as a political prisoner," he told his followers, "I understood why the *Midrash* describes the Satan, the *yetzer hora*, as a fool [commenting on Ecclesiastes 4:13; in *Kohelth Rabbah* 4:15]. Even in prison the *yetzer hora* would not leave me for a moment. Is he not, then, a fool? I was compelled to remain in prison, but who compelled the Satan to do so?"[17]

In Sadigora, Rabbi Yisroel acquired an estate, Zolotoi Potok, and there the glory days of Rizhin began again. Yet his heart was no longer fully in it. At his death he testified that he took with him no enjoyment at all from this world.

We cannot close his book unless this story he loved to tell is retold here for you.

---

15. As told to me by two Lubavitcher storytellers, Levi and Raizal Reiter, and printed in the *N'shei Chabad Newsletter*, *Tishrei* 5755, September 1994, vol. xxiii, no. 1, p. 7.

16. Wiesel, *Souls on Fire*, pp. 150–151.

17. Newman, *Hasidic Anthology*, p. 414.

Once a *misnaged* father-in-law forced his son-in-law, a young *chassid* of the Great *Maggid* of Mezritch, to choose between his wife and the *Maggid*. The son-in-law promised never to return to Mezritch. Yet shortly thereafter he went away. Where? To join his companions and their master. His angry father-in-law petitioned the local rabbi for a judgment. The rabbi consulted the *Shulchan Aruch* and declared that the broken promise was ground for divorce. Overnight the young man found himself without means to subsist alone. Before long, the young man fell sick, and, with no one to care for him, shortly died.

"Well," continued the Rizhiner, "when the Messiah will come, the young *chassid* will file a complaint against his father-in-law and the local rabbi, both guilty of his premature death. The first will say, 'I obeyed the rabbi.' The rabbi will say: 'I obeyed the *Shulchan Aruch*.' And the Messiah will say: 'The father-in-law is right, the rabbi is right and the Law is right.' Then he will embrace the young man and say: 'But I, what do I have to do with them? I have come for those who are not right.'"[18]

Any moment the Messiah will come, and together, right or wrong, we'll be welcomed with open arms by him inside the Messiah's Chamber. There, Moses, Abraham, Isaac, and Jacob will be, and so will every other Jew who ever walked this earth.

For preparing the Messiah's Chamber, we have the Rizhiner to thank. So, thank you, Rabbi Yisroel.

---

18. Wiesel, *Souls on Fire*, and Martin Buber, *Tales of the Hasidim, Book Two: The Later Masters* (New York: Schocken Books, 1991), p. 57.

15

THE MAN WHO
CAME TO DINNER

A feast! Let's have food and drink and invite the Messiah. Let all the saints and sinners come, Jewish, of course! Perhaps it was on such an important occasion that the Dinover Rebbe (Rabbi Tzvi Elimelech Shapiro, 1783-1841) visited the Rebbe of Ziditchov (Rabbi Hershele Eichenstein, died 1837).

At the Sabbath table, when potatoes, then a new vegetable recently imported from America, were placed on the table, the Dinover Rebbe declined to eat them. But the Ziditchover Rebbe persuaded him to partake of them, thereby bringing down an abundance of the "fruit of the earth" in its new home.[1] From this, the Dinover Rebbe learned his lesson well. Every holy meal is important, and welcoming the Messiah is a moveable feast.

One day it became the turn of the Dinover's son to learn the same lesson. His name was Reb Elazar Shapiro of Lanzhut (about 1805–1865), but, at the time, he was known as the rabbi of Strizhov, yet he spent most of his time in his father's house in Dinov. And why shouldn't he? Besides being his father, Rabbi Tzvi Elimelech was known for his ardent love of the Jewish people. He promoted the study of *Kabbalah* and led a valiant fight against the leaders of the *maskillim*, the "enlightened" secularists

---

1. B. Ehrman, *Peer ve-Khavod* (Muncats, 1912), p. 43a. Quoted in Louis I. Newman, *The Hasidic Anthology* (Northvale, NJ: Jason Aronson, 1987), p. 87.

100

who threatened to undermine traditional Judaism.[2] With all that close-
ness between father and son, we can safely assume that Reb Elazar
followed in his father's footsteps. But he wasn't quite there yet as this story
unfolds.[3]

Once a poor beggar—let's call him Menachem—came to the city of
Dinov for the Sabbath, and that poor man was the Messiah. Naturally, no
matter what was about to happen would Menachem permit himself to
pull rank and reveal who he was. So he kept himself in line. He found a
bed at a run-down inn, as they did not let him enter a respectable one.
Arriving before the Sabbath, he left his things with a poor baker, although
he dreaded doing so the moment the baker's sons got on his case. Their
throwing snowballs or mud-balls at him was the least of his problems.
Any way they could, they disturbed his peace. With glee. With malice.
Following him everywhere. Sabbath-time, the boys chased after him
when he began to pray, so that he could not pray, and nobody else around
him could do so either. What those boys needed was a hard smack or a
kick in the right place, but Menachem waved anyone away from them.
This was the Sabbath, he pointed out. And everyone went back to
praying as best as they could. Let the beggar take care of himself, they said.
The baker, feeling overwhelmed, disgusted, and helpless about his sons'
actions, sadly marveled at the beggar, who managed to keep himself in
check.

As far as Menachem the beggar was concerned, no Messiah, in this
situation, could do more. He came to Dinov for a reason.

To bid the Sabbath *adieu*, the rabbi of Strizhov invited his *chassidim* to
the Third Meal,[4] at his father's house, and the aforementioned poor man
also came along. There, too, the boys poked fun at him and disrupted the
holy setting. But rather than deal with the rude behavior of the baker's
boys, whom he was fond of, the rabbi of Strizhov chose to remove the
beggar from his house, as if to say there was one law for the native and
another law for the stranger among them.[5] So, said the rabbi to the

---

2. Avraham Yaakov Finkel, *The Great Chasidic Masters* (Northvale, NJ: Jason
Aronson, 1992), p. 131.

3. This story is based on the text by Ya'aqov Sofer, *Sippure Ya'aqov* (*The Stories
of Jacob*) (Husiatyn: F. Kawalek, 1904), pp. 35–36. Quoted by Raphael Patai, *The
Messiah Texts* (Detroit: Wayne State University Press, 1979), p. 32.

4. *Seudas Shelishis*, the third meal, is held near sunset on the Sabbath.

5. The complete opposite of Exodus 12:49, which states: "One law for the
native and the stranger among you."

beggar: "Go, please, to Rabbi David Ries; he, too, is having a rich meal ushering out the Sabbath Queen, and there you can eat and drink to your heart's desire."

"But," protested Menachem the beggar, "my intention is not to eat and drink, but to hear words of Torah."

Perhaps the rabbi was so distracted that he didn't hear the beggar right. Because the next moment he rose and ordered the poor man from his house. After he left, the rabbi apologized to all his guests for the minor inconvenience, and they went on with their Third Meal. After that, the baker's boys remained perfectly quiet. Which only made the rabbi feel he did the right thing.

As the meal went on, the rabbi suddenly noticed his father had unobtrusively retired to his room to sleep. So he left his guests a moment and went out to lock the front door of his father's room from the outside. As it is written, "He giveth His beloved sleep" (Psalms 127:2). Even more so on the Sabbath.

After they finished eating, the rabbi of Strizhov and his guests recited the grace after meals. When the guests left, he went to open the door of his father's room, but he found that the door was locked from the inside as well. Inside the room, he could hear, were voices discussing mysteries of the Torah. Who else was in his father's room? he wondered as he walked away and repaired to his own room to rest.

The question was finally answered the next morning when he asked his father, "Who was there with you?"

"That man, the beggar you asked to leave the house. I called him back. I had to speak with him. You see, my son, he was the Messiah ben David in disguise."

When his son heard this, he fell to the ground and fainted. When he revived, instantly he ran to the baker to find out whether the beggar was still there, but he found him not.

"Where did he go?" he entreated. "I must find him."

"Where did he go?" piped up one of the baker's sons. "I'll tell you but you ain't gonna believe it."

"Where?" the rabbi asked in great excitement.

"I saw him, too," shouted the other boy.

The rabbi had no time to lose. He almost had one foot out the door when the baker told him what his boys were alluding to. "Reb Elazar, it was this way. The beggar was about to leave when I asked him about a very difficult part of Torah that nobody ever gave me an answer for. And without hesitation he told me what my ears longed to hear. Then, the strangest thing I'd ever seen occurred. A pillar of fire came out of nowhere and took him away from here."

After that the baker and his children could say no more. They looked like they had just seen a ghost, and were burning in place. As for the rabbi of Strizhov, he related this to his father and beat his breast in remorse. "Why did I let this happen—and in your house?" he cried.

Suddenly the Dinover Rebbe did a strange thing: he turned to the author of this story, who in turn turned to this writer, and this writer now turns to you to say, "*Nu*, dear reader, if you know where the Messiah is, by all means bring the man to the next holy meal, and let all the saints and sinners come, Jewish, of course!

"What a feast for the eyes and souls that will be!"

16

GOD'S EVERYTHING

Yes, little Esther,[1] dreams of glory have a Jewish side, too. For only
in such dreams dare a Jewish woman of today see herself as
another Maiden of Ludmir, the "holy virgin," Chana Rochel
Werbermacher (1805-1892). She proved that "dreams do not die if they
bloomed once in the soul."[2]

So, Esther, let me tell you the story of Chana Rochel . . . let me tell
you of her life:

This story is based on the following material: Gershon Winkler, *They Called
Her Rebbe: The Maiden of Ludmir* (New York: Judaica Press, 1991); Charles
Raddock, "Once There Was a Female Chassidic Rabbi," *The Jewish Digest*
(Washington, DC: B'nai B'rith, December 1967), pp. 20–24; *Encyclopaedia
Judaica* (Jerusalem: Keter Publishing House, 1971), 2:554; Menachem M. Brayer,
The Jewish Woman in Rabbinic Literature, 2 vols. (Hoboken, NJ: Ktav Publishing
House, 1986), vol. II, pp. 467–469; J. S. Minkin, *The Romance of Hasidism*, 3rd
ed. (Los Angeles, 1971), pp. 345–347; Y. Twersky, *Ha-Betulah Mi Ludmir*
(Jerusalem, 1950); Yitzchak Alfasi, *Ha-Hasidut* (Tel Aviv, 1973), p. 242; S. A.
Hordesky, *Ha-Hasidut be Hahasidim*, 2nd ed. (Tel Aviv, 1943), vol. 4, p. 68 of the
abridged one-volume edition in English, "The Maid of Ludmir," *Leaders of
Hasidism* (London, 1928); Harry M. Rabinowicz, *The World of Hasidism* (London, 1970), pp. 202–210, and *Hasidism: The Movement and Its Masters* (Northvale, NJ: Jason Aronson, 1994), pp. 345–346.

1. The "Esther" in this story, in real life, is Esther Blau, then seven years old,
the third oldest daughter of the Devorah Leah/Reuven Blau family, whom I

But what's there to tell?
It's all been said and sung—
A Jew's life examined
Is worth the living.
Monesh examined his, so too Leah hers
Then sought the Holy Seer[3] they
Is how little Chana Rochel came to be
By Torah vow of childless parents
In fair Ludmir she was born
"A blessing named Chana Rochel"
But definitely one in disguise!
To have a girl who desired to be a human
Torah—Torah!—What were her parents to do?
The Holy Seer spoke, the parents agreed:
"We'll teach her the Big Book and prayer."
—"Not enough!" she said all along
"I want *Midrash, Kabbalah, Mussar*—
God's everything!"

And she had everything to be—
A warmhearted, affectionate child
A model *cheder* student at seven
Knowing Torah wall to wall
A Jewish soul in bloom
Those holy surges of all!
Wait, there's more:
She lost her momma at nine
Engaged at twelve to wed
A sadness—a melancholy aura
A life without Torah learning
"Who wants friend or foe!"
Comfort's at my Momma's grave
Poppa doesn't know—doesn't care!
Thinks I can live life as a girl!

---

have, as of this writing, never told a story to, yet I remain convinced will be, as
she is now, a special Queen Esther in all the years of her life.

2. Jacob Fichman, *Kol Shire*, ii, p. 23.
3. Rabbi Yaakov Yitzchak Halevi Horowitz, 1745–1815.

—"Not enough!" she said all along
"I want *Midrash, Kabbalah, Mussar*—
God's everything!"

Poppa Monesh threw up his hands
"There's no talking to her
Reading huge tomes of Talmud"
Till a nice boy Monesh put in her path
And now she wore a yellow ribbon
She was only twelve—and Isaac was that too
But then—oh then!—she lost him
In "a time to find, and a time to lose"[4]
The Russian army took him away
Who knew what happened to the boy
Who knew what happened to the girl
Yet she found her Torah true path again
Now father and daughter rarely talked
A visit to Reb Mordechai[5] didn't help
He couldn't take the rabbi out of her
—"Not enough!" she said all along
"I want *Midrash, Kabbalah, Mussar*—
God's everything!"

"Oh Momma," she cried at her grave
"On earth only Torah do I desire
Poppa wants to take that away from me.
There must be a way to live—with God
With Torah to hang my life on
Oh Momma, I'm so alone
With you or without you . . .
Let me rest a while on your tomb
Any moment I feel I may exhume."

---

4. Winkler, *They Called Her Rebbe*, p. 73. This line from Winkler's book seems apropos in describing how the Russian Army conscripted Jewish boys at age twelve and kept them away from their Jewish faith and their families for twenty-five years. Truly, it was a time for Russia to find, and a time for Jews to lose.

5. Celebrated chassidic rebbe, 1770–1837, founder of the Chernobyl dynasty.

And as she slept the wind it did howl
Brushing her leg, bolting her fears
Half-dazed, she ran for her life
Chased by shapes of midnight strife
Her heart with terror bursting
Into an open grave she tripped
—"Not enough!" she said all along
"I want *Midrash, Kabbalah, Mussar*—
God's everything!"

A grave-digger found her in the morn
In a morn dazed beyond repair
Three times a day with *tefillin* on
In never-ending prayer, Monesh watched her
Tranced and hovering between life and death.
Then one morn just like the morn she was found
She opened her eyes and said in a voice so weak
"I've just come back from the heavenly palace
Where they gave me a new, sublime soul."
Monesh said nothing as she rose with new stance
Donning *tzitzis* and *tallis* for the first time
Like King Saul's daughter,[6] she put on *tefillin*.
When her Poppa Monesh died she recited *kaddish*
And annulled her betrothal, to boot
—"Not enough!" she said all along
"I want *Midrash, Kabbalah, Mussar*—
God's everything!"

In secluded meditation she dwelled
Where pious women and menfolks came
to the *grune Stubel*—as the hut was named
Next a small *shul* close to the Lug flow
The lame, the halt, the blind—
Nothing could keep them from their Rebbe
For that's what they called her now
Father Monesh and Reb Mordechai were gone.
Heard but never seen, Rabbi Chana Rochel spoke
When *shalosh seudot* was at hand

---

6. Her name was Michal (see 1 Samuel 14:49–50, and *Bavli, Erubin*, p. 96a).

From her room with open door
In hushed tones men and women outside
heard her discourses breathe
Never could they get enough of her
Nothing her critics said could hurt
—"Not enough!" she said all along
"I want *Midrash, Kabbalah, Mussar*—
God's everything!"

O Maid of Ludmir—how long will you go on
Without a Chofetz Chaim at your side
To warn the wags to guard their words![7]
For what the locals said surely proved
There's death and life in the mighty tongue[8]
Even rabbis who were once her friend
Waxed indignant and drove her out
From the little green hut—her very own Eden
Her Eden beside the waters of the Lug
Now Reb Mordechai loomed again ever so big
At forty she married a *talmid chacham*
Read: a "pallid, long-faced scribe,
her senior by many years"[9]
Who promptly shed her—or did she shed him?
But took her dowry all—for what it was worth
—"Not enough!" she said all along
"I want *Midrash, Kabbalah, Mussar*—
God's everything!"

Things went from bad to worse
Her followers, now a handful by count,
Eyed her sad ending
Excommunicated easily enough
And for this brooding figure

---

7. Rabbi Zelig Pliskin, *Guard Your Tongue: A Practical Guide to the Laws of Loshon Hora* (Brooklyn, NY, 1975), based on *Chofetz Chaim* by Rabbi Yisroel Meir Kagan, 1839–1933.

8. A paraphrase of *Mishlai* 18:21.

9. Raddock, "Once There Was a Female Chassidic Rabbi," p. 23.

Whose green hut she did sell
She was never seen and never heard.
Rumor had it off to Jerusalem she went
By then all her Rebbe power gone
But that's not true—not true at all
By the "Hundred Gates" in Jerusalem old
She at the Wailing Wall bloomed
Offering blessings for sale
This female Rabbi did it all
On Sabbath to everyone's delight
Twelve shewbreads she baked alone
—"Not enough!" she said all along
"I want *Midrash, Kabbalah, Mussar*—
God's everything!"

She did so many things only holy men dared
Setting up a modest chassidic court all her own
Leading processionals with the Scrolls
With prayer shawl and *tefillin* a-bulging
This little grey-eyed woman in purple reticule
Trying to show the Reb Mordechais of each day
That she had "the soul of a great rebbe
Who returned to this world to make some repairs."[10]
O blessed New Moon, O blessed Maid of Ludmir
If not for you on that day, who else would
With female devotees in hand
Marched to Rachel's Tomb—marched to lay down
Such petitions of "matriarchal intercession"
to bring on Messiah! Messiah!
Who knew—"We can't wait!"—who knew!
—"Not enough!" she said all along
"I want *Midrash, Kabbalah, Mussar*—
God's everything!"

So, Esther dear, we come down to that night
That night when all the world stood still
In the cave where Chana Rochel lay in wait

---

10. Winkler, *They Called Her Rebbe*, p. 47.

The Messiah, mounted on donkey, ready to ride
And Elijah poised to do his thing
All she needed was her old *Kabbalist* friend
To give the word a magic—and Messiah would appear.
"We'll sing our hearts out," he had said
"We'll sing the siren song of Messiah—
He has to come, has to come, *Kabbalah* says."
But he the old *Kabbalist* came too late
Some say Elijah held him up—too bad!
The time of the Messiah was yet ripe
In the cave he found stone dead the Maid
What more could the *Kabbalist* say?
—"Not enough!" she said all along
"I want *Midrash, Kabbalah, Mussar*—
God's everything!"

Now I ask you, Esther, some day yourself a queen
Why, without a king must we be left
—"Not enough!" she said all along
"I want *Midrash, Kabbalah, Mussar*—
God's everything!"
In a world where Messiah is heard but never seen?

17

THEY MIGHT HAVE BEEN RABBI AND REBBETZIN MESSIAH

Rabbi Shalom Rokeach of Belz
The First Belzer Rebbe
1783–1855

PRESENTING A POTENTIAL MESSIAH IN HIS TIME . . . REB SHALOM ROKEACH OF BELZ

In *Sefer Hachasidus Mitoras Belz* (*Complete Redemption*, p. 42), it is written: Our teacher, Rabbi Aharon [Rokeach, 4th Belzer Rebbe, 1880–1957], o.b.m., said . . . that according to Maimonides, it appears that in each generation there is one *tzaddik* who is King Messiah and when the time for the Redemption arrives he will be revealed, speedily and in our days, Amen. He further said that his holy grandfather, Reb Shalom, *zt"l*, saw the Messiah twice. The first time, when he was a young man, he saw the Messiah as an elderly man; the second time, when he himself was old, he saw the Messiah as a young man. In the pamphlet *Sha'alu Sh'lom Yerushalayim* (p. 59), an explanation is brought down in the name of the holy Rabbi, Rebbe Yissachar Dov of Belz [grandfather, passed away 1927, of the current Belzer Rebbe, born 1948, who was named after him], o.b.m., who interpreted the above according to Maimonides—that in every generation a *tzaddik* exists who is worthy of being King

Messiah. Accordingly, the first time he saw the Messiah, he was seeing the *tzaddik* of the previous generation. The second time, he was seeing the Messiah of the present generation.

Nobody ever said at the time that the first Belzer Rebbe (Rabbi Shalom Rokeach) and Satan were bound to meet. Nobody—not even Satan himself.

But there was a time that a legendary *tzaddik*, who preceded Reb Shalom into this world, was suddenly confronted by Satan and found not perfect. Let me tell you about it . . .

On one chilly *Shavuos* morning,[1] when it was time to go to shul, the young Rabbi Shalom didn't appear for *davening*. The important members of his congregation were quite surprised as this was unusual for him to be late.

The door was never locked, yet no one among them had the audacity to enter the Rebbe's room without permission. So, they went to his mother, who had her own "in," and asked her to check with the Rebbe why he had not yet come down to *daven*.

When the mother entered his quarters, she saw him heaving a sigh.

"Now," he said to her, "is a time just like the time a thousand years ago. Then, too, was a favorable potential moment for the Messiah to come, Mother dearest . . .

". . . For there was no doubt in any Jew alive that the leader of the generation was worthy of becoming the Messiah. He had never sinned in his life. He always had his two eyes and soul looking upward to God, while his two hands and heart were outstretched to his fellow man . . .

". . . so why not?

"'I'll tell you why not!' Satan insisted to God, carrying his lawsuit all

---

This short biography is based on information from books by Zenta Dayan, Eliezer Yaakov, Roisnitz, "Introduction," *Kol Yaakov*; Avrohom Chaim Simcha Bunim Micholzohn, *Doiver Sholom* and *Ohel Yehoshua* (Pshemishel, Amkrant & Freund, 1910); Rabbi Tzvi Rabinowicz, *Chassidic Rebbes: From the Baal Shem Tov to Modern Times* (Southfield, MI: Targum, 1989); Louis I. Newman, *The Hasidic Anthology* (Northvale, NJ: Jason Aronson, 1987); and *The World of Belz*, eds. Julius Liebb and Yehuda Meth (Brooklyn, NY: Belz Institutions in Israel Publications, Summer 1986), 1:32; and from interviews with Belzer *chasid* Rabbi Lazer Spira, who lives with his family in the Borough Park section of Brooklyn, NY.

1. Micholzohn, *Doiver Sholom*, p. 142.

the way to the highest court in heaven. 'I demand that I be given the opportunity to prove that this greatest holy man of this generation is not exactly perfect.'

" 'How can you say this?' the angels demanded of Satan.

"Simply put, Satan said the obvious: 'He's never been put to the supreme test. Give me a chance to test him. Heaven forbid he will sin, of course, but maybe he will.'

"And in heaven they agreed to this minor request."

In the religious world, Torah scholars never focus on such human curiosities as a stunning blonde. So, Satan came down to earth disguised as a beautiful woman that could attract even Torah scholars. How? Satan made her, in everyone's eyes, the greatest Torah scholar who ever walked this earth—bar no man or woman!

She merely had to open her mouth to speak, and the word of the living God electrified and the earth scorched. Soon her fame spread far and wide, with all her God-given thoughts preceding her from town to town. Was it true, that "everything derives from a woman"?[2]

Taking her time to reach the city where the great *tzaddik* dwelled, the woman traveled from place to place, always ending her talks with an audience of Jewish scholars by saying, "Tell the greatest *tzaddik* of our time to come up and see me sometime. I have things to say about Torah for his ears alone."

And now the word was spread. She and the holy man had to meet!

Then, just as she had long schemed, she reached the very city where he lived.

Coming out to meet her were all the great scholars of the city except the holy man who really mattered to her. Still, the scholars in attendance had to find out if everything really derived "from such a woman"; they didn't have too long to wait. She dazzled them with her Torah brilliance. Nothing was lost on these learned men. Nothing—except those truths she now withheld for the *tzaddik*. He must come, exclaimed the other scholars, he must, if only so they could learn even more! At once three of them set out to the holy man to demand he come to her inn. He must hear what they heard.

Still he refused to come.

So she continued weaving her magic, if such a word has any place in a holy discussion. Before their very eyes, she laid out the deepest secrets

2. Midrash, *Genesis Rabbah* 17.

known only to God Himself until that very moment. He must have personally given them to this unusual woman before she commenced her journey from town to town, reasoned her listeners.

And so these great scholars lapped up these great Torah truths, determined to tell their children and grandchildren they had heard it from an impeccable source.

Then, she held out an even bigger bait for the great rabbi. Every time the holy scholars thought she had revealed everything, she suddenly surprised them and said, with great charm and greater modesty, "If the great rabbi of this city came to my inn, I would say such things that no one ever heard before."

Who could resist such words? No one—not even the great rabbi, who finally fell under the spell. He had to hear the Godly truths from this unusual woman.

And so, surrounded by all the great scholars of his city, he arrived at the inn where she was staying. Once she met him she wasted no time and showed a tremendous power in learning. The great holy man was shocked by what she said.

"Who taught you this?" said the shaken rabbi.

Aha! The holy man was about to fall into the trap.

So she said, "If everyone will step out of the room for a minute, and the rabbi will remain here, then I shall reveal the greatest Torah secrets to him alone, and how I came to know them."

Quickly the room was cleared. The rabbi remained alone with the woman. He had his two eyes and soul looking upward to God. Waiting.

Suddenly he beat his breast. "Aiiieee! I have sinned!"

And indeed, for a few moments, he had, by remaining secluded in a room with a strange woman.

"As a result," Reb Shalom told his mother, "the Messiah did not come."

Bringing it all home, Reb Shalom added, "Well, we almost had the Messiah now also, but he's not going to come. I may as well go *daven*."

Still, in Reb Shalom's time there was hope that the Messiah was coming soon; in fact, many felt he was right there and then—the Belzer Rebbe himself. Still others, hedging their bets, said, "the Messiah is the master; he can wait as long as he pleases."

Reb Shalom's beginnings: Right from the outset, there was something about this Rebbe that his disciples couldn't forget. Through their own religious looking glass, they saw Elijah cast his mantle upon him, as it is written, "Elijah the prophet . . . shall turn the heart of the fathers to the children and the heart of the children to the fathers" (Malachi, 3:23f).

In 1783, the birth of Shalom Rokeach in Brod, Galicia, was greeted with joy. At a young age, Shalom, the son of Rabbi Elazar Rokeach—a prized disciple of Reb Chaim Sanzer of Brod—and a descendant of Rashi and King David, was recognized as a leader who was destined for greatness. "He will lead thousands and tens of thousands," the sainted Seer of Lublin (Rabbi Jacob Isaac Horowitz, 1744–1815) said of the future founder of Belz *Chassidus*.[3]

Once during a Chanukah night, when he was a child of eight or nine, the wind howled and the snow deepened. After the family Rokeach lit Chanukah candles, ate latkes and played with *dreidels*, Shalom asked his father to go to the *beis hamidrosh* to learn.

Ordinarily his father would have automatically granted his request, but he realized that, during Chanukah, some of the other boys from *cheder* played cards in the shul after hours. No, he would not let his son go.

He reassured his father that he would not do that. "All I want to do is study in the shul."

How could a loving father now turn down such a request? Granted! "But wait!" he said as the son moved toward the door. "Wait!" The father had something further to say.

Dutifully, Shalom turned to face his father.

When the father had his full attention, he said solemnly, "I shall give you a very small candle, and you must promise me that when the candle is extinguished you must come home."

Readily the boy agreed, took the candle, and off he went by himself to shul.

There, with his sweet voice and sweeter lips, he sat down to learn. God saw this. The night, the studying, the music: God so loved the boy's learning—"the lips of truth shall be established for ever" (Proverbs 12:19)—that He created another Chanukah miracle: the little candle, which could have burned for only two hours, lasted until the morning.

And when the morning finally came, the candle went out. Being the good son that he was, Shalom kept his promise to his father, closed his *Gemara* and went home.

On his way home, Shalom began to wonder about the candle his father gave him—a candle that burned so long. How could it be? He was still wondering about this when he entered his house.

---

3. Micholzohn, *Doiver Sholom*, p. 5.

Waiting for him was his father, who let the boy have it. "I told you that you had to come home when the candle burned out and you disobeyed me. Why?"

When he was older, the Belzer Rebbe told the story to his *chassidim* of how the candle burned all night. "In reality," he said to them, "I could have answered my father that I did return home when the candle burned out, and my father would have believed me. But the reason I didn't want to answer my father was because I didn't want to use the crown of the Torah to save myself from a punishment."

As the years had passed since his childhood, the hearts of the father and son continued to turn to each other.

Nowhere was this so evident as the time his father accompanied him to another town about a *shiddach* (a proposed marriage). There, a matchmaker said, was an ideal mate for the teenaged Shalom. So off he and his parents went. And as they walked up one street, they saw an old man with a white beard, carrying a large book under his arm.

Suddenly Shalom turned to his father and said, "Please tell that man I would like to see his book."

Never one to approach a stranger, the father declined to do so now. But Shalom implored him further. "I must know what's in that book, Father. Please!"

Finally the father relented and hailed the old man.

"What is your book?" he asked him.

"This book," the old man said, "is a record of all the women in this city who use the *mikveh* [ritual bath]."

"We'd like to look in it, if you please," the father confided to the old man.

"Of course." The old man approached the two strangers and opened the book, allowing them to flip through the pages, if that was what they wanted.

Which they did. And they couldn't find in it the name of the mother of this girl who was proposed for Shalom. Now, this *shiddach* was out of the question. Not with such a family whose females never went to a *mikveh*. Each stream has its own course, but all *mikvehs* have only one direction, the divine path to God. So they turned around and went home.

Many years later, when the first Belzer Rebbe told the story to his *chassidim*, he said he found out later that this city had no such record book of who used the *mikveh*. Then, who was this old man? The old man was Eliyahu Hanovi. And there was no doubt, the Belzer Rebbe said, that he was sent there just at that moment along the road to prevent him from marrying the wrong girl.

Then who was the right girl? Malkah. How did they meet? There came the unfortunate time when Shalom's father passed away at the age of thirty-two in Warsaw, leaving his wife, Rivkah Henya, with three sons and two daughters. After she remarried, the young Shalom went to live with his uncle, Rabbi Yissacher Baer, Rabbi of Sokol. There he met his cousin, Malkah; a match was made for the two teenagers; and after they married, the *shechinah* abided with them forever.[4]

"Shalom, Shalom, Shalom!"

"Every day before daybreak, the dutiful Malkah would wake her husband with the words: 'Shalom, arise to the service of the Creator. See,' she would urge him, 'all the laborers are already at their appointed tasks.'[5] Inspired by his *rebbetzin*, Rabbi Shalom needed but little urging. The *tzaddikim* of that generation applied to Rebbetzin Malkah the verse in *Bereishis* (4:18), 'And Malchizedek, king of Shalom,' interpreting it: 'Since Malkah [the *rebbetzin*] is a *tzaddekes*, then Shalom is king'"[6] (meaning that Shalom shall lead his flock of *chassidim*). There was no question that Malkah was the right wife. Willingly she sold her jewelry so he could sit and study.[7]

Once, early in their marriage, Rebbetzin Malkah asked Reb Shalom how he planned to earn a living. In his humble manner, Reb Shalom responded: "As a bathhouse attendant."

"That's fine with me," she said, "but in time to come, God willing, we'll have marriageable children, and when one of our daughters marries, where will she find the son of a bathhouse attendant of your caliber?"

Reb Shalom smiled at his wise *rebbetzin*. Then, he asked her thoughts on what he should do.

"As the *Mishnah* [*Pirkei Avot*, ch. 5] tells us," she said, "whoever studies Torah with pure motivations merits many things"— "the many things includes a livelihood," she concluded.

After that, Reb Shalom wholeheartedly threw himself into the study of Torah. And it went well for him for a number of days. Then, as he was studying late into the night, Reb Shalom began nodding off. To the

---

4. Ibid.
5. Ibid., p. 7.
6. Rabinowicz, *Chassidic Rebbes*, p. 126.
7. Ibid., pp. 187–188.

rescue came his *rebbetzin*. As Reb Shalom pored over the holy books, with renewed vigor and pure intention, Rebbetzin Malkah held a candle over his shoulder to keep him in deep study. After a few days it worked. Reb Shalom no longer needed his *rebbetzin*'s encouragement to maintain the right Torah spirit.

By 1817, Reb Shalom was appointed rabbi of Belz, Galicia. Under his leadership, Belz sprouted into a metropolis of *Chassidus* and a spiritual center for European Jewry. From his base in Belz, he led the fight against attempts to assimilate the Jews of Galicia.

And pure intention became the foundation in his building of the Great Synagogue in Belz. Once, Reb Shalom's brother, Reb Leibush, came to visit him. When he entered his home, the sound of hammering resounded through the rooms. The town of Belz was constructing the new synagogue. And Reb Leibush couldn't wait to visit the site. After partaking of a cup of tea and some fresh cake with his mother, he went out to check on the progress of the building. There, he saw his brother standing with a shovel in his hand, helping with the work like a member of the construction crew.

Immediately he reprimanded his brother. "Listen, my brother, haven't *chazal* said that a leader should not engage in physical labor in front of three persons? You, the Rebbe of Belz, know this law, so why are you standing here like a common worker?"

Reb Shalom listened quietly to his brother's words before responding. "Leibush," he began. "I will tell you a story that will explain my apparently strange behavior. Many years ago when I was studying in the town of Skohl my two study partners and I learned that if we studied with the utmost dedication and unstinting effort for a thousand consecutive nights without sleeping, we would merit a revelation of the prophet Elijah. When we heard about this, we wanted this holy revelation more than anything else in the world.

"We resolved that we would undertake to study together for a thousand nights in a row. In the beginning it wasn't hard. After all, we were very enthusiastic and burning with our desire to reach our exalted goal. Every night—so that our neighbors would not know or see what we were doing—my dearest Malkah helped me descend from our bedroom window, via a ladder, and I would rush off to the shul. Nights passed in intense study, and we hardly noticed when the morning came.

"But, after a while, it began to be increasingly more difficult to study with the same dedication. We were growing tired and exhausted from the lack of sleep night after night. Thanks to my *rebbetzin*, I kept on going no matter what.

"After a few hundred nights, one of my partners couldn't stand the strain any longer and he decided to drop out. But I continued the nightly session with my remaining partner.

"Finally, it was on the eight hundredth night that he, too, lost the quest, yet I was firm in my will to continue right through to the end.

"I sat alone in the dark shul every night, fighting sleep and utter exhaustion, determined to reach the one thousandth night. When I thought that I had no more strength to continue I still pushed on, so deep was my desire to receive the revelation of the holy prophet.

"On the thousandth night, a mighty storm blew up. It seemed like the gates of Hell had opened and the fierce winds had threatened to destroy the world. Even I, who was normally unfazed by the weather, no matter how violent, was shaken by the unearthly howls and piercing flashes of lightning that zigzagged across the sky. Still, I sat by my open book, determined that nothing would interfere with my reaching my goal. Suddenly there was a loud, frightening crash of glass. The wind had blown out one of the windows of the study hall and its breath had extinguished my candles. Fear overwhelmed me and I tried to run home, but the wind prevented me.

"Here, I had persevered for a thousand nights though my strength was all but gone, and now this. The rain and wind pelted me through the shattered window and my spirits had plummeted to rock bottom. I would have left had I not been so terrified of the raging storm.

"Ovecome with pain and anguish, I went up to the *aron hakodesh* and poured out my heart before God. I don't know how long I stood there pouring out my yearning and frustration to the One Above, but at one point I realized that the storm had ended.

"I came to myself and went over to look out the broken window. I saw an old man walking in the direction of the study hall. I knew it was Elijah, who had come to learn Torah with me. For the rest of the night he taught the entire Torah. The last *halachah* he taught me concerned the building of a *beis haknesses* [synagogue].

"Dear Brother Leibush, this lesson has been so precious to me that if I were able, I would erect the whole building by myself from beginning to end. Alas, this little bit is all I am capable of doing, but even so, it is so dear to me that my entire being is full of joy with each brick that I place."

Reb Leibush smiled, happy with his brother's explanation.[8]

In 1828, Reb Shalom laid the cornerstone to the famous Great

---

8. Micholzohn, *Doiver Sholom*, p. 8.

Synagogue of Belz, whose construction he meticulously supervised. Whatever impression Reb Leibush walked away with, he didn't fully grasp the difficult responsibility his brother had assumed, for building the great synagogue extended over a period of fifteen years. But its history, in a way, extended backward to a thousand years before Reb Shalom's time. In those days lived Reb Avraham in a house on the very spot Reb Shalom laid the foundation of the Great Synagogue of Belz. Reb Avraham's home reminded one of the tent of Avraham Aveinu [the patriarch Abraham, our teacher], with all four sides open to guests to enter. It's recorded[9] that shortly after the construction of the synagogue began, this same Reb Avraham appeared, alive and in the flesh, in the middle of the night, and excitedly asked Reb Shalom where the Messiah was.

"Why do you ask, Rabbi?" Reb Shalom said.

"I've come because the holy commotion above my house could only mean he is here at last. That's why I am here, resurrected from the dead, I believe."

Sadly, the Belzer Rebbe had to tell Reb Avraham he was mistaken, that the Messiah was not yet there.

"Then, how do you explain all the commotion here on earth?"

"Would that the Messiah be here! He would be overjoyed with this holiest of shuls we're building on the sacred ground of your house. It's the shul's holiness that's causing such ecstatic trembling, Reb Avraham."

As much as the rabbi was overjoyed hearing this, he let out the longest and saddest sigh Reb Shalom had ever heard. To console the rabbi, Reb Shalom said: "The time for Resurrection[10] is not here." Then, Reb Avraham disappeared back into the darkness of eternity, gone, waiting for the right moment when the Messiah will finally come.

---

9. Ibid., p. xxx.

10. Many Jewish sources state that the messianic era, and especially the time of the Resurrection of the Dead (*tichiyas hameisim*), is the fulfillment and culmination of the creation of the world, for which purpose it was originally created.

According to Rabbi Israel M. Altein, "the *Zohar* teaches that the Resurrection will begin forty years after all Jews have returned to the Holy Land, and will continue intermittently until all are restored to life. According to the Talmud, those buried in the Holy Land will be restored first, then those of other lands. The *Zohar* writes that the righteous and the Torah scholars will be first. However, everyone will be resurrected eventually, for everlasting life.

"Based on the teachings of the Sages, there will be exceptions to this schedule. Certain individuals will return to life at once, at the advent of the Messiah.

As for Reb Shalom, here was a rebbe who was always perfectly happy to lead his disciples. Here was a rebbe who made his wife an equal partner in every way. Here was a rebbe even other great rebbes came to learn from and from the Rebbetzin Malkah. Reb Shalom said of her, "She has the wisdom of the disciples of the Baal Shem Tov [1698–1760]."[11]

"The soul will return to the body in the Land of Israel. The bodies of those buried in other lands will roll through the earth until they reach the Holy Land, where they will return to life. The righteous, however, will be spared this ordeal.

"The story is told of Andrayanus, who asked Rabbi Yehoshua ben Chananya, 'How will God restore the body in the future?'

"The Rabbi answered, 'From a tiny bone in the spinal column called *luz*.'

" 'How do you know [the bone will not rot away till then]?'

" 'Bring me the bone and I will show you,' the Rabbi said.

"The bone was brought and ground in millstones but was not damaged. It was thrown into fire but was not burned. It was soaked in water but did not dissolve. It was placed on an iron anvil and struck with a hammer until the anvil split in two and the hammer broke. The bone, however, remained unharmed.

"This bone takes nourishment only from food eaten at the Saturday night *melave malka* meal; death and decay are unable to touch it.

"The *Zohar* writes that at the time of Resurrection, God will soften this bone with the 'Dew of Resurrection,' forming a clear and pure liquid. Any other parts of the body remaining at the time will be united with this softened bone until they are one mass. It will then congeal, expand and take shape. Onto this form will be drawn skin, flesh, bones and blood vessels. Finally, God will imbue the complete body with a living spirit.

"Our Sages teach: As the person was before passing away, so shall he be when brought back to life. If when he went he was blind, he shall return blind; if deaf, he shall return deaf . . . ; the garments he wore then he shall wear when he returns. Said the Holy One blessed is He, 'Let them arise as they were before, then I shall heal them.' This God will do by removing the 'sheath' surrounding the sun, permitting the sun's more intense rays, with their Divine healing powers, to reach earth, healing all those who have a share in the Future World." From "The Messianic Era," *De Yiddishe Heim*, vol. 30, no. 1 (Brooklyn, NY: N'shei Ubnos Chabad, Winter 5752), pp. 4–6.

In a similar vein, Queen Cleopatra once asked Rabbi Meir (flourished 130–160 c.e.): I know that the dead will come back to life. But when they rise up, will they arise nude or clad in their garments? Replied Rabbi Meir: You may come to the answer by inference from a grain of wheat. If a grain of wheat, which is buried naked, sprouts forth clad in many robes, how much more and more so the righteous, who are buried in their raiment? (Talmud, *Sanhedrin* 90b).

11. Micholzohn, *Doiver Sholom*, p. 22.

The Sanzer Rebbe (Rabbi Chaim Halberstam of Sanz, the *Divrei Chaim*, 1793–1876) often went to Belz for *Shabbos*. On one such a visit, he was accompanied by his son. This very son later became the Shiniaver Rebbe (Rabbi Yechezkel Shraga of Shiniava, 1815–1899).[12]

Even in his youth, the Shiniaver Rebbe was "uncompromising and unbending as regard to the minutiae of the law. He maintained throughout his life that 'whoever contravenes one of the laws of the *Shulchan Aruch* inherits *Gehinnom* [Purgatory]. . . . While his father interpreted the law leniently, Rabbi Yechezkel took a more stringent attitude. Nor did he support his father in his 'controversy' with the Rebbe of Sadigora, which lasted seven years."[13]

Understandably, his father was very hesitant about his son coming with him to Belz, knowing how outspoken he was on anything he felt was improper.

Now before the Sanzer Rebbe and his son set foot in Belz, we should know that when Rabbi Shalom held a *tisch* [chassidic get-together] Rebbetzin Malkah would often sit beside him.

And why not? Rebbetzin Malkah was always considered a very saintly person. No one doubted that. On almost every problem, Rabbi Shalom consulted his *rebbetzin*,[14] and his example was followed by his *chassidim*. Once, a man came to seek the blessing of the Rebbe. He complained of a painful leg. Rebbetzin Malkah advised him to light a candle every day in the synagogue. He did so, and made a complete recovery. How did the *rebbetzin* know that if the man lit a candle in the *shul*, he would get better? Reb Shalom asked her.

She explained, "It is written in *Tehillim* [119:105], 'Your word is a lamp unto my feet.'"

Finally, the Sanzer Rebbe and his son arrived in Belz for *Shabbos*. They found Rabbi Shalom and his *rebbetzin* sitting in a bare room with plain walls. On their departure, Rabbi Chaim asked his son what impression the couple had made on him and how the room in which they were seated appeared to him.

---

12. According to Micholzohn (*Doiver Sholom*, p. 22), it was Rabbi Baruch of Gorlitz (1826–1906), another of the Sanzer Rebbe's sons, who accompanied him.

13. Sefer Hasidim, 13C, no. 1044, p. 261, based on *Ketubot* 77b; and *A Treasury of Jewish Quotations*, ed. Joseph L. Baron (Northvale, NJ: Jason Aronson, 1985), p. 101.

14. Micholzohn, *Doiver Sholom*, p. 22.

"As we entered," the son replied, "they seemed like Adam and Eve before they sinned and as if their room was *Gan Eden*."

Often the Sanzer Rebbe would tell this charming story to his *chassidim*, summing up with, "At the *tisch*, my son saw only two saintly persons."

Then, the Sanzer would smile the smile of a doting father and say, "I always knew that my son Yechezkel has two good eyes."

Elijah the prophet may be in charge of seating the righteous in *Eden*, but, by their very presence in that modest earthly setting, they had transformed Belz into *Gan Eden*.

The story of their marriage went beyond man and woman, rebbe and *rebbetzin*. It went beyond Rabbi Shalom's building of Belz's Great Synagogue, and the fashioning of the curtain of the *aron hakodesh* with Rebbetzin Malkah's own clothing.[15] It went beyond their earthly lives. It went to the very heart and soul of humanity and divinity.

With these two holy persons in mind, we now come upon David Ehrman (popularly known as Reb David Getzel's), a *chassid* of the third Belzer Rebbe, Rabbi Yissachar Dov Rokeach (1854–1927).

One day he accompanied the Rebbe to the resort town of Marienbad, Czechoslovakia, a city known for its spas. There, the third Belzer Rebbe went to see a certain physician named Dr. Loewy. In his medical approach, Dr. Loewy was totally dedicated to improving the Belzer Rebbe's health. At their first meeting the Belzer was struck by the doctor's basic ignorance of Judaism and the deep sadness in his eyes. When he asked the doctor why he was sad, he paused for a few moments before he said, "I have no children."

As the doctor was leaving the room, he suddenly asked the Rebbe to pray for him and his wife to have children.

After he left the room, the Belzer Rebbe started to traipse back and forth, sighing heavily. Reb David knew well not to interrupt his Rebbe's thoughts at those times. So he waited.

After a time, he turned to face Reb David and said, "*Nebich, nebich,*

---

15. During World War I, the *chassidim* fled Belz. When they finally returned to their beloved city, the first question of Rabbi Yissachar Dov (the third Belzer Rebbe, 1854–1926) was, if the curtain of the *aron hakodesh*, which was made from his grandmother's clothing (because she was a very saintly woman), was still intact? In fact, today's Belzer Rebbe (Rabbi Yissachar Dov, born in 1948, who lives in Jerusalem), once mentioned, "Here we see that a Jewish woman can reach such a high level in serving *Hashem* that even her clothing becomes holy."

nebich, how unfortunate, how unfortunate! David, do you know that the Messiah won't be able to leave this person behind? This person has faith. He believes."

Then the Belzer Rebbe told David the following story:

"My *bubbe* Malkah once told my *zeide*, 'I think that you are going to be the Messiah.' The Rebbe was taken aback by the statement. It was clearly not something he expected to hear, even from his *rebbetzin*. He went into his study, and paced back and forth and gave it a lot of thought.

"When he came out, my *zeide*, now fully composed again, said, 'No, Rebbetzin, I won't be the Messiah, but I will walk alongside the very important people who will be at his side.' He also said, 'Belz will be a foundation stone for Torah and *Yiras Shamayim* [fear of heaven] until the coming of the Messiah!'"

The third Belzer Rebbe continued, "So do you think my grandfather wasn't right, that he didn't want to be the Messiah? I also wouldn't want to be the Messiah. He won't be able to do things beyond the letter of the law. He has to abide by the rules. The doctor believes in God, but he nonetheless is not observant.

"In the Code of Jewish Law it says, that a person who is a sinner because he was never brought up by his parents to be righteous is considered an *oines* (an 'accidental sinner'). He was forced into it from birth. And the Messiah will not be able to leave him and such people behind, because they believe in God. But the way they are in their present situation, the Messiah won't be able to take them along with him.

"So David, what is the solution to this? The Messiah is going to instill a love and fear of God into their hearts, to enable them to do *teshuvah* [repentance], and then he'll be able to take them along with him. If you believe in God and don't sin on purpose, then the Messiah has to take you along to Israel.

"As far as I am concerned," the third Belzer Rebbe concluded, "Dr. Loewy isn't a sinner as he was brought up that way."

Before he and his *chassid* left Mariendbad, the third Belzer Rebbe blessed the doctor.

So too did Reb Shalom abide by the rules. After his *rebbetzin's* demise, he was overheard expressing the following plaint: "Thou knowest, O Lord, that there is nothing in my power I would not have done, to bring my spouse back to life, if it were possible. Yet Thou, the All-Powerful, doth not restore Thy spouse Israel, though Thou are able to do so."[16]

He later added: "The Lord answered me, saying: 'Were Israel as loyal to Me as your wife was to you, I would long ago have redeemed her.'"[17]

Later in his life, Reb Shalom revealed that his soul once was transported to *Gan Eden*. There, he was shown the destroyed walls of *Yerushalayim* (Jerusalem) in heaven. Suddenly, he saw a man walking from one wall to another wall. "Who is that man walking on the walls?" Reb Shalom's soul asked the guardians of the faith in Heaven.

He was told: "This is the Baal Shem Tov, who has sworn he will not step off the walls of *Yerushalayim* until all its walls will be built again on earth."

For obvious reasons, Reb Shalom eagerly awaited the Baal Shem Tov's walk on earth again.

He also awaited, even more so, with every spiritual fiber in his body, the coming of the Messiah. That is why he exerted every effort to build the Great Synagogue in Belz and inspired his children and their children to finish it.

"When the Messiah comes," he often told his *chassidim*, "my shul will be transplanted to Jerusalem. And my shul will be among the most beautiful shuls in Jerusalem. Before the *Kohen Gadol* [High Priest] reaches and enters the *Beis Hamikdosh*, he will stop at twelve shuls to meditate and prepare for *davening*, and my shul will be one of the shuls in which the Messiah and *Kohen Gadol* will enter in Jerusalem."

After the Nazis destroyed the Belzer shul, people asked the fourth Belzer Rebbe Aaron Rokeach (1880–1957), "What about your grandfather's promise? The shul is no longer standing." Said the Rebbe: "Whatever my grandfather said, that is the way it will be. I'm confident that my grandfather's words will be fulfilled."

Toward the end of his life, Reb Shalom became blind. He died on 27 Elul 1855. No *ohel* was built over his grave, in conformity with the traditions of Belz. He was survived by six sons (Elazer, Shmuel, Shmelke, Moshe, Yehuda Zundel, and Yehoshua) and two daughters (Frieda and Eidel). His fifth son, Rabbi Yehoshua, succeeded him.[18]

---

16. Newman, *Hasidic Anthology*, pp. 198–199.
17. Ibid.; also Micholzohn, p. 34.
18. Ibid., pp. 129-130.

In 1984, the cornerstone was laid for the magnificent structure called the Great Synagogue/*Beis Hamidrosh* at Kiryat Belz, Jerusalem. In every way Reb Shalom's Belz synagogue has been transported, awaiting only the Messiah to visit on his way to the Third Temple.

There's a beautiful Belzer *torah* (a talk by a rebbe) based on *Shir HaShirim Rabbah*. The *Midrash* states that when the Messiah comes, and the exile ends, all the Jews will gather at the border of Israel. There, they will stand at the foot of a mountain called *Emunah*—Faith. There, they will sing a song to Hashem. There, they will "sing from the head of faith." Then, they will cross the border into Israel.

And in the Belzer *torah* it's asked, What is the meaning of this *midrash*, this song that will be sung at the border of Israel?

"When Jews are in *golus* (exile), we don't have a clear picture that God is with us all the time. And when He seems hidden from us, a lot of times we have to accept things with faith. When the Messiah comes, the world will be revealed to everyone. We will see it. There will no longer be a need for this type of faith any longer.

"But this type of service—when people serve Hashem through faith—is very important. It's very precious to Him.

"After the Messiah comes, even if you want to sing to Hashem the Song of the *Golus*, you won't be able to do it any more.

"This is why the Jews, after the *golus*, will stop at the mountain on their way to Israel. They're entitled to one last song of the *golus*, one last piece of *Emunah*, one last time to sing this song to Hashem."

And they're entitled to walk with the Messiah as he walks through the Great Synagogue in Kiryat Belz on the way to the Third Temple.

And it all started with a marriage between a holy man called Reb Shalom[19] and a saintly woman called Malkah, who might easily have been Rebbe and Rebbetzin Messiah.

---

19. Reb Shalom left no doubt where he stood regarding the purpose of creation. In *Midbar Kodesh*, p. 247, he wrote: "The main purpose of creating Adam was to bring forth King David and his descendants, the main one being the Messiah. (He should come speedily in our days.) This is hinted at in the acrostic for the Hebrew word for Adam. *Alef* for Adam. *Dalet* for David and *Mem* for Messiah. The main purpose of creation was for the generation of Messiah."

18

THE SPARKS THAT WERE REDEEMED

T wo hundred years ago, there lived in Germany a Jew who was not only learned and God-fearing but wealthy as well. He was blessed with eighteen intelligent and God-fearing children.

One day, the man gathered together his eldest sons and told them: "The time has come for you to follow the teaching of our rabbis: 'Travel even a great distance in order to reach a place of Torah learning.' Today, I give you my permission to go and study in a distant yeshivah. Should you find a suitable match, you also have my permission to marry and establish a proper Jewish home. I make only one request of you, and that is that after three years have passed you return home so that we may all enjoy each other's company and share our Torah learning." Giving each son some money, he blessed them and sent them on their way.

One son, Yechiel Michel, went to Poland to study the new path of divine service taught by the Baal Shem Tov (also called the Besht, 1698–1760, founder of *Chassidus*). He became one of the disciples of the Besht, excelling both in learning and character. So much did he please his teacher that he was given the Baal Shem Tov's only daughter, Adel, in marriage.

L'Chaim weekly publication (Brooklyn, NY: L.Y.O., Aug. 30, 1991), no. 178, p. 4.

When the three years had expired, Yechiel Michel wished to fulfill his promise to return to his father. He asked and received his teacher's blessing to go, but when he requested a blessing to return in time to celebrate Rosh Hashanah in Medzibozh, he received no answer.

When he returned home, Yechiel Michel found his other brothers already there. Their father had invited many scholars of the town to join them at a great feast during which he requested each of his sons to expound upon some of the Torah thoughts he had learned. Each son spoke, and their learned discourses afforded great pleasure to their father as well as to the assembled guests. Only Yechiel Michel seemed unimpressed. When it was his turn to speak, he replied only that he had nothing to say, other than that the meal was delicious.

With tears in his eyes, his embarrassed father called Yechiel Michel to account for his bizarre behavior. Not only had he appeared to be an ignoramus, but a glutton as well! Yechiel Michel apologized, saying that it had not been his intention to offend, and to make amends, he offered to give a Torah discourse at the soonest possible opportunity.

The father agreed and arranged another festive meal, inviting the same guests. Again, the brothers spoke, and again, Yechiel Michel paid inordinate attention to the meal; but this time, after each of the brothers spoke, Yechiel Michel casually tossed out a few questions, the profundity of which utterly destroyed their elaborately constructed discourses. The whole assemblage was dumbstruck.

When it was Yechiel Michel's turn to speak, he told the audience about the new ideas and ways of his master and father-in-law, the Baal Shem Tov, explaining that a Jew must serve God not only with Torah and mitzvos, but in every minute detail of his physical daily life. He continued, explaining that each particular type of food derives its taste from the spark of Godliness it contains, and that from this spark we derive our sustenance and strength to fulfill God's will. His words made a deep impression on his listeners.

Though they asked him to stay and teach them more, Yechiel Michel was still intent upon returning to the Baal Shem Tov before Rosh Hashanah. Therefore, Yechiel Michel set out on his journey, but as he passed through a forest, he was set upon by a group of thieves. After taking all of his possessions, save his *tallis*, *tefillin*, and *shofar*, they sold him as a slave. He was put aboard a ship that sailed for many weeks, until it was hit by a fierce storm and demolished. Grabbing onto a loose board, Yechiel Michel managed to float to the safety of a small island.

Time passed, and Rosh Hashanah approached. When the holiday

arrived, Yechiel Michel prayed with great intensity and fervor, and when he concluded, he blew his *shofar* thirty times, concentrating on the meditations he had learned from the Besht.

Unbeknownst to him, he was being observed by a group of inhabitants of the island who gazed at this strange figure in wonder. Watching him swaying and gesticulating wildly, crying and blowing on a horn, they concluded that he must be a madman. The following day, the king of the island went himself to investigate, and when he felt it was safe he sent his messengers to fetch the stranger.

The king questioned him about his origins and the meaning of his strange behavior, and Yechiel Michel explained his predicament and requested help in returning to his wife and father-in-law. The king was impressed by Yechiel Michel's manner and bearing, and told him that a ship visited the island once a year to trade and do business, and would be arriving within a few weeks. The two conversed further, and the king grew to like Yechiel Michel and invited him to remain on the island. When Yechiel Michel politely declined, the king then asked Yechiel Michel to send him a group of three hundred Jews to establish a colony on the island. Again, Yechiel Michel had to refuse, replying that he lacked the power to send anyone to the island, and that, in any case, if it was the will of God that Jews live on the island, they would arrive there anyway, even as captives in chains.

When at long last, Yechiel Michel returned to his home, his father-in-law greeted him warmly, with the comment: "You answered the king wisely. Know that you were brought to that island by Divine Providence. Since the creation of the world no Jew had ever set foot on that part of the globe, and the holy sparks of Godliness which had fallen there were still in exile. When you prayed and blew the *shofar* in that spot, you redeemed those sparks, enabling them to return to their source and be reunited with God. If you had failed, it would have been necessary for Jews to be exiled there. We Jews have been dispersed all over the world, solely to spread Godliness and redeem the sparks of holiness that wait for our prayers. And when every Jew fulfills his own personal Godly mission, *Moshiach* [Messiah] will come, and all the Jews will be redeemed from exile."

19

5999

It's said that when music composer Arnold Schoenberg (1874–1951) was told his violin concerto needed a soloist with six fingers on each hand, he said, "Very well, I can wait."[1]

Such an improbable waiting period took on the very possible in chassidic circles, where the waiting for the Messiah became a matter of joyous primary concern. Most Jews were willing to wait; chassidic Jews, however, waited—or were willing to wait with a smile on their faces—forever.

Such a typical chassidic rebbe was Reb Moshe of Rozvidoz (the Rozvidozer Rebbe, died 1894), who related that in his youth he visited the Sanzer Rebbe (Rabbi Chaim Halberstam, the *Divrei Chaim*, 1793–1876) on a Sabbath. The Sanzer took the cup of wine and held it up in his hand, as if to drink it, but then began to sing in an agreeable tone the words: "O Creator, Thou Art My Crown." For three hours, he held his cup of wine, not once touching it to his lips, as he continued to sing until the candles were nearly burned down.[2] And if, by some miracle, the candles never burned down, there was no doubt that the Sanzer and his

1. J. M. and M. J. Cohen, *Dictionary of Modern Quotations* (Harmondsworth, Middlesex, England: Penguin Books, 1985), and quoted by Nat Shapiro, *An Encyclopedia of Quotations about Music.*

2. I. Berger, *Esser Tzachtzochoth* (Pitrkov, 1910), p. 123, and quoted by Louis I. Newman, *The Hasidic Anthology* (Northvale, NJ: Jason Aronson, 1987), p. 407.

visitor would have waited till the end of time for God's crowning glory, the Messiah.

Near the end of his life, Reb Moshe was once discussing with a group of his own *chassidim* the different possible dates up to the year 6000 (the time allotted to the existence of this world), when the Messiah might come.

"Believe me," he said, "that even if the year 5999 comes around and we reach sunset of the last day of that year, right before the last minute, and Messiah has not yet come, I will not despair, God forbid. I will confidently await his coming."[3]

Which is, of course, the Jewish way of saying, "Very well, I can wait"—and meaning it.

---

3. *L'Chaim* publication, no. 244 (Brooklyn, NY: L.Y.O., Dec. 4, 1992), p. 3.

20

NOAH WITHOUT AN ARK

This Noah had an island. As such it was "a beautifully wooded island, quiet, isolated, and well stocked with wild game . . . situated on the Niagara River, equally distant from Lake Erie and the Niagara Falls."[1] Grand Island, as it was called, not only comprised 17,381 acres, it also was an inaccessible wasteland in 1825.

To this island, which he promptly renamed "Ararat—a City of Refuge for the Jews," after the mountain Noah's Ark in biblical times landed on, Mordecai Manuel Noah, a jack-of-all-trades,[2] invited all the Jews of the world to come and live until the Messiah came and the Land of Israel would be forever restored to them.

Not one Jew settled there, nor did Noah himself ever set foot on the island, but the story of this man and his island, which he foresaw as an agricultural training school for future Jewish settlers in Palestine, is worth repeating, if only because Noah set a historic first. Long before the early Zionist voices of two Orthodox rabbis, Yehudah Alkalai (1798–1878)

---

1. Anita Libman Lebeson, *Jewish Pioneers in America: 1492–1848* (New York: Brentano's, 1931), p. 278.

2. Gilder, carver, U.S. Treasury clerk, army major, politician, duelist, editor, surveyor, journalist, playwright, New York City sherriff, nationalist, grand sachem of Tammany Hall, judge, philanthropist, and liberator.

and Zevi Hirsch Kalischer (1795–1874), and two secular Jews, Moses
Hess (1812–1875) and Theodor Herzl (1860–1904) (who proposed his
Judenstaat in Palestine), Mordecai Manuel Noah (1785–1851) was considered the "first American Zionist"[3] to suit his actions to his words. As
his biographer said of him, Noah "emerges as an eccentric, surely, but
none the less as an important pioneer in the story of Zionistic endeavor.
If his descendants in the struggle for a Jewish homeland cannot honor his
head, they do all honor to his heart."[4]

Noah's "heart" was born in Philadelphia, 1785. He was the son of a
Sephardic mother, Zipporah Phillips, daughter of a Philadelphia patriot,
and a Revolutionary War soldier, a German-born Ashkenazic who won
the friendship of his commander, George Washington, and had him in
attendance at his wedding to Zipporah.

His growing up in Philadelphia, near a tavern that flaunted a painting
of the Federal Convention, played a vital role in how he would come to
see the rest of the world. As a boy, he used to stand for hours before the
painting, marvelling "at the assembled patriots, particularly the venerable
head and spectacles of Dr. Franklin, always in conspicuous relief," and
conning the inscription:

> Thirty-eight great men have signed a powerful deed
> That better times, to us, shall very soon succeed.[5]

In his lifetime, Noah seemed bent on being the thirty-ninth great man,
but with a distinctively Jewish flavor. There was hardly anything he did in his
life that didn't smack of his love for things Jewish.

There are no contemporary Jewish writers of his day who, in print,
described Noah, but we can get a fairly rounded idea of the body that
housed his *neshomah*: "Physically he was a man of large muscular frame,
rotund person, a benignant face, and most portly bearing. Although a
native of the United States, the lineaments of his race were impressed
upon his features with unmistakable character. . . . He was a Jew,
thorough and accomplished. His manners were genial, his heart kind, and

---

3. Selig Adler and Thomas Connolly, *From Ararat to Suburbia* (Philadelphia:
J.P.S.A., 1960), p. 5.

4. Written in 1937 by Noah's biographer, Isaac Goldberg; quoted by Lee M.
Friedman, *Jewish Pioneers and Patriots* (Philadelphia: J.P.S.A., 1942), p. 115.

5. Lebeson, *Jewish Pioneers in America*, p. 268.

his general sympathies embraced all Israel, even to the end of the earth."[6]
He was also "the first American Jew to emerge as a larger-than-life figure.
A hundred years later he would have certainly become a movie mogul."[7]

If we accept that action is what matters, is the criterion, the proof, of
the divine spirit in men, then the visionary Noah comes as close as any
other Jew who wanted to help his fellow Jews. He wrote a number of
very popular plays in his day, all of the thrilling, melodramatic kind, for
example, *She Would Be a Soldier*, *The Grecian Captive*, and *The Castle of
Olival*, but he saved his favorite lines, "That better times, to us, shall very
soon succeed" and "We will return to Zion as we went forth, bringing
the faith we carried away with us,"[8] for his greatest drama: the founding
of Ararat as a Jewish homeland, or way station.

What drove him to Ararat? His whole life, in a sense, was a preparation
for this enactment. By his actions, he became a gofer for local Democratic
politicians, a major in the Pennsylvania militia, the editor of the *New York
Enquirer*, the *Evening Star*, and the *Union*, and helped James Gordon
Bennett found the *New York World*.

By his actions, he was the first Jew in America to hold a high
diplomatic post in the foreign service of his country. President James
Madison appointed him American consul to Tunis, in 1813, a rather
difficult position because the Barbary states of North Africa were then a
rats' nest of pirates disturbing shipping on the Mediterranean Sea. Noah
represented the United States with diginity and force. In his letter to the
U.S. secretary of state Robert Smith, the major piously suggested that his
appointment would encourage other "members of the Hebrew Nation"
to immigrate to the United States with their funds. Almost as an
afterthought, Noah intimated that his coreligionists would know how to
be "grateful for any testimony of the good opinion of their government."
But he was too generous with governmental funds in redeeming captured
Americans and was accused unofficially of misappropriating funds. In
removing Noah, however, President James Monroe stated officially that

6. Lewis F. Allen, "Founding of the City of Ararat on Grand Island—by
Mordecai M. Noah," in *Publications of the Buffalo Historical Society*, I (Buffalo:
Buffalo Historical Society, 1879), pp. 305–328; also Adler and Connolly, *From
Ararat to Suburbia*, p. 6.

7. Paul Johnson, *A History of the Jews* (New York: Harper Perennial, 1988), p.
367.

8. Noah in 1824. Quoted by Tina Levitan, *Jews in American Life* (New York:
Hebrew Publishing, 1969), p. 50.

"the Religion which you profess [is] an obstacle to the exercise of your consular functions."[9] Noah countered by saying the government well knew about his Jewishness when they assigned him the post.

As it is said, real dreamers never forget their bad dreams—especially dreams that have burnt them in real life. Noah remembered the Jew-baiters in his life, and after that, in the Orient, Germany, and Eastern Europe, wherever Noah came across Jews in his travels, he saw the sorrowful plight of Jews. "Driven into economic ratholes by restrictive measures, this oppressed and persecuted people lived on in memory of its past greatness, and in the hope of some future Messianic miracle which would deliver them from the morass into which they had sunk."[10] Noah determined to change all that.

Once ensconced in New York City, "prematurely stout and flaunting red mutton-chop whiskers, the major became a familiar figure as an unofficial spokesman for Congregation Shearith Israel, a participant in Jewish philanthropic campaigns, defender of Jewish honor against real or fancied slurs. . . . Nobody was allowed to forget that Noah was a Jewish 'leader.'"[11]

Though Noah firmly believed in the coming of the Messiah, "he nevertheless held to the view that the restoration of the Jews must come about through the Jews themselves."[12] He was a Jew, he told the public, and he must do his part. As it is written, "As the generation, so the leader."[13] So Noah without an ark hit upon the plan of establishing, under the flag of the United States, a colony in which the oppressed Jews might found a state of their own. He made it clear that this was in no way to affect hopes for the restoration of an independent state in Palestine whenever in God's good time this became possible.

So he did his part. In 1820 he petitioned the New York State legislature to sell him Grand Island, a 17,000-acre tract above the falls in the Niagara River, near the Canadian border. And when that bill failed, he later persuaded his friend Samuel Leggett of New York City to buy 2,555 acres on that island. What could he hope to do with about

---

9. Johnson, ibid.

10. Lebeson, *Jewish Pioneers in America*, p. 276.

11. Howard M. Sachar, *A History of the Jews in America* (New York: Vintage Books, 1993), p. 47.

12. *The Jewish Encyclopedia*, ed. Isodore Singer, 12 vols. (New York: Funk & Wagnalls, 1907), 6:324.

13. Jerusalem Talmud, *Sanhedrin* 2:6.

one-seventh of an island? According to historians Selig Adler and Thomas Connolly, Noah's "plan was not quite as chimerical as it has sometimes been portrayed. He had chosen a spot which might, with suitable management, have developed into a rival of Buffalo and Black Rock. Capital was needed here at the terminus to exploit the opportunities offered by the newly opened Erie Canal. The community that Noah envisioned might very well have grown into a great metropolis, given the impetus of Jewish capital and immigrant brawn."[14]

Proclaiming that Ararat would be the Jews' "temporary" homeland, until the sounding of the Great Shofar of Redemption, he gave himself the title of "Governor and Judge of Israel," on the model of Gideon and Jephthah of ancient days. Sending out proclamations and manifestos to Jewish communities of Europe, he invited them to settle in this new city, "which was to be under the protection of the Constitution and laws of the United States."[15]

He even adopted for this purpose the old myth that the Indians were the Lost Ten Tribes of Israel and invited them also. To all doubters, he'd say: " 'If the Indians of America are not descendants of the missing tribes, again I ask, from whom *are* they descended?' Noah shouted down the opposition."[16]

So the trip to Ararat began.

Oh yes, there was a Jewish response to Noah and his dream island. At last count there were more than three-quarters of a million words in the English language, but surely the number and kinds of Jewish laughs—which cannot be put into so many words—that Jews around the world expressed at Noah's plan must come close to that figure. The Jews of Germany poked fun at Noah's plan, and those of Russia, smirking, paid no attention to it. American Jews ridiculed his "folly and sacrilegious presumption." Whig politicians gleefully mocked the project as a "mad, mobbing business," a scheme "for swindling the wealthy Jews of Europe."[17]

Nothing daunted Major Noah. "A lively imagination, a Hebraic susceptibility and sympathy for suffering, 'a genial, frank, childlike ingenuousness,' a keen sense of the dramatic, an ardent desire to be the

---

14. Adler, *From Ararat to Suburbia*, p. 6.

15. Levitan, *Jews in American Life*, p. 51.

16. Lebeson, *Jewish Pioneers in America*, p. 276.

17. Sachar, *A History of the Jews in America*, p. 48.

deliverer of his people, an unrestrained, hyperbolic type of mind—of this stuff was the American Messiah made."[18] After all, once said Noah, "My faith does not rest wholly in miracles. Providence disposes of events, human agency must carry them out."

And even on that great day, September 15, 1825, when the parade of dignitaries, with "a salute fired from the courthouse," and music struck up by a band, marched off to the bank of the Niagara River, and there weren't enough rowboats to take them to Ararat, Major Noah, the Johnny-on-the-spot, quickly turned the parade around, and marched through Buffalo to the tallest structure in town, to the little Episcopal Church of St. Paul, there to be received by his friend, the Reverend Addison Searle.

(Of course, it was another matter for the 2,500 inhabitants of the little town of Buffalo, many of whom had repaired with picnic baskets to join the festivities along the bank of the Niagara River. But everybody in those days loved a parade; so they all rose to their feet, baskets and children in hand, and walked along, cheering on Noah, resplendent in a Richard III costume he had borrowed from the local Park Theater.)

For those readers who love a sense of order in their lives, the Grand Parade through Buffalo consisted of:

Grand Marshall, Colonel Potter on horseback

Music

Military

Citizens

Civil Officers

United States Officers

State Officers in Uniform

President and Trustees of the Corporation

Tyler

Stewards

Entered Apprentices

Fellow Crafts

Master Masons

Senior and Junior Deacons

Secretary and Treasurer

Senior and Junior Wardens

---

18. Lebeson, *Jewish Pioneers in America*, p. 274.

Masters of Lodges
Past Masters
Reverend Clergy
Stewards, with corn, wine and oil
Principal Architect
with square, level
Globe   and plumb   Globe
Bible
Square and Compass borne by a Master Mason
The Judge of Israel [Noah himself]
In black, wearing the judicial robes of crimson silk,
trimmed with ermine and a richly embossed golden
medal suspended from the neck.
A Master Mason
Royal Arch Masons
Knight Templars[19]

With them marched the famous Seneca Indian chief Red Jacket and
some of his gaily feathered Indians.

But no Jews besides Noah.

At the church, the cornerstone, with its carefully worded inscription,
was displayed on the church communion table. Its inscription read:

Shema Yisrael, Adonoi Eloheinu, Adonoi Echod
[Hear O Israel, the Lord is our God—the Lord is one]
ARARAT
A City of Refuge for the Jews
founded by Mordecai Manuel Noah, in the month of Tizri 5586,
corresponding with September 1825,
and in the 50th year of American Independence.

There were also readings from the Prophets and Psalms, one in Hebrew,
and the Benediction. Noah, it is said, spoke with great eloquence—at some
length:

"I, Mordecai Manuel Noah, Citizen of the United States of America,
late Consul of the said States for the City and Kingdom of Tunis, High
Sherriff of New York, Counsellor at Law, and by the grace of God,

---

19. Friedman, *Jewish Pioneers and Patriots*, p. 111.

Governor and Judge of Israel, do hereby proclaim the establishment of the Jewish State of Ararat."

Noah also "proclaimed the obligation of all Diaspora Jews to aid any of their brethren who wished to settle in Ararat and to pay a head tax of three *shekels* to defray the expenses of the new Jewish government."[20]

The militia furnished a welcome ending to the celebration with a twenty-four gun salute. The band stopped playing, the dignitaries went back to their homes or reservation tents, the church reverend and the Judge of Israel embraced for the last time, and that was the end of Ararat. But not quite. In 1833, Lewis F. Allen (mentioned in note 6) bought the entire island at a cheap price for its timber, and, in 1852, Grand Island was incorporated as a town. Today, it houses about eighteen thousand persons. The Ararat cornerstone resides in its town hall as a tourist attraction.[21]

As for our Noah, now without even an island, don't cry for him; he never wept over any of his follies. He was his generation's leader and spokesman. Nothing tarnished his reputation as a Jew with *ahavas Yisrael*. In 1840, he organized the Jewish protest against the Damascus atrocities. And in 1845, he wrote a pamphlet in which he advocated Jewish restoration of Zion by Jewish self-effort, and suggested that the land be acquired through purchase.[22] Among other things, he had an illustrious career in journalism and the theater, and wound up a real judge. Yet all his life, he remained foremost a Jew, sincere and reverent, devoted to his people.

When he died in 1851, he already was considered a prophet of sorts, and thousands lined the route of his funeral procession.

As it is written, "One leader, not two, for a generation."[23] So lived and died that kind of Jew—Mordecai Manuel Noah!

---

20. Sachar, *A History of the Jews in America*, p. 47.

21. Ibid., p. 48.

22. "His 1845 address on the restoration of the Jews to their homeland includes a map of Palestine and it became a standard document of reference for American Jews prior to the Civil War." Geoffrey Wigoder, *Dictionary of Jewish Biography* (New York: Simon & Schuster, 1991), p. 375.

23. Talmud, *Sanhedrin* 8a.

21

DAWN OF THE COMING WORLD

Theodor Herzl
1860–1904

PRESENTING A POTENTIAL MESSIAH
IN HIS TIME . . . THEODOR HERZL

In *The Messiah Texts*, Raphael Patai writes: "The Jewish background of Theodor Herzl, the founder of modern political Zionism, was wanting, but it so happens that the concept of the Messiah was familiar to him, as we know from a childhood dream he later remembered and recounted. But even though messianic ideas may have been present in his subconscious, Herzl reached his solution of the Jewish problem, the establishment of a *Judenstaat*, through a political and sociological approach. His secularist attitude, to be sure, did not keep the enthusiastic East European Jewish masses from hailing him as 'King Messiah.'"

If we believe that dreams never die once they bloom in the soul, then such a dream happened to a six-year-old boy named Theodor Herzl. For most of the forty-four years of his short life, he carried it deep inside him without once telling anyone except his biographer about it late in life. Why would—and should—such a prophetic, deeply holy dream happen to a person like Theodor Herzl, who had moved so far from God that it's doubtful he and his Jewish soul were on so-called speaking terms.

140

In his own words, this is what the young Herzl dreamt:

> King Messiah came and he was old and glorious. He lifted me in
> his arms, and he soared with me on the wings of the wind. On one
> of the clouds, full of splendor, I met the figure of Moses (his
> appearance was like of Moses hewn in marble by Michelangelo;
> from my early childhood I liked to look at the photographs of that
> statue), and the Messiah called to Moses: "For this child I have
> prayed." Then he turned to me: "Go and announce to the Jews that
> I will soon come and perform great miracles for my people and for
> the whole world." I woke up and it was only a dream. I kept this
> dream a secret and didn't dare to tell it to anybody.[1]

A dream of glory aside, clearly there was nothing else in his makeup to
suggest any divinity. He was more involved with the sorrows of Werther[2]
than the tears of oppressed Jews. He probably would have grudgingly
admitted there was a difference between "Exodus" and "Egress." Indeed,
he once wrote, six years before his death, "I cannot deny that I went to
school. At first I was sent to a Jewish elementary school, where . . . my
earliest memory of this school was the caning I received for not remembering the particulars of the Exodus of the Jews from Egypt. Nowadays
many a schoolmaster would like to cane me for remembering the Exodus
rather too well."[3]

Of course he knew what the Exodus was, and then some. As one
biographer aptly points out, "Four years of even routine exposure to
Jewish subjects must have left their mark; the young Herzl could not
possibly have been as unfamiliar with the exploits of his spiritual ancestors
as he later claimed."[4]

So let's not make too much of his messianic dream or his later literary
vagaries. He was born in Budapest to a well-to-do merchant who was a
typical, assimilated, middle-class Jew. In his early years, Herzl went to a
Jewish school, where the emphasis was on the sciences, for which he had

---

1. Reuben Brainin, *Hayye Herzl* (New York, 1919), pp. 17–18.
2. "There also exists a fragment of what was evidently conceived as an
epistolary novel in the spirit of Goethe's *The Sorrows of Young Werther*, that
nineteenth-century bible of teenage melancholia." Ernst Pawel, *The Labyrinth of
Exile: A Life of Theodor Herzl* (New York: Farrar, Straus & Giroux, 1989), p. 31.
3. Ibid., p. 12.
4. Ibid., p. 13.

little taste. He soon transferred to the Lutheran High School, one of Hungary's most eminent schools, where there were many other Jewish boys. His bar mitzvah was celebrated at the famous Dohany Street Synagogue, next door to his birthplace.

He had a sister Pauline, who died at the age of eighteen. Her death so disturbed his mother Jeanette that the Herzl family packed and moved to Vienna. Perhaps, as Jewish wisdom tells us, this was a very good thing. By moving they changed their *mazal*. In Vienna, Herzl enrolled at the law faculty of the university and joined the Albia student fraternity, which he left when it passed a resolution not to admit any more Jews.

Although aware of the existence of anti-Semitism, until 1894 his reaction was rather superficial. Later, at the age of thirty-five, he even suggested that the solution to the Jewish question was for all Jews to convert to Christianity. How? Simple in Herzl's mind: now, this very day, en masse, all the Jews should collectively march into the Cathedral of St. Stephen and, in a mass ceremony, convert. No Jews, no Jewish problem.

Before he could work such a plan through in his head, however, another plan took hold of him, and by the time he died, a mere nine years later, he had redefined Jewish identity in terms of a modern secular faith and created a national movement. Within a half century, in 1948, this movement led to the foundation of the Jewish state. Of course, unlike Moses, whom God denied access to the Promised Land, Herzl visited it.

But it took the Dreyfus affair, whose trial in Paris Herzl covered for his newspaper, to get him on the road to Zionism. Suddenly he opened his Jewish eyes for the first time. He wrote a proposal for a political solution for the Jews. With this he turned to the Jewish philanthropist Baron de Hirsh, but the two men did not find a common language.

But by then, we can assume, his *pintele Yid* was well lit, and his Jewish soul would not let his body and mind forget. Over were the years of idolizing Ferdinand-Marie de Lesseps (1805–1894) for promoting the Suez Canal or Count Otto von Bismark (1815–1898), who founded the German Reich. As much as he loved and worshipped his mother Jeanette, and notwithstanding her "passionate Germanophilia coupled with disdain for Jewishness in general and her own [Jewishness] in particular,"[5] he put himself on a path, first and foremost as a writer, that would help lead a lot of other Jews to their own homeland.

---

5. Ibid., p. 10.

Deeply religious European Jews, in his time, didn't take Theodor Herzl too seriously. They remembered the response of Rabban Johanan ben Zakkai (first century c.e.) to the many false Messiahs who claimed to be the true Redeemer in ancient times:

> If you should happen to be holding a sapling in your hand when they tell you the Messiah has arrived, first plant the sapling and then go out to greet the Messiah (*Fathers According to Rabbi Nathan*, version B, chap. 31).

Nothing much had changed in the nearly 2,000 ensuing years, so why should most Jews get excited? False Messiahs came and went. For all it was worth, let Herzl's mother Jeanette claim her son's family tree extended "all the way back to King David."[6] Let others feel that "Herzlian political Zionism was a secularized messianism, divested of its miraculous, superhuman elements, and centering instead on diplomatic negotiation with the modern-day heirs of Armilus—the Tsarist government of Russia, the Sublime Porte of Turkey, the Pope of Rome, the Kaiser of Germany."[7] Let the chief rabbi of Sofia firmly believe that Herzl was the long-awaited Messiah.

A truism: One swallow does not a summer make. One criterion of Maimonides[8]—namely, that the Land of Israel will again be owned by Jews as their national home—does not a Messiah make. And in Herzl's

---

6. Ibid., p. 9.

7. Raphael Patai, *The Messiah Texts* (Detroit: Wayne State University Press, 1979), p. xlviii.

8. Rabbi Moses ben Maimon, also known in Hebrew as the Rambam, an acronym of his name, 1135–1204. In *In the Days of Moshiach* (Kfar Chabad, Israel: Chabad Youth Org., 1993), pp. 119–120, Menachem M. Brod wrote:

> "Contrary to popular expectations of supernatural revelation, Rambam's halachic ruling is that the coming of *Moshiach* [the Messiah] is a natural process by which the Davidic Kingdom will be restored. This process consists of two stages, 'presumably *Moshiach*' and 'definitely *Moshiach*': *If a Davidic king arises who studies Torah and observes the mitzvos prescribed by the written and oral law as his ancestor did, and will compel all of Israel to walk in [the way of the Torah] and reinforce the breaches in its observance, and [he will] fight the wars of Hashem, he is presumably Moshiach. If he does [all the above], conquers all the surrounding nations, rebuilds the Beis HaMikdosh in its place, and*

days, as well as after his time, the Zionist movement did have messianic overtones whose strength depended on the depths of the roots in Jewish tradition. Yet in the West, "where these roots were shallow or withered, Zionism acquired the coloration of a social movement or a philanthropic undertaking in Eastern Europe, where Jewish life was nourished by a vital and throbbing tradition of Judaism; there, the movement had a pronounced messianic character. When, fifty years after the First Zionist Congress (1897), the State of Israel became a reality, as Herzl had foretold it in a prophetic exclamation,[9] Yemenite and other Oriental Jews greeted the event as the undoubted messianic fulfillment of the ancient biblical promise about the Return and the Ingathering."[10]

Yet it came to pass that Herzl soon learned that the notion of a Jewish state did not appeal to most of the contemporary Jewish lay and spiritual leadership. Yet he went on. He had to. He devoted his great administrative talent to organizing the First Zionist Congress in Basel in August 1897. This was his Jewish purpose—this is what God assigned to his Jewish soul.

In January 1904, shortly before he died, Herzl told the king of Italy that when he was in Palestine, "I had avoided a white donkey or a white horse, so no one would embarrass me by thinking I was the Messiah."[11]

By May of that year, Herzl was totally exhausted. In June he went to take a rest at Edlach, Vienna, where he died on July 3, 1904.

We are told that "for much of life, Herzl fought self-destructive and even suicidal tendencies, a struggle that itself affirms his overwhelming and at times desperate will to live."[12] Yet, in his diaries, he wrote the following items—clearly not vagaries of a man still moving away from God:

"First and foremost I have learned to know Jews—and that was

---

gathers the dispersed remnants of Israel, he is definitely Moshiach (*The Laws of Kings* 11:4).

9. On September 3, 1897, Herzl wrote in his diaries: "Were I to sum up the Basel (Zionist) Congress in a word—which I shall guard against pronouncing publicly—it would be this: At Basel I founded the Jewish State. If I said this out loud today, I would be answered by universal laughter. Perhaps in five years, and certainly in fifty, everyone will know it."

10. Patai, *The Messianic Texts*, pp. xlviii–xlix.

11. Ibid., p. xlviii.

12. Pawel, *The Labyrinth of Exile*, p. 523.

sometimes even a pleasure." And: "On being called to the reading of the law on the Sabbath following the first [Zionist] Congress: The few Hebrew words of the *berachah* [blessing] caused me more anxiety than my opening and closing addresses and the whole direction of the Congress."

If we believe that dreams never die once they bloom in the soul, then such a dream was fulfilled in 1948 when the modern State of Israel came to be—all because a six-year-old boy once dared to dream of the Messiah.

After a state funeral took place in August 1949, the remains of Herzl's body were reinterred on Mount Herzl in Jerusalem.

Nothing and nobody can take away from Herzl that, in the end, he and his Jewish soul were on speaking terms, finally reunited in the bosom of God's heart.

STORIES OF THE COMING WORLD

1

"HERE I STAND!"

They came here, beyond time, one after another, these holy men from earth. If you had any feeling for Judaism, your soul would—or would want to—recognize them at once: the Baal Shem Tov,[1] the Great *Maggid*,[2] the Rizhiner,[3] the Rebbe of Berditchev,[4] the Apter,[5] the Rebbe of Lubavitch,[6] and so many others. All they saw—or could see—was a pile of rocks, hewn and shaped by thousands of years of benign neglect. There was nothing but this pile of rocks, and they knew it to be the Garden of Eden. That's why each was here and would go no further until . . .

He wasn't the first nor certainly the last, but when Rabbi Dov Ber, the *Maggid* of Mezritch, felt his end drawing near, he declared, "I will not enter the Garden of Eden until God sends the Messiah." When the *Maggid* passed away, he was brought to the Heavenly Court and told that

---

1. Rabbi Israel ben Eliezer, 1698–1760. Charismatic founder of *Chassidus*, one of the great movements in Jewish history, which emerged in Eastern Europe during the eighteenth century. Also known as the Besht and Master of the Good Name.

2. Rabbi Dov Ber of Mezritch, 1704–1772.

3. Rabbi Yisroel Friedman of Rizhin, 1797–1850.

4. Rabbi Levi Yitzchak of Berditchev, 1740–1810.

5. Rabbi Avraham Yehoshua Heshel of Apta, the *Oheiv Yisrael*, 1755–1825.

6. Rabbi Menachem Mendel Schneerson, seventh-generation Rebbe of Lubavitch, 1902–1994.

a special place was awaiting him in the Garden of Eden. The *Maggid*, however, stood his ground and demanded that God send the Messiah, or else he would not budge.

After much arguing and cajoling, the *Maggid* was offered a spiritual reward that enticed him to forgo his promise.

And in true biblical fashion, the *Maggid* begat his son, Reb Avraham Hamalach (1740–1776). He was known as "the Angel," for he was as disassociated from this physical world as a human being could be, approaching the spiritual level of an angel. Reb Avraham, knowing that his father had been unsuccessful at forcing God to send the Messiah, determined that he would not be dissuaded when his time came, but would refuse to enter the Garden of Eden until he had brought about the coming of the Messiah.

Avraham's end of days approached and he strengthened himself for the celestial battle. When he passed away and stood before the Heavenly Court, he insisted that he would not enter the Garden of Eden until God would send the Messiah.

All manner of spiritual enticements were offered to Reb Avraham, spiritual pleasure and bliss that had not even been offered to the greatest *tzaddikim*. But Reb Avraham stood his ground.

And God stood His ground.

Until finally, God took Reb Avraham by the hand, as it were, and *shlepped* him into the Garden of Eden.

And, again in true biblical fashion, Reb Avraham begat his son, Reb Sholom Schachna of Prohobitch (1766–1802). Through divine inspiration he knew of his father's and grandfather's decision not to enter the Garden of Eden until God would send the Messiah. He knew, too, that neither of them had been successful and eventually entered the Garden of Eden although the Messiah had not arrived.

As Reb Sholom Schachna advanced in years, he, too, determined that he would not enter the Garden of Eden until he made sure that God would send the Messiah.

Upon his passing, Reb Sholom Schachna was led before the Heavenly Court and was invited to proceed to the Garden of Eden. But Reb Sholom Schachna remembered his promise and refused, and with utmost determination and stubbornness declared that he would not proceed until God sent the Messiah. Reb Sholom Schachna did not budge. Not one iota would he move until God agreed to send the Messiah.

Exactly what transpired is not known. But what is known is that God extended the boundaries of the Garden of Eden to encompass that area in which Reb Sholom Schachna stood.[7]

Before he passed away, Rabbi Levi Yitzchak of Berditchev (1740–1810) swore in the presence of his closest followers that once up there, he would refuse all rest until he would be allowed to put an end to man's distress. But in the end, he was fooled. They said *Kedushah* in the *Gan Eden*, and the Berditchever, unable to resist the sanctity of the moment, immediately jumped into the Gan Eden.[8]

The Rebbe of Apta was one of the men who saw what happened to the Berditchever and spoke out. In the moment of death the Apter cried out: "Why does the Son of Yishai [the Messiah] delay?" He wept and said: "The Rabbi of Berditchev promised before his death he would disturb the peace of all the Saints and not cease until the Messiah would come. But they have so overwhelmed him with delights in mansion after mansion that he has forgotten. But I will not forget."[9] The mission of the Apter, as far as anyone knows, was not successful.

Many years later, another great religious leader spoke out. At a gathering in 1989, the Rebbe of Lubavitch related that when Reb Levi Yitzchak of Berditchev passed away he, too, had promised that he would not enter the Garden of Eden before God sent the Messiah. Seeing that Reb Levi Yitzchak was also persuaded to forgo his promise, the Rebbe of Lubavitch then stated:

"What should be done to prevent this from happening again is to take a vow, with the people's consent, not to enter the Garden of Eden until God sends the Messiah. A vow that is accepted with the consent of the multitude cannot be nullified without the consent of the multitude."

Thereupon, the Lubavitcher Rebbe took upon himself a vow that if it came to this point, he would be unable to enter the Garden of Eden without God abiding by the Rebbe's vow.[10]

The Rebbe of Lubavitch passed away on June 12, 1994, and as of this writing, God willing, the Messiah may be with us on earth at last. But then he may not.

---

7. Raphael N. Kahn, *Shmuot V'sipurim*, 2 vols. (Kfar Chabad, Israel: 1973), p. 64; quoted in *L'Chaim*, no. 322 (Brooklyn, NY: L.Y.O., June 17, 1994), p. 4.

8. Ibid.

9. Martin Buber, *Die Chassidischen Buecher* (Hellerau, 1928), p. 507; Louis I. Newman, *The Hasidic Anthology* (Northvale, NJ: Jason Aronson, 1987), p. 69.

10. *L'Chaim*, no. 322 (Brooklyn, NY: L.Y.O., June 17, 1994), p. 4.

Yet there was one holy man who took his lone stand for the Messiah while he was still alive. He was known as the Baal Shem Tov. In a letter,[11] he revealed how his soul went to heaven to speak to the Messiah. This is what occurred:

For on the day of the New Year of the year 5507 (September 1746) I engaged in an ascent of the soul, as you know I do, and I saw wondrous things in that vision that I had never before seen since the day I had attained to maturity.[12] That which I saw and learned in my ascent it is impossible to describe or to relate even from mouth to mouth. But as I returned to the lower Garden of Eden[13] I saw many souls, both of the living and the dead, those known to me and those unknown. They were more than could be counted and they ran to and fro from world to world through the path provided by that column known to the adepts in the hidden science.[14] They were all in such a state of great rapture that the mouth would be worn out if it attempted to describe it and the physical ear too indelicate to hear it. Many of the wicked repented of their sins and were pardoned, for it was a time of much grace.

In my eyes, too, it was a great marvel that the repentance was accepted of so many whom you know. They also enjoyed great rapture and ascended, as mentioned above. All of them entreated me to my embarrassment, saying: "The Lord has given your honor great understanding to grasp these matters. Ascend together with us, therefore, so as to help us and assist us." Their rapture was so great that I resolved to ascend together with them.

Then I saw in the vision that Samael [Satan] went up to act the part of accuser because of the unprecedented rapture. He achieved what he had set out to do, namely, a decree of apostasy for many

---

11. The letter to his brother-in-law, Rabbi Abraham Gershon of Kutow, who was living in the Holy Land at the time, and the following footnotes, nos. 12–18, were excerpted from *The Jewish Mystics*, eds. Louis, Jacobs (London: Kyle Cathie Ltd., 1990), pp. 148–155.

12. The "day I attained to maturity" (lit., "the day I stood on my own mind") means the day on which he began to pursue his own mystical way.

13. The "lower Garden of Eden," as opposed to "the higher Garden of Eden," is a kabbalistic expression for a spiritual state close to the material.

14. The "column" is the means by which the souls ascend by climbing and the "hidden science" is the *Kabbalah*.

people who would be tortured to death. Then dread seized me and I took my life in my hands. I requested my teacher[15] to come with me since there is great danger in the ascent to the higher worlds and since from the day I attained to maturity I had never undertaken such high ascents.[16]

I went higher step by step until I entered the palace of the Messiah[17] wherein the Messiah studies the Torah together with all the *annaim* and the saints and also with the Seven Shepherds.[18] There I witnessed great rejoicing and could not fathom the reason for it so I thought that, God forbid, the rejoicing was over my own departure from this world.

But I was afterward informed that I was not yet to die since they took great delight on high when, through their Torah, I perform unifications[19] here below. To this day I am unaware of the reason for that rejoicing.

I asked the Messiah: "When will the Master come?" and he replied: "You will know of it in this way; it will be when your teaching becomes famous and revealed to the world, and when that which I have taught you and you have comprehended will spread abroad so that others, too, will be capable of performing unifica-

---

15. The teacher of the Baal Shem Tov referred to is Ahijah of Shiloh (1 Kings 2:29f). The legend that Ahijah was the Besht's teacher is referred to by Jacob Joseph in his *Toledot Ya'akov Yosef* (1881) in a number of places, e.g., in the list of sayings at the end of his book (p. 416).

16. The Besht evidently engaged frequently in such ascents of soul and is aware that Gershon knows of this. The two ascents recorded both took place on New Year's day, that is, on the traditional judgment day of the year when the fate of the people is determined on high. The Talmud (*Berakhot* 18b) refers to a saint ("*Hasid*") who remained in the cemetery on New Year's eve and there learned the decrees in heaven to be issued during the coming year. No doubt this well-known passage was in the mind of the Besht.

17. The "palace of the Messiah" is the place in Paradise where the Messiah resides until he is ready to come down to earth.

18. The "Seven Shepherds" (based on Micah 55:4 and *Sukkah* 52b) are: Adam, Seth, Methuselah, David, Abraham, Jacob, and Moses.

19. The "unifications" (*yihudim*) are the various combinations of divine names, as mentioned previously a number of times in this book. By studying the Torah in complete devotion and by having these names in mind, the Besht brought all things together so that the unity of God became established throughout all creation.

tions and having soul ascents as you do. Then will all the *klippot* be consumed and it will be a time of grace and salvation."

I was astonished to hear this and greatly distressed that it would take such a long time, for when will such a thing be possible? Yet my mind was set at rest in that I learned there three special charms and three holy names and these are easy to grasp and expound so that I thought to myself, it is possible by this means for all my colleagues to attain to the stages and categories to which I have attained, that is to say, they, too, will be able to engage in ascents of the soul and learn to comprehend as I have done. But no permission was given to me to reveal this secret for the rest of my life. I did request that I be allowed to teach it to you, but no permission at all was given to me and I am duty bound on oath to keep the secret.

However, this I can tell you and may God be your help. Let your ways be set before the Lord and never be moved, especially in the Holy Land. Whenever you offer your prayers and whenever you study, have the intention of unifying a Divine name in every word and with every utterance of your lips. For there are worlds, souls and divinity in every letter. These ascend to become united one with the other and then the letters are combined in order to form a word so that there is complete unification with the Divine.

Allow your soul to be embraced by them at each of the above stages. Thus all worlds become united and they ascend so that immeasurable rapture and the greatest delight is experienced. You can understand this on the analogy of the raptures of bride and bridegroom in miniature in the physical world. How much more so at this most elevated stage! God will undoubtedly be your help and wherever you turn you will be successful and prosper. Give to the wise and he will become even wiser. Also pray for me, with this intention in mind, that I should be worthy of being gathered into the inheritance of the Lord (the Holy Land) while still alive and pray, too, on behalf of all the remnant still in the Diaspora."[20]

---

20. The advice given to Gershon by the Besht is typical of the latter's approach to the devotional life. The letters of the Hebrew alphabet are far more than mere symbols. They are the material form on earth which the spiritual forces on high assume and are thus the source of all creative activity. When man utters the letters of the prayers in Hebrew he assists the creative acts of God and brings down the flow of divine grace into all creation. In each letter there are

So here we are back at the rock. Outside, we look inside at all the inscrutable ways[21] and signs of the Garden of Eden. Tears of humanity continue to fall, and yet the rock that is the gate of the Garden of Eden makes no sound. But it will, by God, it will when the Messiah arrives.

But, as I stand before you now, why am I telling you this, my God, my Creator? You who stand at your seventh window[22] from the right in the firmament hidden and concealed to the eyes of these holy men, you stand there and dream it all come true.

Until then, man faces his rock, holy man his Garden of Eden, God his seventh window. Not everything is as it should be. That is why Every Man desires to stands outside—if he has the slightest Jewish spark in him—and say "*Ad mosai* - Until when! Here I Stand. *Ad mosai?*"

---

worlds, souls, and divinity, that is, in the letters is mirrored that process whereby human souls are united with God and through them all worlds are united with God. An illustration of the joy inherent in such unification is given from the act whereby bride and bridegroom are united.

21. Such mysteries of the Garden of Eden include "Bird's Nest," which the kabbalists considered the hidden abode of the Messiah, a secret place, embroidered with many colors, and in which are hidden a thousand halls of yearnings (*Zohar* 2:8a). Another mystery includes the time when four men entered the Garden: Rabbis Simeon ben Azzai, Simeon ben Zoma, "Aher" (Elisha ben Avuyah), and Akiva. It is said (Talmud, *Hagigah* 14b) that when Rabbi Simeon ben Azzai looked, he died; when Rabbi Simeon ben Zoma looked, he went mad; when Rabbi Aher looked, he cut off the shoots (referring to his conversion); yet Rabbi Akiva entered in peace and left in peace. What exactly in the inscrutable Garden of Eden were they looking at? "Ben Azzai and Ben Zoma penetrated into the forbidden regions of the Divine mystery and were smitten accordingly. Aher, misinterpreting the mystery, fell into heresy. Only Akiva survived the experience." Hayim Nahman Bialik and Yehoshua Hana Ravnitzky, *The Book of Legends*, trans. William G. Braude (New York: Schocken Books, 1992), p. 235.

22. Reference is from the *Zohar* 2:172b.

2

AN ANSWER TO
THE PEOPLE'S PRAYER

The Chazon Ish
Rabbi Abraham Yeshayahu Karelitz
1878–1953

PRESENTING A POTENTIAL MESSIAH
IN HIS TIME . . . THE CHAZON ISH

Rabbi Isser Zalman Meltzer, in *Derech Eretz HaChaim*, wrote,
concerning the Chazon Ish, one of the greatest Torah scholars of the
previous generation, that the Chazon Ish was the potential Messiah.

He was the young men's vision, and the old men's dream.[1] To Bnei Brak,
where he lived for the last twenty-three years of his life, people flocked to
him, for just about every reason under the sun. Youngsters adored and
venerated him. In fact, one of them said: "If the Chazon Ish was to tell me
my right hand was actually my left one, I would place the *tefillin* on that
hand."[2] He was, for many, the answer to the Jewish people's prayer.

How he did this without even trying to be noticed is worth noting.
This twentieth-century sage saw things not with his eyes but with his
vision: to him a new dawning was the same as an ancient dawning, which
is why he always stressed the continuity of Jewish law.

---

1. A paraphrase of "Your old men shall dream dreams, your young men shall
see visions" (Joel 2:28).

2. Isser Frenkel, *Men of Distinction*, 2nd ed. (Tel Aviv: Sinai Publishing,
1967), p. 142.

He also wrote his revolutionary thoughts down, penning twenty-four works on Jewish law, all under the same title, *Chazon Ish*.[3] Understandably, with his nobility of spirit, imposing Torah scholarship, compassion, and practical wisdom, all inspiring a new vision for his generation to follow, it made sense for Rabbi Abraham Yeshayahu Karelitz to be known forever as the *Chazon Ish*, "the Vision of Man."

Born on 11 Cheshvan, 5639/1878 (or 1879), in the town of Kossowa, in the Russian province of Grodno, he came from parents, Rabbi Shmaryahu Yosef Karelitz and his *rebbetzin*, Rasha Leah, the *Rav* and *Rebbetzin* of Kossowa, who were descended from a distinguished lineage that included Rabbi Zerachiah *HaLevi*, the *Ba'al HaMaor* (tenth century); Rabbi Yehudah Loewy of Prague, the famed holy *Maharal* (sixteenth century); and Rabbi Aryeh Leib Epstein, the *Ba'al HaPardes* (eighteenth century). Through them he was descended from the House of David.

To say that he was, in his youth, a crowd-pleaser may be a bit too much, but it's also true. One can easily grasp the *nachus* his parents must have felt when he stood up at his *bar mitzvah*, already considered a qualified authority on the Talmud, and publicly promised he would devote himself to the Torah *lishmah*, for the sake of study without thought of obtaining a rabbinical post or a position with the rabbinate. To be sure, there wasn't a person in that room who didn't believe he would do as he said. At his funeral, in 1953, the first eulogizer said: "When he reached the age of thirteen, he accepted upon himself to study Torah *lishmah*. I can bear witness that he did just that for more than sixty years."[4]

In time, he became a talmudist, a halachist, an outstanding spiritual world leader of Torah Jewry. He also was well versed in natural sciences, which he studied for the sake of the light they could throw on Jewish law and practice.[5] It was not his style to hold any official position, and he followed in the footsteps of many of our forefathers by agreeing with his

---

3. Although the second word of the title, *Ish*, are "the first letters of his names—*Aleph* for Avraham and *Yod Shin* for Yeshayahu . . . he refused to have his full name appear on the book as the author, explaining: 'The book was not written to advertise my name, but to be of service to the world of Torah. It is, therefore, quite immaterial who wrote it. What is important is the contents of the book and that is all.'" Frenkel, *Men of Distinction*, p. 137.

4. Shimon Finkelman, *The Chazon Ish* (Brooklyn, NY: Mesorah Publications, 1989), p. 262.

5. Geoffrey Wigoder, *Dictionary of Jewish Biography* (New York: Simon & Schuster, 1991), p. 255.

new wife, Basya, the daughter of Reb Mordechai Bei, that she'd work and he'd study all the time. In the city of Kweidan they set up house, and accordingly, Reb Avraham Yeshayahu studied undisturbed and Basya "upheld the pre-marriage agreement in the way of a most exceptional *aishes chayil*."[6] Her income from a small shop selling textile materials provided for their modest needs all their days in Europe and she took great pains to avoid disrupting her husband's studies. However, late at night, when the young scholar was too tired to study or write any more, he assisted his wife with the shop's bookkeeping and helped keep her clients' accounts up to date.

From Kweidan they moved to Minsk, Stuyepitz. Shortly afterward, in 1929, they again moved, this time to Vilna. A very private man, he inclined toward seclusion and anonymity. Although he wrote, under the pseudonym of "*Ta Shmaa*" ("The Solution"), new interpretations of Torah that were published in *Knesset Yisroel*, a monthly journal on religious matters, printed in Vilna and widely circulated, he tried to keep out of the limelight. However, his identity was soon discovered by the then Rabbi of Vilna, the Gaon Rabbi Haim Ozer. There, he also became intimately associated with the world-renowned Torah authority, Rabbi H. O. Grodziensky.

It seemed as if wherever two or more scholars gathered, the Chazon Ish's halachic authority was quickly recognized. Consulted on legal, moral, public, and personal problems, he was deeply respected for his saintly and ascetic mode of life. And why not? For untold millennia, Jews, whose souls break with longing for God's ordinances at all times,[7] had been praying for a messianic figure to take the reins of authority into its hands. Everything about this man from Bnei Brak rang loud and clear.

Once, a friend of the Chazon Ish told a young man, who had a singular encounter with the Chazon Ish: "You think that is something unusual? One day this week, I watched as Reb Avraham Yeshayahu *davened Minchah* in a room off to the side of the *beis hamidrosh*. He wept so profusely that by the time he was finished, a pool of tears surrounded him. On a regular weekday! He thought no one was looking. In public he contains himself. . . ."[8]

Yet the Chazon Ish was God's man, and his own. He loathed appearing in public and conducted his life in ways similar to the Gaon of

---

6. Finkelman, *The Chazon Ish*, p. 31.
7. A paraphrase of Psalms 119:20.
8. Finkelman, *The Chazon Ish*, p. 37.

Vilna (Rabbi Elijah ben Solomon Zalman, 1720–1797, who once said of himself, "Elijah can serve God also without a world to come"[9]).

Yet, in spite of his natural reluctance, the Chazon Ish had too much *ahavas Yisrael* to deny the role of *"manhig hador"* (leader of his generation). His light warmed the hearts of many, near and far. His genuine humility was matchless. Once he wrote: "I am always full of errors in the theory or interpretation of the talmudic text. Yet I am never ashamed. There is no humiliation in the quest of the proper understanding and fulfillment of the *mitzvah.*"[10]

From Shakespeare to the Chazon Ish, there was a connection: "I am a Jew: Hath not a Jew eyes? Hath not a Jew hands, organs, dimension, senses, afflictions, passions? Fed with same food, hurt with the same weapons, subject to the same diseases, healed by the same means, warmed and cooled by the same winter and summer. . . . If you prick us, do we not bleed? If you tickle us, do we not laugh? If you poison us, do we not die? And, if you wrong us, shall we not revenge?"

There you have Shakespeare and, *l'havdil*, there you have the Chazon Ish, who may have lived a life apart from his fellow Jews yet was always part of them, their organs and their souls, their laughs, their tears, their senses and their passions, their bleeding and their healing—their dimension.

So convinced that it would undermine the chastity and modesty of the Jewish daughter who had been reared in a pure religious atmosphere, he intervened directly in the conflict that raged over the conscription of girls for military service in the Israeli Defense Forces. And when then Israel's prime minister David Ben-Gurion trekked to Bnei Brak to seek the holy man out in his little home, concerning the issue of conscripting talmudic students into the army, the conversation quickly turned to the whole problem of coexistence between religious and irreligious Jews. Calmly and wisely, the Chazon Ish explained to Ben-Gurion the secularist leader the emotional and halachic dimensions and depths of the issue. In a famous, widely quoted metaphor, the Chazon Ish cited the talmudic law that when meeting on a narrow path, an empty wagon must yield the way for a loaded one. So, too, he argued, the new State of Israel must

---

9. Quoted by Brainin, *MiMizrah Umi-Maarab*, 1899; also *Treasury of Jewish Quotations*, ed. Joseph L. Baron (Northvale, NJ: Jason Aronson, 1985), p. 320.

10. *Men of the Spirit*, ed. Leo Jung (New York: Kymson Publishing Co., 1964), p. 151.

accommodate a rich, ancient tradition. "Our ship is laden with three thousand years of history, heritage and tradition. Yours, however, is empty, devoid of any real substance. Confrontations are inevitable."[11]

But his special love was for the Orthodox young men and women who had adopted the life of farming and agriculture. Paying particular attention to the neglected agricultural laws of the Bible, he devised milking machines for use on *Shabbos* and permitted use of hydroponics to raise produce in the sabbatical year. He regularly traveled to all their agricultural settlements and *kibbutzim*, encouraging them in the great work they were doing and instructing them in the halachic law as it applied to occupation.[12]

If only the Chazon Ish had more time in the world to help people! In an earlier time, another man of divine goodwill, Reb Elimelech of Lizhensk (1717–1786),[13] once said: "If they had left me alone, if they had left me in peace for two years, I would have made the Messiah come."[14]

If only they had left the Chazon Ish alone!

No one will ever know (until the Messiah comes and reveals the unknown) the full extent the Chazon Ish played in hastening the Messiah on earth, but, in spite of the many problems that required his thoughts and attention, he kept his front door always open, and even though he was often prevented from taking a much needed rest, he refused to limit visiting hours or turn people away. "How can I do such a thing?" he protested when the suggestion was made. "How can I refuse to see anyone who has gone to all the trouble to come out here and who has a problem which is causing him distress? If I can ease or even relieve that distress, should I not do so no matter what the hour?"[15]

And he suited his actions to his words. He involved himself with countless Holocaust survivors, doing his best to mend their broken spirits and hearts, lending them spiritual strength by infusing them with his own unshakable faith. Shortly after World War II's end, the Chazon Ish was asked if one could assume that the Holocaust was the climax of the sufferings which *chazal* speak as a prelude to the arrival of the Messiah. He

---

11. Berel Wein, *Triumph of Survival* (Monsey, NY: Shaar Press, 1990), pp. 414–415.

12. Frenkel, *Men of Distinction*, pp. 139–140.

13. Chassidic Rebbe, popularly known as the *No'am Elimelech*, after the title of his work.

14. Elie Wiesel, *Souls on Fire* (Northvale, NJ: Jason Aronson, 1993), p. 123.

15. Frenkel, *Men of Distinction*, p. 140.

replied: A traveler can map out his journey before he embarks on it and mark off how far he has to go as his journey progresses. Such is not the case, however, with *Kelal Yisrael's* journey through *golus*. Certainly, every travail brings the final redemption that much closer, but what still must transpire is not known to us.[16]

For this and so much more, the Chazon Ish lived—and died. We can well imagine a child ask his *tateh*: "Why did the Chazon Ish die?" The answer has to be simple: "Because he lived."

One *Shabbos* night in 1953 the Chazon Ish passed away. That same night, Rabbi Eliyahu Lopian, legendary *tzaddik* and *mashgiach* at Yeshivah Knesses Chezkiah in Zichron Yaakov, dreamt that a Torah scroll was going up in flames. He awoke shaken. When *Shabbos* ended, he learned the meaning of his dream. The Chazon Ish was no longer with us. "*Chazal* compare the death of a *tzaddik* to the breaking of the tablets bearing the Ten Commandments."[17]

Before we leave the little house of the Chazon Ish in Bnei Brak, and make our way back to Yerushalayim, along a road where we can expect the Messiah at any moment, let me tell you one more touching thing about this extraordinary man.

Until he was utterly satisfied he had found the correct solution to a problem, his mind and body remained focused, neither swaying to the left nor to the right. Suddenly this saintly man, who would physically let himself go only on *Simchas Torah*, would burst into a wordless tune. A sure sign to his family that he had solved yet another difficult problem.[18]

That he saw no possibility for coexistence between the Torah community and the secularist government of Israel, there's no doubt. But wherever the Chazon Ish is now, in the *Gan Eden*, we must conclude, he continues working for *Kelal Yisrael* and hastening the Messiah—until that moment when he again bursts into a wordless tune, so that, God willing, with our ears and eyes wide open enough to hear and see him in this messianic age, we'll know for certain he has solved yet another difficult problem.

For this is what the Chazon Ish and every other searching Jew is all about: an answer to the Jewish people's prayer.

---

16. Finkelman, *The Chazon Ish*, p. 155.

17. "See Rashi's commentary to Deuteronomy 10:6, and the destruction of the *Beis Hamikdosh* (*Eichah Rabbah* 1:39)." Finkelman, *The Chazon Ish*, p. 261.

18. Frenkel, *Men of Distinction*, p. 137.

3

EVERYTHING ENDS
IN A SONG

"And deep things are song," the poet tells us. It is "the very central essence of us, song; as if all the rest were but wrappings and hull."[1] This song—this Divine Light, as we Jews call it—is mystically found in the daily doings of mitzvos ("Each commandment . . . has a unique musical quality . . . which evokes reverent joy and song within us").[2]

Witness the *Maggid* of Mezritch, who once said, "Your kind deeds are used by God as seed for the planting of trees in the Garden of Eden; thus, each of you creates your own paradise."[3]

And witness "the footsteps of the Messiah"[4] as he walked along with a group of thirsting senior citizens. It was the fifth night of the Festival of Lights (Chanukah), 28 Kislev, 5754, and the men and women, freshly fed at the Shalom Senior Citizen Center,[5] and its energetic director, Edith Bloch, and her devoted assistant, Sarah Biolik, all braved the wintry day,

---

1. Thomas Carlyle, *On Heroes, Hero-Worship, and the Heroic in History,* 1841.
2. Rabbi Abraham Isaac Kook, *Eder HaYekot,* 1906, p. 44.
3. Rabbi Dov Ber, 1704–1772, *Esser Orot—Ten Lights.*
4. The phrase *ikvesa diMeshicha* ("the footsteps of *Moshiach*") signifies our era at the very dawn of the Redemption.
5. The Shalom Senior Citizens Center is located at the Young Israel building

marching to "770" (770 Eastern Parkway, home of the Lubavitch World Headquarters, in Brooklyn, New York). There, they would hold a rally to bring on the Messiah. There, Rabbi Menachem Gerlitsky, the organizer of such senior citizen rallies, would tell these oldtimers, mostly from the former Soviet Union, about the "spaceship" that was about to bring the Messiah down to earth. And this very special fifth night of Chanukah was also special because it was the night when the Rebbe of Lubavitch, Rabbi Menachem M. Schneerson, used to distribute Chanukah *gelt* to the children and old people of the community. It was also the Jewish birthday of Cantor Moshe Teleshevsky. This afternoon, he would introduce a new song, as he put it, "to hasten the Messiah."

This too was done in the light of carrying out a mitzvah. This light, this Divine Light, the Koretzer Rebbe (Rabbi Phineas Shapiro, died 1791) described like this: "For thirty-six hours, Adam enjoyed the Divine Light that was created on the first day and was superseded later by the sunlight; then it was hidden. On Chanukah this Divine Light inspired the victory of the ancient *chassidim* [Hasmoneans], and for this reason thirty-six lights are kindled during Chanukah as a memorial of the thirty-six hours that the First Man enjoyed it. Since then this Divine Light has inspired the creation of the thirty-six Tractates of the Talmud. The Messiah will redeem us by this Divine Light."[6]

So come along now and listen to our tale as Amshel Vaynerman, a sprightly Russian man in his seventies, lights the five candles with the *shamash* (the lead candle) and the other senior citizens participate in a rally for the Messiah—each of them wanting to create his or her own paradise.

Long before the senior citizens from all over the city of New York gathered to hear the footsteps of the Messiah in 770 on that fifth Chanukah eve, Rabbi Gerlitsky tells them, a spaceship[7] once upon a time was sent up by earthlings to the nearest star, Alpha Centauri, some eight hundred years away.

---

at 935 Eastern Parkway, in the Crown Heights section of Brooklyn, New York. It is under the auspices of the Crown Heights Preservation Committee and the Crown Heights Jewish Community Council.

6. Louis I. Newman, *The Hasidic Anthology* (Northvale, NJ: Jason Aronson, 1987), p. 162; and Pinchas of Koretz, *Nofeth Tzufum* (Warsaw, 1929), p. 18.

7. Based on a paper by Dr. Roger Revelle entitled, "Sailing in New and Old Oceans," *American Institute of Biological Sciences Bulletin*, October 1962, vol. xii, p. 46, and reprinted in *Challenge: An Encounter with Lubavitch-Chabad* (London: Lubavitch Foundation of Great Britain, 1974), pp. 231–235.

All the details were spelled out in a blueprint. Nothing was overlooked, including the selection of the four absolutely healthy specimens of men and women astronauts, who were expected not only to fly but also to procreate. In the time it would take them to reach their destination, bring back proof to earth that they had been there, 1,600 years would have elapsed. Even if the pioneering four were lucky to live 120 years, they'd never live long enough to reach the end of the mission. So these men and women were subjected to every kind of test to ensure they'd produce generation after generation after generation of offspring to carry out the scientific plan. Nothing was left to chance. Each minute, each second, not a moment too early, not a moment too late, was accounted for. And in carrying out each split-second operation, we can well imagine how nervous the astronauts were. Everything depended on them—lest all might be doomed. The possibility existed that all the earthlings and the land they called earth might not be there when they returned, if the astronauts strayed for one second from their timetable. So the parting words at their takeoff from earth were probably Torah words to the effect of: "Be fruitful and multiply" (Genesis 1:28)—and replenish the capsule.

Rabbi Gerlitsky also told the senior citizens that, "in the interstellar spaceship, the crew would have to learn to tolerate each other, generation after generation. Similarly, we on earth must somehow learn to live with each other.[8]

"Finally came the day the whole world had been prepared to see these people off—these precious four who were ready to sacrifice everything for this mission—to accomplish their objective. At precisely 6:01 they turned their first valve; at 6:01:54 they let air in to the system, and they didn't do it a second before or a second late. They knew how crucial everything was that was written and how crucial it was to follow the instructions. Then they pressed their first switch at 6:02:15. They didn't do it at 14 or 16 but at 15.

"Then, 10, 9, 8, 7, 6, 5, 4, 3, 2, 1, blast off!—and the four astronauts were lifted up, up, and away, and they experienced a shiver they had never felt before. The pressure was so great, the swoon to relieve themselves so tempting, yet they were airborne precisely when the blueprint stated, and everyone in the world sighed collectively for their great start.

"So," Rabbi Gerlitzsky said as he broke into a relieved smile, "the days

---

8. *Challenge*, p. 232.

of the ship in the sky went well, and as the years passed, the astronauts were fruitful; they multiplied and replenished the spaceship. And as the generations stretched one into another, certain vital measures were relaxed, as so often happens in life, too. By the twentieth generation other details were overlooked, dropped, or simply forgotten. The blueprint pages yellowed, the ancient great-grandparents became out of touch with the newer members of the family. And there came a time when even the objective of the launch was lost in a shuffle of pages and lapse of memories."

And suddenly Rabbi Gerlitsky's blue eyes took on a blue as deep as the blue heavens, and he said, "And that was the end of their quest because it was manmade. But our quest, each one of ours as we await the Messiah here on earth, has begun and is as vital to us as it was to our forefathers. All of us have followed the Torah, the blueprint of life, the map of all the world. *Hashem* chose the Jewish people. He put together our mission— make no mistake about that. He gave it to us, each year on Shavuos, from one generation to another generation to another generation. How many of our parents, our grandparents, our great-great-grandparents gave their lives for us to accomplish this mission?

"The hardest part is the landing, it's true, and we're about to land. Messiah is about to come, and we know it's any day. The signs are telling us, and the Rebbe has told us that any moment the Messiah will arrive; we just have to complete this mission of so many generations. We have to do our mitzvos, and hasten the Messiah.

"The fact is you should—*we should all*—continue to shiver when you do a mitzvah because you never know how crucial a mitzvah is. All the things we had to do up 'there' are done. The whole world is waiting for the rocket to come down. All the prize money, all the rewards are ready."

It was especially rewarding that these senior citizens met during Chanukah to rally for the Messiah. The Sachatzover Rebbe (Rabbi Abraham, died 1910, son of Nathan Zeev Bialer) was once asked: "Why does the *Shulchan Aruch* insist that one must buy Chanukah candles even if he/she is destitute and must beg for the money, whereas other duties are not obligatory on the part of one who lacks the means for them?"

The Rebbe replied: "We find in the Talmud the rule, that if a person contemplates performing a precept, but is unavoidably prevented from fulfilling his intention, the Creator allocates to him the credit as if he had actually done the deed [*Berachot* 6]. Chanukah candles, however, must be lighted, it is commanded, in order to give public testimony to the miracles associated with the Festival. Inasmuch as mere intention to perform the duty will not give public evidence, therefore this precept cannot be assumed to be fulfilled, except through its actual performance."[9]

And such a performance by Cantor Moshe Teleshevsky was dedicated to the hastening of the Messiah. "We know from Isaiah [11:1–4]," said the cantor, "that a shoot shall come forth from the stem of Yishai,[10] and with righteousness shall he judge the poor, and with the breath of his lips shall he slay the wicked, and. . . ." And suddenly the cantor broke out into a Yiddish song, composed by Abraham Singer. In English it might be called "A New World." There was no doubt that every ear in 770 was well attuned, including the Messiah's.

> Once upon a time a prophet lived by the name of Isaiah.
> And he told us a prophecy that a new world will come.
> There will be no more wars. All the swords will be turned into plows.
> The wolf and the lamb will live together in peace.
> But when will the time come when we will be able to see the beautiful dream?
> Now I am asking you, dear *Yidden*, wouldn't that be heavenly,
> Wouldn't that be something beautiful?
> But when will the time come that we should be able to live together in peace?
> In yesteryear, the sword was a very prominent weapon,
> But today there's no comparison to the new armaments we have.
> Every land that we go to we see that each and everyone speaks about war.
> So we need a good prophet nowadays!
> He should tell us that the new world is coming right now—with *Moshiach*.

---

9. Newman, *Hasidic Anthology*, pp. 161–162; J. K. K. Rokotz, *Siach Sarfei Kodesh* (Lodz, Poland, 1929), vol. 3, p. 28.

10. The Rabbi of Rozniatov, Rabbi Eliezer Lippmann, a disciple of Rabbi Menachem Mendel Hager of Kossov (1768–1826), persistently asked his rebbe why the Messiah had not come, and why the Redemption promised by the Prophets and Sages had not been fulfilled.

Rabbi Mendel answered: "It is written: 'Why has the son of Jesse not come, either today or yesterday?' [1 Samuel 20:37] The answer lies in the question itself: 'Why has he not come? Because we are today just as we were yesterday.'" I. Berger, *Esser Tzachtzochoth* (Piotrkov, 1910), p. 65.

Wouldn't it be nice, dear *Yidden*, that we live this era as soon as possible?

Wouldn't it be something heavenly!

And we hope the time will come as soon as possible

That we will be able to live through that era.

That a new song for Messiah should be introduced and sung during Chanukah was also apropos, Cantor Teleshevsky pointed out. "It is the time when the Hasmoneans defeated their enemies in battle, another one of God's miracles, and we remained a nation. And the same thing as sung in this song has a lot of the Messiah in it. We continue to have many people who want to oppress us. Yet, we remain with the hope that the Messiah will arrive, that the Rebbe will get well, and he will take us out of *golus*. Even as I say this, I feel that shiver. May he come now! We're ready with our songs and for his Divine Light." The song again came out of the cantor's mouth: "He should tell us that the new world is coming right now . . . wouldn't it be something heavenly!"

As we are about to find out, everything that is heavenly ends in such a song—the Song of the Messiah.

4

HE SANG IT HIS WAY

The rabbis sat there like so many tombstones. For a *melave malka* held in communist Romania, in the year 1954, with the finest array of rabbis from the eastern bloc, and communist officials, some of whom seemed to have more medals on their chests than hair on their heads, it was the kind of communists-and-Jews-at-their-best party any good communist would expect to stage. Every so often, at the insistence of the Romanian government, the Romanian rabbis staged a *melave malka* in Bucharest, to show an invited guest from the free world that communists and religious got along well behind the Iron Curtain, and the communist officials hoped the invited guest rabbi would, in turn, give a glowing report to the outside world—or qualify his condemnation of the Romanian government and its very closed society. To that end, all of the rabbis' prepared speeches sounded a bit different from the others, yet tried very hard to emphasize the positive connection between the Romanian Jews and their earthly masters, or, to put it, as one wag unofficially did, that "all was well in hell."

On this occasion the honored guest was the carefully chosen Rabbi Kurt Wilhelm (1900–1965), the chief rabbi of Sweden. Carefully chosen because, the communists felt, he always advocated a positive and moderate liberalism, similar to Conservative Judaism, seemingly in all his efforts in trying to bridge the gaps between East and West. Born in Germany, he studied at German universities, and at the Jewish Theological Seminary in Breslau and New York. As a Kurt Wilhelm–watcher once noted, Wilhelm "belonged to the circle which supported Arab-

Jewish understanding, and was active in promoting Jewish dialogue with Christianity and other religions."[1] All this mattered very much to the communists, but no little factual nugget was that the rabbi was an old Oxford University school pal of the current secretary general of the United Nations, Dag Hammarskjold (1905–1961). Wasting no time, the Romanian communists proposed, Rabbi Moshe Rosen,[2] the chief rabbi of Romania, extended the invitation, Rabbi Wilhelm accepted it, and there, on that very *motzoei Shabbat melave malka* sat the twenty-five gloomy or stone-faced rabbis and an equal number of smiling communist officials and military generals, their eyes feasting on their guest.

Rabbi Wilhelm was no fool in Paradise; he knew where he was and what the Romanian communists were counting on him for. Yet, in this, his first visit behind the Iron Curtain, where thought was perhaps the only universe of freedom, he had heard nothing rebellious in the rabbis' speeches spoken in Hebrew or Yiddish, so what could he take away from the *simchah* except the taste of overcooked chicken and overcooked speeches? Score one for the communists!

Yet Rabbi Wilhelm had no idea when suddenly a white-bearded man appeared, wearing an unassuming black garment and hat, and methodically and slowly moved to his seat; why suddenly everyone stood up, and the rabbi at the rostrum stopped speaking, to hail the newcomer to the *melave malka*. Rabbi Wilhelm couldn't help notice some of the rabbis wiping away tears in their eyes. All this for a short, thin, pale rabbi named

---

1. *Encyclopaedia Judaica* (Jerusalem: Keter Publishing House, 1971), 16:55.

2. The late Rabbi Moshe Rosen, who passed away in the summer of 1994, had a high regard for the Skulener Rebbe. He was responsible for all the Jewish activities going on during that time in Romania. When his parents passed away he asked the Skulener Rebbe to observe his parents' *yahrzeits* by reciting the *kaddish*. This is something a child usually does. But out of deep respect and believing it would be a privilege to his parents high in heaven, he asked the Skulener Rebbe to recite the *kaddish* as well. Besides that, much later on, the chief rabbi of Romania found out in Paris that he had a malignant growth on his body. Rabbi Rosen dared not share his medical information with any doctor in Budapest. He reasoned: If the communists found out, he would likely lose his powerful position as chief rabbi. At once he contacted the Skulener, who was by then living in New York City. The Skulener blessed Rabbi Rosen and told him to contact a doctor in London and he would see it was nothing. When he found out through this second opinion that the Skulener Rebbe was right, he thanked the Rebbe profusely.

Eliezer Zisha Portugal, familiarly known as the Skulener Rebbe, who, with his eyes, modestly embraced everyone in the room before he took his seat without any further fanfare.

When it came time for the Skulener to speak, he began to approach the dais in what seemed a long time to Rabbi Wilhelm. He had no idea who or what the frail rabbi approaching the microphone was. Why had he come in the middle of the proceedings, two hours late? Perhaps he was and is even now praying along the way to find the right words to say . . . perhaps he might have dressed better if he knew he was going to speak in front of such a well-manicured crowd . . . yet no one but he seemed impatient with the ways of the frail rabbi. So, reasoned Rabbi Wilhelm, he would wait till he heard from *this* rabbi before he formed any more opinions.

If Rabbi Wilhelm had only known why the Skulener came late! Because he always extended the Sabbath for two hours more. Why was that? As the Skulener Rebbe himself liked to quote,[3] "A king built a bridal chamber, plastered, painted, and adorned it. Now what was needed to complete it? Why, a bride! So with the world, after the six days of creation, what was needed to finish it? The Sabbath!" And that took time. Clearly two hours added to the making of the Sabbath was a small price for the Skulener Rebbe to pay.

And if Rabbi Wilhelm only knew what Rabbi Nissan Wolpin would one day add about the Skulener's patience and deliberateness. "In our 'do-it-yourself era' when every man pulls for himself, his *avodah* in *tefillah*—the hours upon hours of all-encompassing concentration when he poured out his heart to God in his prayers, day after day—staggering. *Shacharis* was a four-hour effort. Saying the *Shema* on an ordinary evening *Maariv* took twenty-five minutes. . . . It should be no surprise that when he said his customary *Shema* in the intensive care unit of a hospital during a recent illness, the doctors were alarmed when the cardiogram readings fluctuated wildly with every carefully articulated word."[4]

And this was the little holy man who came his way. And when the Skulener reached the microphone, he excused himself from making a speech. "At that I'm not good," he said in clear-cut Yiddish. But, he raised everyone's hope and expectations, he would sing a song, one he

---

3. Geniba, third-century Babylonian *amora*, on Genesis 2:2 and *Genesis Rabbah* 10:9.

4. *The Jewish Observer*, Sept. 1982, p. 15.

composed just for the occasion. No objections were raised by anyone. When the Skulener sang a *niggun*—music to soothe even the communist beast—everybody craned his neck.

The song was new, but the words were ancient. The musician Asaph sang them in Psalms 79:10–12.

> Wherefore should the nations say, "Where is their God?" Let Him be recognized among the nations before our eyes, as vengeance for the blood of Thy servants that has been shed.
>
> Let the cry of terror of the shackled come before Thee; in keeping with the greatness of Thy arm, cause those condemned to death to survive.
>
> And render to our neighbors sevenfold into their bosom their slander with which they have reviled thee, O my Master!

The words were as old as King David, but the song was the Skulener's, sung his way, expressed in his unforgettable manner, as no rabbi in that room dared to influence the chief rabbi of Sweden. At this *melave malka* most Jews heard the song—"*Niggun Yivoda Bagoyim*"—and understood the message. In it, King David complains about all the nations that suppress the Jewish people in Israel and how they took away their rights, and he asks the Lord to take revenge on all these nations. To the communists, it was an ordinary Hebrew song. They didn't know.

Now the question was, did Rabbi Wilhelm know? Yes, he was clever enough to get it. There was nothing, besides the *niggun*, and later an exchange of hands, to let anyone else know that vital information was exchanged between the two men. There was more to the song than any Jew there would let on. Rabbi Wilhelm learned more from that song than from all the speeches combined. Which meant that when he returned to Sweden he was able to convey to the outside world the true goings-on in Romania.

The Skulener Rebbe—who was this *tzaddik* (although he himself denied it most of his life) who could stir the hearts of the widest possible spectrum of world Jewry? Born in 1898 in the town of Skulen, Bessarabia, his name was Eliezer Zisha Portugal, and he wasn't the scion of a long line of great rabbis. Instead, he was appointed rebbe in his own right. He officiated as Rabbi of Skulen from 1919 to 1936, later to be universally known as the Skulener Rebbe, a much loved and admired *tzaddik* who dedicated his life to helping the needy and oppressed.

Preceding World War II, the Skulener Rebbe moved to the Russian-occupied border town of Chernovitz that sat right next to Romania. In early 1942, the Romanian fascist government, in cooperation with the Germans, deported the Jews of the provinces of Bessarabia and Bukovina to camps in the Ukrainian region of Transnistria, where 100,000 perished from starvation, beatings, hard labor, and frigid cold. Thousands more were executed. Employing ingenious methods, the Skulener succeeded in bringing the survivors to freedom, thanks to his contacts with high government officials. The Skulener and his *rebbetzin* proceeded to "adopt close to 400 orphaned children, and, incredibly, took care of their needs as though they were his own children."[5]

After World War II there were so many Jewish orphans left that the Skulener became a relative for most of them. First, he would adopt each family and then legally ship them out in a circuitous route to Israel. In carrying out this remarkable effort, he supported them, sustained them till they were able to get to Israel. Even if they were strangers, he'd form a family of them by taking two adults and several children, and then made papers out, linking them as relatives to him. As soon as this was in place, he had agents in Romania find the true relatives of these people. How did he get away with this for so long? In those days when he lived in Romania it wasn't as yet strongly communistic, and, besides, the communists well knew all about the Rebbe's undercover activities, and indeed were paid off by him for looking the other way when he smuggled instantly made-up "families" of Jews across the border.

Rabbi Shelomoh Zalman Horowitz, the late Poteker Rav, told the following story:[6] In Russian-occupied Chernovitz, one Friday afternoon during prayer, the Skulener Rebbe approached me and asked, "Since you are a descendant of the Baal Shem Tov,[7] I am asking you to pray for me. I need God's help." The Skulener Rebbe explained: "The Russians arrested a Jewish family who were trying to escape across the border. They may be executed. In similar cases in the past, I have been able to gain the release of the prisoners from the military commander who took a liking to me. But the last time I came he warned me that if I ever approached him again with a request to release 'criminals' he would shoot me on the spot, without blinking an eye. Now this family is in prison and I am going again to see the general, but I am asking you to pray for me."

---

5. Ibid., p. 14.

6. Rabbi Eliezer Zisha Portugal, "Introduction," *No'am Eliezer*.

7. Founder of *Chassidism*, 1698–1760.

The Poteker Rav prayed fervently the entire *Shabbos* for the success of the Skulener's mission. At night he met the Rebbe, who was smiling broadly as he returned from military headquarters.

"Well, how did it go?" asked the Poteker Rav.

Replied the Skulener, "When I came to the general with my petition, he threw me down three flights of stairs—but in the end he did exactly what I asked him to do. He set the family free."

Continued the Poteker Rav: "Things like this happened to him [the Skulener Rebbe] every day."[8]

And "on one occasion he actually gave his hard-won exit visa to a head of a family of eleven. When the official whom he had "paid" for the visa, in a fit of anger and confusion, accused him of reneging on the agreement, the Rebbe replied, 'Eleven souls are more important than one.'"[9]

Based on what the Skulener Rebbe did before, one could write a story of his continued activities on behalf of his fellow Jews—and be right on the money. Over and over he landed in communist prisons, but he did not give up. He treated all of these children as his own, supporting, feeding, and guiding them. In return, the children treated him throughout their lives as their father.

Then, finally, on April 23, 1959, the Skulener Rebbe was arrested in Bucharest, his residence since 1945, and jailed for a few months. In a letter dated July 30, 1959, to *The New York Times*, appealing for help, Professor Reinhold Niebuhr of Union Theological Seminary and Chancellor Louis Finkelstein of Jewish Theological Seminary pointed out that, in coping "with the harsh circumstances of imprisonment and investigation," Rabbi Portugal "is sixty-five, frail and sickly; his weight has repeatedly dropped to ninety pounds, in part probably because he has been unable in prison to obtain the kosher food which his faith enjoins him to eat. His very survival, then, may depend on his being released."

His family (minus one of his sons and some disciples, who were arrested and imprisoned with the Skulener) were told the charges against him seemed very serious and the punishment could be very severe, perhaps the death sentence. Not even his *niggunim*, which were many by that time, could save him.

First the communists accused him of high treason. The communists

---

8. Avraham Yaakov Finkel, *The Great Chasidic Masters* (Northvale, NJ: Jason Aronson, 1992), p. 214.

9. *The Jewish Observer*, ibid., p. 14.

targeted the chassidic custom of *pidyon*. What's that? you may ask. And so did the Romanian communists, who were told they [the *pidyon*] were contributions given to a rebbe. So they accused the Skulener of sending money to Israel. They added fuel to the fire: "People are coming to you with small papers and you are smuggling these messages to their relatives in Israel and America. And they are giving you money to pay for it. That means you are a spy."[10]

Then they brought up charges of smuggling against him. Case after case they cited of his smuggling children across the borders to safety, by claiming they were his own family. If there was any humor in his arrest, it, in an offbeat manner, can be likened to a scene in the movie *Casablanca*. The German officer has just ordered the French prefect of police (Claude Rains) to close down Rick's, a local watering hole. In turn, the prefect orders Rick (Humphrey Bogart) to lock up the Place. "On what charge?" Bogart demands to know. Coolly, Rains says: "On the charge of gambling!" Bogart gives him a dirty look. That very night the prefect of police had been gambling in Rick's Place and won a sizable amount of money. Boldly adds the prefect, "Yes, Rick, I'm shocked, utterly shocked, that gambling is going on here. Shut this place down at once."

So the Skulener Rebbe was imprisoned, and there were fast rumors that he was either executed already or had been shipped off to Russia to be tried there.

Telephones around the world rang, teletype machines clicked noisily day and night. This was a man every Jew and his friends had to save, if only to fulfill the talmudic saying, "He who saves a single soul, has saved a whole world." So the international Jewish organizations combined their efforts for the sake of the Skulener Rebbe. Meetings were held in boardrooms of New York City. International figures worked privately for his release. The U.S. State Department and the Foreign Office in London got involved. In truth, this was a high-anxiety time, barely six years after Joseph Stalin's death in 1953, and nobody really knew how to influence the repressive Romanian government or force the issue, but they *all* were bent on trying.

One Friday night, after the *Shabbos* meal, a young rabbi and teacher named Zelig Sharfstein, now the Lubavitcher *sheliach* and *Rav* of Cincinnati, arrived at the home of the chief rabbi of Cincinnati, Rabbi Eliezer Silver (1882–1968). He was looking forward to hearing a *shiur* presented

---

10. Ibid.

by Rabbi Silver, who was known for his unconventional ways and raconteur stories. The *shiur* was always well attended by the *rabbonim*, so Rabbi Sharfstein hurried to get a seat.

As soon as Rabbi Sharfstein entered the house, Rabbi Silver hailed the young rabbi. "Rabbi Sharfstein, I've been waiting for you. Just this morning [Friday] I got a telephone call from the Lubavitcher Rebbe [Rabbi Menachem M. Schneerson of Lubavitch, 1902–1994], and I'm not joking."

Rabbi Sharfstein waited for his explanation.

"I tell you, Rabbi Sharfstein, your Rebbe personally asked me to go to Washington, DC, right away, and do something there to help free the Skulener Rebbe from the communists."

"Are you going?" asked Rabbi Sharfstein.

"Of course, but I explained to your Rebbe that the people from Young Israel, Agudath Israel, and Agudath Horabonim had already tried several times and nothing came of it. What more could I do? I asked the Rebbe. Still, the Rebbe insisted I should go. 'Don't give up,' the Rebbe told me. 'You have been successful in rescuing Jews in the past and you will succeed.'" Rabbi Silver then told Rabbi Sharfstein that he didn't have much hope for success, but since the Lubavitcher Rebbe asked him, he would go.

And as Rabbi Sharfstein tells it, Rabbi Silver did indeed go to Washington. He contacted I. Jack (Judge) Martin, a White House administrative assistant to then president Dwight D. Eisenhower. Like Rabbi Silver himself, Mr. Martin was a native of Cincinnati, and it was he who was instrumental in having an official letter sent, on official White House stationery, to the U.S. State Department, which thereupon drafted a letter to the Romanian embassy, requesting the freedom of Rabbi Portugal. By a quirk of fate the Romanian embassy had just a few days before drafted a letter and sent it off to the U.S. State Department, requesting that the U.S. government accept the credentials of the new ambassador from Romania.

What happened next could easily be attributed to Divine Providence. When the Romanian embassy officials received the State Department letter they thought that the U.S. officials were requesting release of the Skulener as part of a U.S. deal to accept the new Romanian ambassador. In its way, the State Department letter sounded logical and reasonable. That, coupled with the fact that, in order to change an ambassador in Washington, DC, a foreign country needed U.S. permission, probably tilted the table in favor of the Skulener's release.

Nobody really knows why the Lubavitcher Rebbe phoned Rabbi

Silver the first time. Did the Lubavitcher Rebbe have inside information—
or a Divine message from Heaven—that the time was ripe to spring the
Skulener? Clearly, Rabbi Silver had the right mix for this kind of success.
According to a writer of *Encyclopaedia Judaica*, "[i]n appearance and erudition
to an Orthodox rabbi of the old school, Silver possessed a scintillating and
non-conformist personality and a remarkable sense of humor. His dedication
and selflessness were highly regarded and he was often called upon to mediate
in disputes in communities throughout the United States."[11]

A charming and perhaps revealing story has him riding in a limo one
day. Suddenly his car is stopped for speeding. When the highway officer
reaches the car, the rabbi's driver rolls down the window and says to the
cop: "Don't you know who I have in here?" The cop politely asks who.

"The chief rabbi of the United States—that's who."

And from the back seat comes the voice of the rabbi. "And don't forget
Canada, too."

The cop looks through the car window and sees Rabbi Silver. He
salutes him. Anyone who is wearing a decorated military uniform and a
leather two-cornered military cap deserves his salute. Rabbi Silver has the
whole uniform on—and rightfully so. For a long time he'd been a good
friend of Senator Robert Taft, "Mr. Republican" (1889–1952), who,
because of the outstanding work Rabbi Silver had done for the U.S.
government, got a special law passed so that the colorful rabbi from
Cincinnati could wear a military uniform. This was especially necessary
for the rabbi's work as U.S. representative, when, dressed in a military
uniform, he had to inspect post–World War II displaced persons camps
throughout Europe. As for his claiming to be the chief rabbi of the United
States and Canada, this claim was not at all far-fetched, considering that,
at the time, he was the president of the Union of Orthodox Rabbis of the
United States and Canada.

So the drama of the two letters in Washington played out . . . and a short
time later, everyone got the news that the Skulener Rebbe was freed. Then
the Lubavitcher Rebbe made another call to Rabbi Eliezer Silver to thank
him for what he did on behalf of the Skulener Rebbe. Overwhelmed,
touched, moved—all this Rabbi Silver felt when he received that phone
call, for this was the first time that someone thanked him for his efforts in
rescuing Jews. Said Rabbi Silver: "Most of the time they don't even inform
me that my efforts were successful." Perhaps honor has its deepest source in

---

11. *Encyclopaedia Judaica*, 16:55.

self-preservation, but Rabbi Eliezer Silver, we must conclude, found a higher honor in helping a fellow Jew, and, we must also conclude, that is as it should be.

In an important footnote to this time in history, this surely *was but one effort*, albeit probably the final straw that broke the communist camel's back. Yet, probably closer to the truth was that *all* efforts to release the Skulener Rebbe helped.

Another important effort, which will also bring us back to that *niggun*, "*Yivoda Bagoyim*," the Skulener's music that soothed even the communist beast, was a certain meeting held in New York. There it was suggested that someone contact Dag Hammarskjold. If he could use his personal influence with Mr. Silviu Brucan, the Romanian emissary in the U.N., who, in turn, could persuade his own government to release Rabbi Portugal, the whole Jewish world would have something to really rejoice about in the otherwise dreary world of 1959.

Dag Hammarskjold seemed the right choice: he called his negotiating style "quiet diplomacy"—man-to-man, unpublicized discussions with leaders on both sides of a dispute and neutral statesmen. Such "quiet diplomacy" the Jewish leaders hoped to persuade Hammarskjold to use to help free the Skulener.

The big problem was, no Jewish leader, at that meeting, personally knew Dag Hammarskjold. Finally, somebody came up with the name of Harry Goodman. "Call for Harry Goodman. If anybody knows how to reach Hammarskjold, Goodman does."

"Agreed," everybody said, but who was Harry Goodman? the chassidic leaders especially wanted to know.

Harry A. Goodman was not only a successful trouble-shooter, he also held the London post as chairman of Agudas Israel World Organisation, in London. By the time he got the request from this certain New York meeting of rabbis, Goodman was well aware of most of the other efforts on behalf of the Skulener. He himself decided upon two distinct approaches: (1) he would start a correspondence immediately with the U.N. secretary general and (2), admittedly a long-shot, he would contact a certain Rabbi Kurt Wilhelm, the chief rabbi of Sweden, who was a friend of Hammarskjold from their Oxford University days.

However, some problems: Rabbi Wilhelm had nothing to do with mainstream Orthodox Jewry—he was more like very Modern Orthodox— and Goodman couldn't conceive that such a rabbi would work for a person he didn't know and probably didn't even respect. Still, advised the Satmar Rebbe, Rabbi Yoel Teitelbaum of Satmar (1888–1979), "Let's not miss out on this. If there's even a one percent chance that this can save the Skulener Rebbe from death, let's try it."

As things stood, Wilhelm was on a business trip in London. So Goodman phoned him and the two met a few hours later in the rabbi's hotel room. Said Goodman: "I would like to ask you a favor on behalf of a very respected chassidic rabbi, of whom I believe you never heard. He's now in prison in Romania and we need your help in contacting Mr. Hammarskjold, to help get him released."

The always compassionate Swedish rabbi wanted to know who that rabbi was. As soon as Goodman mentioned Rabbi Portugal from Bucharest, Rabbi Wilhelm began to weep. "He's my Rebbe," he said, "He's my personal friend. There's no need for you to describe him. I personally met him several years ago when I visited Bucharest, and no doubt I'll do whatever I can to accomplish his release. And not only that, but I'll personally travel at once to New York to see Dag Hammarskjold, to take up the Skulener Rebbe's cause."

As promised, Rabbi Wilhelm went straight to the U.N. in New York and told Hammarskjold—"Help free the Skulener Rebbe, my personal Rebbe"—that this was the most important favor he could do for him. Dag Hammarskjold, as we all know by now, put in his crucial effort, and it worked. In September 1959, the Skulener and his son and friends were released and, on March 29, 1960, accompanied by his *rebbetzin* and younger son, he was permitted to leave Romania, arriving on a Sabena airplane from Bucharest to Belgium.

As there are the so-called hidden aspects of the Torah, known as *nistar*, and the revealed parts of the Torah or Jewish tradition, known as *niglah*, now we can see clearly where the *niggun* fits into the scheme of things Jewish. As a matter of *nistar*, it weaved its way through history, and thus helped effect the Rebbe's release.

Upon his arrival in America in 1960, the Skulener continued to be, as Rabbi Wolpin noted,[12] "the epitome of love, sensitivity and forgiveness."

From the Crown Heights section, where the Skulener Rebbe lived in the early 1960s, Lubavitcher *chassidim* still speak reverentially of his abiding, deep humility. Here was a holy man who would sit attentively at *farbrengens* in "770," the synagogue of the Lubavitcher Rebbe, and remain silent for hours on end as the Lubavitcher Rebbe spoke. During those years, there were a number of other rebbes with small followings

---

12. *Jewish Observer*, ibid., p. 15.

living in Crown Heights, but it was the Skulener Rebbe that the Lubavitcher Rebbe singled out to honor and assist, whenever he could, purely out of the deepest respect for this humble rabbi from Skulen. Somewhere it is written, there is no limit to what one can listen to with the humble eye. Which is why the Skulener Rebbe listened and learned until the end of his days.

In his *tzava'ah* (ethical will) read at his Brooklyn, NY, funeral in 1982, it was reported that the Skulener "requested all assembled to forgive him if they gave him contributions for his holy work because they thought him a *tzaddik*—which (he protested) he was not. 'So let all gathered say, "*Machul lach! Machul lach! Machul lach!*" ("We forgive you! We forgive you! We forgive you!").'"[13]

In the ensuing years, thousands of followers flocked to him. With his pure character, his personal warmth, the intensity of his prayers, and the soul-stirring *niggunim* he composed and sang, he electrified his *chassidim*. He built a network of fifty-two schools in *Eretz Yisrael*, spreading Torah to children from alienated Israeli and Russian families.

Not long ago, I had occasion to be in the Skulener Rebbe's shul in Williamsburg, Brooklyn, NY, and the current Skulener Rebbe, Rabbi Yisrael Avraham Portugal, was pointed out to me as he *davened*. Not a movement, not a sigh, nor a word nor a breath emanated from his body. Like father, like son, he was solely with his God, and his soul was, no doubt, humming his father's music as he meditated long on the *Shema*.

That night, I listened for hours to the *niggunim* of the Skulener Rebbe, a picture of his face in front of me. As far as I knew, sixty or seventy of his *niggunim* were published; however, thousands of his *niggunim* were lost because they were never written down. Why I chose "*Niggun Yivoda Bagoyim*" as the final song to hear before bedtime showed me that I too had been deeply moved by this "broad-spectrum specialist"[14] to all Jews. It had to be, I was convinced. Somewhere out there, as long as songs of the Skulener Rebbe exist, no rabbis will ever again sit there like so many tombstones.

---

13. Ibid.
14. Ibid.

Most of the material for this story comes from interviews with two Skulener *chassidim*, Shlomo Yitzchak Weiss and Rabbi Benjamin Heitler, both of whom reside with their families in the Williamsburg section of Brooklyn, NY—close to the current Skulener Rebbe's shul.

5

THE MOUNTAIN JEWS

E ach and every day a Heavenly voice goes forth from Mount
Horeb,"[1] and lately the Mountain Jews of Georgia[2] have been
heeding its call more and more, to "return, return, O Jerusalem!"
Or, as the Baal Shem Tov[3] himself once put it: Whenever a Jew feels an
inner awakening to strengthen his observance of Torah and mitzvos, it is
because his soul is responding to the call that it heard emanating from God
at Sinai.

Of course, for the past 2,400 years, the Georgians, in their comfortable
dwellings in Tbilisi, Abasha, Kobuleti, and other towns like Kutaisi,
nestled in the Catskill-like mountains near the Black Sea, have heard that
Sinai voice but often preferred to ignore it, and, they say, for good reason.

After the First Temple was destroyed, in the year 3338 of the Jewish
calendar, they left Judah, vowing never to return—they had enough
rough "body work" to last a lifetime. Or, as one modern-day rabbi said
(referring to another event), "Though our bodies were sent into exile,
our souls were never sent into exile."[4] The soon-to-be Mountain Jews

---

1. *Ethics of the Fathers* 6:2. Mount Horeb is also known as Mount Sinai.

2. This story unfolded in 1993.

3. Israel ben Eliezer. Also known as the Besht. Charismatic founder of *Chassid-ism*, 1698–1760.

4. The sixth Rebbe of Lubavitch, Rabbi Yosef Yitzchak Schneersohn,
1880–1950.

said they wouldn't return until the Temple was rebuilt. But, some seventy years later, the Temple was rebuilt, and still they stayed away en masse. Why? Now, they claimed, they were waiting for the Messiah to come, and they wouldn't budge a foot off their own mountain until that happened. True? Perhaps. Untrue? Perhaps. But we'll soon see what really went on.

From their very beginnings, they were shrouded in touches of mystery, legends, and blessings. "There's a tradition among the Jews in Georgia (the 'Gurjim') that they are descended from the Ten Tribes exiled by [the Assyrian king] Shalmaneser, which they support by their claim that there are no kohanim (priestly families) among them."[5] According to Rabbi Aaron Kahiashvilli,[6] the Georgian Jewish ancestors were the exiles from Judah under Nebuchadnezzer. And, the rabbi points out, "not only were there any kohanim among us, but the Romans, after destroying the second temple, also shipped the Levites off as well as the treasures of the Holy Temple, so, for quite a time, we were left to our own devices with God."

Another legend comes through the Talmud, based on hard evidence. Rabbi Eleazer ben Pedat[7] declared that one who returns from a journey must rest for three days before he can keep his mind on prayers. He proved this by the fact that when Ezra the Scribe[8] came to the river Ahava, on the way to Palestine from Babylonia, upon the rebuilding of the Holy Temple, he rested for three days before he declared a fast and prayed to God to guide his steps. Behind him literally was the large group of Jewish people exiled to Babylonia, now free to return to Eretz Yisrael—minus the many Jews who preferred to stay in Babylonia and the Mountain Jews of Georgia, of course. When he arrived in Jerusalem he also waited for three days before he commenced his work.[9]

---

5. Encyclopaedia Judaica (Jerusalem: Keter Publishing House, 1971), 7:423.

6. Whose surname is now "Chein." He is a historian and rabbi, born in the yeshivah town of Onyk, south of Kutaisi, Georgia, who now lives in Queens, New York City. He is also the representative of the Lubavitch Youth Organization to the community of Georgian Jews, based largely in Queens, NY.

7. A third-century Talmud amora (a sage who helped compile the Gemara). Died 279 C.E.

8. Jewish priest and scribe of fifth or fourth century B.C.E.

9. Gershom Bader, The Encyclopedia of Talmudic Scholars, trans. Solomon Katz (Northvale, NJ: Jason Aronson, 1993), p. 563.

At once he had to deal with the difficulties of the giving of tithes. He was faced with the refusal of some of the Levites who wouldn't return to Palestine from Babylonia. Quickly he fined those who refused to return by taking away their rights to the tithe. It thus became impossible to include the words "and I gave it to the *Levite*," which are contained in the biblical text of the confession of tithes.[10]

There's little doubt that along the journey from Babylonia to Palestine, the Mountain Jews from Georgia were on Ezra's mind much of the time, as he bathed in and rested along the river Ahava until he and his fellow Jews returned to Jerusalem. Yet he did not penalize them; indeed, he blessed them. First, he sent representatives, perhaps following in the tradition of Moses sending out his spies to check out Canaan, to assess the situation with the Jews from Georgia, and to bid them return to the Holy Land. When the representatives returned to Jerusalem they told Ezra that the situation with the Jews in Georgia was very good; they were prospering economically and religiously.

Ezra shook his head: *No Levites or kohanim among them,* he thought to himself, *yet they are prospering.* "So be it," Ezra pronounced aloud, "if they are doing so well there with their economy and Judaism, better that they should stay over there."

It must have seemed to Ezra that the Jewish people were incomplete in Palestine without the Mountain Jews; yet, no Jew then alive could deny, to Ezra, they were just as important to him as the Jews who elected to stay in Babylonia and whom he fined. He wanted to bring them back into the fold. One explanation comes from Gershom Bader: "It is certain, however, that a large number of Jews refused to return to Palestine even after the Second Temple was built and a Hasmonean ruler governed the land. They did not consider their liberation as the expected redemption and hoped for miracles like those that accompanied the deliverance from Egypt. They awaited a wondrous Messiah from the House of David. They also disapproved of the new Temple which lacked the *urim* and *tummim*, the Holy Ark, and the Cherubim and the sacred fire."[11]

The representatives Ezra sent to Georgia came back with a similar explanation. So Ezra, who was esteemed so highly that it was said, "If God

---

10. Ibid., p. 65.

11. Gershom Bader adds: "But the lack of authentic historical information makes it impossible to give a clear description of that time." Ibid., p. 610.

had not given the Law through Moses, he would have given it through Ezra,"[12] let the Mountain Jews off scot-free.

Yet how did these Mountain Jews manage for 2,400 years in Georgia? How did they retain their Jewish connection? And without Levites and *kohanim*? One way was to "rent out" such priests and Levites, then currently living in Baghdad, whenever a *pidyon haben* (redemption of the firstborn) or another religious matter was at hand.

Another explanation comes from Rabbi Kahiashvilli: "Simply put, Rabbi Yehudah HaNasi,[13] compiler of the *Mishnah*, the oral tradition of the Torah, blessed them. It came about this way:

"Many years after the rebuilding of the second Holy Temple, the Rabbi sent *shluchim* (emissaries) all over the world to collect money for *yeshivahs* in *Eretz Yisrael*. One day one of the *shluchim* returned to Rabbi Yehudah HaNasi with a tremendous amount of money. The Rabbi himself was very wealthy, owning large tracts of land on which he developed agriculture and raised cattle, and he also owned a fleet of boats, on which he exported and imported his own wool and linen; yet he was taken aback by the generosity of this great wealth from a strange land. 'Where did you get so much money?' he asked the *sheliach* (emissary).

"The *sheliach* said the money came from the Jewish people in Georgia. 'They are still there, and well off?' the Rabbi asked, although truly he well knew the answer to his own question, for the Mountain Jews traditionally were well known for their love of Torah and *tzedakah*. In seventy years they had trekked all the way to the shores of the Black Sea, set up their homes in the nearby mountains and established themselves as excellent businessmen, yet never forgot their Jewish responsibilities to other Jews. Their communities continued to thrive. So, no surprise there that the Rabbi would receive *tzedakah* from them, yet the size of it amazed even him.

"Legend has it that he was so moved as to say: 'What is the virtuous path which a man should follow? Whatever brings honor to his Maker and honor from his fellowman. May they have a lot of success and very good religious and living conditions till the days of Messiah.'"

---

12. Geoffrey Wigoder, *Dictionary of Jewish Biography* (New York: Simon & Schuster, 1991), p. 141.

13. Son of Rabban Simeon ben Gamliel. The Talmud always refers to Rabbi Judah the Nasi only by his title of Rabbi. He was also called *Rabbeinu Hakodosh*, our holy teacher, because his contemporaries were convinced that he was the most pious man since the days of Moses.

Much of this is deeply steeped in the long lives of these Mountain Jews, many of whom live well beyond a century. Basically they have been a happy people—"God smiles on us!"—who refuse to admit to anything negative in their long experience living in the exile. Their mistakes are minuscule compared to their good deeds; all this time, maintains Rabbi Aaron Kahiashvilli, the good times have continued rolling on no matter what! This, despite that Georgian and Armenian traditions[14] emphasize the role played by the Jews in the spread of Christianity in this region. This, despite that the Jews of Georgia probably took part in the anti-talmudic messianic movements from the ninth century on.[15] This, despite that Abraham ibn Daud[16] testified to the faithfulness of the Mountain Jews of Georgia to Rabbinate Jerusalem. This, despite the numerous sightings of Georgian Jews, or at least some of them, practicing Christianity.[17] The Georgians, like all Jews elsewhere, had their share of persecution. In 1878, for example, a blood libel case occurred in Georgia, the Jewish villagers in the vicinity of Kutaisi being accused of the murder of a six-year-old girl. The trial took place in 1879, and the accused Jews, who were defended by noted Russian advocates, were declared inno-cent.[18] Little wonder then that the Mountain Jews continued to feel, "God smiles on us."

Although traditionally they are not Torah educated, the Mountain Jews have had a strong faith in the Creator of all things. For centuries they sent their best students to learn in Jerusalem at the oldest yeshivah, Yeshivah Beth El, and when these returning students, revered by their fellow Georgians as *talmidim chachamim* (Torah scholars), they taught all the other people Torah and talmudic tracts. This, they believed, was their reward while awaiting the Messiah, although, admittedly, they some-times forgot, as they lived the good life in the present, the promises from the past about the future messianic era.

What with the communists testing them every so often, they had to have a strong faith in God. "You want to hear a story?" Rabbi Kahiash-villi asked. "I'll tell you one. There was a time when the communists issued an order to demolish the synagogue of one of our mountain

---

14. *Encyclopaedia Judaica*, 7:423.
15. Ibid.
16. Spanish historian, physician, philosopher, and astronomer, 1110–1180 C.E.
17. *Encyclopaedia Judaica*, 7:423–424.
18. Ibid., p. 425.

communities. As the bulldozers rolled toward the holy building, these Mountain Jews lay down on the ground, making it impossible for the synagogue to be leveled. 'First us, then our synagogue,' they railed at the communists, who backed off totally," the rabbi pointed out with a certain pride.

Most of the time, however, they were left alone; indeed, their Georgian rulers infrequently discriminated against them. Like the non-Jews, it was enough that the Mountain Jews were Georgians, and they were treated as such. But these Jews were also known for their love of their fellowman, *ahavas Yisrael*. "According to Jewish tradition, when a person accidentally kills a person, he can flee to the place called *arei miklot*. Georgia was one of these safety zones for such Jews in all of the Soviet Union," Rabbi Kahiashvilli said proudly, probably thinking at the moment of all the Jews saved over the centuries in Georgia.

But, shrugged the rabbi, still no Levites and *kohanim* of their own! That had to be attended to. Finally, the Mountain Jews came up with a plan about eighty years ago. Dressed in their finest outfits, a group of Mountain Jews traveled to the little village of Lubavitch, spiritual home of the Rebbe Rashab, Rabbi Shalom Dovber Schneersohn.[19] As soon as they arrived, many of the townsfolk ran for cover, having had the daylights scared out of them. Undaunted, the Georgian businessmen inquired about the whereabouts of the Rebbe Rashab's yeshivah, and headed for it. When they reached it, they were "greeted" by a group of *chassidim*, who gave them a strong eye. Without understanding the almost hostile welcome, they requested to see the Rebbe Rashab. "What do you want of him?" one *chassid* asked, although knowing full well he might be taking his own life in his hand by even asking a question of these men dressed in cossack uniforms. Despite the feeling that these foreigners were probably up to no good, the *chassidim* agreed to approach their Rebbe and inform him of the visitors' request. "Rebbe, they're dressed like cossacks and wish to see you," said the *gabbai* (secretary to the Rebbe), who also had stood at the door with the other *chassidim*.

"In that case, let them in," smiled the Rebbe. "After *davening* [praying], I will recite with them *t'filat haderech*, the prayer for travelers—of course, omitting God's name in the conclusion, as I generally do."

The *chassidim* fell silent; even the Rebbe couldn't help notice it.

"Are you wondering why I assume they are Jews—these cossacks?

---

19. 1860–1920.

They are. Who else would visit me and knock gently on the door?" The Rebbe Rashab said to his *gabbai*: "They are dressed like Esau, but their voice is Yaakov Oveinu's."

The *chassidim* laughed, and off they went out to usher in the Mountain Jews.

When they entered, the Rebbe had no need to ask them why they were attired as cossacks; he knew that this was their traditional Georgian attire, despite their being successful businessmen, as they at once informed him.

What was their purpose here? the Rebbe wanted to know.

"Can you please send a *shocheit* [a Torah-law animal slaughterer] to our mountain cities? We are in sore need of one."

"Gladly," said the Rebbe, "and what else do you need?"

Another blessing, another success. The first Lubavitcher emissary was Reb Shmuel Levitin, who gave them new chassidic direction and Torah insights. Over the ensuing decades, the Mountain Jews, gaining new religious experiences from the emissaries, allied themselves closely with the Lubavitchers. As the previous Lubavitcher Rebbe (Rabbi Yosef Yitzchak Schneersohn, 1880–1950) assumed the leadership mantle, he too sent *shluchim* to the Georgians. And the Georgians continued to live a double life: they lived as if the Messiah were among them and they lived in expectation of the Messiah.

But then the roof fell in; the unexpected happened. The Soviet Union dissolved and the people of Georgia, wanting their own republic, got caught in the crosshairs of a civil war, among themselves first, and then when Abkhazian secessionists opened an offensive against Georgian troops, or what was left of them. The drive began on Thursday, July 1, 1993, with the apparent goal of isolating Sukhumi, the capital of the Abkhazia district, which was then still under Georgia's control.

During that event, Eduard A. Shevardnadze, the then-leader of Georgia, almost lost his life, according to a report dated July 5, 1993, printed in *The New York Times*. "Georgia state television said the rebels deliberately aimed [a shell] at Mr. Shevardnadze, using the code name 'White Head.' Mr. Shevardnadze has a full head of fine white hair."

But life goes on for the Jews in Georgia as if they had no leader.

"And life is terrible, devastating," said Rabbi Kahiashvilli. "The good times are over. In Georgia, it's very bad. Civil war. A so-called Georgian Mafia has sprung up, robbing everyone, threatening lives. There is little governmental control, so everyone contributes to the chaos. So-called 'Banditen'—hooligans—roam at will, stealing everything and beating up Jews—no, beating up everybody. Just recently [approximately 1993], 5,000 people, who were in jail for vicious crimes, were released outright—free to do anything they wanted; these are 5,000 killers, rapists, arsonists. And who dares to stop them! Nobody seems to care to do anything.

"As for the 50,000 Jews left in Georgia, they're at their wit's end. They must get out, flee elsewhere, leave their businesses and lives behind, if they have to. To stay in Georgia is to invite death, as it is said, 'before the silver cord is snapped asunder, and the golden bowl is shattered' (Ecclesiastes 12:6)."

"I myself visited the Georgian communities, several years ago [1991]," added the rabbi. The rabbi left Georgia as an eleven-year-old in 1972, and is now in his mid-thirties. Today, his old memories—a life of inner and outer peace, no matter who the rulers were—seem like a ruptured cocoon. "In the past, there was work for all, and you still had time to love and care for your family. Every day you accomplished what you wanted to do—with time left for Torah and doing mitzvos."

"Now," the rabbi shook his head sadly, "I can hardly recognize the town I grew up in. Generations of businesses are gone, ruined, burned out. I stood there on street corners, often under a lamppost, taking in sights I never thought I'd ever see in my birth land. Injured bodies lay on the ground unattended. Dazed people walked the streets, not knowing what to do with themselves. Store windows were shattered and boarded up.

"You know, I will tell you something else: As I stood there in all this mayhem, I couldn't help remembering the words of the Talmud: As it is said, 'With the advent of the footsteps of the Messiah, insolence will increase and prices will soar; . . . the government will turn to heresy and no one will rebuke them; the meeting place of scholars will be used for immorality . . . the wisdom of the scholars will degenerate, those who fear sin will be despised, and the truth will be lacking; youth will put old men to shame, elders will rise in deference to the young, a son will revile his father, a daughter will rise up against her mother, a daughter-in-law against her mother-in-law . . . ; the face of the generation will be like the face of a dog; a son will not feel ashamed before his father. So upon whom can we rely?—Upon our Father Who is in Heaven' (Talmud, *Sotah* 9:15)."

For a few minutes the rabbi sat silently with his thoughts.

Then, he blurted out: "Finally, now, we know the Messiah is really coming—maybe he's here already! Why do I say that? Because finally we Georgians remembered the blessing of the Rabbi, Yehudah HaNasi. It's come to pass. We've reached the end of the blessing in Georgia."

Perhaps history repeats itself. In 1969, even though there were no distinct signs that the Messiah was on his way, the urge of the Mountain Jews to settle in *Eretz Yisrael*, after 2,400 years, gained momentum. In November of that year, Israel's then prime minister Golda Meir announced that she had received a letter from the heads of eighteen Georgian families, enclosing their appeal to the heads of the Western Great Powers for help in emigrating from the Soviet Union to Israel. The text reads:

Dear Mrs. Meir:

We, eighteen religious families of Georgia, are still waiting and praying. We have applied with identical requests (there is a difference only in the concluding lines) to the Heads of the Three Great Powers and we are sending you copies of all the three letters. We are doing everything we can; please do also everything you can for our liberation. We again give you the right, if necessary, the full texts of the letters, giving in full our family names, given names, patronyms and addresses. We again ask you to undertake any measures that you consider necessary. Do not think of our safety: the die has been cast and there is no way back any more. We believe: God will help you and us.

God has helped the Georgians, as far as they are concerned. Unlike 1969, it is now 1994, and the Mountain Jews say that the Messiah is expected at any moment.

So, too, are they on their way. Currently (as of 1994), about 100,000 Georgian Jews reside outside of Georgia. Many of them settled in the United States (mostly in New York City,[20] Boston, Baltimore, and San Francisco), Belgium, France, Russia, Austria, and the Netherlands. The preponderance of them, however, are scattered throughout the towns of *Eretz Yisrael*, with forty Georgian Jewish shuls serving their needs.

Perhaps history doesn't always repeat itself.

---

20. Rabbi Aaron Chein and Georgian Jewish scholars and journalists in 1994 published a new magazine—appropriately called *New Life*—which is designed to help Georgian Jews establish their new identity as Jews in the United States. "But," Rabbi Chein points out, "the emphasis in the magazine is always on keeping the faith, studying Torah, doing *mitzvos*, and hastening *Moshiach!*"

"After all, there has never been a time like this," said Rabbi Kahiash-villi. "This is the messianic era. The Messiah—that's what it's taking for even the Georgian Jews to come down from their mountain."

As you read these very lines, most of the Mountain Jews are now safely out of Georgia and in messianic places of refuge—thank God!

6

LIVING ON THE FRINGE

he sky's blue, and so's your old man!"

One kid's taunt to another kid.

But to one man, who now wears a yarmulke on his head and *tzitzis* (fringes on an undergarment used as a reminder of God's 613 Commandments) hanging neatly out of his clothes, this cutting remark made oh so many years ago to him when he was a boy now brings joy to his heart.

"The sky's blue, and so's your old man!"

"It's the first truth I ever knew about myself," says Barry Fader, who hung up his oboe on the wall near his bed, perhaps like King David, hoping to hear the "gentle Jewish breezes stir and play his instrument." Barry holds two degrees in music and one in philosophy, is a returnee to the faith of Israel, and lives simply in Congregation M'Sosnovitz shul, assisting Rabbi Jacob England o. b. m., an Adomsk *chassid*, on a quiet street in the Crown Heights section of Brooklyn, New York.

One chapter of his story begins a hundred years ago, in Poland, where Barry's father comes from. In those days, there was a brilliant sage, Rabbi Gershon Chanoch Leiner, of blessed memory, better known as the Radziner Rebbe. For a number of years he went into seclusion and deeply studied the use of the *techelet*—the ceremonial blue dye. Perhaps the Radziner Rebbe, as a boy, had also heard a similar taunt like "the sky's blue, and so's your old man!" and he too, getting older like many other Jews, wondered aloud: "What does it all mean? This mystery of the origin of the *techelet* dye! The people of Israel are commanded to make use of the special blue dye in the construction of the Tabernacle. Each Jew is told to use it as a dye in the fringes of his *tzitzis*. *Nu?* Where is it now? Why don't we use it?"

Barry, and his father (who was not named after the Radziner Rebbe out of the blue, but to commemorate his great discovery), also learned along the way that the *techelet* dye was derived from a sea creature called the Hillazon, which contains a particular gland wherein the dye is stored. "*Nu*, so where is the Hillazon?" Barry and his father wondered, reflecting perhaps the very same thoughts of the Radziner Rebbe. More importantly, without the Hillazon, who could now carry out the mitzvah regarding the use of the *techelet* dye in the *tzitzis*? Who? The Promised Land-bound Israelites were provided a number of particular clues as to the identity of the Hillazon. Everything—the location where it is found, the geographical distribution of the species, what the Hillazon looks like, a description of the gathering of the Hillazon and the method of extracting the dye from it, as well as how the blue dye is produced, the number of simile images that point to the color of the final product of the dye—everything was revealed to Jews by our Sages and Torah and Talmud commentators. These very Sages, for centuries, had also, in one of the most fascinating chapters in the history of Jewish scholarship, discussed every other aspect of the *techelet*, including:

How many threads were dyed with it?

Does unavailability of the dye disqualify a *tzitzis* garment?

Were cheaper versions of the dye, for example, an imitation produced from vegetable sources, called Klai-Ilan, acceptable in place of the very expensive blue dye?

But it came right down to—*nu*, so where is the Hillazon when we need it? Since the end of the last century, attempts to identify the Hillazon had been almost entirely unsuccessful. Without the blue dye of the Hillazon the sublime, spiritual significance of this mitzvah might fade away forever.

So Rabbi Leiner decided to take a trip to Venice, and like most tourists boarded a boat with a bottom made of plated glass. Through such glass fish life in the waters can be seen clearly. The rabbi knew that water transmits light through plated glass and that only the surface ripples of water make it difficult to see objects clearly in water. And what he saw—the cuttlefish, a little mollusk that has ten arms and a rough, calcareous shell, is common in warm seas, and yields a purple dye—made him rush to the Naples Aquarium, where he found the very sea creature and could study it.

Even after he realized that he had at last found the sea creature from which the dye was extracted to make the blue fringe, the Radziner Rebbe still had doubts about producing it for the public. He anticipated a storm of protest. A great controversy would arise in the Torah communities, he foresaw; everyone would rush to appraise the authenticity of this *techelet*. Taking the first of two worst case scenarios, went his pondering, if in fact the *tzitzis* is no good, that the blue actually ruins the string, then one still has seven white strings left, and seven white strings still make a kosher *tzitzis*. In his second worst case scenario, the blue of his *techelet* does not ruin the quality of the string, yet it's the wrong blue—then, again, there are eight strands with one wrong color. It's still kosher, he agreed. So, at last, in his hand, he was holding the possibility of doing the only real, new mitzvah that could be done in recent centuries! This was the real thing, the Radziner Rebbe felt. Now, holding the blue-dyed string up in the air, he was dumbstruck with inspiration between the meaning of the *techelet* and the blue sky—they were both there to remind us of Hashem's presence. "You have? Hold! You know? Be silent! You can? Do!" From that moment on, the Rebbe of Radzin produced it for the public.

Holding his blue fringes in his hand, Barry says proudly, "My grandfather wore the blue fringes. And my father was named after the original founder of this group. My father's name is Gershon Chanoch. So I too am related to this group. In fact my grandfather's name is in the register of Radzinim *chassidim*, which [the late] Rabbi Jacob Englard has here in this shul at 534 Crown Street."

And that's where we now find Barry, living on the fringe, so to speak. Always wearing his *tzitzis* with the blue fringes. "Perhaps it's the Litvak in me. As you know, a Litvak is so clever he repents even before he commits a sin. So, perhaps, as my own father came from Poland, I wanted to repent—and make certain of committing a mitzvah. I'm convinced that I'm doing just that."

The connection between the Rebbe of Radzin and Barry almost was severed forever during World War II. During the Holocaust, the Nazis destroyed Shlomo of Radzin, the successor of the Radzin rabbinic dynasty, and most other Radzin *chassidim*. Fortunately, the Sosnovitz Rav, the brother of the rabbi of Barry's shul in Brooklyn, Rabbi Avrohom Englard, married into the Rebbe of Radzin's family before the War, and later set up shop in B'nai Brak, Israel, where he continues to make the dye today.

"Anybody who chooses to wear *techelet*," Barry gently warns, should be able to withstand a little static from people who don't see eye to eye about the subject. Rabbi Leiner had his hands full. With his polemical pen and authoritative expertise, he safely walked through the storm of criticism, and he produced his famous three-volume work: *Sefunei Temunei Chol* (*Treasures Hidden in the Sand*), *Petil Techelet* (*The Thread of Techelet*), and *Ein Techelet* (*The Shades of the Techelet*). "And for people who don't wear blue fringes—I warn them too—they may say they doubt the use of *techelet*, and they may only wear white fringes, but if they ridicule it, they degrade the mitzvah and are engaged in a very serious wrong."

The Lubavitchers among whom Barry lives are completely accepting of his wearing his blue fringes. They themselves, however, wear only white fringes, following the Orthodox approach which states: "Innovation in matters of Torah is strictly forbidden." Yet, by his own admission, Barry has altered his life style for good because of the Lubavitcher influence. Still, much of his own current reasoning originated from an incident several years prior to joining the sect of Lubavitchers in Crown Heights. It began, as it usually does, by a seed planted, a vision fleeting, a feeling felt a million times before but never like this before—before he returned to *Yiddishkeit*.

"By trade I'm a professional oboe player," says Barry. "My degree in philosophy brought me to the study of phenomenology, which I study quite a bit. My idea about a *baal teshuvah* is that he should not waste any of his previous education that may have been outside of Torah or against Torah. I advise him to turn it this way or turn it that way until it comes into harmony with and service to Torah. Then all his time spent before he became a b.t. will not be wasted but will be considered time in a divine plan which he brought to use.

"So I too didn't throw my training away. In my studies and philosophical investigations, I've come to realize that the most important aspect of *golus* [exile] is The Eternal—the type of ecumenicalism that's very Jewish and at the same time universal. This is summed up in the overseeing of history by God. The blue sky. That's what I was looking at one fine day in Central Park. I also wore a beard in those days, but dressed as a hippie. Visiting my parents at the time, in 1971, I went to the park with them. The contrast between me and my parents was laughable. Small, ordinary looking, respectable and quiet, they sat on a bench next to me—as I lay stretched out on my back, looking up at the vastness of sky.

"The blue sky. Above me, around me, like a covering, a purpose, a goal, an end, a finality, a direction, a dimensional level. The eye of police, judges, the Tribe of Dan amongst us. This is the blue sky. And now, later, after thirteen years of my wearing my *tzitzis* with the blue fringes, I'm convinced what I saw in the sky then is precisely what I see in my *tzitzis* now: God's watchful ever-blue eye! Yet that took time," Barry laughs aloud.

First he had to deal with the Central Park cop on scooter who suddenly came to a halt at the bench. All he could see were two gentle persons out for a sun bath on a bench and one of those pesky hippies sprawled out next to them, probably scaring the daylights out of them. So the cop poked Barry with his stick and said, "Move on. Don't bother these folks or I'll haul you away!" How shocked the cop must have been when Barry sat up straight and he and his parents walked off arm in arm! And as the cop drove off on his scooter—also blue—Barry turned back and said, as a kid of old, softly, for only the three of his family to hear him, "The sky's blue, and so's your old man!"

Every time Barry looks at his *tzitzis* he also thanks God for being privileged to keep the mitzvah of the blue fringe, and for having such a "blue" father.

7

ORACLE OF THE WORLD

PRESENTING A POTENTIAL MESSIAH IN OUR TIME . . . RABBI MENACHEM M. SCHNEERSON

The Seventh Rebbe of Lubavitch
1902–1994

In which learn of the miraculous events still going on since *Gimmel* Tammuz, June 12, 1994, when the Lubavitcher Rebbe passed away, and why many Jews still consider him the Messiah who will bring the Final Redemption.

"The song is ended, but the melody lingers on,"[1] a Jewish composer tells us, and we have every reason to believe him.

On June 12, 1994, (3 Tammuz, 5754), the Rebbe of Lubavitch, Rabbi Menachem M. Schneerson, passed away. Yet this last of the seven[2]

---

1. Irving Berlin's song from the musical show *Ziegfeld Follies* (1937).

2. Why seven? Why not eight? Why didn't the Rebbe appoint a successor? Because, notes Rabbi Shmuel Butman, "there are seven leaders between Avraham and Moshe [Moses]. *Seven* and not *eight*! By the same token, says the Rebbe, there are *seven tzaddikim* who, each in his generation, helps to bring the revelation of *Moshiach* into the world. . . . Each of the previous six Rebbes

Rebbes of Lubavitch lives—he lives—in the hearts and beliefs of his *chassidim!*

Hear this typical story, which has been retold at many a *farbrengen*: One evening as the Rebbe's personal secretary, Rabbi Leibel Groner, was with the Rebbe in his room, outside a wedding ceremony was taking place under a *chupah*. The *berochos* for the bride and groom to have a fruitful life filled the air. After that, the groom stamped on the glass, and then the crowd shouted "Mazel tov!" The *simchah* began. But after the ceremony, from the Rebbe's room the Rebbe and his aide could hear only voices singing, but not musical instruments. Why was there no *klei zemer* (musical instrument)? the Rebbe wanted to know. Rabbi Groner informed him that both families were very poor and could not afford them. Taking money out of his drawer, the Rebbe told his secretary, "Go out and tell them I shall pay for the *klei zemer*"—and there was music that night at a wonderful *simchah*.

In death the Rebbe's *ahavas Yisrael*, music to every Jew's ears the world over, lingers on, even more strongly.

Hear, then, until we have the Messiah at hand, some strange, mystifying and true tales, these hopes, these songs—all turning word into deed, all beginning at the Rebbe's grave site.

Recently, there was a young man who learned in the *kolel* at "770." The day came when he finished his studies and he had to get on with his life's work. His two options: either take on a *shlichus* and go to a *Bais Chabad* (Chabad House) or become a *rav*. What should he do? When the Rebbe was alive, he could send a note to, or directly ask, the Rebbe, whether he should do this or do that, and the Rebbe would answer him directly. In this way, the young man would receive his direction.

But by then the Rebbe was no longer physically here. So, how could he work it today? the young man asked himself. Like thousands of other Jews, and some not Jewish at all, the young man went to the *ohel*, the Rebbe's burial site, and there, with the same type of note he'd write to the Rebbe when he was alive, he read it aloud. "Rebbe," he said, "I have

needed a successor who would bring the *gilluy* (revelation) of *Moshiach* a step closer to this world. . . . The Rebbe is the *seventh* Rebbe. The *last* Rebbe, who brings the actual revelation down into this world. There is no successor because *there is no need* for a successor. The Rebbe completes the task." *Countdown to Moshiach* (Brooklyn, NY: International Campaign to Bring Moshiach, 1995), pp. 55–56.

a problem: I don't know if I should open a *Beis Chabad* or become a *rav*. Please find a way to tell me what to do." Then he returned home.

Two weeks later, this young man's aunt called him up and said she had a message for him from the Rebbe. Half amused, he said, "Yes, so let me hear."

Said the aunt: "I don't know what it's about, but I just have to tell you. Last night I had a dream in which the Rebbe came to me, and he said, 'Tell your nephew Rafael [the name was changed at the request of the young man], that he should learn to become a *rav*.'"

To the young man, it was, without question, the answer to what he had to do. Why didn't the Rebbe personally come in a dream to him? The following is partly the answer: The Rebbe once explained (*Toras Menachem* 5710, p. 149, in regard to his predecessor, the sixth Rebbe of Lubavitch, Rabbi Yosef Yitzchak Schneersohn, 1880–1950) "that sometimes there are messages a Rebbe wishes to convey to *chassidim* that are not explicitly enunciated; they are intimated through subtle or even obvious hints."[3] Part of the answer can also be explained thus: "[T]hat the Rebbe chose not to command us directly shows us that if he would have done so, it would have eliminated the test—for who then would not have obeyed? The true test of faith at the present time is complying with the Rebbe's wishes by fulfilling his unspoken directives."[4] (The Rebbe's most profound unspoken directive was his public encouragement for more than a year that *chassidim* may publicly identify him as the Messiah.)

Another story: There's a family in *Eretz Yisrael* that had an eighteen-month-old child who was unable to stand; indeed his doctors said the child would never stand because of irreparable muscle damage. Knowing that a cousin of his family was journeying to "770," the child's father asked him, when he reached the Rebbe's *ohel*, to ask a *berochah* for the child to stand. Of course, said the cousin.

Armed with the child's and mother's Hebrew names, he arrived at the *ohel* and, among all the other things he asked for, he asked a *berochah* for the child. A month later, he returned to *Eretz Yisrael* and told his cousin what he did.

---

3. M. B. Cohen, "A *Chasid* Is Not a Game," *Beis Moshiach* magazine, no. 22, 12 Shevat, 5755, p. 54. Adapted from a speech delivered by Rabbi Yosef Yitzchok Wilshansky of Tzfat, Israel, at a special *kinus* in "770," on Dec. 22, 1994.

4. Ibid., p. 53.

The father gave the cousin such a look. The cousin felt hurt. Never did he expect such a response from the father.

"What—what did I say to hurt you?" he asked.

Seeing how he had affected his cousin, the father warmly embraced his cousin, saying, "It *was that.*"

"What?" the distracted cousin again asked.

"Do you know what you did? A few days ago I came into the bedroom of Yitzie, and guess what?"

"What?" the cousin found himself asking, now catching the father's excitement.

"There he was. Standing in his crib. My child. Holding onto the crib's rail. Immediately I called in Rivka. We thought that maybe someone put Yitzie in that position. So we took him and lay him down flat again on the bed. Suddenly, right before our eyes, Yitzie grabbed onto the rail and hoisted himself up. I tell you, since the Rebbe's blessing, he's been standing all by himself."

Another story surfaced. One day a Jewish woman phoned Rabbi Groner. She told the rabbi that her husband was out of a job for eight months. "I heard," said the woman, "that when you go to the Rebbe's grave and people pray, you get help. Please mention my husband's name to the Rebbe so he should get a job." And Rabbi Groner said, "Why not? It'll be my pleasure."

On the following Friday, the secretary was sitting in his office and the phone rang. "Rabbi Groner," the voice said, "would you remember who I am?"

"Tell me your name," he said.

"Oh yes," she said, repeating her name, and added, "and my husband's name is Dovid."

"So," acknowledged the secretary, "what's doing?"

"You won't believe it," she said. "But just yesterday, on Thursday, he landed not one job, but two jobs. One in the first half of the day, and one in the second half of the day." She spoke English with a heavy emotional accent. "Rabbi, I don't know what you did, you must have done something good. I asked for one, and my husband got two jobs."

The bottom line to these stories is: "You gotta believe!" as a famous baseball pitcher called Tug McGraw once shouted as his New York Mets team won their second World Series against overwhelming odds. That's the way it seems at times for most Lubavitchers around the world, who clearly believe the Rebbe, in his new *aliyah* (elevation) away from his body, is not only doing everything in his power to implement revelations and the speedy coming of the Messiah, but that he himself is the very Messiah—dead or alive—who will bring the final Redemption.

Of course, in the eyes of many such Jews, the Rebbe is not dead at all—he's very much alive. Rabbi Groner's *emunah* (faith) in his Rebbe has not been shaken one bit by the events of June 12, 1994, *Gimmel Tammuz*, as his passing is now referred to in *Chabad Chassidus*. "Everything the Rebbe taught us—about *Moshiach*, about the *Geulah*—is 101 percent true," Rabbi Groner declared many times.

But, let us ask, doesn't Maimonides state that if someone is "presumed to be the Messiah," yet passes away, his passing thus proves he is not the one who can be *Moshiach vadai* (the certain Messiah)?

In early 1995, Rabbi Reuven Blau, at one of the many *farbrengens* taking place weekly for men or women in Crown Heights, the home of the Lubavitchers in Brooklyn, NY, had this to say:

"That is a very common misconception. Look inside the Rambam [Maimonides] and read the words very carefully. You will see that it is *not* quite what the Rambam said.

"In 'Hilchos Melachim,' 11:4 [from his monumental work, *Mishneh Torah* code of Jewish law, the only code to detail the halachic rules concerning the identity and rise of the Messiah and the messianic era], the Rambam states that if the presumed *Moshiach* is *killed*, then we know that he can't be the real Redeemer; however, the Rambam does not rule out such a holy man who *passes* away.[5] Killed? Passes away? What's the difference? you ask.

"Think of it this way: What if the *Moshiach* is in the middle of the process of bringing about the Redemption and he suddenly takes a nap for a few minutes or even a few hours? Would you think that while *Moshiach* takes time out to sleep that disqualifies him? Of course not. In only a matter of moments he is expected to awake again and get on with his Redemption business.

"Likewise, as Orthodox Jews, we believe in *Techiyas Hameisim*, the so-called Resurrection of the Dead. Although someone passes away, God can surely resurrect him within a split second, and many references of our sages indicate that this will indeed be the case with *Moshiach*, that he will rise to heaven and then return.[6]

---

5. *And He Will Redeem Us: Moshiach in Our Time*, comp. and ed. Chayalei Beis Dovid (Brooklyn, NY: Mendelsohn Press, Chai Elul, 5754), p. 177.

6. Talmud, *Sanhedrin* 98b; *S'dei Chemed*, 7: 2984; Isaac ben Judah Abravanel,

"However, if he is *killed* (as Maimonides illustrates in the case of Bar Kokhba, who was killed in a war that he was trying to win), then, it's clear that he was defeated by one of God's enemies. The essential nature of the real *Moshiach* is that he cannot possibly be defeated even momentarily, according to the criteria of *Moshiach* put forth by the Rambam. He says it clearly: *Moshiach will fight the wars of God and succeed.*[7] Being killed via defeat in war is the opposite of success in fighting God's battles. *Passing away* is no more of a contradiction than a *tzaddik*'s taking a brief nap until *Moshiach* is resurrected, as our sages have stated."[8]

We've come a long way. In fact, it has been only in "recent years, the Rebbe has transformed the concept of *Moshiach* from some mystical abstract being descending from heaven on a white donkey into a tangible reality that is about to occur now, affecting every individual on a personal level."[9]

Still another story—this one told by a chassidic group of non-Lubavitchers. A young man went to the *ohel* in the month of Elul, when, *Chassidus* tells us, the king is in the field and a good time to ask for a blessing.[10]

When he returned to his *yeshivah*, he told his *rosh yeshivah* he went to

---

Yeshuos Meshicho ("The Salvations of His Messiah") (Karlsruhe, 1828), p. 104; *Midrash Eicha Rabbah* 1:51; Shmuel Ashkenazi, *Yafeh Anaf* (5456) (commentary on *Midrash Eicha Rabbah* 1:51); Chaim Vital, *Arba Mei's Shekel Kesef*, p. 68; *Shaar Hagilgulim*, ch. 13; *Meorei Tzion*, ch. 97; *Zohar, Balak*, p. 203b; *Ohr Hachama* (commentary on *Zohar, Shemos* 7:2); Baal HaTanya, *Maamorim of the Alter Rebbe* 5568, p. 283; Rabbi Sholom Dober Volpa, *Yechi Hamelech Hamoshiach* (Kiryat Gat, Israel, Rabbi S. D. Volpa, 1992), p. 89; and *And He Will Redeem Us*, pp. 131–135.

7. Maimonides, *Mishneh Torah*, "The Laws of Kings" 11:4.

8. See note 7.

9. Butman, *Countdown to Moshiach*, p. 29.

10. "When the king is in his palace, you have to go through the *gabboim*, through his people," to get to see him or to get a message to him, explains Rabbi Leibel Groner. "Maybe they'll let you in and maybe they won't let you in. Maybe they will take your letter in or you don't know if they're taking your letter in [to the king]. Did they read your letter to [the king] correctly? Maybe they did, maybe they didn't. Who knows? [In the field] we are able to go over to the Rebbe now and tell the Rebbe everything we want, tell the Rebbe everything we need, and be assured that the Rebbe will answer us. When we go to the *ohel* now and we read him a *shaaloh* (a question), there's no question that the Rebbe is listening and that he will respond—and that we will see it [the

the Rebbe for three blessings: one, to have a good year; two, for his personal needs to be met; and third, to ask the Rebbe's help in finding out what service to God should be his.

But something quite unexpected happened when he returned to his home, he told the *rosh yeshivah*. He found his child crying on the floor of his apartment. "What are you crying about?" he asked his child. The child said he was playing with the game "Lego" on the window sill and a strong wind blew parts of it into the street. Now, he wept, "I cannot play the game any longer."

"Come," said the father, "we'll look for the pieces together in the street and bring them back into the house."

So the two went out into the street and they gathered whatever they could find. Suddenly, the father saw a page on the ground. It had Hebrew words on it. When he picked it up, he immediately recognized that it was the first page of a translated version of the *Tanya*.[11] "Where does an English translation of the *Tanya* come from out of the blue?" he asked the *rosh yeshivah*. Both principal and yeshivah student stared incredulously at each other.

Finally, the young man, the father, the man who asked the Rebbe of Lubavitch for direction knew, knew the Rebbe gave him his answer. That answer seemed printed on the very page of the *Tanya* he found. To serve God properly, he had to learn *Tanya*, and by doing so, by following whatever the *Tanya* says, he'd know what God wanted him to do with his life.

To serve God properly—this has been the Rebbe's life work. As Rabbi Shmuel Butman pointed out, "Jewish public figures have been struck by the Rebbe's intimate awareness of all details of Jewish life in every corner of the world, and touched by his concern for the material and spiritual well-being of even the tiniest, most remote Jewish communities around the globe. And his devotion to his work has been unparalleled; never, for example, during his forty-four years of leadership did the Rebbe take even a day's vacation!"[12]

Looking back into the past, one can learn a great deal about how

---

results]." Paul and Laura Deckerman, "The King Is in the Field," *Country Yossi Family Magazine*, vol. 7, no. 4, Sept. 1994, p. 56.

11. *Baal HaTanya* (Rabbi Shneur Zalman of Liadi) (Slavita, 1796).

12. "The Rebbe: Leading Our Generation to the Geula," *Country Yossi Family Magazine*, vol. 7, no. 4, Sept. 1994, p. 64.

Chassidus has improved the quality of Jewish life everywhere, merely by observing some of the important dates in the Rebbe's life, and you can look them up in Appendix D. But the one date that will remain forever in my mind is the day I first met the Rebbe. Let me tell you about it via a story I wrote about it shortly thereafter in the *Jewish Press* newspaper. Its title? "The Rebbe's Blessing."

It was the 29th of *Sivan*, 5749, and I was on the line at 770 Eastern Parkway to see the Lubavitcher Rebbe for the first time. If I found out I wasn't a *kohen*,[13] I could remarry my first wife after seventeen years of separation.

Still, scared at fifty-three years of age and far removed from Judaism, I plunged suddenly into the line amongst his followers, and the wait seemed at first pleasant enough. Close up, most of the black-hatters appeared human; but how human was I? Standing on a line that barely moved, I had lots of time to think. In seventeen years, I hadn't moved much—not even in ten times seventeen years. In fact, if anything, I was going back. To remarry my first wife would truly be a blessed thing, but to return to the ancient religion of my childhood seemed a fatal attraction. In my childhood, I had fled from a rabbi who pushed me down a flight of stairs, and now as I looked back there in the rabbi's place was the Rebbe, obviously from his pictures and posters outside the synagogue, a kind face and eyes, calling me to him, beckoning with his open hands to come back up the stairs.

Believing firmly, however, that all things must become man's allies, I began to make friends with the others on the line. They told me they'd traveled from all parts of the world to get the Rebbe's blessing, some each Sunday, some whenever they could. I told them I was here to get only one blessing and that it had to last me a lifetime. Their smiles gave me the benefit of the doubt.

Time went on interminably, and who knew why? After hours of waiting, suddenly I was moving, suddenly I was stalled, suddenly I was pushed, suddenly I pushed back, and suddenly I was all smiles, suddenly I was pressed into smells of human flesh, and dust of Eastern Parkway, with cars parked on every inch of sidewalk in the

---

13. According to Jewish Law, only a *kohen* is forbidden to remarry a divorced woman even if it is his first wife.

middle of the wide avenue, suddenly more hands than I'd ever seen reached almost out of nowhere asking for handouts, suddenly some little boy squirmed through countless legs, including mine, and moved towards the head of the line, suddenly I stiff-armed a teenager trying to follow in the kid's path, suddenly two other little boys squeezed through a crack by me towards the front, suddenly we were moving again, suddenly I was under a beard, above one, inside one, almost growing one, suddenly I felt like I had two heads, suddenly I heard somebody say, "There's a chassidic story of a man who went to see his rebbe. After being asked what he did for a living, he went into a very elaborate and lengthy discussion of his business of making galoshes. The rebbe listened patiently and then commented, 'I have met many people with their feet in galoshes, but this is the first time I have met a person with his *head* in galoshes!'" and suddenly I was doubled over with cramps and gasping for breath, suddenly I was arrogant, suddenly I was humble, and suddenly I met a man from Toronto, Canada, who had traveled from Australia the day before to get here for a chassidic wedding that was going to take place this very day at 5 P.M., in front of "770," and I consoled myself with the thought that at least this ordeal would be long over by that time, only three hours from now, and in my excitement at seeing such a wedding for the first time I asked the Canadian if he were jesting: "Is it really going to take place right here in the street?" and he said, "Where do you want it to take place, in Jerusalem?" and another black-hatter recalled the story about another chassidic Rebbe, Levi Yitzchak of Berditchev [1740–1810], who passionately believed in the coming of the Messiah. Drawing up the engagement contract of the Berditchever Rebbe's grandson, the scribe specified that the marriage was to take place on a certain date in Berditchev. Furiously, Levi Yitzchak tore the contract to shreds. "Berditchev? Why Berditchev? This is what you will write," he told the scribe. "The marriage will take place on such a date in Jerusalem, except if the Messiah has not yet come; in which case, the ceremony will be performed in Berditchev"; and suddenly I couldn't tell myself from my path, or one Wandering Jew from another, or the voice from the call, or beggar from non-beggar, or wise man from fool, suddenly I knew what Jewish fusion meant, and I had no resistance after a time but to move in its mode, until the Rebbe was a mere six feet away, and suddenly (everything, on this line, was suddenly) the rabbi closest to the Rebbe was motioning me to advance. Me? I took a step, then another. All right, I suddenly said to myself, I'd ask the Rebbe with all my heart for a blessing, but I would pay lip-service to Judaism and keep that to myself. And yet just as suddenly all that mishmash was suddenly forgotten as my eyes met the profound eyes of the Rebbe (he knew me and I knew him) and I blurted out, "Rebbe, my name is Mart, er, Mordechai, er, Ben, er, Saul, no, Sol, and I, er, I'd like a blessing to, er, to find out if I'm a, er, not a *kohen*."

What did the Rebbe say to me? Speaking in English, he said something which I was too nervous to hear. Still I could safely assume with the passing of a dollar bill from his hand to mine he blessed me.

And it came to pass, because of the Rebbe's blessing, within an hour I found out I wasn't a *kohen*. Four months later, now living a life of Torah and mitzvos, I was reunited in holy marriage with my first wife, Eleanor, now called Ada, her Hebrew name, after a seventeen-year separation. It was the Seventh of Cheshvan, 5750, Sunday glorious Sunday! *Boruch Hashem*!

Has the Rebbe's song really ended? Is the Rebbe still with us, momentarily to be revealed as the Messiah who will bring us all to our Holy Land? Clearly his melody lingers on. To such a tune, most Lubavitchers continue to chant, sing, shout, clap, dance, the words of which, for them, says it all:

"*Yechi Adoneinu Moreinu V'rabbeinu Melech Hamoshiach L'Olom Voed*" — "May our Master, teacher, and Rebbe, the King Messiah, live forever and ever!"

As for me, who dearly has loved the Rebbe in the short seven years I knew him in his physical state, when next I visit his *ohel*, I shall ask only for what's deep in my heart: "Rebbe, O Rebbe, right now help bring the Messiah, whoever he may be."

8

A BASKETFUL OF MIRACLES

O ne Sunday afternoon last month, a Subaru station wagon drove up to the stadium of the Hapoel–Upper Galilee basketball team in Kfar Blum [Israel]. Out of the car emerged Gershon Fried and Betzalel Kuptchik, two Lubavitcher *chassidim* who run the Chabad House in Safed. They were wearing yellow T-shirts with the message (in Hebrew) "Get Ready for the Coming of *Moshiach* [Messiah]" and were carrying signs that read, "*Baruch Haba Melech HaMoshiach*"—"Welcome King Messiah."

Yossi, the security guard at the stadium, began shouting, "Open the gates. The fellows from *Moshiach* have arrived!"

A bewildered bystander couldn't believe his eyes and went to the directors of the team to inquire whether the team members had suddenly become religious. One of the directors replied, "Those fellows bring us our success!"

The background for that unusual statement started way back on March 8 [1993], when Hapoel–Hagalil hosted the Maccabi–Tel Aviv basketball

This story was authored by Avrohom Shmuel Lewin. Reprinted in *L'Chaim* publication, no. 273 (Brooklyn, NY: Lubavitch Youth Organization, June 25, 1993), p. 2. Originally in *The Jewish Press*. Some details of this story were also carried in the *New York Post* and the *New York Daily News*.

team in the competition for the National League Championship. Maccabi had held the league championship title for the past twenty-three years. To beat them was like breaking a myth.

Kuptchik and Fried were aware that this being a major game, there would be thousands of fans. So they decided to utilize this event by going down to don *tefillin* with the players and the fans before the game. They spoke about the importance of placing *mezuzos* on the doorposts and about *Moshiach*. In the end, Hapoel–Hagalil smashed Maccabi "the Unbeatable," 97–69.

The next day, the Israeli papers were full of the great event. For the first time in twenty-three years, the mediocre Hapoel–Hagalil beat Maccabi–Tel Aviv. The players and managers told reporters and fans that their success was due to the Lubavitchers who alerted the crowd to the subject of *Moshiach*. A month later Hapoel–Hagalil hosted Hapoel–Tel Aviv to compete for the playoffs. Again Kuptchik and Fried went down to the stadium equipped with *tefillin* and posters and brochures on *Moshiach*. Hapoel–Hagalil beat Hapoel–Tel Aviv.

Spontaneously, thousands of fans ran into the court, hugged the players and manager, and began singing the song which has been playing on radio stations in Israel for the past year, "*Moshiach, Moshiach, Moshiach, Aiy, yai, yai*" by chassidic recording artist Mordechai Ben David. The next day, the papers were full of the news of the "Miracle in Kfar Blum."

Kibbutzniks suddenly started thinking that maybe there is something to this whole "religion" bit and contacted the Lubavitchers to arrange for classes to learn more about Torah and the subject of *Moshiach*. In every kibbutz, the hit song was "*Moshiach*" and sports programs on the radio all over Israel started their shows with the "*Moshiach*" song. The Northern Galilee was full of posters, "Get Ready for the Coming of *Moshiach*."

On May 19, 1993, Hapoel–Hagalil hosted Hapoel–Tel Aviv for the final game which was to determine who would win the championship. A day before, the heads of the team sent a fax to the Lubavitcher Rebbe for success in the game. The letter, written on official team stationary and which they later showed the media, read:

> To the Lubavitcher Rebbe *Melech HaMoshiach Leolam Vaed*:
> We members of the administrative committee of Hapoel–Hagalil Basketball team have complied with your wishes to draw the attention of the masses to the topic of *Moshiach* during our basketball games. At every game the crowd of fans spontaneously sing the *Moshiach* song and

we have permitted the hanging of posters on the walls of the stadium advertising the topic of *Moshiach*—free of charge.

During training and before every game our place is opened to Lubavitcher activities among the players and fans. We sincerely believe that our recent victories came as a result of our publicizing the topic of *Moshiach*, and we express our gratitude.

In the merit of the above activities, we request the Rebbe's blessing to win the National League Championship tomorrow. This victory will enable us to play in Europe to compete for the European Cup. And with the help of God, there, too, we will continue to alert crowds of people to the topic of *Moshiach*.

The following day, Hagalil beat Hapoel–Tel Aviv, making them Israel's national basketball champions for the first time. The director of the stadium immediately ordered new *kosher mezuzos* for all the doors of the stadium. But most of all, the team's coach, Pini Gershon, announced that he has taken upon himself to don *tefillin* every weekday from now on and to give *tzedakah* daily. When interviewed on radio and T.V., the only words that came out of his mouth were, "Thank God, thank God," and the song, "*Moshiach*."

The Israeli papers wrote, "If Pini Gershon, the 'atheist,' has decided to don *tefillin*, then we know for sure a miracle certainly happened here. Even the non-Jewish players on the team came to the Lubavitchers before the game and after to put charity in the charity box and asked for literature on the 'Seven Laws of Noah.'"

Kuptchik told *The Jewish Press* that, after the game, numerous secretaries of *kibbutzim*, who had previously been hostile to Torah concepts, have called him and begged him to come to speak to them about Torah and *Moshiach*.

9

"EXTRA, EXTRA—
GET YOUR MORNING
PAPER!"

A curious thing happened a few years ago to a chassidic rabbi named Manis Friedman[1] along the way to the Coming World. As he tells it:

There's a statement attributed to the Alter Rebbe,[2] made some 200 years ago, that when the Messiah comes we'll know about it, not through miraculous means, but we'll read about it in the morning papers. You'll get up in the morning and the paper will say, "The Messiah has arrived!"

Anyway, it was a few years ago, on the news, that a T.V. newscaster said: "The Messiah is coming. More after this . . ." and he immediately switched to a commercial.

After the commercial he returned to say that there was a report out of

---

1. Director of the Bais Chana Women's School, in St. Paul, MN, and author of *Doesn't Anyone Blush Anymore?* (New York: HarperCollins, 1992).

2. Rabbi Shneur Zalman of Liadi, 1745–1812. In 1772 he established the *Chabad* branch of the chassidic movement. His *Tanya* is the "bible" of *Chabad Chassidus*, upon which the hundreds of works and thousands of discourses by seven generations of Chabad/Lubavitch Rebbes and their disciples are based.

Israel that three great rabbis had simultaneous dreams in which they dreamt that the Messiah was coming within 120 days.

And this was on the T.V. news!

Later, I heard from friends in England and South Africa that it was on the news there, too, around the same time. At that time, or around that time, a group of the graduating class from a Lutheran seminary had visited a Lubavitch Chabad House for a lecture, and now the minister of the seminary phoned me at my Chabad House and he said, "Can you tell me any more?"

Now, as yet, I hadn't heard the news item he was referring to.

"Can you tell me any more?" he asked again.

I said, "About what?"

And he said, "Haven't you heard the news?"

I said no.

So he told me about it and then said, "Do you know anything more about it?"

I said no, "but if I hear anything . . . ," but it was interesting that he'd call a Lubavitch Chabad House.

The next day on the T.V. news, the newscaster retracted the story. He said his sources had checked with the rabbis and they all had denied it.

It seems like one story had it that one rabbi said it couldn't possibly be true, because he never reveals his dreams. So even if he had a dream he would never have told it to anyone.

The second rabbi said it wasn't true because he never dreams.

And the third rabbi said it wasn't true because he never sleeps.

The whole story was dismissed and the news people retracted it, and people were disappointed.

But that the Messiah was on prime time news is in itself a very significant thing. The Messiah made it to national news and nobody had even dreamt about it. The dreams weren't even true.

10

THE MITZVAH

On a clear day at the International Moshiach Center one can see forever—as far as the World-to-Come. On a less clear day, there are signs and banners almost everywhere, in every language, proclaiming, "*Moshiach* [the Messiah] Is On His Way—Get Ready!"[1]and "Welcome *Moshiach*."

That is the way it should be, says Rabbi Yosef Shagalov, the (former) director of the center. "The Rebbe, *shlita*,[2] told us that the Redemption is imminent and that we have to get ready to greet the Messiah. The purpose of the Moshiach Center is to spread the Rebbe's message."

---

1. The *Frierdiker* Lubavitcher Rebbe, Rabbi Yosef Yitzchak Schneersohn (1880–1950), declared, "All that remains is to polish the buttons of our uniforms so that we will be ready to go out and greet our righteous *Moshiach*" (from a talk of the *Frierdiker* Rebbe, on Simchas Torah, 5689/1928). "On the above statement the Rebbe [Rabbi Menachem M. Schneerson, *zt"l*] once commented: 'At any time clothes are merely an external supplement; how much more so here, where we are speaking of a garment that is needed not for protection against the cold, but only to glorify the appearance of official garb. Moreover, we are speaking only of a superficial detail—buttons, which merely add tidiness to the appearance. And even these finishing touches, the "buttons," are also in place already. All that remains is to polish them, to give them the beauty of an added mitzvah.'" *From Exile to Redemption: Chassidic Teachings of the Lubavitcher Rebbe Rabbi Menachem M. Schneerson, Shlita, and the Preceding Rebbeim of Chabad on the Future Redemption and the Coming of Mashiach* (Brooklyn, NY: Kehot Publication Society, 1992), vol. 1, p. 109.

2. This story was written and published on May 20, 1994, in *L'chaim* weekly publication, no. 318 (Brooklyn, NY: L.Y.O.), p. 2, less than a month before the

210

Though many were skeptical about whether or not there was sufficient interest to support a *Moshiach* center, the International Moshiach Center (I.M.C.) opened a day before Shavuos, 5753, and, since then, the forty thousand visitors (in one year) to the center, and the untold phone callers, have proven that the time is ripe. Some of the visitors or callers to the Center are not even Jewish, according to Shagalov. "All they know is that the Messiah is coming," says Shagalov, "and they want to be a part of it."

There's one phone call Shagalov cannot explain: Two weeks after he opened his door at 355 Kingston Avenue, in the heart of the Crown Heights section of Brooklyn, NY, he got a phone call from a Reform rabbi in a Pennsylvania town. The rabbi told Shagalov that his congregants had heard the Messiah was coming and insisted that he inform them the minute the Messiah showed up. How he got the phone number of I.M.C. still remains a mystery to Shagalov, but he sent the rabbi all the information he had requested, only to get a second call from the rabbi two weeks later, pleading with him to rush off literature discussing the topic of the Rebbe as the Messiah.

"Gladly," Shagalov said, "but why the urgency?"

Said the rabbi: "Because now my congregants expect me to make a major speech at my temple about the Messiah, and bumper stickers with the Rebbe's picture on them aren't enough. They're really into this, thanks to your Center." This story didn't end there. Two weeks later, Shagalov received a forty-dollar check from the Reform rabbi, making him the first member of the Moshiach Book Club.

The Messiah is not an angel from Heaven, and the Messiah's revelation is not the subject of an idle daydream, but, by all modern accounts, a real flesh-and-blood Jewish man, as holy as can be. And the world is awash with signs of his imminent arrival, as predicted by the Rebbe. It's even been said by the Alter Rebbe,[3] founder of *Chabad Chassidus*, that "the Messiah will come and you will read about it in the newspapers."

So one day recently when a CBS-TV news reporter and cameraman stopped in to check out the I.M.C., no one was the least bit surprised by their appearance.

"Tell me," the female TV reporter asked a store clerk, "What's your biggest Messiah item seller?"

---

seventh Rebbe of Lubavitch, Rabbi Menachem Mendel Schneerson, passed away on early Sunday morning, 12:50 A.M., June 12, 1994, *Gimmel* Tammuz, 5754.

3. Rabbi Shneur Zalman of Liadi, 1745–1812.

"Bumper stickers, pictures, books, you name it—anything that clearly speaks about the Messiah."

"And why is that?"

"Because the Rebbe taught us that the more we reinforce our belief in the Messiah, the more this gives him life and hastens his coming."

Then, as the cameraman continued shooting film, the female TV reporter held up a lavishly decorated tambourine and spoke (this was later shown on Channel 2 News "Live At Five"):

"Good evening, folks. It's said in Jewish teachings that when the Messiah appears, all the women will go out and greet him with music.[4] That is why thousands of Lubavitcher women all over the world right now are buying up tambourines like this. They're decorating them with flower petals and whatever the imaginative mind can dream up in preparation for his imminent arrival" . . . and the camera whirred away until the reporter had finished her segment.

Shortly thereafter, just as the cameraman was putting his camera away and Shagalov was giving the reporter some literature about the Messiah, plus souvenirs, two yeshivah students entered the store, carrying their *tefillin*. Suddenly, Shagalov turned to the cameraman and asked, "Are you Jewish?"

Until then the cameraman had said very little, but in response, now, perhaps taken aback by the question, all he could do was to nod "yes."

"Would you like to put on *tefillin*?"

At first, the cameraman looked confused. He seemed incapable of uttering a single syllable. Suddenly he opened his mouth and this time a word—"yes"—flew out. "But I don't have *tefillin*," he added.

Suddenly the yeshivah students started to put *tefillin* on the newfound Jew—first his arm, then on his head—and all during this time, the only thing he could think of saying was "Yes, yes, yes." But, then, just as suddenly, he blurted out, "But I don't know what to say."

"Repeat after me," said one of the students.

---

4. And it's also said that when "*geulah* comes, 'our mouths will be filled with laughter' (*Tehillim* 126:2), not only because *golus* will have ended, but because creation will have fulfilled its purpose. *Hashem* and the Jewish people will then rejoice together by dancing. As the *Gemara* describes it, 'In the days to come, the Holy One, blessed be He, will make a circle of the righteous, and He will sit in their midst' (*Taanit* 31a)." Menachem M. Brod, *The Days of Moshiach: The Redemption and the Coming of Moshiach in Jewish Sources* (Kfar Chabad, Israel: Chabad Youth Org., 1993), p. 158.

"*Shema Yisroel* . . ."
"*Shema Yisroel* . . ."
"*Hashem Elokeynu* . . ."
"*Hashem Elokeynu* . . ."
"*Hashem Echod* . . ."

When the cameraman had finished saying "*Echod*," he was overflowing with renewed Jewish pride. Jewish phrases that he remembered learning as a boy but had never uttered since that time tumbled from his lips.

As the CBS-TV crew left, the cameraman was overheard to say, "Too bad I couldn't film myself putting on *tefillin*."

But the mitzvah was done. And as it is said, "Let us prepare to accept the Messiah by adding to our mitzvot and Torah study, in accordance with the rulings of Maimonides,[5] that through 'a single mitzvah, one shifts himself and the entire world to the side of merit, and brings redemption and salvation to himself and the world'" (the Rebbe of Lubavitch).

---

5. Rabbi Moses ben Maimon (the Rambam), 1135–1204.

APPENDIX A

OTHER POTENTIAL MESSIAHS OF THEIR GENERATION

Moshiach Forum #2: *Moshiach* in Every Generation
A Free Translation of *Kuntres Moshiach Sheb'chol Dor*
**A Collection of Quotes from Our Sages on
the Subject of *Moshiach* in Every Generation**
Compiled by Rabbi Yosef Yitzchok Keller
Crown Heights, Brooklyn, NY
Commissioned by the International Moshiach Center
355 Kingston Ave., Brooklyn, NY 11213

★ ★ ★

Special thanks to Mrs. Basha Majerczyk
for editing and translating this
material from Hebrew to English

★ ★ ★

It is our fervent hope that our learning about *Moshiach* and
the Redemption will hasten the coming of *Moshiach*, NOW!

Our holy writings are replete with references to *Moshiach* (the Messiah), the one individual who exists in every generation with the potential to redeem the world and usher in the messianic era. The following quotes, spanning a period of thousands of years, provide historical perspective and elucidation on the subject.

1. BABYLONIAN TALMUD, TRACTATE *SANHEDRIN* 98B

Rashi,[1] the great Torah commentator, asks, "What is his (*Moshiach*'s) name?"

The school of **Rabbi Shilo**[2] says: "Shilo is his name, as it states, 'until Shilo comes.'"

The school of **Rabbi Yannai**[3] holds that "Yinnon is his name, as it states, 'His name will be forever before the sun; Yinnon is his name.'" (Comments Rashi: "Yinnon is similar to Yannai—each one interpreted the verses according to his own name.")

The school of **Rabbi Chanina**[4] says, "Chanina is his name, as it states, "That I give you a resting place (*chanina*)."

Others say, **"Menachem,**[5] son of Chizkiya is his name, as it states, 'For a comforter (*menachem*) is far from me, to restore my soul.'"

Rav Nachman[6] said: "If he (*Moshiach*) is living now, it is I, as it states, 'For (Israel's) glorified one will arise from him, and his ruler will emerge from within.'"

Rav said, "If he is living now, it is *Rabbeinu Hakadosh* (**Rabbi Yehudah HaNasi**[7])." (Comments Rashi: "If *Moshiach* is alive today, he is definitely *Rabbeinu Hakadosh*.")

Rabbi Ovadiah of Bartenura,[8] in his Commentary on *Megillas Ruth*:
"In every generation a person is born from the line of Judah who is worthy of being *Moshiach* for Israel (the Jewish people)."

---

1. Acronym for Rabbi Shelomo Yitzhaki, 1040–1105.

2. One of the Sages in Babylonia, passed away after the year 219 C.E.

3. Sage in *Eretz Yisrael*. Lived during first half of third century C.E.

4. Rabbi Chanina bar Hama lived during first half of third century C.E.

5. Menachem bar Chizkiya lived toward the end of the era of the Second Holy Temple.

6. Rav Nachman Bar Yaakov, Babylonian *amora*, died 329 C.E.

7. Respectfully known as *Rabbeinu HaKadosh* (our Holy Rabbi) or Rabbi, 135–200 C.E.

8. Popularly known as Rav or Bartenura, about 1445–1510.

★   ★   ★

Chasam Sofer,[9] Responsa on Choshen Mishpat, Likutim #98:

"Since the day of the destruction of the Holy Temple there has always been someone worthy, because of his righteousness, to be the Redeemer. When the proper time arrives, God will reveal (this) to him, and send him (on his mission). Then he will pour down upon him the Spirit of *Moshiach*, which is hidden and stored Above until his coming."

Rabbi Tzadok Hakohen of Lublin,[10] *o.b.m.*, *Pri Latzaddik, Parshas Devarim* 13; also the Abarbanel,[11] *Yeshuos Moshicho*:

It is written in the Jerusalem Talmud and in the Midrash (*Eicha* 1:70) that *Moshiach* was born on Tisha B'Av, immediately after the destruction. Is it not an explicit passage—"And the Lebanon (Temple) will fall in glory," after which it states, "And a shoot will come forth from the branch of Yishai (King David's father)"? Likewise, every year on Tisha B'Av, *Moshiach* is born, for in every generation there is one soul worthy of being *Moshiach*, if the generation merits, as we find in the Talmud (*Sanhedrin* 98b): "The school of Rabbi Shilo says 'Shilo' is his name etc." That is, each one declared that his teacher is the one soul that is worthy of being *Moshiach*, if the generation so merits.

Sdei Chemed,[12] *Pe'as Hasodeh, Maareches Alef, Klal* 70:

In each generation there must be someone who is worthy. If the generation so merits, he will be the Messenger through Elijah[13] (the Prophet). If they do not merit, he will be like the other *tzaddikim* (righteous) and no different.

If he dies, God forbid, someone else will be worthy in his place, as our Rabbis said (in Tractate *Kiddushin* 2a), "The sun shines, the sun sets." In this manner, each generation arrived at its own conclusion as to who *Moshiach* was. Accordingly, after the destruction of the Second Temple, the name of King *Moshiach* was Menachem, as related in *Midrash Eicha* (1:57). Later, that person was *Rabbeinu Hakadosh*; it was known in his generation that he was the one who was designated. After his passing,

---

9. Rabbi Moshe Sofer, 1762–1839.

10. 1823–1900.

11. Isaac ben Judah Abarbanel, 1437–1508.

12. Rabbi Chaim Chizkyhu Moini passed away in 1905.

13. First half of ninth century B.C.E.

(*Moshiach*) was the person who spoke to Rabbi Yehoshua ben Levi[14] in the Sanhedrin. Afterwards, in the days of Rabbi Nachman, it was **Rabbi Nachman**. Likewise, in each generation, there is someone fitting—perhaps the generation will merit. (Along this line, the students of the **Arizal**[15] wrote that in his day, *Moshiach* was the Arizal.) All this is obvious.

2. RABBI SHACHNA,[16] THE *REMA'S*[17] TEACHER

The sage, o.b.m., author of *Sho'el Umaishiv*, writes in his commentary, *Shai Lamorah*, on names in divorce cases by the *Bais Shmuel* (*Even Haezer*, ch. 129, gloss *shin*):

Shachna is written with a *chof*, as is *Shechinah* (the Divine Presence). Our teacher and sage, Rabbi Shachna, o.b.m., therefore indicated that his name is alluded to in the verse, "You shall seek His dwelling (*shichno*)." He (the *Bais Shmuel*) writes as follows: I have heard that there is extant in Cracow a set of Talmud, annotated by our teacher, the Gaon, Rabbi Shachna, o.b.m., on Chapter *Chelek*, concerning the names of *Moshiach*, in which he comments, "I say Shachna is his name, as it states in the verse, 'You shall seek His dwelling (*shichno*).'" This is the sign given by the *Gaon*, Rabbi Shachna.

Likewise, Rabbi Michel R. Yuzpas of Cracow wrote in the *Siddur Haget* and is also recorded in the work *Kav Naki* (on the "Laws of Divorce," Part 2, "Names," gloss *shin*, footnote 3): I also heard that when the aforementioned sage (Rabbi Shachna) learned (with his students) that portion of the Talmud pertaining to the name of *Moshiach*, in which each (school) brought biblical proof for his opinion, the sage (Rabbi Shachna) said: "If I were there, I would have said that Shachna is his name, as it is written, 'You shall seek his dwelling.'" I likewise saw this printed in a copy of the Talmud annotated from a personal copy of Rabbi Shachna's, at the end of Tractate *Niddah*.

The same thing is mentioned in the work *Margolios Hayam*, on Tractate *Sanhedrin* (98b), where the author writes, "See Responsa of the

---

14. *Amora*, first century C.E.
15. Rabbi Yitzchak Luria Ashkenazi, *Ari HaKadosh*, 1534–1572.
16. Rabbi Schachna of Lublin.
17. Rabbi Moses Isserles, 1525–1572.

Rema (Section 25), in a query from the son of Rabbi Shachna, in which he writes, 'The moment was torn asunder and the Holy Ark was captured. . . . He was requested in the Heavenly *Yeshivah*, the Light of the Exile, the Breath of our Mouths, the *Moshiach* of God, Teacher of Teachers, *Gaon* of *Gaonim*, Leader of Israel—my Master and Teacher, called by his holy name Rabbi Shalom, and known as Shachna.'"

3. THE ARIZAL

In the works *Shivchei Ha'ari* and *Eimek Hamelech* (11:4), it is quoted in the name of Rabbi Chaim Vital,[18] o.b.m., that the Arizal was *Moshiach*. Also see *Toldos Ha'ari* (Jerusalem, pp. 199, 258), on what the Arizal said about himself concerning this.

4. THE MAHARAL OF PRAGUE[19]

A letter to the Maharal of Prague, written by his student, Rabbi Yisroel, appears in Volume II of the Maharal's work *Nesivos Olam*, in section "Nesiv Halashon" (p. 83): "The Angel of God in our midst, may he dwell with honor in our land, our Righteous *Moshiach*, the King at our head, King of Judah . . . the remarkable Gaon, Rabbi Yehuda Liva, may our Master live forever."

5. THE HOLY OHR HACHAIM[20]

The holy Ohr Hachaim wrote about himself (see his commentary on *Parshas Re'ei*, 16:7) that he was *Moshiach*. "Moshiach of God, his name is Chaim." The following story is related in the work *Ohr Hachaim Hakadosh*, the biography of Rabbi Chaim ben Atar, o.b.m. (pp. 213–214): It is well known that the holy Rabbi, Rebbe Pinchas of Koretz,[21] o.b.m., especially treasured the commentary of the Ohr Hachaim. One

---

18. Mystic, 1542–1620.
19. Acronym of Rabbi Yehuda Liva Ben Bezalel, 1520–1609.
20. Rabbi Chaim ibn Attar, 1696–1743.
21. 1728–1790.

time, a printer named Asher brought him a newly published *Chumash* that contained the Ohr Hachaim's commentary. Reb Pinchas was overjoyed, but when he opened the book, it opened directly to *Parshas Re'ei*, in which the Torah states, "If there will be amongst you a pauper, one of your brothers, in the gates of your land. . . ." The Ohr Hachaim interprets this passage according to the *Kabbalah*: "These words are written about King *Moshiach*, who will be impoverished and ride upon a donkey. 'One of your brothers' refers to this most special and chosen of your brothers, who yearns to be revealed 'in your land, which God gives to you.'" The Ohr Hachaim concludes with the words, "The *Moshiach* of God—his name is Chaim." Familiar with the text of the Ohr Hachaim's commentary, Rebbe Pinchas immediately noticed that the words, "his name is Chaim," had been omitted. "Why did you leave these words out?" he asked. "Because he was talking about himself," the printer replied. The *tzaddik* said nothing, but opened the book to *Parshas Naso*. There, Rashi comments (about an unfaithful wife—a *sotah*): "And the woman shall say 'Amen, Amen'—'Amen'—I swear I did not commit adultery with the man who is accused; 'Amen'—nor with any other man" (the Hebrew word for *other* is *acher*). The printer, however, had made a typographical error. His own name, "Asher," had been printed instead of the word *acher*. "Look, here is your signature," the Rebbe said, showing him the error. The man's face turned white. (It later became known that the printer had indeed sinned in this manner.) In the work *Bais Aharon* (on *Chof Bais Tammuz*), the author writes: "Therefore, the *tzaddik*, the Ohr Hachaim, said 'his name is Chaim.' Another *tzaddik* said that the name 'Chaim' is an acronym, standing for Chizkiya, Yinnon, Yannai, and *Moshiach* (or Menachem).'"

6. CHIDUSHEI HARIM[22]—S'FAS EMES[23]

In the *sefer Siach Sarfei Kodesh* (Section V, p. 92), the Gaon, Rabbi Tzvi Yechezkel Michelson, o.b.m. (of the Rabbinical Council of Warsaw), writes in paragraph 17: "I heard that the Rebbe, Rabbi Simchah Bunam of Pshis'cha,[24] o.b.m., said of the Chidushei Harim that the Hebrew

22. Rabbi Yitzchak Meir Alter, first Gerrer Rebbe, 1799–1866.
23. Rabbi Yitzchak Aryeh Leib, second Gerrer Rebbe, 1847–1905.
24. The Rebbe Reb Bunam, 1767–1827.

letters of the word *Moshiach* allude to his name, and his mother's name (see *Derech Tzaddikim*, p. 32). I also heard in the name of the holy Rebbe, Rabbi Avrohom of Parisov, o.b.m., that it never occurred to him that his teacher, the author of *S'fas Emes*, was not *Moshiach* himself, or at the very least would cause our Righteous *Moshiach* to come."

7. REBBE YECHEZKEL OF SHINIAVA[25]

In the work **Makor Chaim** (p. 73), it is written concerning the holy Gaon, Rebbe Yechezkel Shraga Halberstam of Shiniava, o.b.m. (the son of the *Gaon*, author of *Divrei Chaim* of Sanz,[26] o.b.m.): The *Gaon* and *chassid*, Rabbi Avrohom Shlomo Epstein (may he live and be well), who was the son of my brother-in-law, the Gaon of Uzrov (may he also live and be well), traveled to Shiniava on many occasions. He told me that whenever they blessed him (the Shiniava Rebbe) in parting, by saying, "May you live to see the coming of *Moshiach*," he never answered, "Amen." Instead, he always replied, "Together with all of Israel," because he considered himself to be *Moshiach*, if the generation merited.

8. REBBE MENDEL OF VIZHNITZ[27]

The *chassidim* of Vizhnitz said of their Rebbe, the *Tzaddik* of Vizhnitza, o.b.m. (author of the *Tzemach Tzaddik*), that the *gematria* (numerical value) of *Tzemach* is the same as *Menachem*; they therefore held that their Rebbe was *Moshiach*. (From a letter by the author of *Kol Aryeh*, o.b.m., printed at the beginning of Responsa *Vayetzabar Yosef*.)

9. REBBE YISROEL OF HOSIATIN[28]

In the work *Kevutzas Kisvei Aggadah* (published in Montreal, 1947), the author quotes his previous manuscript from the year 1924, which

---

25. The Shiniaver Rebbe, 1815–1899.
26. Rabbi Chaim Halberstam, the *Divrei Chaim*, 1793–1876.
27. Rabbi Menachem Mendel Hager, the *Tzemach Tzaddik*, 1830–1884.
28. 1858–1933.

thoroughly examines the famous section of Tractate *Sanhedrin* (see first paragraph). He writes as follows (p. 502): "In *Sanhedrin* 98b, we find that each student believed that his teacher was worthy of being *Moshiach*, fervently hoping and even searching for hints in Scripture that it was indeed true." Concerning the possibility that *Moshiach* was "one of the living *tzaddikim* worthy of receiving the Spirit of *Moshiach*," he relates a story about his teacher, the holy *Gaon*, Rabbi Yisroel of Hosiatin, o.b.m. (the grandson of Rebbe Yisroel of Rizhin,[29] o.b.m.): The Rebbe of Hosiatin once remarked, "*Moshiach* will not necessarily descend from the heavens. Rather, it is possible that a *tzaddik* will be sitting at his table, nodding off with his head leaning on his hand, and all of a sudden he will wake up and proclaim, 'I am *Moshiach*!' As he was saying this the Rebbe put his own head on his hand to demonstrate."

10. RABBI AHARON OF KARLIN[30]

(From the text *Bais Aharon v'Yisroel*, Karlin, Year 6, gloss 4): "I heard from an elderly *chassid*, Rabbi Shalom Belizhiver, who heard it directly from the holy mouth of our teacher, the Alter Rebbe (author of the *Bais Aharon*, o.b.m.), who said, "Kinderlach! Do you know who *Moshiach* will be? The *tzaddik* of the generation. When the proper time comes he will be informed 'You are the leader!'" (from the writings of the *chassid*, Rabbi Mendel Tzeilingold, o.b.m.).

11. THE FIRST AND SECOND REBBES OF SADIGORA[31]

In the *sefer Otzar Yisroel* ("*Tzaddik* of the Generation," Vol. 5, p. 10), the author writes: The *chassidim* believe that although there may be many *tzaddikim* in a generation, each one of whom is exceptional in his specific area of divine service, possessing his own unique approach and special Godly powers to work wonders, nevertheless, there is always one who

---

29. The Rizhiner Rebbe, 1797–1850.

30. Second Rabbi Aharon, 1808–1872.

31. Respectively, Reb Sholom Yosef (died 1851) and Rabbi Avraham Yaakov (1819–1883) of Sadigora.

stands above the rest, who is called the *"tzaddik* of the generation." He is, in their opinion, in the category of *Moshiach*. When the time for the Redemption arrives, if it is in his lifetime, this *tzaddik* will then be revealed as the *Moshiach* of Israel. But who is the *tzaddik* of the current generation? As one may expect, there are differences of opinion in this; each group prides itself that its teacher is the very one. Faith in this matter is especially prevalent among the *chassidim* of Sadigora, who believe with perfect faith that their Rebbe is the *"tzaddik* of the generation," who is destined to be *Moshiach* only if the time comes in his lifetime. They are unique in that when they bless one another with *"Lechaim,"* they do not wish each other long life, wealth, greatness, or honor. Instead, they say, "May 'our *tzaddik*' be revealed speedily, and may his glory be revealed and apparent on earth and all therein, in our days." In the book *Fun Dem Rebbin's Hoif* (by Rabbi Yitzchok Even), the author likewise writes of his experiences in Sadigora, where he lived for many years. On page 7, he notes that the *chassidim* would toast each other, "'*Lechaim*' . . . May our *tzaddik* be speedily revealed." On page 240, he quotes an elderly *chassid*, Rabbi Avrohom Altcheter, o.b.m., who used to say, "'*Lechaim*' . . . May the pride of Israel be exalted, and may our holy *tzaddik* truly be the Righteous Redeemer."

12. THE SLONIMER REBBE[32]

In the pamphlet *Nachalei Emunah* (p. 31), published by the Slonimer *chassidim* (*Be'er Avrohom*—Jerusalem), appears an article, entitled "The Light of Moshiach," written "in memory of our teacher, the *Sabba Kaddisha*, author of *Chesed L'Avrohom* and *Yesod Ha'avodah*; on the day of his passing, 11 Cheshvan": Who is *Moshiach*? The Kabriner asked this question of the Rebbe Moharash (of Slonim), o.b.m., who was, at the time, a child of eight. The Moharash answered, "It is written, 'The breath of our nostrils, *Moshiach Hashem.*' *Hashem* is the *Moshiach*!" The Kabriner replied, "A Jew such as your grandfather [Rabbi Avraham Weinberg of Slonim, 1804–1884]—he is *Moshiach*, a *tzaddik*, one who keeps the Covenant!" These two opinions— the opinion of the Moharash, o.b.m., that God is *Moshiach*, and the opinion of the Kabriner, o.b.m., that *tzaddikim* are *Moshiach*—are two approaches taken by our Sages long ago. The Moharash's opinion can be found in

32. Rabbi Avraham Weinberg of Slonim, 1804–1884.

Midrash Rabbah (*Eicha Rabasi, Parsha Alef,* 51). The *Midrash* asks, "What is *Moshiach's* name?" and replies, "Rabbi Abba bar Kahanah said that *Hashem* is his name."

The opinion of the Kabriner is found in the same *Midrash,* and also in the Talmud, Tractate *Sanhedrin* 98b, which asks, "What is his (*Moshiach's*) name? The school of Rabbi Shilo say that Shilo is his name, etc.; the school of Rabbi Yannai say that Yinnon is his name, etc.; the school of Rabbi Chanina say that Chanina is his name, etc."

Comments Rashi: "Each school interpreted the verses according to its name." This bears out the second opinion, of the Kabriner, o.b.m., that the *tzaddikim* of the generation are *Moshiach.*

In truth, however, there is no real disagreement. The opinions of the Moharash and the Kabriner do not contradict one another, but rather complement each other. Furthermore, the two approaches of the Sages quoted above can be merged into one, according to a third talmudic discussion found in *Bava Batra* 75b: R. Shmuel bar Nachmeni said in the name of Rabbi Yochonon: Three are called by *Hashem's* name— *tzaddikim, Moshiach,* and Jerusalem. *Tzaddikim,* as mentioned before. *Moshiach,* as it says, "This is the name you shall call him, *Hashem Tzidkeinu.*" Jerusalem, as it says, "And this is the name of the city, *Hashem* is there." Do not read the verse "*Hashem* is there" (*Shamah*), but rather, "*Hashem* is her (Jerusalem's) name" (*Sh'mah*).

Now we can understand the entire matter. God's name, *Moshiach, tzaddikim,* and Jerusalem are all the continuation of a single entity. The revelation of their unity will occur in the longed-for End of Days (the messianic era), when the verse, "And all flesh shall see, etc.," will be fulfilled.

13. REBBE DOVID MOSHE OF CHORTKOV[33]

In the work *Tiferes Adam* (chap. 16, p. 29), the author writes: When he (Rebbe Yisroel of Chortkov[34]) sat . . . in the house of the Alter Rebbe, the *tzaddik,* the foundation of the world . . . he opened with these holy words: "All of Israel hoped and waited for my father, o.b.m. (Rebbe Dovid Moshe), to be *Moshiach.* He was, in truth, *Moshiach,* but

---

33. Popularly known as the Chortkover Rebbe, 1828–1904.
34. 1854–1934.

the generation did not merit it. Nevertheless, do not despair, God forbid, but have faith and trust that surely the Redemption will come soon, God willing." The same is written in the pamphlet *Ateres Yisroel* (4:2), which adds, "My father's pure and holy soul emanated and came down from the Supernal World to this world, for the purpose of building the Redemption. Throughout his life the main portion of his Divine service and holy pronouncements were on the subject of the Redemption."

Rebbe Avrohom of Slonim (of Jerusalem) said about the holy Rabbi, Rebbe Dovid Moshe of Tshorkov, that in his generation it was obvious to all that he would be *Moshiach* (*from an oral tradition*).

14. REBBE YISROEL OF CHORTKOV

Rabbi Yisroel Spiegel, in his *sefer Nezer Yisroel*, relates the words of Rabbi Yechezkel Sarno, o.b.m., who said the following: When his father-in-law saw the Rebbe of Chortkov speaking at the Great Rabbinical Assembly he was tremendously impressed by his radiance and personality. "If only we would merit the Redemption!" he declared, "for we already have the King, *Moshiach*."

15. RABBI SHALOM ROKEACH OF BELZ[35]

In *Sefer Hachasidus Mitoras Belz* ("Complete Redemption," p. 42), it is written: Our teacher, Rabbi Aharon,[36] o.b.m., said . . . that according to Maimonides, it appears that in each generation there is one *tzaddik* who is the Messiah, and when the time for the Redemption arrives he will be revealed, speedily and in our days, Amen. He further said that his holy grandfather, Reb Shalom, *zt"l*, saw the Messiah twice. The first time he saw him, he was an elderly man; the second time, when he was old, he saw the Messiah as a young man. In the pamphlet *Sha'alu Sh'lom Yerushalayim* (p. 59), an explanation is brought down in the name of the holy Rabbi, Rebbe Yissochor Dov of Belz,[37] o.b.m., who interpreted

---

35. The first Belzer Rebbe, 1799–1855.

36. Rabbi Aharon Rokeach, fourth Belzer Rebbe, 1880–1957.

37. Grandfather, passed away in 1927, of the current Belzer Rebbe, born in 1948, whom he was named after.

the above according to Maimonides—that in every generation a *tzaddik* exists who is worthy of being King Messiah. Accordingly, the first time he saw the Messiah, he was seeing the *tzaddik* of the previous generation. The second time, he was seeing the Messiah of the present generation.

16. THE REBBE OF KLAUSENBURG[38]

A student of the holy Rebbe of Klausenburg, o.b.m., writes that he heard the Rebbe explain, during his lectures on Tractate *Makkos*, that when the *Baalei Tosefos* quotes something in the name of his teacher, and concludes with the acronym "*Moshiach*" (standing for the words "*Mori, sheyichyeh*"—literally, "my teacher, may he live"—see *Amar Rabbah* 6a), his intention is to allude to the Talmud in *Sanhedrin* 98b, which refers to *Moshiach*'s name. "We see that the students believed so strongly in the greatness of their teacher that they found hints in the Torah to prove that he was *Moshiach*, for whom the whole world was created (Rabbi Yochanan, ibid.). The *Baalei Tosefos*, therefore, concluded their teacher's words with the acrostic "*Moshiach*" to indicate their faith that their teacher was indeed *Moshiach*.

From the *sefer Ner Yisroel Ruzhin* (Vol. II, p. 151):
Our Master (the holy Rabbi Avrohom Yaakov) of Sadigora, o.b.m., once spoke about the dispute between the *Mahari Bey Rav* and the *Maharalnac*, o.b.m., on the subject of ordination (see end of Responsa of the Maharalnac, and *Shem Hagadolim* by the *Chida*, o.b.m., "Rabbi Yaakov Mahari Bey Rav"). The *Mahari Bey Rav* said that his ordination of the *Bais Yosef* and other students caused a great accusation to be leveled against him in the Heavenly Court, but that he ordained them anyway. Were it not for the controversy they would have merited the Redemption, as it states in Isaiah 1:26, "And I will return your judges as of old, and your advisors as at the beginning; afterward, they will call you the City of Righteousness, a Faithful City." The passage indicates that ordination is required first—only afterward will we merit the ingathering of the exiles. Furthermore, he continued, in the times of the Great *Maggid* of Mezeritch,[39] o.b.m., a similar thing happened. The *Maggid* once asked his students as they sat around the table, "Do you agree that I am the head of the generation?"

---

38. Rabbi Yekutiel Yehudah Halberstam, 1904–1994.
39. Rabbi Dov Ber, 1704–1772.

The students were embarrassed to answer. Three times he repeated his question, but they remained quiet.

Later, he explained: "If you had agreed with me, we would have merited the Complete Redemption. For through my divine service, I had already effected on High that the Redemption would occur."

"Why do you assume more responsibility than the rest of the generation?" they asked.

"Because I am the head of the generation," the *Maggid* replied. "I was trying to gain your approval (the concept of "ordination" before "Redemption"). If you would have agreed, the Redemption would have occurred."

This is also the reason Maimonides[40] authored a book of Jewish legal decisions, *Yad Hachazakah*, which did not mention differing opinions but only included those that were agreed upon by everyone. For Maimonides was descended fom the royal lineage of King David, and wanted to be *Moshiach*. The world, however, was not yet deserving, and criticized him.

From *Stories of Our Master, the Ramach* (by Rabbi Mordechai Slonimer, B'nai Brak, 1989, p. 228):

The holy Rabbi, Rebbe Yisroel of Rizhin, o.b.m., sent letters to the *tzaddikim* of his generation for their consent that he is *Moshiach*. Rebbe Meir of Premishlan, o.b.m.,[41] even agreed to give him the *spodek* (fur hat) that had belonged to his father (the holy Rebbe Aharon Leib, o.b.m.).

In the work *Imrei Pinchas* (Rabbi Pinchas Shapiro of Koretz, p. 203), the author cites the following in the name of Rabbi Gedalia of Linitz, who said, in the name of his teacher, a student of the Baal Shem Tov:[42]

A person who can find good in everyone is in the category of *Moshiach* . . . *Moshiach* will come to the defense of all of Israel, even the wicked.

We now stand at an especially propitious time, for we have recently witnessed many miracles and great wonders around the world, and the *tzaddikim* of our generation have given testimony that we are on the threshold of the redemption.

May it be God's will that we merit the coming of King *Moshiach* of our own generation and his immediate revelation now!

---

40. Also known as the Rambam, from the acronym Rabbi Moses ben Maimon, 1135–1204.

41. 1780–1850.

42. Rabbi Yisrael ben Eliezer, founder of *Chassidus*, 1698–1760.

Appendix B

The Hall of
Shameful Messiahs

THEUDAS

In 44 C.E., the historian Josephus reports a would-like-to-be Messiah—a certain imposter named Theudas. His many followers proclaimed him the Messiah. He urged all his followers to follow him with their belongings to the Jordan River, which, with God's help, he threatened to dry up. The Roman procurator Cuspius Fadus, mindful of the trouble a previous Messiah had caused his predecessor Pontius Pilate, took no chances and ordered the immediate death of Theudas and all his adherents. Fadus sent a troop of horsemen after him and his band, slew many of them, and took others captive. To ensure immediate death, Theudas was beheaded, and then his head was paraded in Jerusalem as a warning.[1]

JUDAS OF GALILEE

Judas of Galilee, founder of the Zealots, led a rebellion against Rome's tax collector Cyrenius, who wanted the Jewish estate holders to open their books; they refused and turned to Judas and his sons Simon and James for

---

1. *The Works of Josephus, Antiquities of the Jews,* trans. William Whiston (Hendrickson Publishers, 1987), p. 531.

divine help; after all, Judas claimed to be the Messiah come to deliver the Jews. The Romans caught up with his sons and crucified them.[2]

BENJAMIN THE EGYPTIAN

Around 59 c.e., the so-called Egyptian Messiah, one "Benjamin the Egyptian," assembled 30,000 followers, with whom he marched up to the Mount of Olives (*Har Hazaysin*), opposite Jerusalem. From that vantage point, Benjamin announced that he would now make the walls of Jerusalem tumble down, a la Joshua before Jericho, but an unimaginative Roman procurator, Felix, broke up the historic meeting. Of Benjamin, "the Lord's anointed" (so he said), no more was ever heard.[3]

MENACHEM SON OF JUDAS OF GALILEE

Around 66 c.e., the inventive son of Judas of Galilee (*inventive* because he skipped his date with death when his brothers got the meat hook) and grandson of Hezekiah, the leader of the Zealots, one Menachem (Josephus, *Wars of the Jews* 2:444–448), announced that he was Messiah and, with men armed from and by a raid on the fortress of Masada, marched upon holy Jerusalem, where he captured the fortress Antonia, overpowering the troops of Agrippa II. He set himself up as—or behaved like—a king, only to incur the wrath of Eleazer, another Zealot leader.

THE FLAMING PROPHET

"Even when Jerusalem was already in process of destruction [70 c.e.] by the Romans, a prophet, according to Josephus suborned by the defenders to keep the people from deserting, announced that God commanded them to come to the Temple, there to receive miraculous signs of their deliverance. Those who came met death in the flames."[4]

---

2. Ibid.

3. Leo Rosten, *The Joys of Yiddish* (New York: Pocket Books, 1968), p. 478.

4. *The Jewish Encyclopedia*, vol. X (New York: Funk & Wagnalls, 1912), p. 252.

MOSES OF CRETE

Moses of Crete was a fifth-century c.e. Messiah—false, of course. He convinced the Jews of Crete that he was the Messiah who had come to lead them to the Promised Land. How to reach it was simplicity itself. He would smite the waters with his staff, which would part as the Red Sea had parted for Moses of Sinai, and they would walk across the Mediterranean Sea to the Holy Land. On the appointed day, the Jews of Crete gathered on the promontory jutting into the Mediterranean and boldly leaped into the sea after their Messiah. History records that those who could not swim were drowned, but fails to record whether or not those who lost their lives saved their souls. Among those who drowned was Moses of Crete himself, for he could not swim either.[5]

ABU ISA AL-ISFAHANI

In the eighth century c.e., an illiterate and plain tailor from Isphatan, Persia, named Abu Isa al-Isfahani pressed the messianic crown on himself and "declared that, whereas Moses was only a prophet, he was the fifth and last Messiah chosen to reveal final revelation and deliver Israel from the yoke of the Gentiles." By conferring prophethood on any rabbi joining his cause, he succeeded in raising an army of 10,000 Jews, which he marched against Caliph Abd ad-Malik in an eschatological showdown to expel the Mohammedans from Palestine and restore that land to the Jews. A forerunner of Anan and the Karaites, Abu Isa held hostile views to prevailing rabbinic traditions of the day. The age was one of revolt against talmudic authority, and sects were springing up in Jewry, culminating in the great Karaite movement of the eighth and ninth centuries. His touching faith in his own invulnerability was cruelly shattered by his death (755 c.e.) on the battlefield at the hands of the Caliph at Rai, and his followers were scattered.[6]

---

5. Max I. Dimont, *The Indestructible Jews* (New York: NAL Books, 1971), p. 127.

6. Abba Hillel Silver, *A History of Messianic Speculation in Israel* (New York: Macmillan, 1927), pp. 55–56.

SERENE

Another eighth-century c.e. wannabe Messiah, Serene, "a gentleman from Baghdad . . . in 720 c.e. threw his credentials into the messianic ring. In promising to restore Palestine to the Jews after expelling the Mohammedans, he gained a large following. Writing in 755 c.e., Isador Pacensis narrates that many Spanish and French Jews, believing implicitly in the Messiahship of Serene, abandoned their homes and their possessions and set out to meet him; there was no turning back as their former ruler confiscated their property."[7] Serene, it turns out, is the only messianic coward on record. When captured and haled before Caliph Yazid II as a rebel, he faced death not like a martyr but was prostrate in fear. Renouncing his messianic crown, he pleaded that he had deliberately planned to mislead and to mock the Jews. No crowds mocked him outside the caliph's palace or shouted "Crucify him," but the caliph nevertheless turned him over to a Jewish court for punishment. His followers were taken back into the fold after giving up their heretical ideas. There is no record of Serene's resurrection, even though he and his followers violated rabbinic law and set at naught many of the traditions originating with the rabbis, even as the followers of Abu Isa had done.

DAUGHTER OF JOSEPH

"Daughter of Joseph" (her name was buried with her body) was probably the world's only female Messiah. Around 1120 c.e., in Baghdad, "the daughter of Joseph, a young woman, just married, saw a vision of the Prophet Elijah. The appearance of Elijah has always been accepted as the forerunner of the Messiah. The Jewish community became convinced that she was their redeemer. The Caliph, after threatening to have her burned, had a change of heart. He himself had a dream which he accepted as proof that she was indeed the Messiah, and as a result he ordered the release of the Jewish men [from prison] and a special dispensation that they be relieved from certain taxes. After this event, the Daughter of Joseph fades into oblivion."[8]

---

7. Ibid., p. 56.

8. Sondra Henry and Emily Traitz, *Written Out of History* (New York: Biblio Press, 1990), p. 76.

MENACHEM BEN SOLOMON

Menachem ben Solomon was born in Kurdistan, but he became famous as David Alroy. Adventurer, magician, and warrior, he appeared about 1147, during the Second Crusade, taking advantage of the disturbed and weakened condition of the caliphate and the discontent of the Jews, who were burdened with a heavy poll tax. He showed miraculous signs to the Jews, declaring that God had sent him to capture Jerusalem and to lead them forth from among the nations. They wanted the Messiah so badly that they rallied round his messianic flag—himself. The warlike Jews of the neighboring district of Azerbaijan and his coreligionists of Mosul and Baghdad at once proclaimed him the Messiah. With his followers, Alroy waged war on the Sultan Muktafi's forces and managed to capture his native town of Amadia in Kurdistan. He then dispatched messengers to many communities, including Baghdad, to prepare for his military advance. His messengers told the Jews of Baghdad to assemble on their rooftops on a certain night in order to be flown miraculously to join the Messiah. Many Baghdad Jews obeyed and spent the night on their roofs. The official Jewish leadership condemned the movement and threatened its adherents with excommunication, while the local authorities began to take energetic measures against his influence. His movement failed: Alroy was captured and imprisoned for conspiracy and political agitation. Rumors of his magical escape from prison are in keeping with the miracles ascribed to the Messiah. Although Benjamin of Tudela, a contemporary, in his itinerary reported that Alroy, "after failing to heed the appeal of the Jewish leaders of Baghdad and Mosul . . . was finally assassinated, while asleep, by his father-in-law, who was bribed by the governor of Amadia." When the Jews of Iraq went to Israel in 1950–1951 they called one of their settlements Kefar Alroy ("Alroy's Village").[9]

YEMENITE MESSIAH

Re the *meshugge* case of the "Yemenite Messiah": Jacob al-Fayyumi drew Maimonides' attention to the appearance of a false Messiah in 1172 C.E. in Yemen. In his *Epistle to Yemen*, he wrote, in answer to al-Fayyumi's letter:

---

9. Geoffrey Wigoder, *Dictionary of Jewish Biography* (New York: Simon & Schuster, 1991), pp. 25–26.

In Yemen there arose a man who said that he was the messenger of the Messiah, preparing the way for his coming. He also announced that the Messiah would appear in Yemen. Many Jews and Arabs followed him. He traversed the country and misled the people, urging them to follow him and to go to meet the Messiah. Accordingly, many Jews and Arabs gathered round him and they followed him into the mountains. He led them astray with such speech as: "Follow me! Let us go forth to greet the Messiah for he has sent me to announce his coming!" Our brothers in Yemen wrote me a long letter in which they apprised me of his practices and customs, of the innovations he introduced into the synagogue service, and in general of what he spoke to them. They informed me of all the miracles they had seen him perform and asked me for my opinion thereon. I understood from what they wrote, that poor man was ignorant although God-fearing, and everything he said or did was either a lie or an illusion. I feared for the safety of the Jews living there, and so I wrote them three letters about the Messiah, about his signs by which men could know him and about the signs of the times in which he would make his appearance. I exhorted them to warn that misguided man in order that he should not go down to destruction and thereby drag the entire community into it with him. The upshot of the matter was that at the end of the year the man was caught and all his followers deserted him. When brought in chains before the Arab king of Yemen and asked for a miracle to prove his assertion that he was born the son of God and not the father of a usurpation, our aspirant unhesitatingly stated, "Cut off my head and I will return to life again."

"You couldn't possibly give me a better sign than that," said the king, "and if what you claim comes true, I and the whole of mankind will believe in you and in the truth of your words, and contrariwise, we will recognize that our fathers practiced nothing but lies, deceits and vanity!"

Thereupon the king commanded: "Bring a sword!"

So they brought a sword and, at the command of the king, they chopped the unfortunate man's head off . . .

May his death serve as his atonement for himself and for all Israel!

Heavy money fines were exacted from Jewish communities in many places. To this day there are ignorant men who believe that he will arise from his grave and appear . . .

ABRAHAM ABULAFIA

Abraham Abulafia had a strong sense of who he was in the thirteenth century (specifically 1240–1291). The number thirteen had to be his lucky number because, he was convinced, this was the right time to declare himself the Messiah for the thirteenth-century Jews. How did he know that? A little birdie inside him told him, he asserted. He was no poor soul looking for something to do with his life. Abulafia, steeped in the *Kabbalah* and other mysteries of life, came from a prominent Spanish Jewish family and was hailed by his followers—and himself—as a new breed of scholarly, European-born, Christian-oriented pretender Messiah. That same whispering birdie, which must have stoked (through words and sound) the vision Abulafia had in the Holy Land, told him to hurry home and declare himself a prophet. With that same voice as a traveling companion, Abulafia went to Rome to convert Pope Nicholas II to Judaism. The miracle was not so much that Abulafia escaped being burned at the stake the next day, the real miracle was that he actually obtained an audience with the pope, told him what his real intention was, and walked out unharmed that very day—and lived to tell about it! Finally, he fled to Sicily; there, Abulafia told the Jews he was their Messiah man for all seasons, but the rabbis, thinking otherwise, excommunicated him, worried lest he try to convert another pope. So, Abulafia disappeared—another sincere but myopic visionary falling into a fading footnote of history.

NISSIM BEN ABRAHAM

In 1295, a Messiah appeared in Avila, Spain. Born Nissim ben Abraham, he announced he would inaugurate the Redemption on the last date of the month of Tammuz. Mass fasting promptly began, worldly possessions were given away, prayers and ecstasies accompanied the impatient wait for the commencement of the kingdom of God. Finally, they came together on the appointed day. But instead of finding the Messiah—alas, poor Jews!—some saw on their garments little crosses, perhaps pinned on by unbelievers to ridicule the movement. Disappointed, some of Nissim's followers embraced Christianity. As for Nissim himself—he went off and away![10]

---

10. *Jewish Encyclopedia*, vol. X, p. 253; and Leo Rosten, *Joys of Yiddish*, p. 480.

ABNER OF BURGOS

Abner of Burgos was a fourteenth-century Jew from Castile, whose "apostasy was abetted by a messianic delusion that had swept over much of Castellian Jewry in 1295. In the ensuing hysteria and irrationality that gripped both the Jewish and Christian communities, all types of dreams, visions and supernatural events were reported. Abner himself claimed to have had a vision that set him on the road to apostasy. . . . After a long period of apparent self-doubt, Abner publicly converted to Christianity in 1320. He wrote a polemic (in Hebrew) asserting the truth of Christianity and this work was widely disseminated by the Church among Jews. This marked the implementation of the Church's first 'Jews for Jesus' stratagem."[11]

RABBI ASHER LEMMLEIN

In 1500, Rabbi Asher Lemmlein, a German Jew, began preaching in Istria, near Venice, of repentance and the coming of the Messiah, which he said would come that year. The year 1500 became known, even among Christians, as the "year of repentance." He appeared in Venice in 1502, modestly announcing that he was the Prophet Elijah. Because of his modesty he was exalted by the Jewish populace as a messiah. Lemmlein asked the Jews to purify themselves in preparation for being whisked to the Holy Land in a heavenly chariot or a pillar of cloud and smoke. David Gans (1541–1613), in his chronicle *Zemah David*, reminisced that his grandfather "Seligman Ganz smashed his oven in which he baked his *matzos*, being firmly convinced that the next year he would bake his *matzos* in the Holy Land." But when neither the chariot nor pillars of clouds appeared on the appointed day, many Jews, who had undergone severe fasting in preparation for the event, felt cheated and had themselves baptized into Christianity on the rebound. As far as anybody knows, the "Messiah" either died or disappeared.[12]

---

11. Berel Wein, *Herald of History: The Story of the Jews in the Medieval Era 750–1650* (Brooklyn, NY: Shaar Press, 1993), p. 197.

12. Max Dimont, *The Indestructible Jews*, p. 200.

DAVID REUVENI

David Reuveni (1490–1535) was an adventurer who inspired the pseudo-Messiah Solomon Molkho (1500–1532, whose Spanish name was Diego Peres). The Jewish gnome Reuveni appeared in Venice in 1523, "said he was commander of the army of his brother, a prince of the tribe of Reuben (hence the name 'Reuveni') who ruled over the lost tribes of Reuben and Gad, and half the tribe of Manasseh in the far-off desert of Habor. Some have suggested he was an Ethiopian Jew. The following year he arrived in Rome, riding a white horse, and was received by Pope Clement VII. . . . His presence in Portugal (1525– 1527) [where King John III received him with great honors] aroused intense fervor among the Marranos, the crypto-Jews . . . one of them, Diego Peres, left a high position in the government, declared himself a Jew, and dedicated his time to the study of the Torah. He changed his name to a Hebrew name, 'Solomon Molkho,' and set off for Salonika and Safed, attracted by the study of the *Kabbalah* there."[13] Solomon Molkho later joined David Reuveni in a campaign to enlist the aid of Emperor Charles V of Rome in a combined crusade against the Turks. Charles clapped them in irons and turned them over to the Inquisition. When asked if he was the messiah, in much the same manner as Jesus was asked by Pilate if he was "King of the Jews," Molkho's answer was, "God forbid," which proved to the Inquisition that he was a blasphemer. Molkho was burned. Reuveni escaped from prison and vanished from history.

SHABBETAI TZEVI

At a young age, Shabbetai Tzevi declared himself to be the Messiah. A Sephardi Jew of Spanish descent, he was born in Smyrna in 1626, on the Ninth of Av, his press releases would herald, the Ninth of Av being the traditional date of *Moshiach*'s birth known since the Second Temple was destroyed in the year 70 of the Common Era. He was by all accounts a

---

13. Wigoder, *Dictionary*, p. 417.

man of such personal beauty and extraordinary charm that Jews accepted his messianic pretensions unquestioningly. He also suffered from manic-depressive states. Packaged by Nathan of Gaza as the Messiah, this young man, whose father was a broker to an English merchant, was sent to the finest schools and was fluent in Hebrew and Arabic; this young man, who sang psalms very sweetly, was much loved by children and was so deeply taken up by the mystical teachings of the famous kabbalist, the Holy Ari, Rabbi Yitzchak Luria Ashkenazi; this man, who heard voices from heaven ordering him to redeem Israel, seemed to have been able to induce prolonged ecstatic states in himself. In Salonika, in the prophetic year 1648, as a twenty-one-year-old Turkish Jew, he announced that he was the Messiah. This strange man's evangelistic itinerary took him to Egypt and his celebrated marriage there to a prostitute who literally walked into his life. It was for the enterprising Nathan of Gaza, to whom the pseudo-messiah Shabbetai Tzevi turned, to put the finishing touches on him. From that point, together with his mentor Nathan and wife Sarah, Shabbetai Tzevi proceeded to turn the Jewish world upside down. "One Sabbath in the synagogue, he defiantly pronounced the tetragrammaton name of God, traditionally forbidden to all except the high priest on the Day of Atonement, and announced the cancellation of certain fast days, notably the 9th of Av."[14] He also married a Torah scroll under a *chupah*, publicly kept the holidays of Passover, Shavuos and Sukkos all in one week, declared that mitzvos were abolished, turned fasts into feasts, abolished the separation of men and women in shul, and "substituted his own name for that of the sultan in the prayer for the authorities. He also announced that he would now have intercourse with his wife for the first time and next morning produced the traditional 'evidence' of her virginity! He then announced that he was dividing his territories into twenty-six kingdoms, to be allocated to his colleagues, each being given a biblical title, with his brother being called 'King of Kings.'"[15] Despite his being excommunicated and banned and expelled by the Orthodox rabbinate of many areas, most Jews, including prominent rabbis and

---

14. Ibid., p. 472.
15. Ibid.

scholars, ate him up; by 1665 the whole diaspora was under his spell; over one million Jews, "from every stratum of society, rich man, poor man, scholar and worker, from Turkey to England, all hailed him as the long-awaited deliverer."[16] It appeared as if Jews couldn't get enough of him. Shabbetai Tzevi was not a leader nor a sage learned in Torah. His life was characterized by distorting Torah law rather than by strengthening it. Had the Jewish masses known and paid attention to the halachic definition of the potential *Moshiach*, they would not have put any faith in him and this unfortunate chapter in our history would never have occurred. Yet it did, and before Shabbetai Tzevi sailed from Smyrna to Constantinople to depose the sultan and set up his messiahship in 1666, Nathan his advance man announced that he had a new vision revealing that 1666 would be the Year of the Redemption, "when Shabbetai Tzevi would ride into Jerusalem on a lion, with a seven-headed serpent, as its bridle."[17] God surely works in mysterious ways: in this case, the sultan arrested Shabbetai and gave him an ultimatum: Choose Islam or die! Shabbetai chose Islam, and left it to his press agent Nathan to turn things around in his favor. Without a blink of his shameful eyes, Nathan of Gaza did another mirror trick, telling the world that it was perfectly natural for his prodigy to do exactly that. Hadn't the Messiah voluntarily undertaken suffering in order to ease the sufferings of Israel! Yes, yes, and so must Shabbetai Tzevi. He went along with the sham as reason took a holiday. In 1676, on Yom Kippur, the Day of Atonement, Shabbetai Tzevi died a prisoner of the sultan, yet the Shabbetean psychosis continued to be borne out by many of his adherents up to the twentieth century. For them Shabbetai Tzevi was the Messiah who definitely would return one day.

JACOB FRANK

Jacob Frank (1726–1791) regarded himself as the reincarnation of Shabbetai Tzevi. "However," wrote Geoffrey Widoger, "he developed a

---

16. Max I. Dimont, *Jews, God and History* (New York: Signet Books, 1994), p. 275.

17. Wigoder, ibid., p. 473.

simpler theology, with a trinitarian basis that paralleled Christianity (God, the Messiah, and the *Shechinah*, a female hypostasis of God)."[18] "Anybody, according to him [Frank], could find redemption through purity. The unique way of finding redemption was through impurity."[19] He and his daughter Eve lived in palaces, thanks to his many followers. The "rabbis excommunicated him in 1756 for his heretical teachings, antinomianism, and transgression of the commandments. . . . The Frankists for their part put themselves under the protection of the Catholic bishop of Kamienic-Podolski. . . . Frank declared himself a living embodiment of God's power and said that he and his adherents were destined to adopt Christianity as a guide."[20] "The Frankists . . . marched in giant numbers to the baptismal font, with the nobles of Poland as their godfathers and the king of Poland himself as the godfather of Frank. . . . Frank died in 1791 of apoplexy, but Frankism was a few more years in dying. It was carried on by his charming daughter Eve, in the tradition of her father. She preserved the dues-paying membership of Frankism by combining the scholasticism of the *Zohar* with the mysteries of her bedroom into a lucrative religion which enabled her to live in the grand style of her father."[21] Eve Frank died in 1817, in heavy debt and poverty.

---

18. Widoger, ibid., p. 150.
19. Dimont, ibid., pp. 277–278.
20. *Jewish Encyclopedia*, vol. X, p. 255.
21. Dimont, *Jews, God and History*, p. 28.

APPENDIX C

OUTSTANDING TORAH PERSONALITIES, TALMUDIC SAGES, RABBIS, AND CHASSIDIC REBBES MENTIONED IN THIS BOOK

Aaron, Moses' brother and first high priest, thirteenth century B.C.E.

Aaron of Karlin, Rebbe, 1736–1772.

Abraham, biblical patriarch and traditional originator of monotheism, nineteenth century B.C.E.

Abraham Gershon of Kutow, Rabbi, brother-in-law of the Baal Shem Tov.

Abraham of Sachatzov, Rabbi, son of Rabbi Nathan Zeev Bialer, died 1910.

Abraham Yeshayahu Karelitz, the *Chazon Ish*, Rabbinic authority, 1878–1953.

Aharon of Belz, fourth Belzer Rebbe, 1880–1957.

Akiva ben Yosef, Rabbi, 40–135 C.E. Jewish Sage and martyr in Palestine.

Amos, biblical prophet, eighth century B.C.E.

Avraham Hamalach, Rabbi, son of the Great *Maggid*, 1740–1776.

Avraham Mordechai Alter, third Gerrer Rebbe, *Imrei Emes*, 1886–1948.

Avraham Yehoshua Heshel of Apta, the Apta Rabbi, the *Oheiv Yisrael*, 1755–1825.

Ben-Gurion, David, Israeli statesman and first Prime Minister of Israel, 1886–1973.

Chaim Halberstam of Sanz, the Sanzer Rebbe, the *Divrei Chaim*, 1793–1876.

Chaim Vital, Rabbi, kabbalist, and mystic, 1543–1620.

Chana Rochel Werbermacher, Holy Virgin of Ludmir, 1805–1892.

Chiya bar Abba, *amora*, third generation.

Cordovero, Moshe, known as the *Remak*. Mystic and moralist, 1522–1570.

David, King, second and greatest king of Israel, 1037–967 B.C.E.

Dov Ber of Mezeritch, the Great *Maggid*, 1704–1772. Successor to the Baal Shem Tov.

Dov Ber Schneersohn of Lubavitch, second Lubavitcher Rebbe, the Mitteler Rebbe, 1773–1827.

Eibeschutz, Jonathan, circa 1690–1764. Rabbi, talmudist, and kabbalist. Author of the famous works *The Tumim* and *Ya'arot Devash*.

Elazar Shapiro of Lanzhut, Strizhover Rebbe, circa 1805–1865.

Eleazer ben Pedat, died 279 C.E. *Amora*, third century, who helped compile the *Gemara*.

Elijah ben Solomon Zalman, the Vilna Gaon, 1720–1797. Lithuanian scholar of the most powerful influence on his own and succeeding generations, and an opponent of the chassidic movement.

Elijah, *Eliyahu Hanovi*, Israelite prophet, first half of ninth century B.C.E. Regarded as the precursor of the Messiah. "According to the narrative in II Kings, ch. 2, he did not die, but rather rose into heaven. Tradition maintains that he descends to our material world from time to time and reveals himself to the righteous. Ultimately, it will be he who will announce the coming of the Messiah (see Malachi 3:23)." Rabbi Eliyahu Touger, *As a New Day Breaks* (Brooklyn, NY: S.I.E./ E.M.E.T., 1993), p. 132.

Elisha, Israelite prophet, ninth century B.C.E. Successor to the prophet Elijah.

Enoch, the earliest biblical figure, about whom it is said in Genesis (5:24) that "Enoch walked with God, and he was not; for God took him."

Esther, Queen, consort of the Persian ruler Ahasuerus (Xerxes) and heroine of the biblical book named for her.

Ezra the Scribe, fifth or fourth century B.C.E. He led a large group of exiles from Babylonia to Jerusalem, and instituted religious reforms, based on Torah, which molded the future of Judaism.

Hershele Eichenstein, Rabbi, Ziditchover Rebbe, died 1837.

Herzl, Theodor, founder of political Zionism, 1860–1904.

Hezekiah, King of Judah, reigned 727–698 B.C.E.

Hillel, Pharisee leader and outstanding sage, late first century B.C.E.–early first century C.E.

Hillel, Rabbi, "A brother of Rabbi Judah II" (*Sanhedrin* Soncino, p. 669, no. 4).

Hillel ben Gamliel III. One of two sons of Rabban Gamliel; the grandson of Rabbi Yehudah HaNasi.

Isaac, Patriarch, son of Abraham, about the eighteenth century B.C.E.

Isaac Luria Ashkenazi, the holy Ari, 1534–1572. His teachings deeply influenced modern Jewish mysticism and the chassidic movement.

Israel ben Eliezer, the Baal Shem Tov, the Besht, Master of the Good Name, charismatic founder of *Chassidus*, 1698–1760.

Isserles, Moses, 1525–1572, known by the acronym *Remah*, Rabbi, scholar of religious law, and codifier in Poland.

Jacob, also called Israel, one of the three Patriarchs; son of Isaac, about eighteenth century B.C.E.

Jose ben Chalafta, Rabbi, *tanna*, fourth generation.

Josephus Flavius, Jewish military commander and historian, 38–100 C.E. His *The Jewish War*, an account of the uprising against Rome and the destruction of the Second Temple, 70 C.E., and its aftermath, throws much light on this tragic period.

Judah Loew ben Bezalel, the Maharal of Prague, 1520–1609. A recognized leader of Askenazi Jewry and prolific writer. He is credited with making a *golem*, a man artificially created by kabbalistic rites.

Karo, Yosef, 1488–1575, codifier of *halachah*.

Levi Yitzchak of Berditchev, the Berditchever Rebbe, 1740–1810.

Maimonides, Moses, the Rambam, 1135–1204. Possibly the greatest medieval Jewish scholar, halachist, and philosopher.

Meir, Golda, Israeli prime minister, 1898–1978.

Menachem Mendel Morgenstern, the Kotzker Rebbe, 1787–1859.

Menachem Mendel of Hodorok, leading disciple of the Great *Maggid*, 1730–1788.

Menachem Mendel Schneerson of Lubavitch, seventh Lubavitcher Rebbe, 1902–1994.

Meshullam Zisha of Hanipol, Rabbi, 1718–1800.

Michael the Angel.

Mordechai of Chernobyl, 1770–1837.

Moses, popularly known as *Moshe Rabbeinu*—"Moses Our Teacher." Thirteenth-century B.C.E. leader, lawgiver, and prophet. Played key role in emergence of Judaism, founder of the Jewish nation.

Moses de Leon, Rabbi, 1240–1305, Spanish kabbalist.

Moses Ibn Ezra, Spanish Hebrew poet, about 1055–after 1135.

Moshe of Lellov, 1775–1851.

Moshe of Rozvidoz, the Rozvidozer Rebbe, died 1894.

Moshe Teitelbaum of Ujhel, the Yismach Moshe, 1759–1841.

Nachmanides, Moses, the Ramban, 1194–1270. Best known as a biblical commentator, talmudist, and philosopher. He stoutly defended his people in the Christian-Jewish disputations forced upon them in Spain.

Nachman of Bratzlav, the Bratzlaver Rebbe, 1770–1811.

Nathan of Nemirov, 1780–1845.

Noah, Mordechai Manuel, first American Zionist, 1785–1851.

Phineas Shapiro, the Koretzer Rebbe, died 1791.

Rachel, wife of Jacob. Matriarch of the Jewish people, eighteenth century B.C.E.

Rav, Rabbi Abba bar Aibu, *amora*, most active 219–247 C.E.

Rothschild, James de, 1792–1868. Son of the famous family of bankers.

Samuel, eleventh century B.C.E. Jewish prophet.

Sandalfon the Angel.

Saul, King, first king of Israel, twelfth century B.C.E.

Shalom Dovber Schneersohn of Lubavitch, fifth Lubavitcher Rebbe, the Rebbe Rashab, 1860–1920.

Shalom Rokeach of Belz, first Belzer Rebbe, 1783–1855.

Shemuel Eliezer Eidels, the *Maharasha*, 1555–1631.

Shelomo Yitzchaki, Rashi, 1040–1105. French rabbinical scholar whose commentary on the Bible and Talmud is considered definitive.

Shimon Bar Yochai, 100–160 C.E. Rabbinical authority and mystic. Outstanding pupil of Rabbi Akiva.

Shlomo ben Aderet, the *Rashba*, 1235–1310.

Shneur Zalman of Liadi, the Alter Rebbe, 1745–1812. In 1772 he established the *Chabad* branch of the chassidic movement. His *Tanya* is the "bible" of *Chabad Chassidus*, upon which the hundreds of works and thousands of discourses by seven generations of Chabad/Lubavitch rebbes and their disciples are based.

Sholom Schachna of Prohobitch, son of Rabbi Avraham Hamalach, 1766–1802.

Simcha Bunam of Pshis'cha, Rebbe Reb Bunam, 1767–1827.

Simeon bar Kokhba, leader of Jewish revolt against Rome in Judea, died 135 C.E.

Simeon ben Gamliel II, Rabban, president of the Sanhedrin, first–second centuries C.E. Father of Yehudah HaNasi.

Simeon ben Halafta, Rabbi, first half of third century C.E.

Sofer, Moses, popularly known as *Chatam Sofer*. Hungarian rabbinical authority, 1762–1839.

Tzvi Elimelech Shapiro, the Dinover Rebbe, 1783–1841.

Yaakov ben Wolf Krantz, the Maggid of Dubno, 1741–1804.

Yaakov Yitzchak Halevi Horowitz, the Seer of Lublin, 1745–1815.

Yechezkel Shraga of Shiniava, the Shiniava Rebbe, 1815–1899.

Yehoshua ben Chananiah, Rabbi, *tanna*, second century C.E.

Yehoshua ben Levi, *amora*, third century C.E.

Yehudah Aryeh Leib Alter of Ger, *Sfas Emes*, second Gerrer Rebbe, 1847–1905.

Yehudah HaNasi, Yehudah the Patriarch, *Rabbeinu Hakodosh*, "Our holy teacher," son of Rabban Simeon ben Gamliel II, late second–early third century C.E.

Yishai, King David's father.

Yisrael Meir haKohen Kagan, the Chofetz Chaim, 1838–1933.

Yisroel Friedman of Rizhin, the Rizhiner Rebbe, 1797–1850.

Yissachar Dov Rokeach, third Belzer Rebbe, 1854–1927.

Yitzchak Meir Alter of Ger, Rabbi, first Gerrer Rebbe, the *Chidushei Harym*, 1799–1866.

Yochanan ben Zakkai, Rabban, *tanna*, first century C.E.

Yohanan ben Torta, Rabbi, *tanna*, third century C.E.

Yosef Yitzchak Schneersohn of Lubavitch, sixth Lubavitcher Rebbe, the Rebbe Rayatz, 1880–1950.

APPENDIX D

A CHRONOLOGY OF EVENTS OF THE REBBE OF LUBAVITCH

As there are hundreds of thousands of Jews who considered Rabbi Menachem M. Schneerson the potential Messiah in our time and still do, despite his physical body passing away on June 12, 1994, I offer this chronology of his life in the hope of satisfying many curious questions about him. As it is said, when the Messiah comes, we'll know everything we ever wanted to know, including all the incredible holy efforts of this unique man.

The following was compiled by Boruch Jacobson, English Editor, "The Rebbe's Life and Vision: A Chronology of Events," Algemeiner Journal 23: 1169 (June 17, 1994—Tammuz 8, 5754): B1–B4.

• The Rebbe, Rabbi Menachem M. Schneerson, was born on Friday, April 18, 1902 (11 Nissan, 5662) in Nikolayev, Russia, to Levi Yitzchak and Chana Schneerson. He was the firstborn, followed by two brothers, Dovber and Yisrael Aryeh Leib.

• The Rebbe's father . . . was a direct descendant of the third *Chabad* Rebbe, Rabbi Menachem Mendel (1789–1866), also known as the *Tzemach Tzeddek*; the grandchild of the first [*Chabad*] Rebbe, Rabbi Shneur Zalman (1745–1812), author of the *Tanya* and *Shulchan Aruch*

Harav. The Rebbe was named after the third [*Chabad*] Rebbe, Menachem Mendel, who was his great-great-great-grandfather.

• The Rebbe's father was appointed as rabbi of Yekatrinislav-Dnieperpetrovsk in 1909, and the Rebbe and his family moved there from Nikolayev.

• When the Rebbe was eighteen (1920), the fifth *Chabad*-Lubavitch Rebbe, Rabbi Sholom Dov Ber Schneersohn (born 1860), passed away and his only son, Rabbi Yosef Yitzchak (1880–1950), assumed the leadership as the sixth Rebbe.

• The Rebbe met the Rebbe Rayatz, Rabbi Yosef Yitzchak, for the first time in 1923 in Rastov. In 1924 the Rebbe's mother, Rebbetzin Chana, went to visit her future daughter-in-law in Leningrad.

• The Rebbe visited the Rogotchover Gaon, Rabbi Yosef Rozen, in Leningrad in 1925, where they would discuss Torah law and commentary.

• The Rebbe left home in 1927 to be with his future father-in-law, Rabbi Yosef Yitzchak, in Riga, Latvia.

• The Rebbe's [future] father-in-law . . . was arrested in 1927 and sentenced to death, but was miraculously freed a month later.

• The Rebbe spent Rosh Hashanah, 5688 (1927), with his parents in Yekatrinislav-Dnieperpetrovsk before departing Russia for Riga to be with his future father-in-law. The Rebbe and his father, Reb Levi, spent much time together, fearing this would be the last time they would see each other. The Rebbe's mother, Rebbetzin Chana, escorted the Rebbe to the Latvian border, not to see each other again for twenty years.

• The Rebbe moved to Berlin in 1927 and would return to his [future] father-in-law in Riga for holidays. While in Berlin the Rebbe spent most of his time in Torah study while also attending the University of Berlin.

• The Rebbe married Chaya Mushka Schneersohn, the second daughter of the sixth *Chabad*-Lubavitch Rebbe, Rabbi Yosef Y. Schneersohn, on Kislev 14, 5689 (1928), in Warsaw. The Rebbe's parents celebrated the wedding night in Dnieperpetrovsk.

• The Rebbe and Rebbetzin returned to Berlin after their wedding and stayed there until 1933. They visited Rabbi Yosef Yitzchak in Riga, and he visited them in Berlin on several occasions.

• The Rebbe and Rebbetzin received many letters from Rabbi Levi Yitzchak, the Rebbe's father, many of which are published in a volume of letters written by the Rebbe's father.

• The Rebbe and Rebbetzin were forced to escape the growing

anti-Semitism of the Nazis in Germany and relocated to Paris in the winter of 1933. They remained in Paris for eight years until 1941. The Rebbe continued his Torah studies while also attending the Sorbonne [University].

• The Rebbe's brother, Yisrael Aryeh Leib, escaped Russia to Berlin and Paris. The Rebbetzin Chaya Mushka put herself in great danger to acquire papers to provide her brother-in-law safe passage to Israel, where he settled in 1934.

• The Rebbe's father was arrested and jailed by the N.K.V.D. in 1939 as a "counter-revolutionary" for his efforts to strengthen Judaism. After ten months in jail, Rabbi Levi Yitzchak was sentenced to exile in the city of Tzeili in Kazachstan, where he died five years later.

• The Rebbe's brother, Dov Ber, was murdered by the Nazis together with the rest of the Jews in Igrin. Sheina, the newly married sister of the Rebbe's wife and the youngest daughter of Rabbi Yosef Yitzchak, and her groom, Menachem Mendel Hornstein, were murdered by the Nazis in Treblinka.

• The Rebbe's father-in-law, Rabbi Yosef Yitzchak, escaped At-watsk, Poland, when World War II broke out. He reached America in March 1940.

• The Rebbe and Rebbetzin for one year lived under the shadow of the Nazis, who invaded France in 1939. They boarded one of the last trains out of Paris and escaped to Vichy, where they arrived only minutes before the holiday of *Shavuos*, 1940. They remained in Vichy until the end of the summer of 1940, when they continued to Nice in the south of France, which was under Italian rule. The Rebbe and Rebbetzin remained in Nice for nine months until the early summer of 1941. Despite the great danger, they made every effort to help their fellow Jews in every possible way. Rabbi Yosef Yitzchak used every means at his disposal to arrange for the safe passage of the Rebbe and Rebbetzin from German-occupied Europe.

The Rebbe and the Rebbetzin traveled to Marseilles, where during *Chol Hamoed Pesach*, 1941, they received their visas to America. Once they were ready to begin their journey to America, they needed to acquire passage visas for a stopover in Portugal. They successfully reached Portugal, from where they later traveled to Barcelona.

The journey from Barcelona to America was very dangerous because of the constant assaults by the Nazis.

On 28 Sivan, 5701 (1941), the Rebbe and the Rebbetzin safely arrived in New York on the [ocean ship] *Surpa Pinta* at 10:30 A.M., after which they reached 770 Eastern Parkway in the Crown Heights section of Brooklyn, New York.

• In 1942, the Rebbe's father-in-law and predecessor . . . appointed the Rebbe to lead Machne Israel, the wide-ranging social service and outreach institution of Lubavitch; Merkatz L'Inyonei Chinuch, the educational arm of Lubavitch; and the Kehot Publication Society.

• The Rebbe was appointed editor-in-chief of the Otzer Hachasidim Lubavitch Library in 1943. He also compiled and published the *Hayom Yom* daily almanac in 1943.

• The Rebbe's father, Rabbi Levi Yitzchak, passed away on 20 Av, 5704 (1944), in Alma Ata, Soviet Union.

• The Rebbe's mother, Rebbetzin Chana, traveled to Moscow in 1945 and later to Poking, Germany.

• The Rebbe compiled and published an in-depth commentary on the Passover *Haggadah* in 1946.

• In 1947 the Rebbe's mother reached Paris. The Rebbe, together with the Rebbetzin, traveled from New York to greet his mother after being separated for twenty years. The Rebbe stayed in Paris for three months after which he and the Rebbetzin traveled back to New York by ship.

• The Rebbe's mother reached the United States in 1948 where she started a new chapter in her life. She moved into an apartment on President Street in Crown Heights, Brooklyn, only a few blocks away from her son, the Rebbe.

• On Shabbat morning, 10 Shevat, 5710 (1950), the previous Lubavitcher Rebbe, Rabbi Yosef Yitzchak, passed away in his home at 770 Eastern Parkway.

• One year later, on 10 Shevat, 5711 (1951), the Rebbe assumed the leadership of the *Chabad*-Lubavitch movement and recited his first chassidic discourse, in which he outlined the goal of his generation: to bring about the Final Redemption from the long, bitter exile.

• Throughout the early years of his leadership, the Rebbe established educational and outreach organizations, schools, and institutions in South Africa, Israel, Australia, Canada, and many other countries.

• The Rebbe's brother, Yisrael Aryeh Leib, passed away in Liverpool, England, on 13 Iyar, 5713 (1953).

• The Rebbe's mother . . . passed away on Shabbat, 6 Tishrei, 5725 (1964), at the age of eighty-five. Up until the day of her passing, the Rebbe visited his mother every day.

• The Rebbe launched the "Mivtzah Tefillin" campaign in 1967 followed by the other nine mitzvah campaigns of *mezuzah*, *Shabbat* candles, Jewish books, *kashrus*, family purity, Jewish education, loving one's fellow Jew, Torah study, and charity. Mivtzah mobiles and mitzvah tanks began combating the plague of assimilation by strengthening the awareness of Jewish laws and traditions in all communities.

• In 1970 the Rebbe called for the completion of the Moshiach Torah Scroll, which the previous Rebbe had begun to write decades before, but never completed. The Rebbe also began to battle the omission of the words "according to Jewish law" from the Israeli "Law of Return," defining who is a Jew.

• The Rebbe declared the year 1976 as the "Year of Education." The Rebbe also continued to establish educational institutions in scattered cities around the world.

• In the following years the Rebbe continued to launch various campaigns, including free loan societies, Torah study for senior citizens, the Tzivos Hashem (Army of God) children's organization, writing of Torah scrolls with the participation of all world Jewry, relief and religious freedom for Russian Jewry, dissemination of the Seven Noahide Laws for all mankind, promotion of a "Moment of Silence in Public Schools," and the petitioning of God to send *Moshiach*, using the words, "We Want *Moshiach* Now."

• In 5738 (1977), on *Shemini Atzeres* during *hakofos*, the Rebbe suffered a serious heart attack. He remained in his room at "770" until 1 Kislev, under the care of his Rebbetzin and doctors.

• In 1984 the Rebbe encouraged Jews to demand the coming of *Moshiach*. The Rebbe also launched a program of the daily study of Maimonides' *Mishneh Torah* and *Sefer Hamitzvoth*.

• In 1986–1987, the books, manuscripts, and belongings of the Lubavitch movement, collected by Rabbi Yosef Yitzchak [the previous Rebbe], which had been taken from the Lubavitch Library, were found by a New York judge to rightfully belong to Agudast Chasidei Chabad, headed by the Rebbe.

• The Rebbe's Rebbetzin, Chaya Mushka, passed away on Tuesday night, 22 Shevat, 5748 (1988), leaving the Rebbe mourning in their home on President Street in Brooklyn, where tens of thousands of visitors came to comfort the Rebbe.

• On 25 Adar, 1988, the Rebbe called for Jews to celebrate their birthdays with festivities and resolutions of good deeds and Torah study.

• The Rebbe throughout the years welcomed visitors from all different circles. In the earlier years, the Rebbe held private audiences that would last into the late hours of the night. In later years the Rebbe would distribute dollar bills for charity every Sunday for many long hours, offering blessings, advice, and words of encouragement to hundreds of thousands of visitors.

• In recent years the Rebbe illustrated how the worldwide revolutions of democracy and freedom, including the collapse of communism, were evident signs that the ultimate redemption was imminent. The Rebbe further pointed to the Persian Gulf War as a miraculous sign that "the time of the ultimate redemption is here."

• The Rebbe urged Jews and non-Jews to prepare for the glorious Redemption by practicing to live a life of peace, harmony, and education. The Rebbe used his weekly addresses to encourage celebrations and acts of joy to hasten the Final Redemption.

• The Rebbe further elaborated on how the recent ingathering of Jews from all corners of the globe to the Land of Israel was another divine demonstration that the Redemption was upon our generation.

• On 28 Nissan, 5751 (1991), the Rebbe declared that his work to bring the Redemption was complete and that now it was up to World Jewry to do their part to bring an end to the exile and begin the era of the Final Redemption. In the following weeks, the Rebbe specified the studying [about] *Moshiach* and the Redemption and increasing in commitment to *mitzvos* as the means to participating in bringing on the Redemption.

• On *Shabbos Shoftim*, 5751 (1991), the Rebbe declared the prophecy of "Immediate Redemption!" and right away, "Behold! Here comes *Moshiach!*" The Rebbe indicated that he was making this declaration as his role as a prophet.

• On Monday, 27 Adar I, 5752 (1992), the Rebbe was praying at the grave site of his father-in-law, the previous Rebbe, Rabbi Yosef Yitzchak, when he was felled by a serious stroke that paralyzed the right side of his body and left him speechless.

• Three months later, on the holiday of *Shavuos*, the Rebbe appeared briefly for the first time since his stroke, at the front doorway of the Lubavitch World Headquarters at 770 Eastern Parkway.

• On the day before Rosh Hashanah, 5753 (1992), the Rebbe began to participate in the main synagogue at 770 Eastern Parkway, by means of a balcony that was built to link his office and the synagogue.

• The Rebbe, on some occasions, spent several hours with the men, women, and children in the synagogue, partaking in the dancing and singing of chassidic melodies (including the song acknowledged by the

Rebbe's emphatic encouragement, "Long live our master and teacher and Rebbe, King Moshiach, forever and ever"), making *lechaims* and nodding in response to the prayers and greetings for his speedy recovery.

• Following the stroke in 1992, the Rebbe underwent gall bladder surgery at Mount Sinai Hospital and cataract surgery at the Eye, Ear and Throat Hospital in Manhattan.

• Two years to the day after suffering the stroke paralyzing his right side, on 27 Adar, 5754 (1994), the Rebbe suffered a stroke to his left side, leaving him in critical condition at Beth Israel Hospital in New York until *Gimmel* Tammuz, 5754—June 12, 1994—when, at approximately 3 A.M., the Rebbe returned to his office at 770 Eastern Parkway, Brooklyn, to bid farewell for now to his followers, World Jewry, and all mankind.

May we merit to celebrate his immediate return, even before we go to press.

GLOSSARY

Abishter Father in Heaven.

Abya Acronym of initials of the four worlds—*Atzilut, Beriah, Yetzirah, Asiyah*—in *Kabbalah*.

Adar Twelfth month in the Jewish calendar. In a leap year, an extra month is intercalated after Shevat (the eleventh month) and is called Adar Rishon (the first Adar), immediately followed by Adar Sheni (the second Adar); Adar Sheni is then the regular or principal Adar for purposes of observing Purim and other special occasions related to that month.

Ad mosai Until when?

Admor Acronym of Hebrew words meaning *Adonenu, Morenu, v'Rabbenu*, "Our Lord, Master, and Teacher," a general title of respect given to chassidic rabbis or rebbes.

Aggadah Nonhalachic portions of the Talmud, composed mainly of ethical teachings based on the non-literal exposition of biblical texts.

Ahavas Chinam Loving someone for no reason.

Ahavas Yisrael "Love of fellow Jew"—"Love of Israel" as enjoined by the biblical precept "Love your fellow-man like yourself" (Leviticus 19:18).

Aishes Chayil "A woman of valor." Verses describing the virtuous wife are chanted or sung in the home on Friday night before the *Shabbos* meal.

Aleinu The last prayer of all the daily prayers as well as of the Sabbath and Festival prayers.

251

Aliyah (pl., aliyot) "Ascent"; being called up to partake in the communal reading of the Torah; immigration to *Eretz Yisrael*.

Amora (pl., Amoraim) Sages who compiled the *Gemara*, approximately 165–500 C.E.

Aravah (pl., aravot) Willow twigs (of the *etrog-lulav* set).

Arei Miklot A place of refuge, especially in Israel, for a Jew who kills another person by mistake, in which he cannot be harmed by anyone, including grieving friends and relatives of the victim.

Aron Hakodesh (Aron Kodesh) The Ark, the place where the Torah scrolls are held in synagogue.

Asiyah The world of action, in the *Kabbalah*.

Atzilut The world of emanation, in the *Kabbalah*.

Av Fifth month in the Jewish calendar, corresponding to July–August; also referred to as *Menachem Av*.

Avodah The service of God, whether in sacrifice, prayer, or self-effacement.

Baal Shem Tov Rabbi Israel, founder of Chassidism; born Okup, 1698 (18 Elul, 5458), died Medzibush, 1760 (6 Sivan, 5520).

Baal Teshuvah (pl., baalei teshuvah) One who returns to God; a penitent who returns to the Torah way of life after having been astray.

Babylonian Talmud (Talmud Bavli) Compiled by Rav Ashi; also known as the Gemara.

Bar Mitzvah "Son of the Commandment"; term relating to boy's attainment of religious maturity at thirteenth birthday.

Bas Daughter of.

B.C.E. Before the Common Era.

B'chor The firstborn of royalty.

Beis Din (lit., "house of law") Assembly of three or more learned men acting as a Jewish court of law.

Beis Hamidrosh A synagogue and place of study.

Beis Hamikdosh The Holy Temple (First or Second) in Jerusalem.

Beis Harknesses A synagogue.

Beis Midrash See *Beis Hamidrosh*.

Ben Son of.

Beriah The world of creation, in the *Kabbalah*.

Berochah (pl., berochos) Blessing.

Besht Acronym of the Baal Shem Tov, Master of the Good Name.

Birkas Hamazon Grace after meals.

Bochur (pl. bochurim) An unmarried young man.

Boruch Hashem Thank God.

Bubbe   A term for grandmother.

C.E.   Common Era.

Chabad   A chassidic movement founded by Rabbi Shneur Zalman of Liadi, 1745–1812. The word comprises the initials of *Chochmah, Binah, Daas*: Hebrew for wisdom, understanding, and knowledge.

Chabad House   A place where visitors come to view the chassidic way of life as it's lived by Lubavitchers.

Challah   A loaf of bread baked in honor of the Sabbath and festivals.

Chanukah   (lit., "dedication") An eight-day festival that begins 25 Kislev, commemorating the Maccabees' rededication of the Holy Temple in the second century B.C.E. and marked by the kindling of lights.

Chassid (pl., chassidim)   (lit., "a pious man") A follower of a rebbe, or adherent of the chassidic movement.

Chassidic   Related to *Chassidism*.

Chassidism   The movement of spiritual reawakening within Judaism founded by the Baal Shem Tov.

Chassidus   See Chassidism.

Chazal   Acronym for *Chachameinu zichronam li'verachah* (our Sages of blessed memory), referring to the talmudic Sages.

Cheder   Jewish primer school.

Chelm   A real town in Poland, but in Jewish fanciful legend, a center of innocent stupidity, peopled with wise (foolish) characters.

Cheshvan   Eighth month of the Hebrew calendar, corresponding to October–November.

Chevlei Moshiach   The birth pangs of the Messiah; the period of suffering immediately before the appearance of the Messiah.

Chevra Kaddisha   Burial society.

Chiddush   Newly derived Torah thought that had not been known before.

Chupah   The wedding canopy under which the marriage is solemnized. Also, the ceremony itself.

Chutzpah   Nerve; insolence.

Dalet   The number four.

Daven   Yiddish colloquialism meaning to pray.

Diaspora   See *Golus*.

Dreidels   Small tops, having four sides, that are spun with the fingers. Jewish children traditionally play with them on Chanukah.

Dveikus   The ecstatic state of cleaving to God.

Elul   The sixth month of the Jewish year, corresponding to August–

September; a month devoted to repentance and soul-searching in preparation for the Days of Awe.

Emunah   Faith in God.

Eretz Yisrael   The Land of Israel.

Erev   The day preceding.

Exilarch   (lit., "Head of the Exile") From the Aramaic, *Resh Galuta*. The head of Babylonian Jewry, a hereditary office held only by descendants of the House of David.

Farbrengen   (a) an assemblage addressed by a rebbe; (b) an informal gathering of *chassidim* for mutual edification and brotherly criticism.

Frei   A Jew who is not practicing Judaism.

Freilach   Joyous.

Freylachs   A cheerful dance.

Frum   A Torah-observant Jew.

Gabbai   In the chassidic community, the Rebbe's personal aide and attendant.

Gabriel   God has given this angel the task of revealing His messenger, namely, Elijah. Described as a leader of the angels, Gabriel is the only angel mentioned in the Bible (Daniel 8–10) and in apocryphal and rabbinic literature.

Gan Eden   Garden of Eden; also used to refer to the abode of the souls in the spiritual realm in their afterlife.

Gaon   (lit., "genius") Title given to outstanding talmudic scholars.

Gartel   A prayer belt.

Gehinnom   Purgatory.

Gelt   Money.

Gemara   The Talmudic traditions, discussions, and rulings of the *amoraim*, based mainly on the *Mishnah*, and forming the bulk of the Babylonian Talmud and Jerusalem Talmud.

Gematria   The numerical value of the letters that compose a word in the Holy Tongue, and the derivation of insights therefrom.

Gentile   A non-Jew.

Geulah   The final Redemption in the messianic era.

Gilgul (pl., gilgulim)   Reincarnation.

Gimmel Tammuz   3 Tammuz, 5754 (June 12, 1994), the day the Rebbe of Lubavitch, Rabbi Menachem Mendel Schneerson, passed away.

Gog and Magog   Forms the talmudic and medieval basis of the global Armageddon of evil forces that will wage war with the forces of the Messiah.

Golem   A man or woman artificially created by kabbalistic rites.

Golus (Golah)   The Exile; the diaspora.

Gonif   A thief.

Goy (pl., goyim)   A non-Jew.

Goyishe   Describing non-Jewish things or matters.

Groschen   Small German silver coin whose old value was about two cents.

Guf   The celestial hall of the souls.

Haftarah   The prophetic lesson read after the Torah reading on *Shabbos* or *Yom Tov*.

Haggadah   (lit., "telling") The *Haggadah* is the book that tells the story of the Jewish Exodus from Egypt.

Hakofos   The sevenfold procession made with the Torah scrolls in the synagogue on *Simchas Torah* and accompanied by singing and dancing.

Halachah   Code of Jewish Law; a particular law.

Har Hazaysin   Mount of Olives.

Hashem   God.

Haskalah   (lit., "enlightenment") A movement originating in eighteenth century Germany to acquire culture and customs of the outside world. An adherent was called a *maskil*.

Hatov v'hamaytiv   Blessing in honor of very good news in the world.

Hoshanah Rabbah   (lit., "the great *hoshanah*") The name given to the seventh day of Sukkos.

Ikvesa diMeshica   Footsteps of the Messiah.

Iyar   Second month of the Hebrew calendar, corresponding to April–May.

Jerusalem Talmud (Talmud Yerushalmi)   The Talmud edition compiled in *Eretz Yisrael* at the end of the fourth century C.E.

Jude   A Jew.

Judenstaat   A Jewish state.

Kabbalah   The body of classical Jewish mystical teachings.

Kabbalistic   Exponent of the *Kabbalah*.

Kaddish   (lit., "sanctification") A prayer recited in memory of a deceased person.

Kashrus   Observance of the kosher laws. Dietary proprietary of foods by Torah law.

Keitz   A particularly auspicious time for the Messiah to bring the Exile to an end.

Kelal Yisrael   The entire Jewish nation.

Kethuvim   The Holy Writings, beginning with the Psalms.

Kibbutz (pl., kibbutzim)   A collective farm or settlement in Israel.

Kiddush   Blessing over wine expressing the sanctity of the Sabbath or a festival.

Kinus   A special meeting.

Kipa   A yarmulke, skullcap.

Kislev   Ninth month of the Hebrew calendar, corresponding to November–December.

Klei Zemer   Musical instrument.

Klippot   Shells or evil covers of man's spiritual core that form a barrier between man and God.

Kohen (pl., kohanim)   Priest of the Holy Temple; descendant of Aaron.

Kohen Gadol   The high priest.

Kol Nidrei   Opening words of the evening service of Yom Kippur.

Kopeck   Small Russian copper coin, there once being 100 kopecks in a ruble.

Kosher   (lit., "fit for use") An adjective used to indicate that food or religious articles have met the standards Torah law prescribes for their use.

Kotel Ha-Ma'aravi   The Western Wall of the Temple.

Kup   A head.

Kuthim   Samaritans.

Kvitel (pl., kvitlach)   A note to a rebbe, requesting a blessing, usually accompanied by money.

Lag B'Omer   The thirty-third day of the counting of the *Omer*. Also commemorates the cessation of the plague that carried off many disciples of Rabbi Akiva.

Landesrabbiner   Chief rabbi.

Latkes   Potato pancakes traditionally served on Chanukah.

Lechaim   (lit., "to life") Traditional words of a toast on alcoholic drinks.

Lechoh Dodi   A song to welcome the Sabbath.

Levanon   Reference to the Holy Temple, in the Torah.

Levite   Descendant of the tribe of Levi. A person who assisted the priest in the Holy Temple.

L'havdil   Word to separate sacred from secular matters, in speech and in print.

Lilith   Wife of Satan (Samael).

Lishmah   To study Torah for the sake of holy study.

Livyasan   The Leviathan, the great fish.

Lubavitch (lit., "town of love") The town in White Russia that served as the center of Chabad Chassidism from 1813 to 1915 and whose name has become synonymous with the movement.

Maamar (pl., maamarim) (lit., "the words") In *Chabad* circles, it means a formal chassidic discourse first delivered by a rebbe.

Ma'ase rav Great authorities of the Torah.

Maggid (pl., maggidim) Usually, a popular, roving preacher, a teller of stories.

Maggid Shiur A lecturer of the Talmud.

Manhig Hador Leader of his generation.

Masada A gray fortress on brown rock rising 1,200 feet, where the Roman army defeated the Jews in 72 c.e.

Mashgiach An Orthodox rabbi who oversees the proper *kashrus* method of food preparation.

Mashpiah (lit., "source of influence") In chassidic circles, a spiritual mentor.

Mashke Strong alcoholic drink.

Maskil (pl., Maskilim) Enlightened Jewish secularists who threatened to undermine traditional Judaism; exponent of the *Haskalah*.

Master of the Good Name Rabbi Israel ben Eliezer, the Baal Shem Tov, 1698–1760.

Matzoh (pl., matzos) The unleavened bread eaten on Passover.

Mazal In the context of the *maamar*, "source of influence," the soul as it exists in the spiritual realms that exert influence over the soul as it is enclothed in the body; also means "good luck."

Mekubal A scholar well versed in the mystical teachings of Judaism.

Melave Malka A festive meal eaten after *Shabbos* is over.

Menorah Seven-branched candelabra in the Holy Temple; eight-branched candelabra used during Chanukah.

Mentsh A gentleman.

Mesirus Nefesh (lit., "sacrifice of the soul") The willingness to sacrifice oneself, either through martyrdom, or through a selfless life, for the sake of the Torah and its commandments.

Mesorah The Jewish observant tradition that was handed down from generation to generation, dating back to Moses at Mount Sinai.

Metatron The Archangel of God who spoke to Moses in the name of the Lord of the Universe, and who received the mission to lead the Children of Israel into the Holy Land. Metatron is also the preserver and guardian of the law and of the Holy Writ.

Mezuzoh (pl., mezuzos)   (lit., "doorpost") A tiny parchment scroll affixed to a doorpost.

Midrash (pl., midrashim)   The classical collection of the talmudic sages' homiletical teachings on the Bible.

Mikveh   Body of water used for ritual immersion.

Milah   Ritual circumcision.

Minchah   Afternoon prayer service.

Minyan   Quorom of ten Jewish men required for divine service.

Mishnah   Basic collection of the legal pronouncements, discussions, and interpretations of the *tannaim*, edited by Rabbi Yehudah HaNasi (the Patriarch) c. 200 C.E., early in the third century. Serves as the basis for the Talmud.

Mishneh Torah   Maimonides' magnum opus, which serves as a compendium of the entire Oral Law.

Misnaged (pl., misnagdim)   An early opponent of the chassidic movement.

Mitzrayim   (lit., "the land of Egypt") Figuratively, a state of limitation.

Mitzvah (pl., mitzvos)   (lit., "command") A religious obligation; one of the Torah's 613 commandments.

Modeh Ani   The first words of prayer said upon awakening in the morning.

Moshiach   Messiah.

Moshiach ben David   The elect of God, the true Messiah.

Moshiach ben Ephraim   See *Moshiach ben Yosef.*

Moshiach ben Yosef   Also called *Moshiach ben Ephraim.* Imagined as the first commander of the army of Israel. Is slain by Armilus, but is resuscitated by *Moshiach ben David.*

Moshiach Vadai   The Messiah for certain.

Motzoei Shabbos   The time of the departure of the Sabbath.

Mussar   Ethics; chastisement. Designates books and traditions of moral and ascetic theology.

Nachus   Pleasure.

Nasi   (a) In biblical times, the head of any one of the Twelve Tribes; (b) in later generations, the civil and/or spiritual head of the Jewish community at large.

Nebich   Poor fellow.

Neilah   Concluding service of Yom Kippur.

Neshomah (pl., neshomos)   Jewish soul.

Neviim   Prophets.

Niggun (pl., niggunim) A wordless song, generally, that accompanies chassidic praying.

Niglah The revealed parts of the Torah.

Ninth of Av Anniversary of destruction of the First and Second Temples.

Nissan Seventh month of Jewish calendar, corresponding to March–April, in which Passover, the Exodus from Egypt, occurs on 15 Nissan.

Nistar The so-called hidden parts of the Torah.

Nu Yiddish expression, usually a question meaning "so?"

Nun The number fifty.

O.B.M. Of blessed memory.

Ohel Edifice over a grave of a chassidic rebbe.

Oines An accidental sinner.

Olam Haba The World-to-Come.

Omer Dry measure. Denotes the period between Passover and *Shavuos*.

Oral Law The *Mishnah* of the Talmud and laws derived from it.

Passover Pesach, seven-day festival (eight in the diaspora), beginning on 15 Nissan commemorating the Exodus from Egypt.

Perushim Torah explanations and insights.

Pesach See *Passover.*

Pidyon Contributions given to the rebbe.

Pidyon Haben A ritual in which a father redeems his firstborn.

Pintele Yid A spark of Judaism.

Pirkei Avot "Ethics of the Fathers." Part of the *Mishnah* of the Talmud. This tractate is traditionally learned every Shabbat between Pesach and Shavuos and in many communities also between Shavuos and Rosh Hashanah.

Pnimiyut haTorah The inner dimension or soul of the Torah; the esoteric tradition, in general, and *Chassidus* in particular.

Potch A smack.

Pshat The plain meaning of (e.g.) a scriptural passage.

Purim (lit., "lots") A one-day festival falling on 14 Adar and commemorating the miraculous salvation of the Jews of the Persian Empire in the fourth century B.C.E.

Rabbi A qualified authority in Torah learning.

Rabbonim A selective group of gathered rabbis.

Rambam Acronym for Moses ben Maimon, Maimonides, Spanish physician, theologian, jurist, codifier of the Jewish law, 1135–1204.

Rav   A rabbi; the halachic authority and spiritual guide of a Jewish community.

Reb   Mister.

Rebbe (pl., rebbeim)   Religious leader of a chassidic community.

Rebbetzin   The wife of a rabbi, rebbe, or *rav*.

Reb Yid   An informal term of address to an individual whose name is not known.

Responsum (pl., responsa)   Written replies by qualified authorities given to all questions on aspects of Jewish law.

Rosh Chodesh   Sanctification of the New Moon.

Rosh Hashanah   The New Year festival, falling on 1 and 2 Tishrei.

Rosh Yeshivah   Yeshivah principal or rector.

Samael   Satan.

Samekh   The number sixty.

Sanctuary   The term used in two different contexts: (a) The Tabernacle in which the Divine Presence dwelled during the Jews' journeys through the desert. (b) The portion of the Temple building before the Holy of Holies, which contained the inner altar, the table for the showbread, and the menorah.

Sandalfon   Name of an angel.

Sanhedrin   Supreme judicial authority in the Holy Land during the Roman period, consisting of seventy-one ordained scholars; also a tractate of the Talmud.

Seder   The order of the festive meal at home on the first and second nights of Passover.

Sefer (pl., seforim)   Book.

Sefer Torah   A Torah scroll.

Sefirah (pl., sefiros)   The kabbalistic term or the attributes of godliness that serve as a medium between His infinite light and our limited framework of reference.

Seudah   Meal.

Seudas Shelishis   The third meal on *Shabbos* eaten before sunset.

770   770 Eastern Parkway, Brooklyn, NY—the address of the Lubavitch World Headquarters.

Shaaloh   A question.

Shabbos   The Sabbath.

Shacharis   Morning prayers.

Shalos Seudos   The third meal eaten after the afternoon service on *Shabbos*. Often the setting for chassidic teachings.

Shamash   A beadle. A man responsible for the cares of the synagogue.

Shavuos (lit., "weeks") Festival commemorating the giving of the Torah at Mount Sinai; in *Eretz Yisrael*, falling on 6 Sivan; in the diaspora, on 6–7 Sivan. On this day, the Baal Shem Tov and King David died.

Shechinah Divine Presence. The spirit of the Omnipresent as manifested on earth; the indwelling presence of God.

Shechitah The Jewish ritual method of slaughtering animals for food.

Sheliach (pl., shluchim) An emissary of the Lubavitcher Rebbe who is involved in Jewish outreach work.

Shema Yisrael The opening words, which are part of the confession of Jewish faith, "Hear, O Israel, the Lord our God, the Lord is one!" It's one of the central sections of the *siddur*.

Shemini Atzeres The last day of Sukkos.

Shemoneh Esrei The prayer that is central in the three daily services.

Shevat Eleventh month of Jewish calendar, corresponding to January–February.

Shiddach A proposed marriage.

Shiloh (Shrine) The location of a sanctuary that housed the Holy Ark, and that served as the center of sacrificial worship for the Jewish people. The Shiloh Shrine stood for 369 years.

Shiur A Torah lecture.

Shlepp To proceed or move slowly, tediously, or awkwardly.

Shlichus Asssignment of the Rebbe's emissary.

Shlimazl A luckless fellow. As one wit once put it, "A *schlemihl* [a bumbling yokel] is a man who spills a bowl of hot soup on a *shlimazl*."

Shlita Acronym for the Hebrew words meaning, "May he live a long and good life."

Shocheit Ritual slaughterer.

Shofar A ram's horn, blown on Rosh Hashanah and at the termination of Yom Kippur.

Sholom Aleichem A greeting that means "Peace be with you"; in response, one says, "*Aleichem Sholom*."

Shomayim Heaven.

Showbread The bread offered on the sacred table in the Sanctuary each week. See Leviticus 24:5–9.

Shtender A wooden stand to rest open books.

Shtickle A piece.

Shtiebel Small *chassidic* house of prayer and study.

Shtreimel Fur hat usually worn on the Sabbath and festivals.

Shul   A small synagogue.

Shulchan Aruch   Code of Jewish laws.

Siddur (pl., siddurim)   Prayer book.

Simchah   Joy or festive occasion.

Simchas Torah   (lit., "the rejoicing of the Torah") The final day (in *Eretz Yisrael*, the eighth day; in the diaspora, the ninth) of the festival of Sukkos on which the annual cycle of Torah readings is completed; this event is celebrated with exuberant rejoicing. Celebrated on Tishrei 23.

Sivan   The ninth month of Jewish calendar, corresponding to May– June.

Sod   Secret; the level of the Torah that plumbs kabbalistic or mystical depths.

Spodek   A chassidic fur hat often worn on weekdays in Ropshitz or other chassidic places.

Sukkah   Thatched hut Jews live in and/or eat in on the holiday of Sukkos.

Sukkos   (lit., "booths") Feast of the Tabernacles, celebrated 15-22 Tishrei.

Tallis   Prayer shawl with four fringes.

Talmid Chacham (pl., talmidim chachamim)   Torah scholar of standing.

Talmud   Comprehensive term for the *Mishnah* and *Gemara* as joined in the two compilations known as the Babylonian Talmud (*Talmud Bavli*; completed in Babylon in the sixth century) and the Jerusalem Talmud (*Talmud Yerushalmi*; completed in the Holy Land, beginning of the fifth century).

Tammuz   The fourth calendar month after Nissan, around June.

Tanna (pl., tannaim)   Talmudic teachers of the *Mishnah* period, in contradistinction to the *amoraim* who followed them.

Tanya   The classic text of *Chabad* chassidic thought authored by Rabbi Shneur Zalman of Liadi, the Alter Rebbe.

Tateh   Term for father, dad, or pop.

Techiyas Hameism   Resurrection of the Dead.

Tefillin   Small black leather cubes containing parchment scrolls inscribed with *Shema Yisrael* and other biblical passages, bound to the arm and forehead and worn by men at weekday morning prayers.

Tehillim   Book of Psalms.

Teku   The term *teku* is used in the Talmud at the end of a discussion when no definitive answer was reached. Its basic meaning is that the question is unanswerable despite all attempts. Also an acronym for four Hebrew words that mean: "Elijah the Tishbite will solve all difficulties and inquiries," that is, we shall know the answer when the Messiah comes.

Teshuvah Repentance.

T'filat hadarech The prayer for travelers.

Tikkun (pl., tikkunim) The process of refining, restituting, and rehabilitating the materiality of this world.

Tisch (pl., tischen) Festive table at which a chassidic rebbe presides and delivers a discourse.

Tisha B'Av The ninth day of the month of Av; fast day commemorating the destruction of both the First Temple and Second Temple in Jerusalem.

Tishrei Seventh month of Hebrew calendar, corresponding to September–October.

Tor Turtle.

Torah "Teaching"–in the narrow sense the *Chumash* (Five Books of Moses; Pentateuch); in the general, comprehensive sense, the entire body of Jewish law and teachings; also a talk by a rebbe.

Totrish Hungarian.

Tu Bi-shvat New Year for Trees festival.

Tummim See *Urim VeTummim*.

Tzaddekes A female chassidic saintly rebbetzin.

Tzaddik (pl., tzaddikim) A completely righteous person; a rebbe.

Tzedakah Charity.

Tzimtzum The voluntary restriction of divine light.

Tzitzis Fringes on a *tallis*.

Urim VeTummim According to some Jewish authorities, the stones embedded in the high priest's breastplate. They served as oracles in the time of the First Temple.

Vav The number six.

Yahrzeit Anniversary of the passing of a near relative.

Yamim Noraim Days of Awe, High Holy Days.

Yarmulke Skullcap that is worn by Torah-observant Jewish males.

Yayin Wine.

Yechidah The innermost of the five levels of the soul.

Yechidus Private interview with a rebbe.

Yeidel Little Jew.

Yerushalayim Jerusalem.

Yeshivah (pl., yeshivot or yeshivahs) Talmudic academy.

Yetzer Hora   Evil impulse.

Yetzirah   The world of formation, in the *Kabbalah*.

Yid (pl., Yidden)   A Jew.

Yiddish   (lit., "Jewish") The dialect of German spoken by the Jews that became their mother tongue.

Yiddishkeit   The Torah way of life.

Yiddle   A young Jew.

Yiras Hashem   Respect for God.

Yiras Shamayim   Fear of Heaven.

Yod   The number ten.

Yom Kippur   Day of Atonement, fast day falling on 10 Tishrei and climaxing the Days of Awe.

Yom Tov (pl., yom tovim)   Holy day or festival.

Zeide   Term for grandfather.

Zohar   "Book of Splendor." Title of basic work of the Kabbalah, essentially composed by the second century *tanna* Rabbi Simeon bar Yochai.

Zt"l   Acronym for *Zecher Tzaddik Livracha* (the memory of the righteous one should be for a blessing).

INDEX

About the Author

Mordechai Staiman is the author of *Niggun: Stories behind the Chasidic Songs That Inspire Jews* (1994), *Diamonds of the Lubavitcher Rebbe* (1977), and *Everything You Ever Wanted to Know about Moshiach but Didn't know Whom to Ask: A Complete Messiah Encyclopedia* (1997). He is currently working on a book about children with Down's syndrome. His articles have appeared in *The Jewish Press, Algemeiner Journal, Beis Moshiach, Chabad, Country Yossi Family Magazine, L'Chiam, Wellsprings,* and *N'Shei Chabad*. A prolific writer, editor, publicist, and copywriter for 32 years, he lives in the Crown Heights section of Brooklyn, New York, with his wife, Ada, and his mother-in-law, Sophie.